USA Today bestseller Annette D. dozen novels including the fiv Chambers mystery series about rural Pennsylvania. Her standalor Dr. Tony Ryan Book Award for ex............ .. ..g...... .. literature. *Where the Guilty Hide* is the first in her new mystery series set along the shores of Lake Erie. Annette and her husband live in the United States on ten acres of what was her grandfather's Pennsylvania dairy farm with one very spoiled cat.

www.annettedashofy.com

 twitter.com/Annette_Dashofy
 facebook.com/Annette.Dashofy

Also by Annette Dashofy

Zoe Chambers Mystery Series

Circle of Influence

Lost Legacy

Bridges Burned

With a Vengeance

No Way Home

Uneasy Prey

Cry Wolf

Fair Game

Under the Radar

Til Death

Fatal Reunion

Crime in the Country

Helpless

Standalone titles

Death by Equine

Detective Honeywell Mystery Series

Where the Guilty Hide

KEEP YOUR FAMILY CLOSE

A Detective Honeywell Mystery

ANNETTE DASHOFY

One More Chapter
a division of HarperCollins*Publishers*
1 London Bridge Street
London SE1 9GF
www.harpercollins.co.uk
HarperCollins*Publishers*
Macken House, 39/40 Mayor Street Upper,
Dublin 1, D01 C9W8, Ireland

This paperback edition 2023
1
First published in Great Britain in ebook format
by HarperCollins*Publishers* 2023
Copyright © Annette Dashofy 2023
Annette Dashofy asserts the moral right to be identified
as the author of this work

A catalogue record of this book is available from the British Library

ISBN: 978-0-00-857982-1

To Todd and Marianne Main

Chapter One

Detective Matthias Honeywell had responded to hundreds of back alleys in his twenty-one years with the Erie City Bureau of Police. Compared to most, this one exhibited none of the usual stenches he attributed to dank, narrow spaces, especially on a steamy June morning. Situated in a mostly residential part of town, the alley made for a convenient short cut between streets, a good place to walk a dog without the risk of speeding traffic.

Until one dog walker encountered a dead body.

Detective Brad Frazier approached, having spent the last fifteen minutes talking to the crowd gathered outside the yellow police tape. "No one claims to have seen anything." He aimed his pen at a young woman holding the leash of a small furry dog. "She called it in. Said she was walking her mutt around the block just after daybreak when she came across the stiff."

The woman in question was wearing a glittery pink top that perfectly matched the T-shirt on the pup. Matthias had a feeling she would take offense at her purebred something or other being referred to as a "mutt."

Frazier, with his broad shoulders and movie-star looks, was a good cop but had three flaws. One, his people skills needed work, although Matthias held little hope they'd ever improve. Two, he had no sense of humor. None.

Three, he was well over six-feet tall. Matthias matched Frazier in the broad shoulder department but had neither the movie-star face, courtesy of two pronounced scars, nor the height. Even with the thick soles of the tactical boots he preferred over street shoes, Matthias barely topped out at five-nine.

Next to the body, Felix Hamilton, Erie County Coroner, climbed to his feet and gestured the detectives toward him. Sprawled on his back, the dark-haired male victim's open eyes were opaque. Matthias guessed he was in his late twenties or early thirties. He wore white sneakers, skinny jeans, and a T-shirt that might've had an image on the front, but the blood obscured it. His neatly trimmed mustache and goatee framed a gaping mouth. He appeared surprised at how his Friday morning started. Or at how his life had ended.

"Do you have an ID on him?" Matthias asked.

Hamilton, who looked like he belonged on a beach in California, shook his head. "I checked his pockets. No wallet."

"Robbery gone bad," Frazier mused.

"Maybe." The coroner lowered his gaze to the man on the ground. "What I can tell you is he sustained three gunshot wounds. Two to the chest, which, due to the residue on his shirt, appear to be contact wounds. The third GSW to the forehead appears to have been made from slightly farther away."

"How far away?" Matthias asked.

"Can't say for sure yet."

"Assailant stuck the gun in his chest," Frazier said. "Bang, bang. Victim goes down. Assailant stands over him and fires one more to finish the job."

Hamilton nodded. "That would be consistent with my preliminary findings."

Frazier grunted. "Professional hit?"

"That's one possibility."

"What about an approximate TOD?" Matthias asked.

"Considering his state of rigor, I'd estimate time of death as late last night or very early this morning." Hamilton peeled off his gloves and waved to his deputy coroner waiting by the van. "Anything else will have to wait until after the autopsy."

Frazier stepped closer to the body and held his phone over the man's face, snapping a picture. "Not the best image to be showing around, trying to identify him, but it'll have to do." He returned to Matthias's side. "I'm going to talk to the patrolmen. See if they've learned anything." Frazier strode toward the alley's intersection with the street.

Matthias let him go and took another look around the scene, which nestled midway between downtown Erie and the touristy area near Presque Isle State Park. Within a matter of a couple of miles, one could encounter multi-million-dollar homes, poor, high-crime neighborhoods, downtown's museums and restaurants, and old warehouses gradually being converted into business and living spaces. Erie, Pennsylvania, had it all. Luxury. Beaches. Tourist spots. High culture and low living.

This alley and the blocks surrounding it edged a poverty-stricken area known for drug activity. The homes here were modest. Well kept. But that meant nothing. An addict looking for money to feed his habit could easily walk here.

Matthias studied the man on the ground. Is that what happened to him? Or was this a professional hit, as Frazier had suggested? If so, who was this guy and what had he been into?

Matthias turned a slow 360, taking in every detail.

The narrow alley was lined with a high brick wall on one side with residences beyond. He glimpsed peaks of roofs above it, but no windows. Across the alley was the side of a two-story building, also brick and windowless. According to faded lettering on the wall, the now-vacant structure had once housed an upholstery business. Beyond the crime scene, he could see a green dumpster and a few scattered trashcans. What he didn't see—anywhere—were security cameras.

Facing the street, his back to the victim, he took in the faces of the gathered looky-loos. Men, women, young and old, some aiming their cell phone cameras at him. No, not at him. At the victim.

Was the mugger among them? The old trope about the killer returning to the scene was often true. He looked at each person. Was anyone acting odd? Nervous? Smug? Did anyone turn away when they noticed him watching?

Frazier rounded the corner and waved to him.

Matthias moved his way. "What have you got?"

"I spoke with the first officers on the scene. They searched the alley. No wallet. No weapon. No bullet casings. They and the other uniforms have been canvassing the surrounding homes. A few people report hearing what they thought were fireworks around midnight."

Fireworks. With the Fourth of July only a couple of weeks away, it was a plausible mistake.

"I guess that's all we can do around here," Frazier said. "Let's get back to the office."

Matthias didn't move. He looked left, down a tree-lined street with small but tidy homes. Then right. Houses across the road. The old upholstery business on the corner. A couple more residences. And a bar on the next corner. "Let's check one more thing." He strode down the sidewalk with Frazier trailing.

Pauly's Polynesian Pub's façade, with its cedar-shake siding and fake thatch overhang, gave the place the appearance of being a tiki bar. The solid steel door and the small windows filled with neon lights advertising national brand beers made it look like any other dive. Matthias grasped the door's handle and jerked. It didn't give.

Frazier framed his eyes against the glare and squinted through the windows. "It's closed."

"You have a knack for stating the obvious," Matthias muttered. "It's only nine in the morning. I just thought someone might be inside cleaning the place."

"I'll have one of the uniforms check back tonight."

Matthias spotted a scrawny young guy walking toward them. He slowed, apparently taking in their matching polo shirts embroidered with an image of their badges, trousers, and sidearms, all of which shouted, "*Cop.*" His eyes widened and if his body language meant anything, he was about to turn and head the other way.

Matthias moved toward him and raised a hand. "Hey. You."

The scrawny guy stiffened and pressed one finger into his own breastbone.

"Yeah, you. I want to ask you a question." Matthias pointed at the tiki bar. "What time does the owner usually show up?"

Scrawny Guy visibly relaxed. "Pauly? He's always here by one, two at the latest. Don't open until five though."

Matthias shot a smile at him. "Thanks for your time."

His nod looked more like a spasm. After a few moments of visibly trying to decide whether it was safe to continue on his way, Scrawny Guy decided it was. He stepped out into the street, giving wide berth to Matthias and Frazier, apparently not willing to risk being grabbed.

Frazier scowled after him. "There's something going on with that dude."

"Probably. But I doubt it has to do with our homicide."

Frazier's focus came back to Matthias. "Why are you interested in this bar anyway?"

"A hunch. Did you see how the victim was dressed?"

"Black T-shirt a size too small. Black skinny jeans. White sneakers."

"White sneakers that were spotless, save for a few drops of blood." Matthias walked away from his partner, turned the corner, and strode down the sidewalk with Frazier trailing. "Our victim was dressed for a night out. The neighbors reported hearing gunshots around midnight. This is the only bar for blocks. I bet he was coming from here."

"That's a lot of supposition."

Matthias's usual partner, Cassie Malone, would agree. But she'd also agree it was a good working theory.

He reached the back corner and the gravel lot behind the building. A lone pickup, a black Tundra, was parked facing the street. Without explaining, he strode toward the truck, pulling out his phone.

When dispatch picked up, Matthias identified himself and asked her to run the pickup's plate. A few seconds later she said, "Comes back to a Thomas Jenkins." She read off an address about five blocks away. "No wants or warrants."

"Thanks. Do me a favor? Send me a copy of Mr. Jenkins's driver's license photo?"

"Will do."

Matthias ended the call. Less than a minute later, his phone pinged. He opened the message and clicked on the attached image. Frazier moved to his shoulder, and Matthias angled the device so he could see. "At least we don't have to use the photo with the hole in his head when we show it to potential witnesses."

Chapter Two

"Now begin to bring your awareness back to your breath."

The soft and melodic voice of the yoga instructor filtered into Emma Anderson's brain as she lay on her mat, covered with a wool blanket. She always knew what to expect from Kira Petersen's class, especially these final moments of *shavasana*. Corpse pose. Expected. But still resisted. Those words drew her back to reality.

"Slowly begin to wiggle your fingers and your toes," Kira continued, drawing out the long Os. "Roll your wrists. And your ankles."

Emma obeyed reluctantly.

"Bend first one knee, then the other, bringing your feet flat to the floor. And whenever you're ready, slowly roll to your side and continue to rest there."

Emma knew what came next. Pressing up to sit, eyes closed meditatively. Within a few moments, she and the other five students brought their palms together at their hearts and joined Kira in chanting, *"Om shanti, shanti, shantihi,"* and concluded with a bow. *"Namaste."*

Emma climbed to her feet, folded her blanket, and rolled her mat. Most of the students at Namaste Yoga owned their equipment. Emma still borrowed hers. While the others filtered out of the large, dimly lit room, she carried the mat and blanket to the shelf in the corner and replaced them where she'd found them.

"I'm glad to see you back in class."

Emma looked up to find Kira at her side. "Work's been keeping me busy. That's a good thing, right?"

"Not necessarily."

Emma huffed a laugh. "After months of hit-or-miss income freelancing, having a real job as staff photographer with a real news outlet is a good thing for my bank account."

Kira crossed her arms. "Not if it keeps you from doing the things you want to do."

Emma thought she meant taking these yoga classes.

But Kira asked, "How's your search for your sister going?"

Emma's younger sister, Nell, was the main reason Emma had moved to Erie and the sole reason she stayed. As far as she knew, Nell was somewhere in this city, lost in the world of drugs and addiction.

Emma started toward the wall of cubbies where she and the other students stashed their personal items during class. "About the same. In other words, I'm getting nowhere. I keep making the rounds of the area bars, hoping to find her working there. Or that someone has seen her. I leave my number, but I have a feeling these guys toss it in the trash the moment I walk out."

Kira made a face. "I don't like the idea of you going into those places alone. It's not safe."

Emma couldn't argue. More than once, she'd hustled to her Subaru, jumped in, hit the locks, and tore out of a parking space before some sleazebag could catch her.

"Next time you do something like that, call me. I'll go with you."

She looked at Kira in her turquoise unitard that hugged her very curvy figure. Over it, she wore a gauzy knee-length drape, which matched her hair, once purple but now light blue. "I couldn't ask you to do that."

"You're not asking. I'm volunteering. Safety in numbers and all that. Besides…" Kira struck a sultry pose. "I don't just look hot. I can kick ass too."

Emma laughed. "I don't doubt it." She pulled her handbag and phone from a cubby and swiped the device's screen to unmute it. "Huh. I missed a call during class."

"From whom?"

"I don't recognize the number. They left a message." Curious, Emma tapped the icon to listen to the voice mail.

"This is Zeke at Mercury Tavern and Grill. I may have information about your sister. I'll be here until two this afternoon if you wanna stop by."

Emma's throat tightened. She met Kira's curious gaze.

"What is it?" the yoga instructor asked.

Emma set the phone on her palm, hit speaker and replay.

Kira's eyes grew wide as they listened to Zeke. "How's that for timing?" She glanced at the clock on the wall. "It's noon. I've never been to Mercury Tavern and Grill, but I hear they have good food."

"Really?"

"Hell, I don't know. But I do know you're going, and I'm not letting you go alone. Besides, I'm hungry enough to eat whatever slop they serve."

From the passenger seat, Kira chatted about an assortment of topics while Emma drove without registering a word her friend said. At least until Kira twisted to face Emma. "You're ignoring me."

"No, I'm not."

"Then what did I just say?"

ANNETTE DASHOFY

Emma struggled to pull up the line of chatter from her subconscious and failed.

"Like I said. You're not listening."

"Sorry. I guess I'm wrapped up in what this guy might tell me."

"I know. I was trying to distract you." Kira faced front and pointed through the windshield. "I think it's up here on the left."

"Yep." Emma was embarrassed to admit how well she'd become acquainted with Erie's bar scene in the four months she'd lived here.

She found an open spot on the street, maneuvered the Subaru into it, and turned off the ignition.

Kira unclicked her seatbelt. "I'm impressed."

"Because I can parallel park?"

"Because you can manage it in one try. And you're not a city girl. Didn't you say you grew up on a farm?"

"I can drive a tractor, too. I'm multi-talented where motor vehicles are concerned."

"Like I said. I'm impressed."

Emma stepped out into the noonday heat and studied the front of the Mercury Tavern and Grill across the street. Lights shown from inside the large window, and an "open" sign hung in the full-glass door.

Kira came around the car to join her. "Looks less like a dive than I expected for the location."

Emma checked for traffic and jogged toward the opposite curb. "Maybe you were right about the food being good."

Inside, blissful air conditioning and a circa 1970s glass display counter greeted them. Once upon a time, the shelves probably held varieties of chewing gum. Or possibly pies and pastries. Now it was empty. A cash register and a bowl of plastic-wrapped mints sat on top along with a plastic rack holding laminated menus. Next to the display case, two doors were labeled Men and Women.

10

A large sign directing them to seat themselves hung beside a doorway to the left. The dining room's tables and chairs appeared to be of the same vintage as the display case. Two of the tables were occupied, both with men wearing work uniforms. There wasn't a waitress to be seen.

Kira selected a menu, wrinkled her nose, and put the laminated page back. Frowning at her fingers, she said, "I'll spring for lunch as long as we eat anywhere but here."

"Deal."

A door to the right of the entrance opened into the tavern half of the establishment. Dark wood and burned-out lights provided the ambiance of a cave. A man wearing an apron over tight jeans was wiping down tables. He looked up at them. "Can I help you, ladies?"

"I'm looking for Zeke," Emma said.

The man turned toward the mahogany bar. "Hey, Zeke. You have company."

Emma stepped farther into the room as a second man entered through a swinging door. She approached him and took a seat on one of the stools. Kira, she noticed, veered over to the first guy. "You're Zeke?" Emma asked.

He appeared guarded. "Yes, ma'am."

"I'm Emma Anderson. You called—"

Recognition registered in his expression. "About your sister. Yeah."

"You've seen her?"

"I think so. I mean, I'm pretty sure."

Emma's high hopes started to sink. "Pretty sure?"

He rested his inked forearms on the bar. "I was at a wedding reception weekend before last over at the Royal Palace Hotel." He paused. "Do you know the place?"

"The big convention center down in Millcreek, right?"

"That's it. I saw this woman there and thought she looked familiar. It's been bugging me, where I knew her from, for two

11

solid weeks." He straightened and reached under the bar. "Then this morning, I spotted this." He pulled out a photo and placed it in front of Emma. She immediately recognized the picture of Nell. Emma had printed dozens of copies of it, scrawled her name and number on the back, and left them at every bar in the northwest corner of the state.

She fingered the photo. "This is the woman you saw?"

"I'm sure of it." Zeke made a face. "Well, ninety-five percent sure."

Emma's pulse echoed in her ears. This was the first lead she'd had since Nell left her a cryptic voice message last month. And that hadn't been a lead at all.

Still, Emma kept the recording on her phone.

She tapped the photo. "Was she working at the hotel?"

Zeke scowled. "No. At least, I don't think so."

Emma's racing heart slowed. If Nell worked there, Emma stood a good chance of finding her, even if it meant camping out in the lobby.

"I think she was staying there," Zeke said. "Same as I was. The bride and groom got us a special rate on rooms so me and my girl took advantage. Better than driving home drunk, you know?"

Emma was getting lost in Zeke's ramblings. "Nell was at the wedding?"

But before Emma could ask who the bride and groom were, Zeke shook his head. "I don't know. Maybe. I just saw her in the hallway. She must've been staying in a room on the same floor as us."

"You only saw her in the hallway and remembered her?"

"This photo's been here for the last month. It stuck in my memory. When I saw her in the hotel, I had a feeling I'd seen that face somewhere before." He tipped his head toward the picture on the bar. "That's her. I'm sure of it."

Ninety-five percent sure, Emma thought. "You mentioned your girlfriend was there too. Maybe she saw her."

He shook his head. "No, she didn't."

"Are you sure? Maybe—"

"She didn't." The bite of his words left no room for further discussion.

Still, Zeke had given her more than she had before. If he recognized Nell from the photo, maybe someone at the Royal Palace would too. "Thank you. I appreciate you calling me."

"You want to take the picture with you?"

"No. I have more." Emma pushed the photo across the bar toward him. "Keep it."

She turned away and spotted Kira still chatting up the other man. She had one hip cocked and her fist resting on it. What Emma called her runway-model pose. Clearly the man was enjoying the conversation. Or the way Kira's unitard fit like a second skin.

Emma crossed the room and tapped her on the shoulder. "I'm done here."

The man pouted.

"Nice meeting you, Rafael," Kira told him. "You got my number. Call me." She mimed pressing a phone to her ear.

He held up his palm where he'd jotted her number. "Count on it."

Once outside, Emma faced her friend. "I didn't realize you were back on the prowl. Aren't you dating that cop?" Matthias Honeywell. Emma knew his name but didn't want to let on.

Kira gave a nonchalant shrug. "We go out on occasion. But neither one of us is interested in monogamy right now. He's free to see other women. I'm free to see other men." She looked both ways and started toward the car.

Emma trailed. "I'm surprised. I thought you really liked him."

"I did. I do." Kira shot a wicked grin at Emma. "He's hot."

She beeped the doors open without responding. Hot. At one time, Emma would've laughed. After he'd saved her life, she'd begun to see his appeal.

Plus, she couldn't shake the memory of those fleeting seconds when she'd thrown her arms around his broad shoulders, and he'd returned the embrace.

Kira rounded to the passenger door but stopped, meeting Emma's gaze over the roof. "Unfortunately, he has one big flaw."

"Oh? What's that?"

Kira winked. "He talks entirely too much about *you*."

Chapter Three

By the time Matthias and Frazier returned to Pauly's Polynesian Pub, the Tundra was gone, towed to the garage beneath the police station for processing. Frazier parked their sedan where the pickup had been. Unlike this morning, there was a second vehicle in the lot. A blue Hyundai SUV was nosed in toward a back door to the establishment.

"Someone's home," Frazier said.

As they headed down the sidewalk to the front door, Matthias pulled up Thomas Jenkins's driver's license photo on his phone. A faint light shown through the dirty window, but when Matthias tried the steel door, it didn't budge. He made a fist and pounded.

No one responded.

He pounded again. When he still received no response, he pounded and kept pounding. As expected, he heard the lock click and the door swung open.

"Son of a bitch, we ain't open until—" The man Matthias presumed was Pauly must have noticed their attire because he stopped mid-sentence, his mouth agape.

In case there was any doubt, Matthias held up his badge. "You the owner?"

"Yeah?" He didn't sound too sure.

"Mind if we come in and talk?"

Pauly had the physique of a boxer and looked more like a bouncer than a business owner. With flame-red hair, he definitely didn't look Polynesian. He gave the request serious consideration before shrugging and stepping clear. "Sure. I got nothing to hide."

"I'm sure you don't," Frazier said.

Pauly shut and locked the door behind them. "What can I do for you gentlemen?" he asked as he crossed to the bar where one lone lightbulb shone on a stack of paperwork.

Matthias followed him and set his phone on top of the pile. "Have you seen this man before?"

Pauly picked up a pair of reading glasses and propped them on his hawk-like nose. "Oh, sure. That's Tom. Tom Jenkins. He's a regular." He frowned. "What's he done? I mean he seems like a stand-up guy from what I've seen."

"When did you last see him?"

Pauly took off the glasses and held them by one of the temples. "Last night. He comes in every night around seven or eight."

"What time did he leave?"

Pauly tossed his glasses onto the papers. "What kind of trouble is he in? Pissed off some gal's husband?"

"He do that much? Piss off husbands?"

"Sometimes. Just like you're pissing me off right now. If you're looking for Tom, you'll have to come back later."

Matthias picked up his phone. "We're not looking for Tom. We know exactly where he is."

"The morgue," Frazier said.

The words took a moment to register before Pauly's mouth went slack. "He's dead?"

"Murdered." Frazier crossed his arms. "A few blocks from here."

"Holy Mother of God." Pauly gripped the bar with one trembling hand. "What the hell happened?"

"That's what we need to figure out," Frazier said.

"Let's try this again." Matthias pocketed his phone and dug out his notebook and pen. "What time did he leave here last night?"

"Around midnight, I think."

"Was he alone?"

Pauly huffed. "Nope. Tom always came in alone. Rarely left that way, if you catch my drift."

"Pissing off husbands," Matthias said.

"Sometimes. But only if the broad wasn't wearing a ring. Tom got into it a couple of times with jealous boyfriends, but he mostly tries to stick to the unattached ones."

"What about last night?"

"Never saw the lady before. She wasn't one of the regulars. Don't think she was wearing a ring, but I wasn't paying attention to her hands."

"Can you describe her?"

"Blonde. Pretty. Cute figure. Short skirt, tight top. You know the type. She was looking for Mr. Right. Or at least Mr. Right Now."

"And that was Tom?"

"Apparently."

"Did you catch her name?"

"Hell, no. She paid cash for the first round. Then she latched onto Tom, and he paid for all the rest."

"And they left together?"

"Arm in arm like a couple of lovebirds."

Matthias surveyed the bar and pointed. "That security camera work?"

"Most of the time."

"Mind if we take a look at the footage?"

"If it'll help catch who did that to Tom, sure." Pauly came out from behind the bar and waved them toward a door leading to the back. "He was a real stand-up guy. Ladies' man, sure, but always polite and gentlemanly."

Matthias and Frazier followed the bar owner to a cramped and cluttered office. The camera system could've been classified as antique. Pauly pushed a button and a VHS tape popped out. He handed it to them.

Neither Matthias nor his partner reached for it.

Matthias wagged a finger at the player on the desk. "Do you mind?"

"Not at all." Pauly moved to a second machine attached to a vintage television. The set-up reminded Matthias of watching rented movies when he was a kid.

Pauly inserted the bulky cassette and punched another button. The machine emitted a disturbing whir and hiss as it rewound. It took a few tries, selecting play, rewind, play, and fast forward, but Pauly finally settled on a spot in the recording and let it run. "There." He pointed at the screen. "That's him."

The black and white image was probably grainy when the equipment was new. With the tapes having been over-recorded a few thousand times, the image was barely recognizable as Thomas Jenkins. A woman moved into the frame. She was definitely blonde. Beyond that, Matthias couldn't make out if she was tall, short, underaged or a grandmother.

Pauly excused himself to get back to his bookkeeping and left them to watch the rest of the evening's footage. The blonde and Jenkins became quite cozy as the evening and the drinking progressed. She tottered away at one point, probably to use the restroom, but came back to Jenkins's side, leaning against him. Eventually, the couple stepped back from the bar. Jenkins raised a hand to wave goodbye to someone off camera. Then, arm in arm, they left.

Not once did Matthias get a good look at the blonde's face. "We need to find out who she is."

"Pauly said she's never been in before." Frazier reached over and pressed the eject button.

Matthias pondered the situation. "It's possible she lives nearby."

"Why do you say that?"

"They walked. We know where Jenkins lives. Opposite direction from where he was shot. He left his pickup in the parking lot, so they must've planned to walk to her place."

"She might've parked down the street somewhere."

"Maybe. Either way, between here and there, something went wrong."

Frazier held the VHS tape in his hand and studied it as if it could provide answers. "Maybe she lured him to that alley and pulled a gun."

"That's one possibility."

"What else could it be?"

Matthias ran the scenario through his mind, letting it play out. "Jenkins and the woman were walking back to her place. Or her car. A mugger jumps them. Jenkins plays the hero. Tells her to run. Or she runs without being told. Either way, Jenkins is left to tussle with the mugger. And loses."

Frazier considered the theory. "I hate to say it, but there's a third possibility. The mugger takes out Jenkins and then kidnaps the woman."

Matthias hated this third option. He already had a missing person's case on his desk. A young woman who vanished while walking home from work.

Two missing young women if he added Emma's sister to the mix.

"We don't know who Blondie is," Frazier said. "And we don't know if she's a killer, a victim, or a witness."

"We need to talk to her," Matthias said.

"Which means we need to find her."

And fast.

Pauly agreed to let them take the VHS tape with them, provided they returned it ASAP or replaced it with a new one.

Matthias wasn't sure the latter option was even possible. Did they still make those things?

Pauly also agreed to call if the blonde came back to the bar.

They entered police headquarters through the garage. Frazier veered off to check on the team processing the victim's pickup. Matthias headed upstairs with a stop to leave the tape with the AV guy, who snorted coffee through his nose at the sight of the cassette.

"There's footage of a woman who may be a killer or a kidnap victim," Matthias told him. "I'm not expecting miracles but do what you can."

He climbed the steps to the detective's floor and stopped in the kitchenette for a cup of coffee. Wincing at the bitterness, he entered Major Crimes. The long, narrow room housed eight cubicles along one wall, reminding Matthias of the horse stalls in the barn where he grew up in Oklahoma. Instead of horses, these stalls held desks and computers. He slid into the chair at his station. The cubby behind his had been empty all week. His recently promoted partner, Detective Sergeant Cassie Malone, was on vacation with her husband and granddaughter, who they were caring for while Cassie's daughter was deployed overseas. Cassie had texted photographs of the smiling family at Disney World and Epcot, along with

Wish you were here.

Which would've been sweet except for the multiple laughing emojis attached at the end. This morning, she'd sent a text, sans photos.

Be back Monday. Have all our cases cleared by then.

And another laughing emoji.

His phone rang. He didn't recognize the number on the screen. "Detective Honeywell," he answered.

"Detective, this is Lucille Watson. Gillian's mother?"

The name triggered an emotion that Matthias hated. The sense of dread which came with an ongoing open case. Gillian Watson had been missing for a full week now. A hostess at an upscale restaurant, she was last seen leaving work last Friday. She often walked from work to her downtown Erie apartment. But last Friday, she never arrived home.

"Yes, Mrs. Watson." He didn't ask what she wanted. He knew.

"My daughter, Stephanie, and I are about a block from the police station. Would we be able to meet with you to talk about Gillian's case?"

"Absolutely." He told her to park in the lot west of the department and he'd meet them there.

He found two women standing in front of a tan Toyota sedan. The mother was stooped over, as if the weight of the unknown had crushed her spine and her spirit. The sister looked remarkably like the image of Gillian that Matthias kept burned into his brain, except the sister was a brunette instead of a blonde. He wondered if this might be Gillian's natural color.

They spotted him crossing toward them and offered hands which he shook before asking them to follow him inside. Neither woman spoke as they trailed him up the stairs to the Major Crimes Unit's interview room. He dragged two of the chairs away from the table, positioning them against the beige wall of the small room, and motioned for Gillian's mother and sister to have a seat. Before settling into a third chair facing them, he flipped on the ceiling fan to circulate the stale air.

"How are you holding up?" he asked, hoping his voice

21

radiated his genuine concern. He'd been told his manner tended to scare people. He did not want these two women to be scared.

"I'd be better if my sister would get her ass home," the younger one snapped.

Mrs. Watson placed a hand on her daughter's arm. A nonverbal shush. To Matthias, she said, "You remember my youngest girl, Stephanie?"

He'd met the sister once, last Saturday during the initial interview. "Yes, I remember. I gather you haven't had any word from Gillian?"

"Nothing." Tears welled in her eyes. "I was hoping you might have something for us. A clue as to where she might've gone?"

"I wish I did." He thumbed through his notebook. "The four-block area between the Blue Pike Restaurant and her apartment has been thoroughly searched several times. We haven't found any evidence. Her credit cards haven't been used. We've pinged her cell phone but the last signal from it was ten-thirty p.m. Friday, before she reportedly left work. Our officers have interviewed her neighbors. No one saw her arrive home that night. Her bed was made, and her kitchen was clean."

Stephanie's lips drew into an impatient sneer. "Maybe aliens abducted her."

"Stop it," Mrs. Watson said. "This is serious."

"I know it is." The daughter shifted in the chair, resting an elbow on the armrest opposite her mother. "It just seems to me like you cops should've found something by now." She directed her sharp gaze at Matthias. "Did you talk to the bums who live on the streets in that area?"

His jaw clenched at Stephanie's flippant use of the derogatory term. "There are a few homeless people who camp in the vicinity. We've questioned those who were willing to talk to us, but no one claims to have seen anything."

Mrs. Watson shook her head. "I don't understand Gillian. She

22

has a lovely car. We made sure of that. But she insists on walking. Even after being on her feet all day."

"Have you been able to think of any friends from out of town she might have gone to visit?" he asked. "Someone who might have picked her up after work?"

"She would've told me," Mrs. Watson said. "She knows I would worry."

Matthias caught the deepening crease between Stephanie's brows. "Did you think of something?"

She blinked. "Maybe. If Gillian was going to run off to Tahiti with some sugar daddy, she might not tell us. But I know who she would tell." She looked at her mother. "Didi."

Mrs. Watson shook her head. "Gillian wouldn't run off."

Stephanie's shrug said she might.

Matthias flipped back a couple of pages to find the name. "You're talking about Didi Reed?"

Stephanie nodded. "Gillian's BFF."

"Two peas in a pod," the mother added, although from her expression, Matthias sensed she considered this best-friend-forever to be a rotten pea.

Didi had been out of town when he tried to reach her and hadn't returned his calls. He made a note to try again. Then he studied Stephanie, evaluating her. She seemed impatient and annoyed but not worried. The mother held the monopoly on anxiety where the pair was concerned. "Is there anything else you can tell me that might help us locate Gillian?"

Stephanie shook her head without hesitation. Mrs. Watson thought about it for a couple of beats before mirroring her daughter.

Matthias reminded them that they had his number if they remembered anything, even the smallest detail. They stood and he offered his hand, which the mother grasped but Stephanie ignored.

As he escorted the pair out of the station, he wondered about

Gillian. Was she the type to run off with a rich man as the sister suggested? Or was she the good girl who wouldn't think of leaving without telling her family?

Outside, he watched the women walk away, and his mind drifted to another missing woman and her worried sister. For the last month, he'd spent a good deal of his spare time trying to track down Nell Anderson. Her disappearance was intentional, and as an adult, she had every right to do as she wished, but her history with drugs and alcohol gave her older sister a legitimate reason to want her found.

Emma and Matthias had exchanged a couple of text messages, but he hadn't seen her since that day at her camper. He'd returned her stolen merchandise and offered his help in locating Nell. Her smile was seared into his soul along with the feeling of her arms around him. That embrace. It was simply gratitude on her part. But he couldn't shake the memory of her warmth. Her scent. Those Caribbean blue-green, almost teal, eyes…

He tamped down the surge of emotions that overpowered his better judgement every time he thought of her.

Which had become way too often.

Chapter Four

Kira made good on her offer to buy lunch. Afterward, Emma dropped her off in front of Namaste Yoga so she could get ready for her late-afternoon class.

As Kira climbed out of the Subaru, she turned and leaned into the open passenger window. "You're going to that hotel without me, aren't you?"

"I have to. It's been almost two weeks since the bartender saw Nell there." If it really was Nell. He'd claimed to be ninety-five percent certain. But Emma had been guilty of seeing people she thought she knew, only to be proven wrong.

Kira nodded. "I understand. At least the Royal Palace is a nice place and in a safe part of town. I won't have to worry about you."

Emma gave her an appreciative smile. So few people remained in her life who gave a flying fig what happened to her. "I'll text you and let you know what I find out."

Kira patted the window frame and straightened. "You do that."

Emma watched her friend sashay into the yoga studio, checked the rearview for vehicles, and pulled out.

Traffic was heavy on a June Friday afternoon in Erie. Tourists flooded north on I-79, eager to spend the weekend at the beach or Waldameer Park. Emma joined the southbound traffic on the interstate, locals leaving work a little early and trying to get home.

The Kearsarge exit into Millcreek was backed up. Between nearly a dozen hotels, twice as many restaurants, the Mill Creek Mall, and several satellite shopping plazas, this southern Erie community was a magnet for locals and out-of-towners alike. Emma sat through a red light on Mall Boulevard, another once she'd crossed over the interstate, and finally waited for her chance to make the right turn into the Royal Palace Resort and Convention Center.

She'd been to the Royal Palace once, but not as an overnight guest. A month or so ago she'd attended a photography conference here. Today, she parked at a different entrance. The one with a sign reading Registration.

The lobby soared at least two stories high but otherwise looked nothing like a palace. Emma's sneakers made no sound on the wood flooring as she crossed an open area decorated with modern furniture gathered in assorted seating groups. A half dozen people stood in line to register with one of the two women working the desk. Clutching a photo of Nell, Emma joined the queue and looked around. A husband and wife with three children in various stages of screaming or whining clustered around a trio of roller bags while juggling a pair of backpacks and several totes. Nearby, a young woman in a housekeeping uniform mopped up a mess of what looked like a spilled soft drink mingled with scattered potato chips.

Emma immediately suspected the accident had been caused by the yowling kids, only because she had vague memories of her and Nell at that age, vacationing with their parents.

"I can help you here," the polished woman behind the desk said.

Emma blinked. Apparently all six of the others in line were together and were being taken care of by the other receptionist.

Emma stepped up to the counter and introduced herself. "My sister has been missing for two-and-a-half years. I have reason to believe she may have been a guest here the weekend before last." Emma placed the photo on the counter and slid it toward the woman. "Her name's Nell Anderson."

The receptionist appeared concerned but didn't look at the photo. "I didn't work that weekend," she said as her fingers tapped over the computer keyboard. She scowled at the screen before giving Emma a tight smile. "*If* a Nell Anderson was a registered guest, it would go against company policy to give out that information."

Emma studied the woman, trying to understand what she wasn't saying. "If. You mean she wasn't registered."

The woman squirmed. "I'm really not allowed to say. But I have a kid brother who disappeared for a year before we tracked him down." She glanced at her co-worker who was busy with the group checking in. "No," she whispered to Emma. "There's no Nell Anderson in the system."

Emma regrouped. "You said you didn't work that weekend. Is there anyone else here who did? Maybe they saw her."

The woman looked at the other receptionist. "Roberta, did you work the weekend before last?"

Roberta thought a moment and shook her head. "I was on vacation."

Emma exhaled a sigh. "Would you mind showing that photo around? My email and phone number are on the back. If anyone remembers seeing her, I'd appreciate a call."

The woman smiled sadly. "Certainly. I'm sorry I wasn't more help. Truly."

"Me too." Emma turned and discovered a line had formed behind her. She stepped out of their way and moved toward the door, disappointed yet again.

"Excuse me."

Emma spotted the housekeeper, who'd been cleaning up the spill, approaching and stopped.

"I couldn't help but overhear," the young woman said softly. "Do you have another one of those photos? I worked here that weekend."

Emma dug into a side pocket on her handbag and withdrew another picture. The housekeeper—her name tag identified her as Katie—took the photo in hand and studied it. Emma watched her. Katie appeared to be all beige. Light-brown hair, lightly tanned skin, beige uniform, no makeup. To the hotel guests, this young woman was likely invisible unless they wanted extra towels.

She slowly shook her head. "I'm sorry. I don't recognize her." Katie held up the picture. "Do you mind if I keep this? I can show it around to the others working housekeeping at the time."

"That would be great. Thank you."

Beige Katie smiled. "You seem like a nice person, worrying about your sister like that. I'd like to help."

Emma thanked her again after pointing out her contact information on the back of the image.

"I'll be in touch," Katie said and walked away.

Emma had heard that promise more times than she could count. She watched Katie go and said to herself, "I hope someone will be."

Emma detoured through Wegman's to grab some groceries before joining the northbound traffic on I-79 to her current home, Sara's Campground at the entrance to Presque Isle State Park. As expected, Sara's Restaurant, a local landmark in vivid red and white, was packed and had a long line of cars at the drive-through window. Picking up groceries and cooking in her camper had been the wise choice.

While she'd moved to Erie to find Nell, Emma had settled at Sara's to hide. She no longer needed to hide, but chose to stay. For one thing, she was paid up through the end of the season. For another, she felt safe within this community. No one bothered her. She sensed her neighbors, while keeping a respectful distance, also kept an eye out for her. Word had gotten around about what happened last month.

She eased through the campground and its mix of seasonal camps with a smaller number of un-reserved sites. The man who always walked his shelties waved to her. She smiled and waved back. At the far end of the level grounds, beyond the shower house, she made a right, up a slight hillside to her shaded corner of the world.

She parked, grabbed her groceries from the cargo compartment, and stepped onto her covered wooden deck. After kicking off her shoes, she unlocked the door and swung it outward, securing it with a bungee. Not pretty, but functional.

Inside, the seventeen-foot camper provided the comforts of home and little else. The futon at the front converted into her bed. The galley kitchen consisted of a small sink, a four-burner gas range, and a fridge suitable for a college dorm. Her table doubled as her office workspace, holding two laptops connected to a pair of monitors—a digital version of the darkroom she'd used back home when she played around with film cameras.

As Emma put her groceries away, her thoughts wandered to the events of the morning. The bartender who was "ninety-five-percent sure" he'd seen Nell. And the front desk clerk who had *not* seen her and couldn't find a registration under Nell's name.

Could Nell have used an alias? Absolutely. Emma felt certain Nell was well acquainted with the kinds of people who provided fake IDs. Or she might've stayed with someone else, the room registered in that person's name.

This morning hadn't provided much of a lead on Nell's location. But it was the best Emma had.

She popped the lid from a ready-made salad, which after the big lunch Kira had bought them, would suffice as supper.

Matthias entered Emma's whirling thoughts. He'd offered to help find her sister. She knew he'd been trying. She also knew Nell did not want to be found. But he was a detective. A city cop. He had resources and contacts that Emma lacked. She should call him about what she'd learned.

The thought stopped her in the middle of pouring dressing onto the salad. The idea of reaching out to Matthias tugged her heart in opposite directions. Part of her longed to see him again, a fact which terrified her. For one thing, she'd sworn off men. To call her last relationship a disaster was a monumental understatement. For another, he was dating Kira, her only real friend these days.

Except Kira said they weren't. She'd flirted with that guy in the bar, after all. "He's free to see other women," she'd said. But Emma didn't think Kira would appreciate her being one of those other women. Yet, what was the other thing Kira said?

"He talks entirely too much about *you*."

Emma shook her head to clear her muddled thoughts. Kira had been teasing her.

After adding some salted sunflower seeds to the salad, Emma licked her fingers, and carried her lunch to the futon where she curled up in one corner to eat. Despite her best efforts, her thoughts detoured back to Nell and the Royal Palace.

And Matthias.

Her phone lay where she'd dropped it on the other end of the couch. She set the salad bowl on the ledge next to her and reached for the cell.

Chapter Five

"Where'd you go?" Brad Frazier asked when Matthias returned to Major Crimes.

"Gillian Watson's mother and sister wanted an update on the case."

Frazier made a sour face. "You want to know what I think?"

"Not really." Matthias already knew.

"I think she took off with some rich dude. She's probably floating in some fancy swimming pool or cruising the Mediterranean on a millionaire's yacht. There's no sign of foul play. She turned off her cell phone so no one would bother her. And she hasn't used her credit cards because the rich dude is footing all the bills." Frazier gave a self-satisfied nod.

"Tahiti," Matthias said, too low for Frazier to hear.

"What?"

"Gillian's sister apparently agrees with your theory."

Frazier opened both arms wide. "Well, there ya go."

"But her mother does not."

"Maybe she doesn't share the details with her dear old mom."

Matthias pulled out his notebook and found the page he'd been looking at. "Didi Reed."

"The friend we haven't been able to reach?"

"We need to talk to her. The sister says Gillian might not have shared her plans with the family, but she'd have told this Reed woman."

"I say we focus on the Jenkins homicide. We know this one's a crime. There's no law against a grown woman taking off without telling anyone."

Matthias disregarded Frazier and pulled out his phone. "Have we found anything in the pickup yet?"

"Not so far. No wallet, anyway. They're still going over it for fibers and prints."

Matthias keyed in the number from his notebook. After four rings, Didi Reed's voicemail picked up. He left the same message as the past three attempts.

"Ms. Reed is probably with Ms. Watson," Frazier said. "Double date." He smirked. "Or a threesome."

"You're a sick bastard, you know that?" Matthias growled.

Frazier chuckled but quickly turned serious. "We should talk to Jenkins's ex-wife. Officers Kollman and Lyle already notified her of her husband's demise. I spoke with Lyle. According to him, she wasn't too broken up over the news."

"Yeah. We need to piece together Jenkins's recent history. She might be able to help. After that, we'll go to his apartment. Talk to his neighbors." As Matthias stood, his cell rang.

Emma Anderson. All of his conflicting emotions regarding this woman boiled up inside him. Attraction, resistance, joy at the thought of hearing her voice. Dread because he'd experienced firsthand how relationships ended.

"I have to take this," he told Frazier. "I'll catch you at the car."

Once Frazier left the room, Matthias reclaimed his seat and thumbed the green button. "Hey," he said softly. "How are you?"

There was a momentary pause. "I'm okay. How about you?"

He cringed at the whole small talk thing. If Emma was calling him, it wasn't to check on his wellbeing. "What can I do for you?"

Another pause. "I may have a lead on Nell."

He listened while she talked about some guy named Zeke from Mercury Tavern and Grill. Matthias knew the place. Knew it was one step up from a nuisance dive bar. Knew of the number of times law enforcement had responded there over the years. Emma was talking about this guy and a wedding at the Royal Palace, but Matthias cut her off. "You shouldn't be going into places like the Mercury. I don't want another missing woman's case on my plate. Or worse." He hated the heavy note of concern in his voice and hoped Emma didn't catch it.

"I wasn't alone. Kira went with me."

Kira. He kept forgetting she and Emma had become friends. He wondered what Kira told Emma about him and immediately stopped. He was an egotistical ass for thinking they talked about him. Kira was someone to spend an occasional evening with. Nothing more. And Emma was only interested in him as a cop who could help find her sister. "Kira shouldn't be going into places like that, either."

"Kira can take care of herself." He could hear the amusement in Emma's voice. "She may teach yogic living and being calm and centered, but I'm pretty sure she could kick ass with the best of them."

He couldn't argue the point, but it didn't assuage his fears about the two of them going into bars like the Mercury. "What were you saying about a wedding at the Royal Palace?"

"Zeke thinks he saw Nell there the weekend before last. I talked to a woman at the front desk and to one of the housekeepers." Emma shared her findings. Or lack of them.

"That was two weeks ago," he reminded her. "If this Zeke character was correct about seeing her—and I wouldn't put a lot of faith in anyone who works at the Mercury—she could've gone anywhere since then."

"I know."

Her obvious pain made him instantly regret his words. But he couldn't help remembering what Frazier had said about Gillian Watson. Nell wasn't breaking any law by avoiding her sister either. Still, Matthias remembered the devastation in Emma's eyes when she'd told him about Nell's dive into alcohol and drugs after their parents were killed. Nell didn't fall into the official definition of a missing person, but was definitely an endangered one. "I'll try to go over to the hotel this weekend and ask around."

"Thanks." She sounded more disappointed than relieved. Not his intention.

"This is good news, right?" he said, wanting to hear the sparkle in her voice again. "She's still in Erie. And she's alive." He didn't tell Emma how he'd been paying close attention to every Jane Doe who came into the morgue. How he had a friend at the trauma center who kept him abreast of overdose victims. He may have failed at finding Nell, but his failure wasn't the worst thing that could happen.

"So you believe Zeke?"

"Do *you* believe him?"

Yet another pause. "I believe he's telling the truth. He didn't come across as trying to con me. But I also believe he's not a hundred percent certain it was Nell he saw." Emma huffed a forlorn laugh. "If he said she was living on the street, I wouldn't have questioned it. But the Royal Palace? What would she be doing at an expensive conference hotel?"

Matthias knew of one reason she'd be there, but if Emma hadn't come up with the world's oldest profession, he wasn't going to add to her worries. "I'll ask around and get back to you."

"Thanks." This time she sounded genuinely grateful.

They ended the call. Matthias sat at his desk looking down at his phone. Somehow he would find a few minutes to drive down to Millcreek. Maybe he'd even swing by the Mercury Tavern and Grill and size up this Zeke character. If he found out anything at all, it would give him an excuse to drop in at Sara's Campground and site 518.

He swiveled in his chair and glanced at the empty desk behind him. Good thing Cassie was away on vacation. He could just hear her getting on him about the Cute Photographer Chick, as she so fondly referred to Emma. If Cassie really knew how he felt, she'd have a field day over this latest phone call.

"Mrs. Jenkins?" Matthias held up his badge.

"Petrovich." The pretty brunette had eyes that could flash-freeze an active volcano. "Olivia Petrovich. When Tom and I divorced, I wanted nothing from him. Not even his name."

"Mind if we come in and ask you a few questions?"

She stepped clear and allowed them into the modest two-story house.

The small living room was packed with oversized furniture including a sofa positioned so close to the front door that Matthias nearly tripped over it. Thomas Jenkins's ex-wife ushered them around the maze and flopped into a well-used recliner. Matthias and Frazier lowered onto a portion of a massive sectional that faced her.

"I don't know what I could possibly tell you," she said before they had a chance to ask their first question. "I haven't had anything to do with Tom for over a year."

"When was the last time you spoke with him?" Frazier asked.

She leveled her gaze at the detective. "Over a year ago," she replied, sounding like a kindergarten teacher explaining the word "no" to a youngster.

Matthias struggled to maintain a straight face. "Do you know who any of his friends were?"

She sighed. "A few." She rattled off a list, which Matthias jotted on a new page of his notebook. "But I haven't been in contact with any of them. Tom may have alienated them, too."

"Too?"

"He used to have more friends. That was before he started hitting on their wives."

Sweet guy. Matthias thought of the bartender and what he'd said. Ladies' man. Polite. Gentlemanly. "Is that why you divorced him?

"Yes. He was never faithful. It wasn't in his nature."

Matthias had to wonder why she married the guy in the first place.

She must've read his mind. Exhaling, she looked down, the ice in her eyes thawing. "We met back in high school. He was the quarterback. I was the head cheerleader. We were the ideal couple. Homecoming king and queen. In hindsight, his true colors were already showing. He could be mean. He'd play pranks on the unpopular kids. Act like he wanted to be friends only to humiliate them in front of everyone." She lifted her gaze and spotted Matthias looking at her. "I know, I know. I should've known better, but he was always a terrific boyfriend. It was after we married that reality reared its ugly head." She brushed a loose strand of hair from her face. "Or maybe it took that long for me to see who he really was."

"That must've made you angry," Frazier said.

Her gaze shifted to him. "It did. At the time. To be honest, I was as angry at myself for being an idiot as I was at him. But that was years ago. I'm over it."

Matthias wasn't so sure. He made a note. Had it really been more than a year since Olivia Petrovich saw her ex? "Mr. Jenkins was last seen leaving Pauly's Polynesian Pub with a blonde."

Petrovich shrugged. "He lives near there. Makes sense that's where he'd hang out."

"Any idea who the blonde might be?" Matthias asked.

She hiccupped a laugh. "Hell, no. And I'd be willing to bet Tom didn't either."

"Did he have a thing for blondes in particular?"

36

"Tom was an equal opportunity sex fiend. He didn't care if she was blonde, brunette, or a redhead. If she had boobs, he'd hit on her."

Despite her claims to be over it, Matthias picked up a hint of bitterness in her voice.

"Look," she said. "I know what you're thinking. The wife is always a suspect, am I right?"

Matthias didn't answer, hoping Frazier wouldn't either.

But he did. "It's just routine."

Her eyes froze over again. "I may not have liked him very much, but I wouldn't wish this on him. You're looking for his killer? My money is on a jealous girlfriend or husband."

"What's your take on Ms. Petrovich?" Frazier asked when they were back in the car with the air conditioning cranked on high.

Matthias contemplated the question. Smart. Attractive. But he couldn't get those frosty eyes out of his mind. "I think she's carrying a lot more hostility toward her ex than she's willing to say."

"I got that too. What do you think? She put on a blonde wig and met him at the bar? Lured him into the alley and shot him?"

Matthias choked back a laugh. "A blonde wig wouldn't conceal her identity from the man she was married to."

Frazier shrugged. "No, but they might've been into some kinky role-playing shit."

Matthias considered the idea and wanted to dismiss it, but couldn't entirely. "I don't see Jenkins going off to an alley with a woman he knew despised him."

"Maybe she doesn't despise him as much as she lets on. I say we show Pauly her photo. I can doctor it up on my computer to make her a blonde."

Matthias started the car. "Good idea. But first, let's head over to Jenkins's apartment building and do a knock-and-talk. Maybe his neighbors can shed some light on his habits. Who he was seeing. Olivia Petrovich might be right about a jealous husband or girlfriend. If his apartment's walls are thin, the folks next door might have a lot to say."

Matthias skirted the main arteries to avoid Friday's late afternoon traffic. Still, the trip took almost twenty minutes.

The apartment complex reminded Matthias of an old motel. Two stories, exterior entrances. A stairway led to the second-floor balcony that ran the length of the building. About half of the units had decorated their small outdoor patches with potted plants and cheap lawn chairs.

The CSU truck was parked in front of the first-floor apartment matching Jenkins's address. The forensic techs were finishing up as they arrived. Billy Everett, who looked to be all of fourteen, shook Matthias's hand. "We're done here," Billy said.

"Find anything interesting?" Matthias asked.

"Won't know until we analyze it and, in some cases, have something to match it to." Billy's eyebrows waggled. "Our victim didn't wash his sheets very often. Potentially lots of DNA there."

Matthias made a mental note to do laundry on his next day off.

Billy grew serious. "I can tell you we found no blood evidence. Everything was neat and in place. Dusty, but no signs of any rough stuff. Beyond the bed, that is."

"Don't suppose you found a calendar or appointment book?" Matthias asked.

"Or a little black book," Frazier added.

"Maybe on his computer. We already have it bagged and tagged. I'll let you know what we find."

"Thanks."

"I'm outta here," Billy said. "Lock up when you're done."

Matthias and Frazier did a slow walk-through of the apartment. One bedroom. A decent-sized bath. A kitchen open to the living space. One huge television.

Lots of fingerprint dust.

Matthias didn't think they would find anything here linked to Jenkins's murder. Except maybe for the body secretions from the bed. It was up to the lab to sort that out. "Let's go talk to the neighbors."

No one responded at either of the apartments sharing walls with Jenkins's unit. A burly man with bloodshot eyes answered their knock on the next unit but mumbled a few expletives and told them he minded his own business before slamming the door in their faces. Most other residents on the ground level were equally unhelpful.

They headed up the concrete stairs to the second floor.

At the first two apartments, either no one was home, or they pretended not to be. Matthias paused at the third one, which he deemed as the winner for best outdoor décor. Red, white, and blue bunting hung from the railing. Large terracotta pots filled with flowers had small American flags stabbed into the dirt. A Fourth of July banner plastered the door even though the holiday was still a couple of weeks away. Expecting nothing, Matthias knocked.

From inside, a dog started baying.

"Wow," Frazier said. "Sounds like a big one."

The dog fell silent, and a woman who looked to be in her sixties appeared at the door, her gray hair pulled into a ponytail. "How can I help you?"

Frazier showed his badge and introduced them. "Do you happen to know your neighbor downstairs in 1B?"

"Tom? Oh, sure. He feeds and walks my dog when I go out of

town." Concern creased her forehead. "Is he in some sort of trouble?"

"I'm sorry to have to tell you, he's dead."

"What?" The word came out in a squeak as her hand covered her mouth. "What happened?"

"That's what we're trying to find out. May we come in?"

She stepped back. "Please."

The apartment was a duplicate of Jenkins's but with a definite feminine flare. And a dog the size of a small horse. The beast immediately advanced on them. Matthias noted its tail was not wagging.

"Oh," the woman said. "Let me put Pinky in the bedroom."

Matthias met Frazier's gaze and mouthed, "Pinky?"

Frazier shrugged.

The woman returned and introduced herself as Viola Beele. They turned down her offer of something to drink but accepted seats in her spotless living room. Spotless except for a coating of dog hair.

Frazier continued to take the lead. "How long have you known Tom Jenkins?"

She plucked a tissue from a box next to her chair. "He was living here when I moved in two years ago. To be completely honest, he's the only one in this entire building who's ever said a word to me. I'll miss him. You didn't say what happened. I assume it wasn't an accident since the police are questioning his neighbors."

"It doesn't appear to be an accident, no," Frazier said. "When was the last time you saw him?"

She thought about it. "I guess it was yesterday morning. I have insomnia, so I'm always up before most folks." She pointed to her window and the upholstered chair next to it. "I like to watch the sun come up and the world come alive outside with my cup of coffee. I always see Tom leave for work at seven a.m." Viola's expression turned glum. "I didn't see him this morning. I should've known something was wrong."

"Did you ever see Tom come home after work?"

Her face grew guarded. "Sometimes."

"Did he ever bring company home with him?"

Viola's chin came up. "I may like to look out the window, but I'm not a nosy neighbor. What Tom did was none of my business."

Matthias leaned forward. "Ma'am, Tom was shot to death in an alley after being seen leaving a bar with a blonde woman. We're not suggesting you're nosy, but you may have seen something that could help us find his killer."

His words had their intended effect. Viola stiffened. She sat back in her chair as if he had physically shoved her. "Oh, my God," she said. "How horrible."

"Have you ever seen him bring a blonde back to his apartment?"

Viola hesitated, then nodded. "Lots of times."

Matthias brought the tip of his pen to his notebook.

"But I've also seen him with dark-haired women and redheads."

Not surprising. Not exactly helpful either.

"Like I said, Tom was always a gentleman to me. Always willing to help. So I overlooked his..." she struggled to find the words. "...playboy lifestyle."

"Did he see any one woman on a regular basis?" Matthias asked.

"No. At least not that I noticed. It was always someone new. As far as I could tell, he never...*dated*...the same woman twice. If you can call what they did 'dating.'"

Matthias looked down at his notes. As much as he missed working with Cassie, right now he was happy she wasn't here. She often accused him of the very same thing. He could well imagine the heckling she'd be giving him.

They thanked Viola for her time and left her apartment. After she'd closed her door behind them, Frazier turned to Matthias. "Looks like we can rule out a jealous girlfriend."

"Not necessarily. One of his conquests might've read more into a one-night stand than she should have."

"Maybe. But my money's on one of his conquests having a husband with a temper. And a gun."

Chapter Six

The price of having Friday off was having to work Saturday and Sunday. Emma didn't complain. After months of scraping by on a freelance photographer's income, she was now scraping by on that of a staff photographer. The money was only marginally better, but she had regular paydays to plan around.

The staff room for ErieLIVE had seen its last remodel sometime in the seventies. Gray metal filing cabinets and desks that were never intended to hold computers anchored the décor. At least newer ergonomic chairs had been purchased at some point.

Emma's boss, Laurie Kassim, handed out the day's assignments in her usual take-no-prisoners manner. Emma knew Laurie had a softer side—she'd seen it when she shared her story about Nell—but handling a staff of mostly men forced Laurie to maintain a strict, all-business façade.

Laurie teamed Emma with Rocco Vitale to cover the local youth soccer games. Rocco fancied himself a sportswriter destined to report on the NFL. Barely out of college, he let everyone know about his big dreams. He also treated Emma as if she had one foot in the grave. She'd pointed out that she was only thirty. He responded by calling her a crone.

ANNETTE DASHOFY

Laurie knew about the exchange and had whispered to Emma, "Feel free to kick his ass."

Despite Rocco's ageist views, Emma didn't mind working with him. He may have thought she was old, but he also respected her skill with a camera.

As she checked her gear and made sure her lenses were free of smudges, her phone rang. A month ago, not recognizing the number would've sent her into a panic. Thanks to Matthias, her stalker was no longer an issue.

"Is this Emma Anderson?" a meek voice asked.

"Yes."

"This is Katie. We met yesterday at the Royal Palace Resort."

Beige Katie from Housekeeping. Emma's pulse quickened. "Yes, Katie. I remember you."

"I may have some information about your sister."

Emma checked her watch. Eight-thirty a.m. The first soccer game didn't start for an hour. "I can be at the hotel in fifteen minutes to meet you."

"I have today off. How about coffee?"

"Do you know where Prime Cuppa Joe is?" Emma asked.

"Downtown on Peach Street?"

"That's it."

"I can be there by nine."

That would be cutting it close, getting to the game. "See you there," Emma said.

Emma told Rocco she'd meet him at the field.

Prime Cuppa Joe occupied a narrow but deep store front in downtown Erie. The interior matched the exterior brick, playing on the industrial look of the building. A half dozen tables and mismatched chairs occupied the front of the coffee shop. Shelves and a glass display case housing pastries and sandwiches lined one side of the space about a third of the way back, with a few more tables against the opposite wall.

Emma ordered a white chocolate mocha and grabbed a seat facing the window with plenty of time to spare. She hoped Katie might be early.

She wasn't, but she was punctual. Katie entered at promptly nine o'clock, wearing khakis and a tan blouse. Beige Katie even when she wasn't in her housekeeping uniform.

She bypassed the line for coffee and slid into the chair across from Emma. "Hi," she said, her voice little more than a whisper.

"Thanks for meeting me." Emma tried to remain relaxed, battling her urge to lean over the table and demand answers.

"I showed your sister's picture to the other housekeepers. One of the ladies recognized her."

"She was there?"

Katie gave a quick nod. "But as far as I've been able to learn, she wasn't registered under her name."

"I know."

Katie appeared surprised.

Emma remembered the woman at the front desk mentioning she was going against company policy and decided against explaining how she knew.

When Emma didn't elaborate, Katie continued. "Not being registered doesn't really mean anything, though. There was a wedding and a big graduation party that weekend. Both booked huge blocks of rooms. People share to cut costs. If she was doing that, the room could've been booked under her friend's name."

Nell's friend. Emma didn't have the faintest idea who her little sister's friends were anymore.

"Or," Katie went on, "she might not have been a guest at all and was using a friend's room to change clothes for one of the parties."

Or, Emma thought, it wasn't Nell at all. "Is this woman absolutely positive the person she saw was Nell?"

Katie brightened. "Oh, yes. Everyone teases Betty about having a photographic memory. She remembers everything down to the tiniest detail. For instance, she remembered your sister was wearing a floral sundress. Lots of color. And yellow sandals."

Nell loved bright colors. Always had. The memory raised an unexpected flood of hot tears. Emma blinked hard to keep them at bay. "Sounds right," she managed to choke out, her voice raspy.

"There's something else." Katie glanced around furtively. She dug into her tan handbag and withdrew a USB flash drive. She pinched it between her finger and thumb, holding it in front of Emma.

"What's that?"

"I have a friend in Security. Since Betty knew when she'd seen your sister, what she was wearing, and what floor she was on, he was able to find her on the CCTV footage. We copied it here." Katie waved the flash drive.

Emma reached for it, but Katie pulled back, closing her fingers around it. Her face suddenly tightened with worry. "If anyone ever found out about this, my friend and I would both get fired. And no one else in this business would ever hire us."

"I understand. I won't tell a soul."

Katie's smile returned. She opened her palm.

Emma snatched the drive before Katie changed her mind. "Thank you. Really. You have no idea how much this means to me." Emma needed to repay the young housekeeper and reached for her purse. "Let me give you something for your trouble."

Katie raised both hands. "You're so sweet, but you don't need to do that. I'm glad to help." She climbed to her feet. "I'll let you know if I find out anything else."

Emma thanked her again and watched her leave. She looked down at the flash drive in her hand. It probably wouldn't get her any closer to finding Nell. But if the image did show her at that hotel two weeks ago, at least Emma would know she wasn't wasting her time staying in Erie.

At least she'd know Nell was still alive.

Chapter Seven

The morgue was housed in the basement of the Erie County Courthouse, an easy three-block walk from the police department.

Easy, but not one Matthias enjoyed making.

He stood well back from the stainless-steel table where Thomas Jenkins's body lay open to the world. Or at least to the forensic pathologist, the coroner, and a pair of autopsy techs.

Matthias felt no need to see any of it for himself. Frazier stood at his side, craning his neck for a better view.

"They'll let you watch from up close," Matthias told him.

"That's okay." Frazier made a show of crossing his arms and leaning against the wall behind them. "I'm good."

Felix Hamilton exchanged a few words with the pathologist, gave a nod, and moved away from the body. He stripped off his gloves and other protective gear, deposited them in a bin, and approached the two detectives.

"Any surprises?" Matthias asked.

"Not really," Hamilton said. "Victim was a healthy, fit male in his mid-twenties. He measured six-feet tall and weighed one hundred eighty-two pounds. He was struck by three bullets. One ripped through the small intestines. The second perforated the descending aorta, which in of itself would've proved fatal. But the head shot was the cause of death. He suffered massive brain trauma. All three bullets entered from the front. None exited the body."

"Is that the order in which he was struck?" Frazier asked. "Intestines, aorta, head?"

"It's difficult to say which of the gunshots to the abdomen was first. But they were both up close and personal. In my expert opinion, those two, either singularly or together, dropped him. Then the killer stood over him to deliver the final and fatal shot to the head."

Frazier elbowed Matthias. "Professional hit. I'll bet you ten bucks."

Hamilton shrugged. "It's a possibility."

Matthias looked toward the counter where a small pan held the extracted bullets, and a brown bag contained the victim's clothing. "Did you come up with anything else that might help us?"

The coroner crossed his arms. "There were no defensive wounds."

Interesting. "So he knew his attacker," Matthias said. "He'd never have let a mugger—or a hitman—get that close. Not without a struggle."

"I bet a professional hitman could get close. It's his job." Frazier fingered his mustache.

Matthias had to admit Frazier made a good point. But there was more to the case. "We haven't tracked down the blonde woman yet," Matthias said, hating where his mind returned to next. "What if his attacker managed to grab her after killing Jenkins?"

Frazier met Matthias's gaze. "We need to find this mystery blonde."

Hamilton cleared his throat. "Not that it'll provide any

immediate help, but we did retrieve several blonde hairs from the victim's shirt. Those and the other trace fibers are already on their way to the lab."

Matthias thanked the coroner and headed for the door, Frazier right behind. They had a lot of work to do and not a lot of time to do it.

Back at the station, they met with Lieutenant Armstrong and the uniformed officers working the current caseload for a briefing. There was still no activity on Gillian Watson's credit cards, bank accounts, social media, or cell phone. Another sweep had been made of the streets and alleys between her home and the restaurant at which she worked. This time, they'd widened the scope in case she'd taken a different route. Or in case she'd been dragged off her usual path.

Matthias tried to ignore the other option that haunted him. If she'd been grabbed and stuffed in a car, she could be anywhere. Including Lake Erie or the bay. "Ms. Watson's sister seems to think she may have run off with a man."

"The friends I spoke to all mentioned her attraction to the wealthy type," one of the officers said. He read from his notebook. "Age and looks don't matter to her nearly as much as a fellow's portfolio."

Matthias hoped that was the case. He'd be beyond happy to learn Gillian Watson had shown up tanned and blissful following a private cruise of the tropics. "One friend we haven't reached is Didi Reed. The sister says if Ms. Watson told anyone her plans, it would be Reed."

"Maybe the friend went with her and the rich boyfriend," the officer suggested.

"Let's not settle for maybes," Armstrong said. "Honeywell, Frazier, double down on this Didi Reed. If you can't track her

51

down, look into her family, social media, employment. You know the routine."

The discussion moved on to Thomas Jenkins. Matthias let Frazier report on the autopsy findings and his theories.

The tech wizard reported on his progress—or lack thereof—with the VHS tapes. "I've digitized the footage and done everything I can to clean up the images." He shook his head. "For one thing, those tapes are ancient and have been recorded over so many times, I'm amazed there's any viable image at all. For another, there isn't a clear view of the woman's face. There's one shot of them leaving." Tech Wizard indicated a printout of the image in question, which was being handed around the room. "Again, no recognizable facial features. But knowing Jenkins is a six-footer, we're estimating the woman is roughly five four. Average weight and build."

Which they already knew thanks to Pauly at the bar.

Assignments were handed out. The neighborhood where the body was found would be revisited, especially the houses where no one responded yesterday. Matthias and Frazier would continue to search for the woman with whom Jenkins was last seen, as well as continuing to track down Gillian Watson's wayward best friend.

"What do you want to do first?" Frazier asked once the meeting broke up.

Matthias already had his phone out and his notebook open. "I'm trying Didi Reed's number. If we can manage to talk to her, we might get some answers."

As in previous attempts, the call went to voicemail. Matthias once again left a message, this one sterner than the first four.

Frazier leaned against the wall. "You think she's dodging us?"

"If she is, it's not gonna work," Matthias said. He was tired of spinning his wheels on these two cases. "Let's go pound on her door."

Didi Reed's address was a small bungalow west of town. What

were once flower beds now boasted a healthy crop of weeds. The small lawn hadn't been mown recently. Maybe she really had joined her friend in a threesome aboard a yacht. Or maybe Gillian —and Nell—weren't the only missing women.

Then there was the mystery blonde.

Matthias climbed the three concrete steps to the stoop and pounded on the aluminum storm door. There was no response. No sounds from inside. Frazier wandered over to the detached garage and framed his eyes against the dirty windows.

"There's a car inside," he said.

Matthias didn't like this. He descended the steps and peered into the large, picture window. The interior of the house was dark. He made out furniture in the shadows. As far as he could tell, everything was in order. No signs of a scuffle.

From the house next door, he heard children laughing.

He started across the yard. "I wonder if Didi has nosy neighbors."

A privacy fence blocked the view but included a latched gate between the properties. Matthias lifted the latch. Not locked. He stepped through, Frazier right behind.

The kids he'd heard were climbing on a massive play set. A woman sat on the white painted brick home's porch with a cup of coffee. She spotted Matthias and Frazier and came to her feet. She reminded Matthias of a mother bear ready to take out anyone who threatened her cubs.

"Can I help you?" Her tone was definitely more mother bear than neighborhood welcoming committee.

Matthias unclipped his badge and held it out as he approached. "Detectives Honeywell and Frazier, Erie Bureau of Police. Do you mind if we ask you a few questions?"

Mother Bear folded her arms across her chest, her gaze darting from them to the gate they'd come through and back. "What's this about?"

Matthias hiked a thumb over his shoulder. "We're trying to track down Didi Reed. Do you know her?"

"Sure I know her. She's not in any trouble, is she?"

Matthias closed the distance between them. "Not that I know of. I need to talk to her about a friend of hers, and she isn't returning my calls." He gave her his practiced cop smile.

"She's out of town."

He pulled out his notebook. "I'm sorry. I didn't get your name."

Mother Bear hesitated. She glanced at her kids before replying, "Marie Connor."

"How do you know Didi's out of town?"

"She told me. Asked me to pick up her mail for her."

"Do you know where she went?"

Mother Bear Marie squirmed. "I don't think she'd want me giving out that information. She's very private."

Matthias lowered his head, exasperated. "Mrs. Connor, the friend I mentioned? She's missing. Her family is very concerned. Didi may have knowledge of where she is."

"Or Didi may be missing as well," Frazier said.

Matthias shot a look at his partner.

"No," Marie said, shaking her head. "Didi's fine. I spoke with her just the other day."

"You saw her?" Matthias asked.

"She phoned me. Told me she was expecting a delivery and asked me to keep an eye out for it. I did and I brought it over here, just as she asked."

"What day was this?"

"Do you mean the day the package arrived?"

"No, the day Didi called you."

Marie brought one hand to her mouth and tapped her lips. "Let me think. Today's Saturday. The package arrived Thursday. Must've been Tuesday or Wednesday. Wednesday, I think."

He scribbled a note and lifted his gaze to meet hers. "Since

Didi isn't returning my calls, would you be willing to call her for me? Maybe she'll answer if she sees your name on caller ID."

Marie brought her phone from her pocket. "I doubt she'll pick up. It's been my experience that when she's on vacation, she's *on vacation*, if you know what I mean. She unplugs from everything."

"Could you try? If she doesn't answer, leave a message and ask her to call me. She should have my number."

Mother Bear Marie agreed with a nod and worked her thumbs over the screen. She must've put the device on speaker because Matthias could hear the ring back tones.

Just as when he'd called, voice mail picked up. Marie left the message he requested and hung up. "Sorry."

"I appreciate your help." He handed her one of his cards. "If you hear from her, please let me know." He decided to pull a Columbo. "One more thing. Do you know where she went on vacation?"

His attempt to trip her up failed. "Like I said, I shouldn't tell you."

He held her gaze and waited.

Marie's resolve gave way. "Tuscany. She's part of a group tour."

Tuscany? Damn. He wouldn't answer his phone either.

Major Crimes was quiet. Only those detectives working on time-sensitive cases—like the Jenkins murder—worked weekends. That left Matthias and Frazier alone at their desks.

They split the tasks. Matthias worked on Didi Reed's social-media pages while Frazier focused on Jenkins's background.

Matthias was having no luck. Everyone else in the world posted their vacation photos as they were happening. Normally, it bugged the hell out of him. Go ahead and announce to all the burglarizing trolls on the internet that you weren't home. Please, come rob my house.

Not Didi. The last images she had posted showed her in a tight, short dress with a group of young men and women, also dressed for clubbing. That had been ten days ago.

He started composing a list of Didi's friends, especially local ones. Then he clicked over to Gillian's page and made a column of their mutual friends. He hoped Mother Bear Marie would have Didi get back to him before he had to start contacting each one of the names. It was a long list.

Frazier appeared next to Matthias's cubby. "Having any luck?"

"Define 'luck.'"

Frazier apparently took that as a no. "I'm making some progress on Jenkins's past."

Matthias swiveled his chair to face his partner. "And?"

"No wants or warrants. No criminal history at all. If he ever had a run-in with a jealous husband or boyfriend in the past, no one reported it. He graduated seven years ago from Erie High School and ranked in the middle of his class. Like his ex told us, he was the team's quarterback." Frazier clenched a fist. "Go, Royals. He attended Edinboro but dropped out after a year at which time he went to work for his uncle's construction company. I spoke with Billy Everett about what the CSU investigators came up with. He found Jenkins's bank records on his computer. Looks like he maintains a small balance on each of three credit cards but has enough in his bank accounts to pay them off if he wanted to."

Matthias rolled the information around in his mind. Something stuck. He thumbed through his notes and found it. "Jenkins went to Erie High School? So did Gillian Watson."

"So did I," Frazier said. "So did just about anyone who grew up around here. What high school did *you* go to?"

Matthias leveled a flat stare at him. "East Central High. Tulsa, Oklahoma."

"I forgot you were a cowboy."

Before Matthias had a chance to comment, Lt. Armstrong strode through the door. "We have a dead body." He read off an address on 16th Street.

An address dead center of the area in which they'd been searching for Gillian Watson.

Matthias and Frazier approached the block in question. Police cruisers barricaded the streets but waved the unmarked black Impala through. Matthias parked, climbed out, and took in the scene before him. Backed against the old railroad tracks, several blocks of 16th Street consisted of redbrick warehouses, abandoned and gradually being transitioned into trendy businesses with loft apartments. Including the restaurant where Gillian Watson worked. But that was at the far end of the block. The coroner's wagon and marked police vehicles were gathered around a gap between two of the structures which had yet to be renovated.

Matthias and Frazier headed toward the passageway, wide enough for a vehicle but not designed for one. A uniformed officer at the opening directed them down a crumbling and weedy sidewalk. Roughly forty feet into the shadowy walkway, more officers gathered next to a pipe railing. Concrete steps lead to a subterranean level and a heavy steel fire door, which was currently propped open. "Down there," one of them pointed. "It's not pretty."

"Dead bodies never are," Matthias muttered as he descended into the warehouse's basement.

The space inside the door was dark, the sole lighting provided by officers' flashlights aimed at what Matthias assumed was the body.

At the bottom of the steps, two more uniforms stood like stone sentries, their faces equally pale. Matthias only had to inhale to know why. The stench of decomp was something he was familiar with, but that first rancid whiff always turned his stomach. "What have we got?" he asked.

"There was a team of developers upstairs, looking the place over," the youngest of the uniforms said, clearly trying to speak while not breathing. "One of them found her. He said he thought a rat or a stray dog had wandered in and died so he went looking for the source of the smell and found her."

"Female?" Frazier asked.

The uniform nodded. "Judging by her clothes. You sure can't tell by looking at her face."

Frazier glanced at Matthias. "Gillian Watson."

"Probably," Matthias said. "Let's go talk to Ham."

They moved toward the ring of light and the body. Felix Hamilton was climbing to his feet and spotted them. "Long time, no see," he said without a hint of humor. Without being asked, he added, "Female victim, probably mid-twenties. Hard to tell how long she's been deceased, but considering the rate of decomp, I'd say at least a week to ten days."

"Did you find ID on her?" Matthias asked.

"Yep." Hamilton held out a palm to one of the officers who placed a sodden wallet in it.

"Gillian Watson," Matthias said.

"Nope."

Not the answer Matthias had expected. Didi Reed? No. Her neighbor had spoken to her more recently than that.

Hamilton unsnapped the wallet. "There's no cash or credit cards." He spread the wallet open and turned it so Matthias could see the driver's license. Matthias looked at it. Blinked, certain he'd read it wrong. But he hadn't. In the last month, he'd become familiar with the photo. And the name.

Nell Anderson.

Chapter Eight

E mma couldn't wait to get home after a long day of capturing photos of young soccer players. She still had hours of work to do once she uploaded the images to her computer, sorting through hundreds of shots, picking out those that not only captured the action but also the emotion on the players' faces. With any luck, she'd end up with a half a dozen to send to the editor at ErieLIVE.

She hadn't had a chance to view the flash drive's contents. While she knew she should focus first on the paying work, she also knew she'd be distracted until she viewed the footage Beige Katie had provided.

Emma made the turn into the campground. Sara's Restaurant was jumping with oldies' rock and roll playing over the outdoor speakers, and families crammed the picnic tables. She eased her way through the entrance gate to the campground, cautious of kids on bikes and grownups out for a stroll. As she made the turn up the hill toward her camper, she noticed a black Chevy Impala sitting in her parking spot.

Matthias? He must have news on Nell. Why else would he

drop by to visit? Part of her wished he was there strictly to see her, but she knew better.

Emma pulled in next to the Impala, climbed out of her Forester, and looked toward her deck. Matthias sat in one of her lawn chairs. Alone. No partner accompanied him. "Hi," she called.

"Hey," he called back. His tone was gruff and low, but he had that kind of whiskey-smooth, slightly sandpapery voice.

She snagged her camera bag from the back seat and slammed the door. "I'm surprised to see you here," she said as she approached her deck.

He leaned forward but didn't rise. Instead he gestured to the empty chair.

She held up her keys. "Let me put my camera equipment inside."

He rose to his feet and blocked her way. He took her keys in one hand and the strap of the bag in the other. "Sit down."

Emma met and held his gaze, searching those intense blue eyes. This wasn't good. She'd seen him angry and distrustful. She'd become familiar with the veil he used to cloak his emotions —what she'd come to call his cop face. She'd also seen him relaxed, teasing. And scared.

This? This was something new. Somewhere in the back of her brain, in the pit of her stomach, she knew what he was here to tell her. But she couldn't let herself go there.

Her fingers released their hold, and he took her camera bag and keys and set them on the shelf next to the camper's door. "Sit down," he said again, softer this time.

Her knees no longer wanted to hold her, and she dropped into the chair. She didn't—couldn't ask the question. What happened? She already knew.

Matthias moved his chair to face hers. Set it so close that when he sat, their knees touched. He again took her hands, holding them as if trying to hold her together. "There's no easy way to tell you this. We found Nell's body this afternoon."

Emma had read it in his eyes, in his tight jaw. Hearing the words should've made it real. And yet, she couldn't grasp the concept. "No. That can't be right. She—she was just seen at the Royal Palace." Not *"just"* a voice inside her brain whispered. *Two weeks ago.*

Matthias kept holding her hands in his. Kept holding her gaze.

She pulled one hand free. "I have proof." She dug into her pocket and withdrew the flash drive. "It's on here. Proof that she was at the Royal Palace." *Two weeks ago.*

He closed his fingers around the drive and around her hand. "What is this?"

"I told you about that wedding. This is a copy of the hotel's security tape showing Nell. I haven't had a chance to look at it yet—"

He cut her off. "This was a couple weeks ago, right? Or was she seen there more recently?"

Emma's throat was tightening. "No," she squeaked. "It was…" *Two weeks ago.* Two long weeks during which anything could've happened. Nell could've…Emma looked down at her hands in his. Hers were trembling. "You saw her? This afternoon?"

He nodded.

The world was closing in around Emma, darkness encompassing her peripheral vision. "It was her?" She heard the question. Knew it was coming from her lips. But her own voice seemed miles away.

"It was."

She knew he wasn't lying. Yet she couldn't accept his words as true. "No. You're wrong."

He remained silent, steady.

Emma couldn't breathe. Air refused to pass the emotional clot in her throat. Matthias was wrong. He had to be. "I want to see the body."

He shook his head. Slowly. Without breaking eye contact. "That's not a good idea."

"Why?" Emma snapped, harsher than she'd intended. She summoned fortitude she didn't feel. "You think I can't handle it?"

"There just isn't much to see."

"What's that supposed to mean? Were you there? Did you see her?"

"Yes."

"Then take me to her. I need to see her for myself."

"They've moved the body to the morgue."

"The body?" Emma heard the shrillness in her voice. "You mean my sister. She's not just *the body*."

He lowered his eyes. Emma read the pain in his clenched jaw. This wasn't easy for him.

But it was a helluva lot harder for her. "Where did she die?"

"The—" Matthias winced. "Nell's body was found inside the basement of one of the old warehouses downtown."

Emma's imagination ran amok. She pictured a dark, musty, industrial cavern. Spiderwebs. Rats. And Nell. Dying alone. "I want to see her."

Matthias released one of her hands. He shifted his weight to one hip and brought his phone from his pocket. Still clinging to her other hand, as if afraid she'd bolt, he thumbed the screen, tapped, and thumbed again. Finally he found what he was searching for and looked at her. "I won't take you to the morgue. You're right. I don't think you can handle it."

She started to protest.

"But I have a photo."

She held out her free hand. He turned the screen toward her and let her take the device.

She'd had trouble drawing a breath before. Now she sat in a vacuum, staring at an unrecognizable image. The face was gone, eaten away by time and bugs. The hair was dark blonde, shoulder-length. Neither were proof this poor soul was Nell.

As if reading her mind, Matthias reached over and swiped the screen to the next photo.

Emma stared at the driver's license. Nell's face. Same dark blonde hair as in the previous picture. Her name. The address was her old one from back home in Washington County. A hundred-and-fifty miles away might as well have been a thousand miles. The license, the photo, the address all blurred in a rush of hot tears.

"We found that on the body," Matthias said so softly she barely heard him.

Emma closed her eyes against the tears and the encroaching darkness of reality. Images danced frenetically across her mind. Nell as a little girl, Emma's bratty kid sister, always wanting to tag along. Wanting to go to school with her, even though Emma was six years older. The two of them, riding horses, their shared passion. Emma protecting Nell from bullies. Going to the fair together. Sharing secrets. The long-forgotten man Emma had been in love with at twenty-four until he broke up with her only to ask out a then-eighteen-year-old Nell, who'd turned him down flat. Nell reluctantly telling Emma.

They'd shared grief. Losing their beloved grandparents. Losing their parents. They'd shared their guilt over that last one, both believing they could have prevented it.

That was when Nell started drinking. Then taking drugs. And eventually she ran away. Disappeared. Ended up here in Erie.

Ended up dead.

The phone slipped from Emma's fingers. Matthias caught it before it hit the deck.

Nell. Was dead.

Emma staggered to her feet. Swayed. Matthias leapt from his chair and caught her as he had his phone. She allowed him to wrap her in his strong arms. Suddenly, the fear she'd carried for over two years—the fear of finding out that Nell had overdosed—had come true. The worst-case scenario had happened. Emma

63

buried her face against Matthias's shoulder and let the sobs and the anguish and the emptiness devour her.

Chapter Nine

Matthias held Emma, feeling her body convulse with tsunami waves of sobs. He was vaguely aware of her neighbors across the road staring at them. This deck was far too public for such a private display of grief. Once he felt her legs gaining strength, he guided her, half stumbling, to the camper door only to find it locked.

She still clung to him but managed to reach for her camera bag on the shelf where he'd put it and retrieved a key ring from one of its exterior pockets. He took the keys from her and made three attempts before finding one that fit the lock.

Once inside, he eased her down onto the futon. She slouched, rocked forward, and braced her elbows on her knees, burying her face in her hands. She no longer quaked. Instead, she grew still as granite.

He couldn't simply leave her there. He reached outside to bring the camera bag in and placed it next to her. Looking around, he searched for something tangible he could do to help and spotted an empty four-cup coffee maker next to the sink. He rummaged through cupboards, quickly finding a plastic bin filled with ground coffee. Next to it, a box containing filters.

As he busied himself making a fresh pot, Emma pushed up to her feet and brushed behind him. He thought she was headed for the small bathroom at the rear of the camper. Instead, she slid into the bench seat at the table. Furtive glances told him she was booting up her computer. He resisted the urge to tell her she needed to rest. He'd seen enough grief in his job to know everyone dealt differently. Having cried it out, maybe she needed the distraction of work.

Once the coffee maker began to bubble and hiss, Matthias moved to Emma's side. She didn't look up at him but slid over, making room. He claimed the vacated space.

He'd forgotten about the flash drive, which was now plugged into the laptop. The image on the screen made him instantly regret not demanding she lie down and close her eyes. Security footage showed a hotel hallway. Which hotel didn't matter. Their hallways all looked the same. But he knew this was the Royal Palace. In the distance, a woman exited a room and moved toward the camera.

Emma's sharp intake of breath was audible. He saw it too. She hit a key on the computer, freezing the video. The woman in the image was Nell.

Tears streamed down Emma's face again. Matthias knew she was focused on seeing her sister. He noticed two other things though.

The timestamp at the bottom of the footage. A little after six p.m. Saturday evening, two weeks ago. He fumbled with his phone to confirm the second. The photo from the crime scene was still queued up.

The badly decomposed body was wearing a floral sundress and yellow sandals.

So was Emma's sister in the hotel footage.

"Oh, God."

Matthias had been so engrossed in the comparison, he failed to notice Emma looking at his phone. Too late, he turned it over.

"It's her." Emma's voice sounded as ragged as shattered glass. "The clothes match."

"I'm so sorry." He wanted desperately to offer some hope. He couldn't.

"She's really gone."

His detective's training kicked in and he pointed at the computer. "Who gave you that flash drive?"

Emma's lips parted, but she closed them again.

Why was she reluctant to tell him? "Emma?"

She breathed a loud sigh. "I gave my word I wouldn't tell."

He debated arguing, pressing her for an answer. Instead, he settled on silence.

It worked. Emma squirmed. "She could lose her job if her boss found out she gave this to me."

"I'll do my best to see that doesn't happen." He modulated his tone, seeking a balance between firm and compassionate. "Tell me."

She lowered her gaze. "A housekeeper at the hotel."

"Did you get her name? Number?"

"Katie," Emma said. "Beige Katie."

"What?"

Emma huffed. It might've been a laugh if she wasn't so distraught. "I don't know her last name. I didn't get a number. I'd given her one of those photos with my contact info on the back. She called me."

"Beige Katie?"

"That's just a trick I use to remember names. She was all beige. Tan uniform. Sandy brown hair. No makeup. She was just…"

"Beige Katie. I get it. I use the same trick sometimes."

She met his gaze. "What did you used to call me? Before we got to be friends, I mean."

Cute photographer chick. No, that's what Cassie had dubbed her. It took all his willpower to resist reaching over, caressing her cheek. "I never had a problem remembering you."

The cheek he longed to touch flushed crimson. She returned to the computer screen, shattering the moment—a moment that he shouldn't have let happen. Not now.

He clenched his fists under the table and focused on his job. "You said she called you."

"Yeah."

"Her number should be on your phone log."

"Oh." She handed her cell to him. "You're right."

He took the device and clicked on the incoming-call list. Selecting the one he suspected was Katie, he showed the screen to Emma. "Is this it?"

She nodded.

"I'll track her down."

Emma's gaze returned to the image on her computer monitor.

"There's something I need to ask you," he said, hating that police business had to intrude.

"Anything." She sounded like she meant it. Anything.

Focus. "We need to positively identify the body." Her expression signaled she misunderstood. "There's no way you—or anyone—could do that by viewing the—her," he said quickly, then added, "Dental records. Do you know who her dentist was?"

"Oh." She thought about it. "Dr. Androulakis from back home in Washington."

Matthias opened his notebook. "A name like that, I should be able to find a number for him."

"No." She was gazing out the window, but he had a feeling she wasn't seeing the campground.

"No?"

"I'll drive down and get them."

"That's not how it works."

"It's not a problem. I've been thinking about making the trip for a while. Ever since Clay…"

She didn't have to finish the sentence. Or the name. Matthias knew. Clay Bauer. Her stalker who was no longer a threat.

"Ever since it's been safe to go home," she said instead. "I have business I need to take care of. Now feels like a good time for a road trip. It'll clear my head."

"I could go with you." The words were out before he could stop them.

"No. You need to find out how my sister died."

"You're right." He shouldn't have suggested it. For so very many reasons. "But the dental records are a police matter. Subpoenas and all that."

"Ah. Right." She continued to stare at the computer for several long moments before shifting her gaze to him. "I'm still going to make that trip home."

"Do you think you're safe to drive?"

"Well, not right this minute." She almost grinned. Then it was gone. "Tomorrow. I'll drive home tomorrow. Take care of Nell's—" Her breath caught. She looked away from him and choked back another sob. When she spoke again, her voice was almost a whisper. "I'll take care of funeral arrangements on Monday. I'll be back Monday night or Tuesday."

He wanted to make her swear an oath that she'd be back. She'd said she was going *home*. Back to where she'd grown up and lived until a few months ago. Now that Bauer was no longer in the picture and the hopes of finding Nell wasn't keeping her here, what if Emma never returned to Erie?

Matthias chastised himself the entire drive south to Millcreek and the Royal Palace Resort and Conference Center. He'd shown way too much of his heart to Emma. He mentally spelled out a long list of reasons why he was a fool for doing so. Emma was distraught over losing her sister. Her memories of what might otherwise have been sweet moments would forever be tainted, linked to this horrible day. Never mind his own shitty history with women.

Cassie teased him about never dating the same woman twice. It wasn't far from the truth. He'd cared too deeply once—twice—and then developed an impenetrable shell. He was a cop. A real relationship wasn't in the cards.

And now he was having feelings for Emma. The kind that, if he wasn't careful, could shatter him into a million pieces all over again. Not to mention what it would do to her.

At the hotel, he strode through the electronic doors and assessed the people in the lobby. One rail-thin man stood behind the registration desk, head down, occupied by his computer. A pair of teenage girls mulled over the selections in a closet-sized market next to registration. The place was quiet this afternoon.

As Matthias approached the desk, the guy at the computer looked up. "Do you have a reservation?"

Matthias held up his badge. The man blinked but didn't show any adverse reactions to facing a cop. "I'm looking for a young woman who works in housekeeping here. Her name's Katie."

"Katie who? We have four of them."

Beige Katie wouldn't do. "I don't have her last name." He used part of Emma's description. "Light brown hair."

"That describes three of them."

Dammit. Matthias's phone rang. Frazier, according to caller ID. He excused himself and moved toward the high windows surrounding the lobby.

"Where are you?" Frazier demanded. "I thought you were doing a death notification."

"I was. I did. I'm following up on a potential lead." Why was Matthias bothering to explain himself to Frazier? "What's up?"

"We have a potential lead here too."

"On the Nell Anderson homicide?"

"No, on the Jenkins case. Finish up what you're doing and get back to the office." Frazier hung up before Matthias could tell him he sounded like a jealous wife.

He returned to the skinny guy at the desk. "Are any of these Katies working today?"

The man tapped his keyboard and scanned his monitor three times. "Two of them were on duty this morning. None of them are here now."

Matthias reached into his pocket and shelled out three business cards. "Tell you what. Give one of these to each Katie with sandy brown hair and ask them to call me. I'll sort out which one I need to talk to."

Back at the station, Matthias found Frazier at his desk. "Okay, what's this potential lead?"

Frazier didn't look up from his computer. "For starters, Jenkins's wallet's been found."

"Where?"

"A local resident found it in a trash can. No cash or credit cards in it. Just a driver's license and gas rewards card. Confirms our mugging theory."

Maybe for Frazier, but questions popped like fireworks in Matthias's brain. "You say a resident found it in a trash can?"

"Yep." Frazier still never looked up.

Matthias pictured the trash receptacles in the area. Large, black municipal things. Not the sort of can where a person was likely to walk by, glance in, and see a wallet. "Where?"

Visibly annoyed, Frazier turned away from his monitor to look at a printout on his desk. "Corner of Eighth and Cherry. About two blocks from the crime scene. Mugger blew Jenkins away, took the wallet, cleaned out the cash and plastic, and tossed it while getting away."

"What's the name of this civic-minded resident?"

"Sebastian Wilcox. He lives over on Liberty. And I don't know how civic-minded he is. According to the report, the first thing he wanted to know was if there was reward money involved."

Matthias imagined the dude's disappointment. "No good

deed," he said under his breath. To Frazier, he asked, "Is Sebastian Wilcox a city refuse worker?"

"No."

"When did he find the wallet?"

For the first time since Matthias's return, Frazier brought his gaze to bear on him. "What difference does it make?"

Matthias was quickly changing his mind about Frazier being a good cop. "This is Saturday afternoon. Jenkins was mugged Thursday night, Friday morning. What took Wilcox so long to turn it in? And how the hell did he find it? Was he dumpster diving? Was he digging for something else in the trash and just happened to find a wallet? I could maybe see if he was working trash collection for the city, but for a citizen to just happen to find it? I'm not buying it."

Frazier went back to looking at his computer, but Matthias could tell he wasn't seeing whatever was on the screen. Matthias had stumped him, and Frazier didn't like being stumped.

"Where's the wallet now?" Matthias asked.

"At the lab."

"Did you question Wilcox?"

"No."

Matthias gave Frazier a few more moments to process before asking, "Don't you think we should?"

"Yeah. I guess so."

"Then let's go."

"Wait. I told you the wallet was for starters. There's more."

Matthias hoped what was coming next didn't raise more questions.

"When we spoke with Jenkins's ex-wife, she failed to mention she had a boyfriend." Frazier no longer looked like a chastised schoolboy. He looked more like the Cheshire Cat.

"And?"

"She does. The guy's last name is Nuccetelli. First name is

Paul." Frazier eyed Matthias as if the name should mean something.

It didn't. "So?"

"Nuccetelli goes by Pauly."

"As in Pauly's Polynesian Pub?"

"That's the one. Funny. Pauly never mentioned having a girlfriend either."

"Especially one who used to be married to his now-deceased regular patron." Wilcox and the wallet suddenly seemed much less interesting. Still, his address and that of the pub were mere blocks apart. "I'm driving."

No one came to the door at the address they had for Sebastian Wilcox. Matthias tried the phone number they had for him. The call went to voicemail. So much for talking to the finder of the wallet tonight.

Pauly's Polynesian Pub was already standing-at-the-bar-room-only, possibly due to the buy-one-get-one-free happy hour special. The blackboard sign at the door also listed a discount on wings and fried fish. Considering the size of the crowd, Matthias wondered if he should place an order to go.

It seemed the only person *not* at the pub was the one they were looking for.

"He ain't here." The burly, bearded, and inked man behind the bar barely looked up from drawing a draft when Frazier asked about Pauly.

"Any idea when he will be?"

That earned his attention. "Will be what?" From his expression, Matthias gathered he was sincerely puzzled.

"Here," Frazier repeated. "When will he be here?"

The man grunted. "Not tonight. Not tomorrow. Maybe Monday."

Matthias made a show of surveying the crowd. "Is that common? The boss taking off on a busy weekend?"

"He's the boss. He can do whatever he damned well wants."

Matthias rested an elbow on the bar, leaned toward the bartender, and gave him the look Cassie told Matthias was intimidating. "That wasn't my question."

The look worked. "No. It ain't usual. I usually work as a bouncer, not a bartender. Pauly handles this job all on his own. But he called me a couple hours ago and asked me to fill in."

"Did he say why?" Frazier asked. "Or where he was going?"

"All he said was he and his girlfriend made last-minute plans. For what? I got no idea."

Frazier looked at Matthias and shrugged. "Guess we'll have to come back on Monday."

But Matthias scrolled through his phone, found Jenkins's photo, and turned the device toward the bouncer-turned-bartender. "Do you know this guy?"

"Yeah. That's Tom. I heard he got killed not far from here. Damn shame. He was a nice guy. The ladies all loved him."

"Did anyone around here not love him?"

When the man got that perplexed look again, Matthias elaborated. "Did he ever piss anyone off? Maybe for hitting on a dude's girlfriend or wife?"

He made a face. "Not that I ever saw."

"How about Pauly?"

"You mean, did Pauly ever piss anyone off?"

Forget the wings and fish. Matthias was going to need a good, stiff drink by the time he finished talking to this guy. "Did Pauly ever get pissed off at Tom?"

"Oh. Not that I know of. Tom was a good customer. Why would Pauly get pissed at him?"

"Maybe because Tom used to be married to Pauly's girlfriend?"

"What?" The bartender's shock was genuine. He wasn't smart

enough to be that good an actor. "I didn't know that." He squinted. "I wonder if Pauly knows."

Good question. Matthias intended to ask Pauly when they tracked him down. "Were you working here Thursday night?"

"Thursday? Yeah. As a bouncer. Not as a bartender."

A harried waitress elbowed in between Matthias and Frazier. "I need four drafts," she said and scurried away.

Before the bartender could fill the order, Matthias asked, "Did you see Tom Jenkins leave?"

"Yeah. With a hot blonde. What a babe. New customer. I'd have remembered if she'd been in before. Those two, Tom and the blonde, were all over each other. Lucky bastard."

Matthias waited for the bartender to realize what he'd said. He didn't.

Frazier leaned forward, bracing both arms on the bar. "Have you ever seen Pauly's girlfriend?"

"Nah. She don't come around here." He tipped his head toward the waitress. "I need to get back to work before she gets mad." Lowering his voice, he added, "You don't wanna see that little gal get mad."

Matthias and Frazier thanked him and made their way out to the street. "What do you think?" Frazier asked. "Do we revisit the ex?"

"Try getting her on the phone."

Frazier placed the call as they strode down the sidewalk to the parking lot. "Voicemail," he said, pocketing the device. "Seems like everyone's out on the town tonight."

Ahead of them, Matthias spotted a skinny young man coming their way and realized it was the same scrawny guy they'd encountered yesterday morning. He obviously spotted them too. This time, he didn't give them a chance to stop him. He pivoted, almost falling in the effort, and hurried back the way he'd come.

Matthias pointed after him. "I'm beginning to take his rejection personally,"

Frazier looked at him. "You should. You're one scary-looking dude."

Matthias met his gaze. Was Frazier attempting to be funny for once? Without a hint of a grin, he kept walking toward their car.

Nope, Matthias decided. Humor wasn't Frazier's thing.

Chapter Ten

Sunday morning, a steady rain thrummed the Forester's roof as Emma set out. She grabbed breakfast at one of the takeout windows along West Twelfth before picking up I-79 south. The rain lessened to a drizzle by the time she made one rest stop. And the sun came out as she reached home by ten a.m. Except home wasn't home anymore. The property was still there but both houses were gone. Burned to the ground. A bulldozer had buried the foundation of the smaller one, leaving no sign of the single-story bungalow her father had built.

The circa 1850 farmhouse had burned last month, the acrid stench faint but still there. Two chimneys remained standing, flanking a fieldstone foundation and the charred remains of Emma's youth.

Having left the clouds behind, she stood under a hazy blue sky in knee-high weeds at the edge of the yard. She clutched her Nikon in hand, except she couldn't bring herself to make images of the forlorn landscape. The breeze whispered voices of ghosts through the tall pines. Grandma shouting for everyone to come in for dinner. Grandpap cursing his tractor for not starting. Mom chastising the girls for not feeding the chickens.

Emma's camera couldn't see Nell racing around the yard with puppies nipping her heels. But Emma could. And she could hear her sister giggling and squealing in delight.

The old barn still stood well beyond where the house had been. Beyond where Grandma grew her impressive vegetable garden. Beyond the springhouse, above which Grandpap and Dad housed their workshop. Both Emma and Nell had learned to drive on the farm lane between the house and the barn.

Emma's entire life was here on this land. And now it was gone. All of it.

She bent down and stuffed the camera back in its bag.

"I am so sorry I'm late."

She wheeled and came face-to-face with Eric Baker, her best and truest friend.

"I meant to be here before you," he said, opening his arms wide.

Emma fell into them and surrendered again to her grief. She buried her face into the middle of his chest, which was as high as she stood. Eric, tall, broad-shouldered, fair-haired, handsome, and very gay, had been her guardian and protector-of-secrets all through school. When she made the decision to leave Clay, Eric was the only person she trusted with her plans and location.

In turn, always a genealogy geek, he'd hired her to photograph tombstones of his ancestors in Erie.

After receiving the news about Nell, Eric was Emma's first phone call.

The second was to Laurie at ErieLIVE, who told her to take all the time she needed.

Emma sniffled and drew back, digging a well-used tissue from her jeans pocket. "I'm sorry. I thought I'd already cried myself out."

"Don't apologize. I can't believe Nell's gone."

"I can. I mean, I can't grasp it yet, but I've been expecting this ever since she ran away."

He surveyed the remnants of the old farmhouse. "You think Clay was behind this?"

The shift in gears caught her by surprise. "Oh. You mean the fire."

"Yeah."

"I do. Both of them." She swung around to look toward the corner of the farm property where her father had built the bungalow. "You'll never convince me otherwise."

"I'd never try." Eric slung an arm around her shoulders. "What are your plans?"

She dabbed at her nose and pocketed the tissue. "Tomorrow morning, I have a meeting with the funeral director to make arrangements. And I suppose I should talk to the guy who bulldozed Mom and Dad's house and ask him to do the same here. It's probably a hazard the way it is now."

"No one should come up here and mess around. I posted the no trespassing signs like you asked."

"Signs don't mean anything. If someone came snooping around with a metal detector looking for old coins and fell in or had a brick from the chimney fall on their head…"

Eric snickered. "I remember your grandfather. He was a tight old buzzard. I can't fathom him ever losing a coin."

"True. He'd have been on his hands and knees going through each blade of grass until he found it."

"Yep." Eric's expression turned somber. "What I really meant when I asked about your plans was, are you intending to move back here?"

Her laugh hiccupped into a sob. "Here? Where?" She swept both arms, gesturing at the two missing houses.

"You have insurance money from the fire. You could rebuild."

"I haven't given it much thought." Not true. She'd thought about it a lot, but not like this. In her dreams, she would bring Nell home with her. Reconstruct a modern version of the farmhouse. Maybe even create the bed and breakfast they'd always talked of running. But now? "I don't know," Emma said.

He gave her a squeeze. "You don't have to decide right this minute."

"It is something to consider though," she admitted. "My campsite in Erie is paid for through the end of the season. I might as well make use of it."

"True, but don't forget. If you do decide to rebuild, it's not going to happen overnight."

"Hey." She elbowed him. "You just told me I didn't have to decide right now. First, I need to focus on burying my sister."

Eric pressed a kiss to the top of her head. "Absolutely. Just know I'm here for you."

"I do. Thank you." The problem, Emma realized, was there wasn't anything luring her back here. No house. No parents. No sister.

But there was a dark-haired, blue-eyed detective up in Erie. She hadn't been truly aware of the hold Matthias had on her heart until she'd driven a hundred-and-fifty miles away.

No. She'd let her misguided feelings for a man direct her decisions once already. She wasn't about to make that mistake again.

Yet even as she steeled her resolve, she remembered the feeling of his strong arms around her yesterday. The feeling of safety when she was most devastated.

She shook her head as though she could shake off the attraction threatening her good sense.

"What's wrong?" Eric asked.

"Nothing. Do me a favor?"

"Anything."

"Take me out to eat. I'm starved."

Chapter Eleven

M atthias arrived at the station early Sunday morning to take advantage of the department's gym. If it hadn't been pouring rain and if he didn't have two fresh homicides and a missing person's case on his plate, he'd have driven to Presque Isle to run the trail.

He was kidding himself, using the cases or the weather as an excuse. His real reason for avoiding the state park was its proximity to Emma's campground. With her sister lying in the morgue, he was struggling to keep her off his mind.

He bypassed the machines, choosing to power through his workout with the free weights and barbells. Even with the strain, the clank of steel, and the stench of sweat, Emma's devastation battled its way into his mind and his heart.

He'd promised to find her sister. But not this way.

After a grueling hour of squats, curls, and bench presses, he hit the shower, changed into his official polo shirt and trousers, and climbed the stairs to the detective division.

He'd expected to find Major Crimes empty, but the tapping of fingers on a keyboard greeted him, as did the aroma of freshly brewed coffee. He filled a cup and stepped into the office.

Detective Sergeant Cassie Malone looked up from her computer. "How are you?"

"Surprised," he said truthfully. "What are you doing here?"

"I work here."

"You're still on vacation until tomorrow."

She rolled her chair halfway into the aisle between the row of cubbies and the wall. "I decided to get up to speed a little early. Now that I outrank you, I can't have you being more informed about our cases than I am."

He snorted. She'd always outranked him merely on the basis of seniority. The addition of "sergeant" to her title was a long overdue acknowledgment by the powers that be. He was happy for her, but knew the promotion didn't change the mutual trust and respect between them.

"You didn't answer. How are you?"

"You think I can't get along without you for a week?" He set his coffee on his desk.

Cassie didn't smile. "I know you can. I also know about the body that was discovered yesterday. Maybe I should be asking, how's Emma?"

Matthias broke eye contact. "She lost her sister. How do you think she is?"

"You made the death notification."

He didn't see the need in confirming what Cassie already knew. He waited for her to chastise him for getting too personally involved.

Instead, she kept her voice soft. "That had to be difficult."

Cassie Malone, tall and fit with dark skin and close-cropped white hair, could be as formidable as a warrior or as compassionate as a mother hen. More often than not, he was at the receiving end of her warrior side and razor-sharp wit. He wasn't used to being mothered by her.

Frazier bustled through the door, bumping into Matthias and saving him from Cassie's therapy session. Frazier appeared clueless to having interrupted anything. "I got the report on the wallet."

"What wallet?" Cassie asked.

Frazier reacted as though he hadn't noticed her before. "Belonged to our murder victim, Thomas Jenkins. A fellow by the name of Sebastian Wilcox turned it in yesterday. Said he found it in the trash."

"Trash?" Cassie scowled. "Was he dumpster diving?"

Matthias lowered his face to conceal a grin.

Frazier aimed a thumb at Matthias. "That's what *he* asked. We haven't spoken with Wilcox yet but intend to. Turns out the only prints on the wallet were his. Wilcox's."

"Interesting," Matthias said, exchanging a knowing look with Cassie.

"Who wiped it down?" she asked. "Wilcox or someone else?"

"The killer," Frazier said.

"Maybe Wilcox *is* the killer." Matthias crossed his arms. "Other than his number and home address, what do we know about him?"

Frazier slipped past Cassie to his own cubicle and sorted through some papers on his desk. "Wilcox is employed at Erie Sand and Gravel as a heavy machine operator. He's lived here all his life. Not married. No wants or warrants."

Cassie rolled her chair toward Frazier's desk and held out a hand. "Give me his number. I'll give him a call and set up a meeting."

Frazier had also been on the receiving end of Cassie's warrior side. Without arguing, he scribbled on a sticky note, tore it off, and handed it to her. She wheeled into her own cubicle and picked up her phone.

"We need to reach Jenkins's ex and Pauly," Matthias said.

"I'm on it." Frazier retreated to his desk.

Which left Matthias to ponder Nell's murder. The autopsy was scheduled for tomorrow morning. They'd already canvassed the area where the body was found, but their questions had been focused on a photo of Gillian. He needed to revisit the residences, businesses, and workmen along those streets.

Gillian's disappearance still bugged him. Nell Anderson's killer walked the same streets as Gillian. They needed to search the vacant buildings and basements. He had a gnawing sensation in his gut that Gillian may have met the same fate as Nell.

Unless her sister was right, and Gillian really had run off with a rich boy toy.

Matthias bumped locating Didi Reed to the top of his priority list. Along with another walk-and-talk around Nell's murder scene, and questioning Pauly Nuccetelli and Olivia Petrovich.

Cassie rolled her chair out of her cubby. "Sebastian Wilcox is on his way in. Should be here in under a half hour."

"At least someone is answering our calls," Frazier said. "I left voicemails for both Pauly and the victim's ex-wife."

"While you gentlemen interview the dumpster diver, what do you want me to do?" Cassie asked.

"Go home," Matthias told her. "You're still on vacation."

"I've spent the last eight days with my husband and granddaughter, twenty-four-seven. There's such a thing as too much togetherness. The two of you are juggling two homicides and a missing person's case. I need to get back to work. You need help." She rocked forward in her chair and repeated, "What do you want me to do?"

Matthias picked up Gillian Watson's file from his desk and handed it to Cassie. "Didi Reed is our missing woman's best friend. According to the sister, if anyone knows where she'd have gone, it would be Didi. But she's off the grid, in Tuscany according to her neighbor."

Cassie flipped through the folder's contents with a scowl. "What are you thinking? Are the two women together?"

"Your guess is as good as mine. See if you can track down

Didi's family members or friends who might be able to put us in touch with her."

"On it." Cassie rolled back to her desk.

Frazier stepped from his cubby, carrying a legal pad. "Are you ready to go talk to Sebastian Wilcox?"

Matthias checked the time. "Yeah. Then let's head down to Sixteenth Street and find out if anyone saw Nell Anderson within the last couple weeks."

Sebastian Wilcox towered over both Matthias and Frazier as they escorted him into one of the interview rooms. On size alone, Wilcox could easily have played lineman for the Steelers or the Bills. He hesitated once inside, assessing his new surroundings.

"I'm not being arrested, am I?"

"Have you broken the law?" Matthias gave him a well-practiced smile meant to put the guy at ease.

"No." He took the chair they indicated and continued to look around. "At least there isn't one of those two-way mirrors," he said with a nervous chuckle.

"Nope." Matthias didn't mention there were video cameras and a fellow cop watching from another room. For now, both audio and video recordings were off, although available at a moment's notice.

Wilcox accepted their offer of coffee. Matthias gave a nod to Frazier, who ducked out, returning a few moments later with a steaming paper cup and a handful of creamers and sugar packets. Matthias watched as the big guy tried a sip, winced, and proceeded to doctor it. Matthias knew from experience there wasn't enough sugar or half-and-half in the entire state of Pennsylvania to make that crap taste good.

Matthias sat across from Wilcox and leaned back, settling into a relaxed posture. "Tell us exactly where you found the wallet."

Wilcox tried another sip, again making a sour face. He pushed the cup away. "I spotted it in the trash can over at the corner of Eighth and Cherry."

About two blocks from the crime scene. "How did you spot it?"

"Excuse me?"

"I realize you're tall, but most folks don't walk down the street peering into the trash."

Wilcox nodded. "I see what you're getting at. I was on my way to a job interview and was studying the notes I'd made and drinking coffee." He eyed the cup on the table. "Better coffee than that, I have to tell you."

Matthias gave him another exaggerated smile. "Go on."

"I finished the coffee and tossed the empty cup in the trash. Except I was so distracted by my notes and the interview, I forgot I was still holding my car keys in the same hand, so I ended up tossing them in the trash too." He rolled his eyes. "Yeah, I'm a klutz and an idiot. While I was digging around for my keys, I found that wallet and opened it to find out who it belonged to. The first thing I saw was the driver's license, and I recognized the name and the photo from the news. It was that Thomas Jenkins dude who got shot last week, so I called 911." Wilcox stopped talking and folded his hands on the table.

Matthias studied him. His story was reasonable and answered all their questions. In a sense, he *had* been dumpster diving. "When exactly was this?"

"Yesterday morning." Matthias could tell Wilcox was thinking. Maybe a little too hard. "I guess around ten."

"How did the interview go?"

The change in direction threw Wilcox. "Huh? Oh. Okay. I haven't heard from them yet. You know, it takes a few days."

"Who were you interviewing with?"

"Who?"

"What company?"

"Oh. Lake View Real Estate."

Matthias made a note to confirm his story. "Are you a real estate agent?"

"Not yet. I work over at Erie Sand and Gravel, but I've been doing some house flipping as a side gig. I thought getting my license would help, so I've taken a few online classes. I'm only five hours away from completion."

"What time was your interview?"

"Ten o'clock."

"So you were late."

"Huh? No."

"You said you found the wallet around ten."

"Yeah. Around. As in a little before."

"Did you call 911 before your interview or after?"

"After."

Matthias tapped his chin with his pen. "Did you ever find your keys?"

"Oh, yeah." Wilcox smiled broadly. "I'd have turned the whole freaking can over to get to them if I had to."

"One last question. What was in the wallet? Besides the driver's license."

The smile faded. "I don't know. I didn't look."

"You didn't check for cash or credit cards?"

"Uh-uh."

Matthias made one last note before thanking Wilcox for his time.

"I can go?" he asked.

"Unless you want another cup of coffee."

The smile was back. "I'll pass."

Matthias let Frazier escort the big man out. Once he was alone in the room, Matthias pulled a pair of nitrile gloves and a couple of small paper evidence bags from his hip pocket. He deposited the used creamers into one. After labeling the bag, he gingerly picked up the still full coffee cup and carried it across the hall to the restroom to dump the contents. The empty cup went into the second evidence bag.

Frazier returned and caught him in the hallway. "What are you doing?"

"Collecting fingerprints and DNA."

"You think Wilcox is guilty of something?"

"I know he's guilty of lying."

Frazier crossed his arms. "About what? All of it?"

Matthias replayed the interview in his mind. "I don't know about all of it. The job interview part is easy enough to confirm. Dropping his keys in the trash is a reasonable excuse. But I'm not buying the part about not looking in the wallet."

"Maybe he's an honest man."

"Honest men are still curious. But even if he doesn't have a curious bone in his body, the logistics don't add up." Matthias handed the evidence bags to Frazier and pulled out his own wallet. "You find this in the trash. You want to see who it belongs to." He opened his billfold and pointed. "I keep my driver's license right there in that window cut-out. Most people do. Right?"

Frazier nodded, but Matthias could tell he still wasn't catching on.

He turned the wallet toward Frazier and ran his finger along his collection of plastic. "Every wallet I've seen has slots for the credit cards next to the space for the license."

Frazier's shoulders sagged as reality started sinking in.

Matthias closed the wallet and stuffed it back in his pocket. "I could maybe buy Wilcox's claim that he didn't check for cash. Maybe. But he had to notice whether or not there were any cards."

Frazier's expression hardened. "If he lied about one thing, there's a good chance he lied about more."

As Matthias bustled through the doorway into Major Crimes with Frazier on his heels, he nearly collided with Cassie. He pulled up short, and Frazier slammed into him from behind.

"Dammit," Matthias growled at both of them.

"I tracked down the missing-woman's friend," Cassie said.

"Didi Reed? Where?"

"Technically speaking, I didn't track down Didi, but I managed to locate a phone number for one of her social-media friends."

He held out a hand. "Give it to me. I'll call her."

"Him. And I already talked to the kid. He didn't know anything about Didi's whereabouts or who she was with, but he did have a number for her parents."

"And you've already called them."

Cassie grinned. "You know me so well. Yes, I talked to her mother."

"And?"

"She confirmed most of what you learned from the neighbor woman. Didi is vacationing in Tuscany as part of a tour and is limiting her texting and phone calls to save money. Rather than buy an international calling plan, she only checks her messages when she's at a hotel with free Wi-Fi."

Matthias swore.

Cassie shushed him with a raised finger. "However, she's supposed to check in with her mom tonight. Mrs. Reed will make sure she calls us first thing in the morning."

"Our time or hers?"

Cassie shrugged. "Beggars can't be choosers."

"Did you ask her if Gillian was with her daughter?"

"I did. Mrs. Reed said Didi was traveling with several close friends but didn't know if Gillian was one of them."

"I guess we'll have to take what we can get," Matthias said. He just wished they could get it sooner rather than later.

"How did your interview with the man who found Thomas Jenkins's wallet go?" Cassie asked.

Frazier slipped past her and Matthias. "I'm going to do some checking on his story."

Cassie eyed Matthias. "Checking?"

He gave her the short version of the interview and watched her expression transform from interested to skeptical.

"No way he didn't notice whether the credit cards were missing," she said. "I'm not even giving him the benefit of the doubt where the cash is concerned. You find a wallet, you check to see how much money's in there. Even the most honest person does that. So they can say 'there's five hundred dollars in there' when they turn it in. Keeps *everyone* on the up-and-up. You know what I'm saying?"

"I do."

"No answer at Lake View Real Estate," Frazier called from his desk. "The recording says everyone's out doing open houses. But I did find Wilcox's Facebook page. He was telling the truth about flipping houses."

Matthias and Cassie slid into Frazier's cubicle behind his chair to look over his shoulder. Wilcox's About Me page did indeed list him as a remodeler. "Maybe he was telling the truth," Matthias said. "Or maybe he's using social media to back up his alibi."

Cassie eyed him. "When did you become so cynical?"

"When I was sixteen."

She snorted a laugh, not realizing Matthias wasn't kidding.

He waved a finger at Frazier's monitor. "Scroll through his posts and photos."

Most consisted of memes. But the pictures Wilcox had posted seemed to confirm his secondary employment. Images of houses he was working on. Selfies with him in plaid shirts and hard hats. Before and after shots of remodeled kitchens.

"Do you believe him now?" Frazier asked.

"I believe he fixes up houses. But there isn't anything there about studying for a real estate license."

Cassie stretched. "It's Sunday. Looks like we aren't going to get any answers today." She tapped Frazier on his shoulder. "Why don't you go home? Get some rest and get a fresh start in the morning."

"Sounds good."

Matthias opened his mouth to complain. They'd had two strikes—one on the Gillian Watson case and one on the Jenkins homicide. But they still had Nell Anderson's homicide to work.

Cassie had a talent for reading his mind. She met his gaze and touched a finger to her lips.

He closed his mouth, gave her a single nod of understanding, and returned to his own desk. After Frazier strode past with a wave, Matthias faced Cassie.

Before he could speak, she said, "Nell Anderson. Let's you and me go do a walk-and-talk down on Sixteenth Street and find out what happened to that girl."

Chapter Twelve

Emma had planned to get a hotel room twenty miles away in the county seat of Washington, Pennsylvania. When Eric offered his guest room only ten minutes from her family farm, she accepted. She'd forgotten what a fabulous cook he was until he set a veggie omelet in front of her in the early hours of Monday morning.

"What's the plan?" he asked between sips of gourmet coffee.

She blew on a forkful of eggs to cool the bite. "I meet with the funeral director at nine o'clock."

"I'll come with you."

"You have to go to work."

"Have you forgotten? It's called *Baker* Consulting. *I* own the company. That gives me the freedom to take time off when a friend needs me."

She set the fork down. "I've missed you."

"I've missed you, too." Eric reached over the kitchen island and picked up her mug. "You need a refill." He crossed to the fancy coffee maker in the corner. As he measured a scoop of beans into the grinder, he glanced her way. "Tell me about him."

"The funeral director?"

"No, you moron. *Him*. The man in Erie who's caught your eye."

Matthias. She almost spoke the name but didn't. How the hell did Eric know? She'd never mentioned anything to him. Had she? "There is no man in Erie."

Eric feigned shock. "No men in Erie? Well, damn. I'm never going there."

She choked on her eggs. "There are plenty of men. Just none who've caught my eye."

"Liar liar, pants on fire."

Emma couldn't help but shake her head in amusement. "Stop being so gay. We both love Randy Rainbow, but you aren't him."

He chuckled. "Oh, come on. You know you're the only one around here that I can joke with. I may not be in the closet but if I want to keep my clientele, I don't dare advertise." He made air quotes.

"I've always wondered why you don't move into Pittsburgh."

"To be closer to my own kind?"

She could tell he was only half joking. "So you'd have someone other than me to laugh at your Randy Rainbow impersonations."

"I know what you mean." Eric inserted the ground coffee into the machine and pressed a button. "Truth is, I'm not about to let those narrow-minded idiots around here run me out of the home I love. Besides, I can see we're making progress a little at a time." He stood taller. "I want to be known as a leader of the Pride Movement."

"I thought you were worried about your clientele."

"It's a fine line." He pushed another button on the machine.

Emma listened to the gadget hiss as he added steamed milk to her cup and thought about her tiny Mr. Coffee back in her camper. Not only could she not afford a professional-grade contraption like Eric's, but she'd also never figure out how to use it.

He returned to the kitchen island and placed her steaming

mug in front of her. "I see what you're doing. Changing the subject. Tell me about the man from Erie."

Eric was right about her changing the subject. "What makes you so convinced there's a man?" she asked.

"Because you can't look me in the eye and say otherwise."

He was right. She kept her focus on what she was doing as she added sugar to her coffee.

"Emma?" He dragged her name out.

He wasn't going to let this drop. She lifted her eyes to meet his, opened her mouth, and closed it again. "I gather you're not going to accept 'it's complicated' as a suitable response."

"You gather correctly."

Emma allowed her mind to wander back to Saturday on her deck. The utter devastation of the news Matthias brought, merging with the comfort of being in his arms. Her memories rewound further. Last month, when she'd been convinced she was about to die, Matthias, already battered, bruised, and bandaged, had stepped into the line of fire.

"Wow. It really *is* complicated," Eric said, although she hadn't spoken a word.

"How can you tell what I'm thinking?" she demanded.

He held up a finger. "You're changing the subject again, but the fact is your face gives everything away."

"Because you've known me since first grade."

He held her gaze, waiting.

She wasn't getting out of this. "All right already. There is a man. But he's dating a friend of mine." A partial lie, but it might get her out of talking about something she wasn't ready to even think about.

Eric's expression melted into a glum scowl. "Oh. Damn."

Kira's words echoed inside Emma's head. *He talks entirely too much about you.* She blinked them away before Eric's mentalist abilities read her mind.

"Is he hot?" he asked hopefully.

"Only if you think dark hair, blue eyes, and a gym-rat's physique is hot."

Eric moaned. "How good a friend is this other woman?"

"Very." Emma heaped on a heavy dose of regret for Eric's sake.

"All right. I'll let the subject drop." He narrowed his eyes. "For now."

She couldn't help but smile. "Thanks."

"For dropping the subject?"

"No. For distracting me from what I have to do today."

Sitting in a dark-paneled office with a handful of tissues and Eric at her side, Emma answered the funeral director's questions. Date of birth was easy. Date of death, less so. She promised to get him a copy of the coroner's report as soon as it was available. Cremation or burial? Cremation. Public service or private? "Private," Emma said.

As for the obituary, Emma named herself as the sole person in the "survived by" column. Preceded in death by? Grandparents and parents. No husband. No children.

She felt Eric's arm reach around the back of her chair as he gave her shoulder a squeeze, which was when she realized she was trembling.

Most of the arrangements were left as pending, but as soon as the Erie County Coroner released Nell's body, it would be transported back here.

Back home.

"You okay?" Eric asked on their way to his car.

She choked out a short laugh.

"All right. Stupid question. What's our next stop? The liquor store?"

She envisioned getting sloppy drunk, weeping while sitting in Eric's living room. Passing out. Except she knew better. Her history with getting drunk enough to forget her woes always ended with her bent over a toilet. "No liquor store."

Eric swore. "Well, it's not like I don't have a fully stocked wine cellar."

No sooner had she settled into the passenger seat than her phone rang. She didn't recognize the number. "Hello?"

"Is this Emma Anderson?" a woman's voice asked.

"Yes. Who is this?"

"Katie from the Royal Palace Resort and Conference Center. I found out what room your sister was in, and the name on the reservation."

Emma's vision clouded. Twenty-four hours ago, she'd have welcomed this news as a potential link to locating Nell. A name on the reservation. Someone to contact about finding her little sister. The hotel sighting was over two weeks old. Emma no longer thought of it as recent. Now it felt like eons ago.

"Emma?" The voice on her cell jarred her back to the present moment.

"I'm here, Katie."

"I'd rather not talk about this over the phone," Katie said, her voice dropping to a whisper as if someone had walked into the room. "Can we meet later this afternoon?"

Emma almost told her that Nell was dead. Almost told her to call the police and give the information to them. But Katie sounded so secretive, afraid of being found out. Afraid of losing her job for divulging information on hotel guests. She probably wouldn't want to talk to a cop. Emma checked the car's clock. Almost ten. By the time they got back to Eric's place it would be close to ten-thirty. It wouldn't take long to throw her stuff back in her overnight bag. She could be on the road by eleven. Three and a half hours to drive back to Erie—provided she didn't stop to use the restroom. "I could probably meet you around two-thirty."

"How about three-thirty?"

"Even better."

"How about at that same coffee house on Peach Street."

"Prime Cuppa Joe?"

"Yes, that one."

"I'll see you then."

Eric was watching her when she looked up from the call. "What was that about? Who's Katie?"

"She's a housekeeper at a hotel where Nell was last seen. She may have information about who Nell was with." Emma flapped a hand toward the car's ignition button. "I need to get back to Erie as soon as possible."

Instead of starting the car, Eric continued to study Emma. Then he nodded. "Okay. But you're in no shape to drive. I'm going with you."

Chapter Thirteen

Yesterday's stroll along 16th Street had yielded nothing. A small homeless encampment set up on the sidewalk was empty. Only one of the residents in the low-income housing across the street responded to their knock. He claimed he hadn't seen anything before Matthias could even mention a date and immediately slammed the door in his and Cassie's faces.

Monday morning, Matthias entered the morgue, expecting to find Frazier observing the postmortem on Nell Anderson. Instead, Cassie looked up as he came through the door. "Where's Frazier?" he asked.

"He gets squeamish about autopsies."

"No he doesn't."

"Oh. Right. That's you."

Not that he'd admit it. "Seriously. Where's Frazier?"

"Armed robbery call came in. I told him and Roth to take it."

"You missed me," Matthias said, laying on the sarcasm.

She snorted. "In your dreams."

He grew serious. "Hear anything from Didi Reed?"

"Not yet."

The coroner stepped away from the body after conferring with the pathologist. Stripping out of his protective gear, he approached Cassie and Matthias.

"Well, Ham?" she said. "What'd you find out?"

Hamilton tossed his scrubs and gloves into the biohazard hamper. "Cause of death was a broken neck. She also sustained multiple skull fractures."

"She was beaten?" Matthias dreaded sharing that news with Emma almost as much as he'd dreaded the death notification.

"Maybe. But considering the number of contusions and abrasions accompanying the neck and skull injuries, I'd say her death was more likely the result of falling down a flight of cement stairs. Like the ones at the building where the body was found."

Matthias pictured the crime scene. "She was found inside the basement. Are you telling me she fell down those stairs and, with a fractured skull and a broken neck, managed to open the steel fire door and crawl inside?"

"No, that isn't what I'm telling you. With this kind of injury, there's no way she crawled anywhere. But there are signs of the body being moved within a few hours of death."

Matthias tried to make sense of this development. Nell fell down a flight of stairs. Died at the bottom, just outside the door. And someone came along and dragged her inside. "Why?"

"Finding that answer is your job, detective."

"Any evidence of recent drug or alcohol use?"

"There weren't any needle marks, and her liver, kidneys, and heart are all in good shape, but I won't know for sure until I get the toxicology reports back."

After collecting the bags holding Nell's clothing and personal effects, Matthias and Cassie left the morgue and walked silently down the hallway toward the doors to the parking lot. She stopped him just inside. "Maybe you should let Frazier and I handle this one."

Matthias studied the concern on her face. "Why? You're the one who sent Frazier on another case."

"Because you're too personally involved."

"I never met the victim."

Cassie's concern grew into annoyance. "Emma."

He broke eye contact to look through the glass doors to the parking lot. "I'm not personally involved with Emma."

"No?"

"No."

He could feel Cassie's gaze scorching the side of his face. She remained still for several moments. When she spoke again, her voice was softer. "The real reason I sent Frazier on the other call was because I wanted to work this one. I like Emma. She's a sweet young woman who took a long walk through Hell in recent years. Now this."

"Maybe *you're* too personally involved." Matthias heard the gravel in his voice.

"Don't be an ass. That's Frazier's MO, not yours."

Matthias's gaze snapped back to Cassie. Her expression held more compassion than her words.

"You have feelings for Emma." Cassie showed him her palm. "No. Don't deny it."

He swallowed hard. "All right. I have feelings for her. But other than informing her of her sister's death, I haven't seen her since I returned her stolen computers. I am not turning this case over to Frazier. Or anyone else."

"Okay."

"Okay?" He'd expected a bigger—or at least longer—argument.

Cassie shrugged. "I just wanted you to admit to yourself that you do care for her." He started to growl a reply, but she stopped him again. "And I want you to be aware that once more, she's involved in a homicide case. Peripherally, but involved nonetheless."

"Got it." He hadn't planned to ask Emma out. Wanted to but wasn't going to. Especially now.

That was part of the problem of building any kind of relationship while being a cop. The timing always sucked.

He pushed through the doors. "See you back at the office." He started off to where he'd parked. The sound of Cassie's phone ringing stopped him. He watched as she answered, then motioned for him to come back.

"Yes, Ms. Reed. This is Detective Sergeant Cassie Malone with the Erie Bureau of Police. I'm going to put you on speaker, if that's all right." Without waiting for approval, Cassie tapped the screen and held the phone so Matthias could hear. He yanked his notebook and pen from his pocket.

"My mother told me to call you." The voice on the other end of the call sounded irritated.

"And we appreciate you doing so. I understand you're close friends with Gillian Watson. Is that correct?"

"Yes."

"Does she happen to be on this trip with you?"

"No," Didi Reed said, as if that was the stupidest idea ever. "Why are you asking?"

"Do you know where Ms. Watson is right now?"

"I have no idea."

"Her family hasn't heard from her in over two weeks and is understandably concerned. Her sister suggested she might have gone off with a boyfriend and thought you would know if that was the case."

"Like I said, I have no idea where Gillian is. Why don't you check at the restaurant where she works?"

"We have," Matthias said.

"Who's this?"

"Detective Matthias Honeywell. The last anyone saw her was when she left work a week ago Friday night."

The line fell silent.

"Ms. Reed?" Cassie said.

"I'm still here." She sounded more worried than annoyed. "That's not like her. You said her sister thinks she's with a man?"

"She thinks it's a possibility."

"You've talked to her boss at the restaurant?"

"We have."

"Russ Carlisle?"

Cassie shot a questioning look at Matthias. He flipped back a few pages. "That's her manager," he said to Cassie. To the phone he replied, "Yes, we spoke to him."

"He's not just her manager. She's been dating him for the last six months."

Funny. He hadn't mentioned that part. Matthias scribbled a note. "I'll question him again."

"I honestly don't know where she would be," Didi said, "but I'll try to get in touch with her."

"Ms. Reed," Cassie said, "when do you plan to return from your trip?"

"I'll be home this Thursday."

"Good. If you manage to contact Gillian, please have her call me at this number."

"I will. And please let me know if you hear anything."

"Absolutely," Cassie said.

Provided Didi answered her phone.

Cassie tucked her cell into her handbag and faced Matthias. "What was that about her boyfriend?"

"He never told us that part." Matthias skimmed through his notes before closing the book and putting it away. "He didn't show any concern beyond that of a boss for a missing employee."

Cassie grunted. "Maybe we should pay him another visit."

"Another? You weren't there the first time. You bumping Frazier from this case, too?"

"I'm assisting. Besides, Didi has *my* phone number, not his or yours."

Chapter Fourteen

E mma searched the customers' faces as she and Eric entered the coffee shop.

"Is she here?" he asked.

"I don't see her."

He flicked a hand toward an empty table by the front window. "Grab a seat. I'll order us a couple of coffees."

Emma snagged the table and positioned herself so she had a view of the door. She placed her phone in front of her. The screen showed the time as three twenty-five.

Customers came and went. No Katie.

Eric approached, carrying two large to-go cups. He set one in front of her. "White chocolate mocha with an extra shot."

"You remembered the white mocha part," Emma said. "But I don't usually get extra espresso."

"You do today." He lowered into the chair next to hers. "You should see yourself. You look like hell."

"Just what a girl loves to hear." She didn't mention she felt like hell, too. "But thanks." Emma spotted Katie through the window, crossing the street. "Here she comes."

Instead of a housekeeping uniform, she wore jeans and an

oversized button-down shirt. Beige, Emma noted as she waved to her.

Katie made her way toward them, and Eric, ever the gentleman, stood. "I'm sorry," she said. "Am I late?"

"Not at all. We just got here." Emma noticed Katie cautiously eyeing Eric and made the introductions. "This is Eric Baker, a friend of mine from back home."

Katie shook the hand he offered but looked at Emma. "I thought we'd be talking alone."

Eric thumbed over his shoulder. "I can go sit in the back."

Katie considered the offer. "No. That's okay. I just don't want my bosses to find out I'm sharing guest information. I'd lose my job."

He gave her his famous killer smile. "I totally understand. What can I get you to drink? I'm playing waiter today."

"Oh. Hot tea?"

"One tea coming up." He swept a hand at the chair he'd vacated. "Have a seat. I'll be back in two shakes."

After he strode away, Katie sat, watching him go. "Boyfriend?"

Emma might've smiled or laughed under different circumstances. "Just a good friend. Tell me what you found out."

Katie dug into the small cross-body bag she carried and came up with a folded slip of paper. She placed it on the table and smoothed it open before sliding it in front of Emma.

She read the block-printed note. "E.A. Dyson. Room 433."

Katie pointed at it. "By looking at the video footage I gave you, we were able to figure out which room your sister came from. Four thirty-three. It was registered to an E.A. Dyson. I don't know what the initials stand for. And please don't ask me how I got this information." Katie made a looping motion with one finger. "The address he gave is on the other side."

Emma flipped the note. She didn't recognize the street name, but it was in Erie.

Katie leaned forward, resting her arms on the table and

smiling eagerly. "Maybe you'll find your sister there."

Emma had been holding it together pretty well until then. From Katie's expression, Emma could imagine what her own face looked like.

"Oh, my gosh," Katie said. "What's wrong? Has something happened?"

Eric picked that moment to return and set a steaming cup with a tea bag tail sticking out from under the lid. "Emma's learned her sister is dead."

She closed her eyes, hoping to keep the hot tears at bay and heard Katie's sharp inhale.

"Oh, no. Oh my gosh. Oh..." Her voice trailed off. "I'm so sorry. If you'd told me, I wouldn't have bothered you."

Emma heard the hiss of paper sliding across the table and opened her eyes. She reached out, pinning Katie's hand beneath her own as the young woman tried to retrieve the note. "No. I wanted to hear what you learned. I want this name and address."

"Why? What does it matter now?"

Emma caught Eric's eye and glanced toward an empty chair, silently asking him to sit, which he did. She swept her free hand across her face, tackling the escaped tears. "It matters. My sister is —was—a drug addict. She died alone in a vacant warehouse."

Katie paled. "Good heavens."

Emma released her hand and tapped the note. "This E.A. Dyson might know who gave her the drugs. Might know how she spent her last day. Days." Emma didn't say it but couldn't help thinking *this E.A. Dyson might* be *the one who gave her the drugs.*

Katie folded her hands around the cup of tea as if they were cold. Her mouth opened and closed twice. Whatever she was thinking, she obviously decided to keep it to herself.

For which Emma was grateful. She'd heard too many sanctimonious comments over the years regarding Nell's addiction. Snide remarks made by people who clearly had never known or loved someone held captive to drugs and booze. Nell wasn't lazy. Wasn't weak. Willpower wasn't enough. She'd tried. Lord, she had tried. Rehab, once, twice, three times. But the demon, strengthened by guilt and agony, had its talons buried deep in Nell's heart and soul. And in the end, had won.

A hand on Emma's back jarred her free of her nightmarish reverie. She blinked at Eric's concerned face and forced a fleeting smile to let him know she was okay. His expression told her he wasn't buying it.

Katie had removed the plastic lid and was blowing on the tea, sending steam swirling away.

Emma stood and felt the ground tilt beneath her feet. She gripped the table as Eric grabbed her arm. A deep breath in and out steadied her. "I'm going to the restroom," she said. "I need to splash some water on my face."

Eric gave one nod. "Good idea."

As she shuffled away, she heard Katie's almost whispered voice asking him, "Tell me what happened? When? Where?"

Emma couldn't blame her for wondering. She'd dragged the poor young woman into her quest. It was human to be curious. Thank heavens Eric was there to field the questions that Emma couldn't.

———

"Now what?" Eric sat behind the wheel of Emma's Subaru at the curb in front of the coffee shop while she occupied the passenger seat. She rarely relinquished the driver's spot—at least voluntarily —but she was grateful beyond words that he'd insisted.

"Now what?" she echoed, her voice thick with exhaustion. She looked down at the note she still clutched. Who the hell was E.A. Dyson? She should call Matthias and turn the information over to him, and she would.

Just not yet.

"Let's go back to Sara's."

"Who's Sara?"

Emma huffed a short laugh. "Good question. I honestly don't know. But her name is on the campground where I live."

"Ah." He turned the key. "You'll have to navigate. I haven't been up here since I was a kid."

She pointed to the windshield. "That way." She directed him toward the scenic Bayfront Parkway so he could see the marinas before the road swept away from the water. The strip malls along West Eighth were less scenic. As they approached the light at Peninsula Drive, she told him to turn right. "Unless you want to visit the cemetery where your ancestors currently reside." She'd done some tombstone photography for him several weeks ago. As soon as she made the suggestion, she regretted it. That cemetery is where she'd first laid eyes on Matthias Honeywell.

"Not today," Eric said. When the light turned green, he swung onto Peninsula.

The thought of Matthias made her realize her next move. She pulled out her phone. "When we get to the bottom of the hill, you'll see a couple of restaurants and a bait shop on the right. Pull into the parking lot. The entrance to the campground is between the businesses."

From the corner of her eye, she saw Eric glance her way. "Who are you calling?"

"The cop who's working the case." No way was she going to tell Eric she was calling the man he'd questioned her about. She got a recording and a beep. "Detective Honeywell, this is Emma Anderson." She was well aware Eric was listening. "I have some information you might be able to use. Please call me when you have a minute."

"Is this the place?" Eric asked as the terrain leveled.

"Yep." She directed him to the gate and through the campground to her site.

He parked where she indicated, turned off the ignition, and handed over her keys. "You live here?"

"Home sweet home." She climbed out, dragging her overnight backpack with her.

Eric exited the SUV and studied her trailer. "I've seen dog houses that are bigger."

"Quit being a snob." Emma crossed in front of her car, careful to not smash her knee on the trailer's hitch for the fifth time. She'd contemplated building some sort of barrier around it. Decorative stone or maybe a miniature picket fence. And plant flowers. Several of her neighbors had done that.

She came to a stop with one foot on her porch deck, realizing she might not live here long enough to bother sprucing it up.

But where would she go? Back home wasn't home anymore.

Eric gave her a gentle nudge from behind. "What's wrong? Is there a snake?"

His exaggerated tone of fright lightened her spirit. When they were kids, she was always the one terrified of snakes. Not Eric. He'd pick them up and toss them safely into the weeds.

"I was just thinking." She stepped onto her deck and crossed to the door.

"Me, too. I'm thinking I guess I won't be staying here tonight."

"There's a bunk over my bed." Emma unlocked the outer door and secured it with the bungee. "I use it for storage, so I'd have to throw all of my stuff on the floor. And I think there's a hundred-and-twenty-pound weight limit." She stepped inside, hung the keys on the hook next to the door, and tossed her backpack on the futon.

"That leaves me out." He followed her and stood in the threshold surveying her home. "I saw some hotels on top of the hill when we were driving in. With a little luck, I can get a room."

"I'm sure you can. It's not a weekend. But unless you're leaving right now, come in and shut the screen door before the mosquitos take up residence."

She was about to dig into the fridge for soft drinks when her phone rang. The screen lit with the name Matthias Honeywell.

"Detective Honeywell," she answered, conscious of Eric's presence. "Thanks for getting back to me."

Silence filled the air. Emma could imagine his confusion surrounding her formal tone. Their friendship—or whatever it was—had surpassed the first name milestone.

"I may have some information about who my sister was in contact with prior to her death. Do you want me to meet you at the police station in the morning?"

"Where are you now?" He sounded wary.

"I just got home."

"Your camper?"

"Yeah."

"I'll be there in fifteen minutes."

Emma was about to protest but the line went dead. She realized why he'd hung up. After what had happened with her stalker ex-boyfriend, Matthias took her professional tone as code for her being in trouble. A large part of her appreciated his protective tendency. But...

"Why are you smiling?"

She looked at Eric, who was watching her with the intensity of a mother bear patrolling her cubs. "I'm not smiling. I'm wincing. The cop said he wasn't far away and is on his way here."

Eric appeared to accept her partial lie.

"I was hoping I could just meet him at the station tomorrow. I'm tired and hungry and don't want to deal with anything else today." She added what she hoped was a sufficiently whiny note to her words.

Eric bought it. "No wonder. We drove straight through without stopping for lunch. I'm famished too. What say we head back out after the detective leaves and grab something to eat?"

"I have a better idea. Why don't you take my car and go get takeout and bring it back? I really don't feel like venturing out again." And with a little luck, Matthias would be gone by the time Eric returned.

Chapter Fifteen

M atthias and Cassie's attempt to question Russ Carlisle had failed. The restaurant hostess informed them Monday and Tuesday were his days off.

His home address was listed as a unit at Bay Front Place, a luxury apartment complex west of downtown. Despite its name, it was located several blocks from the water, but close enough to pull in outlandish rental fees.

Cassie surveyed the structure and surrounding manicured grounds as they approached the main entrance. "You wouldn't think a restaurant manager makes this kind of money."

"No, you wouldn't," Matthias agreed.

No one responded when they pressed the buzzer, so they had to settle for a phone call, which went to voicemail.

Frazier's armed robbery turned out to be the easiest case of the bunch. He and Roth got their hands on a clear shot of the perpetrator on CCTV footage, tracked down their suspect, and made the arrest.

"You should've taken that one," Matthias told Cassie, "and stuck Frazier with me, spinning our wheels."

She snorted. "What's the fun in that?"

Matthias left Cassie at her desk and snagged Frazier to head over to Pauly's Polynesian Pub. The bouncer once again tended bar and had no idea when his boss would be back. "If he ain't back tomorrow, I quit," he said.

Jenkins's ex still wasn't home or answering her phone either.

"Dammit," Matthias muttered on the way back to the station. "I thought cell phones were supposed to make it easier to keep in touch."

"Only if the person wants to be reached," Frazier said.

As of four that afternoon, none of their messages had been returned. When Matthias's phone did ring, it was Emma, acting weird.

The call puzzled him. No. Not the call. The whole "Detective Honeywell" thing. Had he done something to piss her off? He didn't think so.

Someone was with her, he decided. At first, he thought she was signaling that something was wrong. But as he drove toward the campground, he reconsidered. If she was in trouble, she wouldn't have used his official title. She wouldn't have wanted whoever was there to know he was a cop.

Would she?

Unless she wanted to scare the person away.

Did she have another stalker?

Even more concerning, Emma's car wasn't there. Matthias eased his Impala up the slope toward her campsite, every nerve on edge.

Then she appeared on her deck. She seemed fine. He relaxed. A little.

"Where's your car?" he asked as he stepped out of his.

She crossed her arms. Shifted her weight. "I loaned it to a friend."

He interpreted her body language as anxious. "What friend?"

"A friend from home who came back with me. I was a mess after all the funeral planning stuff this morning."

Reasonable. In fact, he was glad she hadn't been alone. As he stepped onto her porch, she gestured at one of her chairs and sat in the other. "Are you holding up okay?" he asked, keeping his voice soft.

"More or less." Her eyes glazed, and she turned her head as if suddenly interested in what was going on down the hill.

He guessed her answer should've been "less" instead of "more" but didn't push it. "You mentioned some information?"

She made a quick swipe at her face before looking at him again. "I got a name and address of someone you might want to look into." She pulled a folded paper from her pocket and handed it to him. "That's the room number Nell was in at the Royal Palace. And that's the name the room was registered to. His address—or *her* address—is on the other side. E.A. Dyson. I don't know if it's a man or a woman."

Matthias studied the name. Flipped the page to check the address. Local rather than out of town. He pulled his phone from his pocket and keyed in Cassie's number. When she picked up, he said, "I need you to run a name and address through the system. Person of interest in the Nell Anderson case." He watched a cloud of pain cross Emma's face.

"Go."

He read the information to Cassie and listened to the sound of keystrokes.

"Comes back to an Ezekiel 'Zeke' Allen Dyson. No current warrants but he has a list of past arrests and charges. Drug possession. Burglary. Simple assault. Served light sentences and is currently clear."

"Thanks."

"This is in connection with Emma's sister's homicide?" Cassie asked before he could end the call.

He glanced at Emma who was again gazing down the hill. "Yeah."

"You with Emma now?"

"Yeah," he said again.

"Give her my best. I'll see what else I can find out about this guy."

Matthias ended the call. "Cassie sends her best."

Emma brought her gaze back to him. "Tell her thanks. What'd you find out?"

"E.A. stands for Ezekiel Allen. Goes by Zeke."

"Zeke?" She brought her fingers to her lips, thinking. With a quick headshake, she said, "I'm sure there's more than one Zeke out there."

"Who are you thinking about?" But he remembered before she could reply. "The guy from the Mercury Tavern."

The color drained from Emma's face. "He claimed he saw her at the hotel but never mentioned her being in his room."

Matthias leaned forward, longing to touch her, comfort her. "I'll head over there as soon as I'm done here."

She gave him a quick nod of thanks. Then her expression shifted from gratitude to sullen and her eye's filled. "What about Nell's autopsy?"

"The coroner did it this morning."

"Did she die of an overdose?"

This was the last topic he wanted to discuss, but better Emma hear it from him than from a stranger. "We won't know if there were drugs or alcohol in her blood until toxicology comes back. But the cause of death was a broken neck likely sustained in a fall. There was an exterior flight of concrete stairs leading down to the basement where she was found."

Emma moaned. Matthias could tell she was running the scene through her mind. "Nell fell?" she asked. "Probably because she was under the influence."

He debated telling her the rest but knew she'd find out eventually. "There's more."

She brought those blue-green, almost teal, eyes to bear on him.

"She was moved."

"Moved?" Emma echoed.

"She fell down the stairs. Because her neck was broken, the coroner believes she either died instantly or was paralyzed." Matthias became vaguely aware of a vehicle coming up the hill. "But we didn't find her body in the stairwell. Someone dragged her through the fire door, into the basement."

Questions and horror played across Emma's face. "But...who? Why?"

"We don't know. There wasn't any cash or plastic in her wallet."

From his peripheral vision, Matthias noticed Emma's white Forester pull in next to his sedan. Her friend was back.

If she noticed, she didn't react. "Nell was robbed?"

"Maybe. But why take the time to move the body?" He winced. *Nell's* body, he thought but continued rather than correct himself. "And why bother to put the wallet back in her handbag?"

Emma's gaze shifted, staring at the deck flooring, although Matthias was certain that wasn't what she was seeing. "Nell wasn't alone. Someone was with her. They pushed her down the steps." She looked up at him. "Zeke?"

Matthias put a hand on top of hers. "I intend to find out."

"Emma?"

Matthias had registered someone getting out of the Subaru carrying two takeout bags, but at the sound of a male voice, he released Emma's hand and turned to face the newcomer. Not a woman friend as he'd expected, but a tall, well-dressed male who bore an uncanny resemblance to a dude who played one of those superheroes in the movies.

"Eric," she said, brushing a hand across her face. "This is Detective Matthias Honeywell. He's investigating Nell's death. Detective, this is Eric Baker, a friend from back home."

Matthias stood. Baker shifted both bags to one hand and extended the other. Matthias shook it. Baker had a firm grip, but when he winced, Matthias realized he may have used too much muscle and quickly released.

Emma climbed to her feet as well. "Could you do me a favor?" she asked Baker. "I left my camera gear in the car. Could you grab the bag from my back seat."

He handed her the takeout bags. "Sure thing."

While the friend backtracked to the car, Emma excused herself to put her dinner—hers and the friend's, if the size of the bags was any indicator—inside the camper. Matthias watched Baker, assessing. Was he *just* a friend? Was he staying here with Emma? He didn't appear to have his own car to go somewhere else.

He didn't have his own car to go back where he'd come from and leave her here. She'd have to return with him. The idea stirred feelings Matthias hadn't experienced in ages. He hated the sensation.

Emma returned and reclaimed her chair.

Baker slammed the car's back door and strode toward them carrying Emma's camera bag, which he set on the floor next to her. "What'd I miss?"

She gave him the short version. Baker moved behind her and rested his hands on her shoulders. "Oh, sweetie. I'm so sorry. Poor Nell."

Sweetie?

She met Matthias's gaze. "You never told me. Where did she die?"

"I did tell you. An abandoned warehouse downtown."

Emma shook her head. "I know that. Which abandoned warehouse?"

"You're not going there."

Her posture grew rigid. "I need to see where my sister died."

He pictured the spot. The same part of town where Gillian Watson had gone missing.

"I'll be with her," Baker said.

As if that should reassure Matthias.

"I don't intend to disturb evidence. I just need to…" Her face contorted, revealing her pain. She lowered her face.

Still standing, all he could see was the top of her head. Friend or boyfriend be damned. Matthias dropped into the chair and scooted it even closer, so their knees almost touched. "It's not the kind of neighborhood you should wander around in." He looked up at Baker before he could repeat his offer to go with her. "Even accompanied," Matthias added firmly.

Baker's expression hardened. "I can take care of her. I've been doing it most of my life."

Emma shot a look at Baker that Matthias couldn't interpret. But he bit back the words that gathered on his tongue. *Where the hell were you when she was dealing with Clay Bauer?*

"I'll just drive by," Emma said to Matthias. "And I'll keep the doors locked."

She wasn't going to let this go. Matthias tried to imagine having a sibling who had died tragically. It didn't take much effort. He was an only child, but he'd experienced losing his mother. He knew where she'd died. In her home. Violently. But if she'd been killed in a lonely warehouse, how would he feel?

He would need to see for himself too. "Sixteenth Street between French and Holland. Do you know the area?"

She shook her head.

"We'll find it," Baker said, massaging Emma's shoulders.

Matthias pushed his chair back, its plastic feet scraping the wooden deck, and rose. "You have my number," he said to her.

She popped up. "Let me know what you find out about Zeke."

He tried to answer but didn't trust his voice. Instead he nodded to her, met Baker's gaze, and strode away from the couple.

Chapter Sixteen

Emma spun on Eric the moment Matthias's car disappeared at the bottom of the hill. "What the hell was that all about?" she demanded, then mimicked, "*I've been taking care of her most of my life.* What a crock of bullshit."

Eric folded his arms as a knowing smile crossed his lips. "I was right. Detective Honeywell is *the* man from Erie."

She balled her fists to keep from choking him. Stuttering, she settled on saying, "It's none of your business," and realized how lame she sounded.

"I can't say that I blame you. He's hot if you like the scarred and brutish type."

She fell back on her old excuse, even though it no longer appeared to be true. "He's dating a friend of mine."

"Oh?" Eric sounded deeply disappointed but recovered. "Are you sure about that? Because if I'm any judge of relationships—and I am—Detective Honeywell is extremely attracted to *you*, my dear."

"No, he's not."

Eric erupted in laughter. "Sweetie, the look on his face when I put on my straight routine and pretended to be your knight in shining armor was priceless. He wanted to rip my head off."

"Stop calling me Sweetie."

He ignored her. "Do you mean to tell me you didn't see how jealous he got when I promised to take care of you?"

She dropped into the chair Matthias had sat in, still warm from his presence, and buried her face in her hands. Arguing with Eric was useless. Always had been. Kira's words danced in her brain.

He talks entirely too much about you.

The thought of Kira brought another memory to the surface. Kira had flirted with Zeke's co-worker at the Mercury.

Emma bounced back up to her feet and held out a hand. "I need my keys."

"I may have been messing with your policeman, but I was serious about not letting you go to that warehouse alone."

"Then let's go. I have someone I need to see first."

Eric looked longingly at the camper door. "What about our supper?"

She followed his gaze. "I've lost my appetite."

Five minutes later, Emma climbed behind the wheel while Eric sat in the passenger seat with his takeout burger and fries. Her mind spiraled as she drove through the campground, adhering to the five mile-an-hour speed limit. She needed to talk to Kira. According to the clock on the dashboard, it was almost five o'clock. Kira had a yoga class at five-thirty. Emma hated to hit her with this right before she had to teach, but it couldn't wait.

"You mentioned someone named Zeke. Is that who you're in such a big hurry to see?" Eric asked as he picked onions from his burger.

"No."

"So who is this Zeke person?"

"Remember I told you about a bartender who called and told me he'd seen Nell at the Royal Palace?"

Eric's affirmative grunt was muffled as he took a bite.

"His name was Zeke. The E.A. Dyson on the note Katie gave me? The E stands for Ezekiel. And he goes by Zeke."

Emma braked when she reached Peninsula Drive and waited for the steady stream of traffic to clear.

"You do realize Zeke isn't a rare name."

"It's not a common one, either. Especially when you're talking about two of them being in the same hotel at the same time."

"If we aren't paying a visit to this Zeke fellow, who *are* we going to see?"

"My friend, Kira."

"The yoga teacher you told me about?"

"Yep."

Eric chuckled. "I guess you do need your chakras cleared."

Emma couldn't argue that point. "That's not it. Kira may have learned something about Zeke."

"How?"

Emma spotted a gap between cars and hit the gas. The sudden acceleration and turn into traffic sent Eric's meal sliding and him scrambling to keep it on his lap. "The last time I saw her," Emma said, "she was exchanging phone numbers with the other guy working at the bar. If they went out on a date, maybe he mentioned something about Zeke."

Burger and fries corralled, Eric shifted sideways to face her. "You believe this Ezekiel Zeke fellow, providing they're one and the same, knows more than he's told you."

"It's more than that," she said. "If they are the same person, he lied to me. He never mentioned knowing Nell. He claimed he wasn't even sure it was her he saw. Now I find out it was his room she was seen coming out of. And if that's the case, he's the last person I know of who saw my sister alive."

Emma had to circle the block twice before a parking space opened near Namaste Yoga on Peach Street. A stiff breeze was blowing dark clouds and the promise of more rain in from the north. "You can wait in the car," she told Eric.

"No way. You've told me so much about this gal, I want to meet her." He stuffed the last bit of burger in his mouth, crumpled the wrapper into the bag, and set the trash on the floor at his feet.

They trailed a dark-haired young woman with a rolled yoga mat under her arm into the building. Kira stood at the front counter and flashed a smile at Emma while accepting the student's punch card for class. Once the brunette disappeared down the hallway to the studio, Kira assessed Emma and Eric. "Neither of you is dressed for class."

"That's not why I'm here," Emma said. She introduced Eric as an old friend from back home and immediately expected Kira to shift into seductress mode.

Instead, she maintained her calm, professional yoga instructor persona. "It's a pleasure to meet you." She focused on Emma. "What's up?"

"I guess you haven't heard."

Kira's easy smile faded. "Heard what?"

Emma had to force the words she'd never wanted to say from her throat. "Nell's dead."

"Oh, no. Oh, honey." Kira bustled from behind the counter, her gauzy drape billowing, and pulled Emma into her arms. "I'm so sorry."

The outpouring of sympathy rekindled Emma's tears. She choked them back. "No. I'm the one who's sorry. I shouldn't have dumped this on you when you have a class in a few minutes."

Kira drew back but kept a grip on Emma's arms. "Don't you dare apologize. Tell me what happened. I know you've been afraid she would overdose."

"The coroner is waiting on toxicology results." Emma wasn't about to pour out the whole story to Kira. Not right now. "The reason I'm here...have you been out on a date with that guy from the Mercury Tavern?"

A hint of Kira's seductive side flickered across her eyes. "Rafael? As a matter of fact, we had dinner Saturday night. Why?"

"Did he happen to mention Zeke?"

"Zeke?" Kira appeared puzzled.

Emma's spark of hope faded to black. "I'll take that as no."

"Wait. Zeke. That's the bartender you were talking to, right?"

"Yeah." Emma told her about Ezekiel "Zeke" Dyson and the room Nell had been seen leaving."

"You think they're one and the same?"

"I don't know. That's why I'm here. I thought Rafael might have mentioned something." As Emma said it, she realized what a long shot her idea had been.

Kira held up a finger. "Just hold on a minute. We didn't do a lot of talking, but he did say something about a guy he worked with. Rafael didn't mention him by name, but he told me his buddy at the bar was stressed out over problems with his girlfriend."

Emma struggled to make sense of this tidbit. "You think he was talking about Zeke?"

"I don't know. I'm sure there are other men who work at the bar, but Zeke is the only one I've met. I'm probably jumping to conclusions, assuming it was him."

But if it was Zeke having problems with his girlfriend...and if Nell had been staying in Zeke's room at the hotel...did that make the two of them a couple? And if so, why did Zeke call Emma and then pretend he didn't know her sister?

If, if, if.

Kira shot a glance at the clock on the wall. "Have you mentioned Zeke to Matthias?"

Emma could feel Eric's eyes burning holes in the back of her head. "I did. He said he'd track him down."

"Good. I know he'll move heaven and earth to get answers for you." Kira gave Emma a gentle shake. "I have to go teach my class. How about we have lunch together tomorrow and chat? If you feel up to it, that is."

"Thanks. I'll let you know."

Kira released her and gave a polite, professional nod to Eric. "Nice meeting you."

"Likewise," he said.

Once they stepped outside, Kira locked the door behind them. As Emma headed toward the Subaru, Eric hummed. "Matthias will move heaven and earth to find answers for you," he echoed Kira's words.

Emma swept her wind-tossled hair from her face. "He's a good cop."

"And Kira happens to know he's the good cop you would go to with your findings."

"It's his case."

"*Matthias*. Not Detective Honeywell."

They reached the Forester, and Emma beeped it open before turning to face the man who was close to becoming her *ex*-friend. "Kira's the one who's been dating him. That's how she knows him."

"What about Rafael?"

Emma stepped off the curb, checked for traffic, and hurried to her door. "It's not a monogamous relationship. But it's a rule we women have. You don't date someone your girlfriend has feelings for."

Eric waited until they'd climbed in and buckled their seatbelts before saying anything else. "I understand that. It's a good rule." He turned to face her. "But what I want to know is which of you really has feelings for Detective Matthias Honeywell?"

"That must be it." Eric pointed at a strip of yellow police tape fluttering on the breeze next to a warehouse on 16th.

Emma pulled over across the street from the redbrick structure. Unlike Peach Street, parking spaces were abundant on this stretch of road. She shifted into park and turned off the engine.

"You're not getting out." Eric's words were a warning, not a question.

She leaned back in the seat without answering and looked out the window. Despite the deep shadows cast by heavy clouds, she could make out the sidewalk cutting between two warehouses. What she couldn't see was what lay beyond. On impulse, she opened her door, then thanked the heavens that a car or truck hadn't driven past in that moment. Belatedly checking for vehicles, she stepped out.

Eric scrambled from the other side. "We're only supposed to drive past. You told your cop you weren't—"

"He's not my cop," she said softly, but she was already crossing the street and knew Eric couldn't hear.

"Wait!"

Emma was focused on the yellow tape and the gap between the buildings. Eric's footsteps slapped the pavement behind her.

He caught up and grabbed her arm as she made it to the opposite curb. "Will you just wait, already."

She tried to tug free, but he held on, anchoring her in place. "I need to see where Nell died." The words choked her.

Eric glanced left and right before leaning his face close to hers. "Look around, Emma. This is not life on your farm. It's not your campground. It's not even the street where the yoga studio is."

She wanted to ignore him but took in their surroundings. Crumbling sidewalks. Broken windows. A couple of blocks away, scaffolding against another in the string of warehouses promised rebuilding and renovation. Between there and here, several makeshift tents leaned into the brick walls. She'd seen similar communities of the homeless scattered around Pittsburgh back

127

home. But she didn't see anyone near the tents. She didn't see anyone at all. Except for a terrified Eric Baker. "What's your problem?" she asked. "It's not like we're being circled by some murderous motorcycle gang."

His eyes widened as if she'd added one more boogieman to fear.

Emma turned her attention to the narrow passageway. The police tape had once blocked the entrance but was now torn. Twenty or so feet back, she made out a pipe handrail jutting away from the brick, turning and running parallel to it. She wrenched free from Eric's grip and headed between the buildings as the first fat raindrops fell.

Eric exhaled an exasperated groan and followed.

She stopped at the pipe railing and gripped it, looking down into a dark pit. Fractured concrete steps led to a steel door. Just as Matthias had described.

This was where Nell had fallen to her death. Emma pictured her sister, crumpled at the bottom of the stairs. In pain. Crying out for help. Dying. Emma gripped the pitted pipe so tightly, the rust dug into her palms. For one fleeting moment, she thought about continuing along the railing to the top of the steps. Imagined going down there. Pushing through the door.

The world around her started to spin.

Eric caught her before her knees buckled and turned her toward him, crushing her against his chest.

She gasped, choked on tears clogging her throat. With his support, the vertigo passed.

"Hey, you! Leave her alone!"

The shout jarred Emma, and Eric flinched. They spun and looked for the source.

A towering figure loomed out by the street, blocking the opening of the walkway. She tried to make out his features, but between his camouflaged baseball cap and a scruff of beard, he might as well have been wearing a ski mask.

The tents. He had to be one of the homeless, living in the tents down the street. Suddenly, Eric's concerns for their safety made a lot more sense.

Lightning illuminated the dim alley, immediately followed by a ground-shaking crash of thunder. Emma flinched, and in that moment, the man vanished. She blinked. Had she imagined him?

The rain became a deluge, instantly soaking them.

Eric started trembling. "Holy crap."

Emma wasn't sure if he referred to the homeless man or the downpour. Which was when she realized that man might have witnessed Nell's fall.

Emma launched down the passageway, through the rain, toward the street. Eric called after her. She ignored him. In seconds, she exited the shadows and staggered to a stop across from her car. She looked toward the makeshift tents.

The sidewalk was empty. She tried to wipe the rain from her eyes and turned the other way. No one.

Where the hell had he gone?

Chapter Seventeen

Still seething, Matthias parked in front of the Mercury Tavern and Grill. He shut off the ignition and stared through his rain-streaked windshield at the bar front, but his mind was still back at Emma's campsite.

Eric Baker. Her "friend" from back home. Clearly, they were comfortable together. And they made a good couple. She was beautiful. The natural kind of beauty. Matthias had never seen her with makeup on. She didn't need it. Baker—Mr. Superhero—had the kind of looks that would make women swoon.

Matthias forced thoughts of Emma and Baker from his mind. Who she saw was none of his business. Allowing feelings for this woman to build was a huge mistake. He needed to focus on the case at hand. Nell Anderson's murder. He stepped from the car and jogged across the street through the rain.

Inside, a dining area to the left appeared in dire need of a remodel. About half of the tables were occupied by exhausted-looking couples and families seeking a meal that didn't involve heating their kitchens at home. Matthias had never eaten here. The sticky vinyl floors, dingy 1970s décor, and stench of overused fryer grease did nothing to make him reconsider. He turned right and entered a murky pub where the air smelled of hops and whiskey with a hint of burnt popcorn. The stools at the bar were filled, mostly with men watching a baseball game on a TV mounted high on the wall. A woman in jeans, a tank top, and an apron moved among the small tables delivering drinks to the patrons who preferred to talk to each other rather than watch sports.

Matthias didn't see anyone else working and wondered if the waitress was pulling double duty. He watched and waited until she finished taking an order and headed back toward the bar.

"Excuse me," he said, stepping in front of her. "I'm looking for Zeke Dyson. Does he work here?"

She eyed him distastefully. "You're a cop."

He flashed a smile. "Afraid so. Does it matter?"

"Not to me." She glanced back at the tables she'd been serving. "Might to some of our customers."

"I'm only here to follow up with Mr. Dyson as a possible witness. I understand he may have spotted a woman who's been missing."

Her expression eased. "Yeah. Zeke's here." She looked toward the bar. "He must have gone into the back for something." After another quick glance at the tables, she said, "Why don't you wait by the front door. I'll send him out to talk to you."

Matthias gave her a grateful nod and left the bar, but not before checking out the seated patrons and wondering who the waitress didn't want him to see.

No one set off any alarm bells in his head.

He only had to wait near the unattended cash register for a couple of minutes before a man with a goatee and full-sleeve tattoos on both heavily muscled arms approached him.

"I'm Zeke Dyson. You lookin' for me?"

Matthias shook his hand and introduced himself. "I understand you spoke to Ms. Emma Anderson about having spotted her sister at the Royal Palace Hotel. Is that correct?"

"Yeah. It is."

He pulled out his notebook and pen. "Do you mind telling me how you came to encounter the missing sister?"

"Like I told Emma, I'm pretty sure I saw her in the hallway there a couple of weeks ago."

"In the hallway. Did you pass her?"

"Yeah. I mean, I think it was her. She looked familiar at the time. It was later that I noticed the photo her sister left here and realized that's where I'd seen her before."

"But you aren't sure it was her?"

"Not a hundred percent, no."

Matthias pretended to ponder Zeke's answer. "If you saw her in a hallway, I assume you were a guest there?"

"My buddy was getting married and got us a reduced rate, so yeah. Me and my girl stayed the night."

His girl. Interesting. "What room were you in?"

The question appeared to startle Zeke. "Hell, I don't remember."

"You said you were with your girlfriend. What's her name?"

Zeke crossed his arms and gave Matthias an intimidating glare. "I don't think it's any of your business who my girlfriend is."

"You may be right." Matthias thumbed a page in his notebook. "I understand you and your girlfriend have been having some problems."

Zeke grinned unconvincingly. "Women. You know how they are."

"I hear ya." Matthias made a show of reading his notes. "Room 433."

"Huh?"

"You're Ezekiel Allen Dyson, right? E.A. Dyson?" Matthias added the home address he had on the guy.

Now Zeke was the one looking intimidated or at least uneasy. His lips moved as if to reply, but he reconsidered.

"E.A. Dyson was registered in room 433 at the Royal Palace Resort and Conference Center two Saturdays ago." Matthias retrieved his phone from his pocket and acted as though he was randomly scrolling. "That *is* you, right?"

Zeke still didn't say anything.

Matthias opened the clip from the hotel's video file—the one showing Nell in her floral sundress exiting room 433. He turned the screen toward Zeke and played the recording.

Zeke's eyes widened at the same time his lips thinned.

"Is this the woman you saw? The one you believe to be Nell Anderson?"

His nod was barely perceptible.

"Care to explain why this shows Miss Anderson coming out of room 433?"

Zeke's gaze snapped up to meet Matthias's, but he still didn't reply.

Matthias decided to give him a way out. "Maybe she and your girlfriend are acquainted?"

Zeke's lips remained glued together, but he shook his head and shrugged, which Matthias interpreted as maybe, I don't know, neither of which he believed. He swiped his phone's screen to bring up the next photo. The one from the crime scene. "Would you like to see another photo of Miss Anderson in that same dress? I have to warn you. This one's a bit more graphic since it shows her decomposed body." He had no intention of showing the image to Zeke, but the mere suggestion brought a reaction.

Even in the inadequate lighting, Matthias could see the color drain from Zeke's face, replaced by a greenish pallor. "She's...dead?"

"She is."

He jerked one hand to cover his mouth, mumbled, "Oh, my God," and bolted into the men's room next to the cash register.

Matthias stashed his phone seconds before a middle-aged couple carrying a take-out container made their way from the dining room and out the front door with an uninterested glance at him.

Long minutes passed. The waitress from the bar appeared in the doorway wearing a scowl. "Where's Zeke?"

Matthias tipped his head toward the restroom.

She huffed. "When he comes out, will you please tell him to get his ass back behind the bar." An order, not a request.

Matthias continued to wait and began to wonder if there was another exit to the restroom. Zeke's reaction was stronger than Matthias had anticipated. He'd expected shock. Or more accurately, feigned shock.

The men's room door creaked open, and Zeke returned, water droplets still clinging to his goatee. His color remained pale, but he now appeared dazed rather than ill. "I have to get back to work."

"You haven't answered my question yet. What was Nell Anderson doing in your room?"

Zeke's lower lip trembled. "I have to get back to work," he repeated slowly. "Unless you're arresting me, I have nothing else to say. And if you are arresting me, I want a lawyer."

Matthias raised both hands in surrender. "You're not under arrest. Yet."

Zeke sidestepped and headed for the bar.

"We'll talk again soon," Matthias called after him.

The chat with Zeke Dyson continued to replay through Matthias's thoughts the following morning as he walked to work. The previous evening's showers had passed, leaving a sunny sky overhead and air thick with humidity. By the time he completed the three-block stroll and arrived at the police station, sweat trickled down his back. He hit the gym, then the showers, before changing into his work garb. He slid into Major Crimes minutes before the daily briefing.

Lt. Armstrong called out for updates on the Thomas Jenkins homicide and the search for the female patron with whom he'd been seen.

"I stopped in at Pauly's Polynesian Pub over the weekend," Frazier said. "Still no sign of the woman. But I think I know why."

Every head in the room turned to him.

Frazier waved a folder. "I just got the lab report back. First of all, the victim's blood alcohol was at .09."

Over the legal limit for driving, but Jenkins hadn't been behind the wheel.

"Toxicology showed no drugs in his system." Frazier continued to read. "Here's the interesting part. A long blonde hair was found on Jenkins's shirt."

Matthias wasn't sure what was "interesting" about that. They already knew a blonde hair had been sent to the lab.

"So?" Armstrong said. "He was seen leaving the pub with a blonde."

Frazier gave him a sly grin. "That's what most of us assumed. Problem is the hair, while it was indeed human, was determined to have come from a wig."

The detectives in the room fell silent. Matthias tried to process the revelation. They'd been asking about a blonde. No one could identify her. No one claimed to see her return to the pub. But if they weren't looking for a blonde, they had nothing to go on. No images of her face. No inkling of her identity.

Cassie was the first to speak. "Why was she wearing a wig? Does she have thinning hair? Was she being stylish? Or was she intentionally trying to throw off our attempts to ID her?"

"Good questions," Armstrong said. He aimed a pen at Cassie. "Find out. And find *her*. She knows what happened in that alley and may be the only person who does." The lieutenant brought his gaze back to Frazier. "Anything else in the report?"

"Nothing helpful."

"Honeywell, have we learned anything new about Jenkins's past?"

"He worked for his uncle's construction company, but the uncle hasn't returned our calls. The receptionist said he's been out of town and should be back today."

"Make sure you follow up on him." Armstrong studied his clipboard and moved down the list of open cases. When he got to Gillian Watson's missing-person's case, Cassie reported on having spoken with Didi Reed. "Ms. Reed told us Gillian was romantically involved with her manager, Russ Carlisle. He hasn't answered our calls, and his days off were yesterday and today."

The last case on the lieutenant's list was Nell's homicide. "The officers who were first to respond reported finding the exterior door to the basement unlocked. While canvassing the area, they found one homeless man who was willing to talk to them. He claimed the lock's been broken for ages. Last winter, vagrants used the space as an unofficial homeless shelter."

Matthias raised his hand. "Did he mention knowing the victim?"

"He says he did not. But according to the officer who questioned him, he wasn't very forthcoming. After telling them about the basement encampment, he spooked and ran off. Wouldn't give them his name either."

Matthias couldn't help wondering if Nell had been part of the homeless community. He scribbled a note to locate the minimally talkative vagrant. A hot meal might encourage him to answer a few more questions.

The briefing broke up with Armstrong's admonishment to bring some answers to the table by tomorrow. Matthias and Frazier gathered around Cassie's cubicle.

"We've got three stalled cases," Cassie said. "It's getting embarrassing."

"Roth and I cleared our armed robbery case yesterday," Frazier said, sounding entirely too smug.

Cassie glared at him. "Good for you. Since you're on a roll, go down to Thomas Jenkins's uncle's company and nose around." She shook her head. "I can't get past the way he was killed. Double tap to the chest and one to the head. Sounds like a professional hit to me."

"That's what I said." Frazier backhanded Matthias's shoulder. "You know what else I said? The wig. Remember? I think Jenkins and his ex-wife were getting into some kinky role-playing stuff with her wearing a wig."

Matthias wasn't buying it now any more than he had the first time Frazier suggested it. "We talked to the ex," Matthias said to Cassie. "I don't see her as wanting anything to do with Jenkins, kinky or otherwise." He pondered Cassie and Frazier's other idea and still wasn't sold on it, either. "As for it being a professional hit, why leave the body in an alley? Why not dump it in a foundation and pour concrete on top."

"You've been watching too many old movies." Cassie returned her focus to Frazier. "Since you agree with me, chase down that angle."

"On it." He spun away and slipped into his cubicle.

She shifted to Matthias. "I'm going to do my best to locate and talk with our elusive restaurant manager, Russ Carlisle." She hiked one eyebrow. "I assume you want to focus on the Nell Anderson case."

"Yeah. I'm heading back to the crime scene. If the homeless are familiar with the building, maybe they can shed some light on what happened."

Cassie's expression darkened. "You're not going back there alone."

Her concern amused him. "You don't think I can take care of myself?"

"I'd rather you didn't have to find out." She wagged a finger at the partition between their cubicles. "Why don't you see what you can find out about Nell online. I'll make my phone calls. If I can get Carlisle to agree to meet with us, we can talk to him and then head over to 16th Street."

"I've already searched online for Nell." He didn't mention that Emma had as well. "There's nothing. She's been off the grid for most of the last few years."

Cassie glared at him. "Try again. Or work on your reports. Or go get some coffee. Either way, I'm going with you just as soon as I track down Russ Carlisle."

Matthias knew better than to argue with her. The decision became whether to do as he was told or slip out without letting her know. His phone rang before he had a chance to consider the options. The county coroner's office lit the screen.

"Detective Honeywell, this is Felix Hamilton." The voice on the other end of the line sounded oddly strained.

Matthias eased into his desk chair. "What can I do for you?"

"I'm afraid we have an issue."

Chapter Eighteen

With Eric at an affordable hotel on West 12th Street and planning to attend Zoom meetings for work all morning, Emma hopped on her bike at first light. She hit the trail that connected Sara's Campground with Presque Isle State Park and continued along a fourteen-mile loop around the peninsula. She was grateful to be free of Eric's well-meaning but overwhelming concern for a few hours. Pedaling steadily, Emma dodged other bikers, joggers, walkers, and rollerbladers, brought out by the clear sky. Once she cleared the Perry Monument, trail traffic lightened, and she bore down, pumping hard to burn off her frustration and grief.

By the time she reached the lakeside, the heat of the sun combined with her exertion started taking their toll. Sweat soaked her shirt and trickled down her back. She pulled off the trail at Beach Six, parked her bike, and hiked across the sand to plant her feet at the water's edge. Wind blowing across the lake buffeted her, tossing her hair. Eyes closed, she listened to the rush of the crashing waves, the cries of the seagulls, the whoosh of the wind. As Lake Erie washed over and around her ankles and calves, she allowed the past to wash over her soul.

Her parents used to bring Emma and Nell here every summer. Then, the lake, the park, the city held nothing but happy memories. Two sisters frolicking in the water, Dad never far away. Mom would set up a beach umbrella and an old blanket and would settle in with a book.

It was natural for Nell to run here to escape the tragic loss of their parents. Emma had run here, too, to escape a psycho boyfriend. These waters had soothed her pain. Unfortunately, Nell had never found comfort. She'd deepened her addictions, fallen further into the abyss.

The only solace Nell found was in death.

The realization pummeled Emma harder than the stiff winds blowing across the water from Canada. She inhaled a shuddering breath, determined not to cry again. She'd done enough of that last night, alone in bed. And earlier, in Matthias's arms.

She forced that last memory away.

Emma looked out across the lake and its wind-driven surf sending bursts of spray over the man-made rock breakwaters. She had no idea how long she stood in that spot, but when she checked her watch, it was already well past ten. Cell service was hit-or-miss out here, which was usually a good thing, but Eric would be trying to reach her soon, and she still had a long bike ride back to the campground.

Reluctantly, she trudged back to where she'd left her bicycle, swung a leg over, and pushed off.

She knew the moment she got back in cell range. Her phone pinged. She pulled over and stopped to check her messages, expecting to see one from Eric. Instead, there was one missed call from a number she didn't recognize along with a voice message. She clicked to listen.

"Emma, it's me. I need to see you."

Still straddling her bike, Emma's knees weakened at the voice, which had to be a hallucination. She staggered, dropping the bicycle into the sand at the edge of the trail and toppling onto her hip. The phone slipped from her fingers.

A man passing by braked to a stop. "Are you okay?"

She forced a smile, uncertain if it appeared sheepish, as intended, or panicked. "I'm fine. Just being my usual klutzy self."

He returned her smile, waved, and continued on his way.

Frantic, Emma searched the sand for her phone. Found it. Without dusting it off, she hit replay and listened to the full message.

"Emma, it's me. I need to see you. You probably think I'm dead by now. I'm not, but please, whatever you do, don't let anyone else know. If you do, I will be. Call me back at this number as soon as you can. But make sure you're alone."

The message ended. Emma stared at the screen. A hysterical, giddy laugh burst from her throat, unbidden.

She hadn't been imagining her sister's voice on the phone. Nell was alive.

Emma had never pedaled so fast in her life. By the time she skidded into her campsite, she was breathless and drenched with sweat.

She staggered onto her porch, fumbling with her keys. Finally inside, she pulled the exterior door closed behind her and made her way around the small space, cranking closed the windows above the futon bed and over the galley sink. She slid into the bench at the kitchen table, which served double duty as a desk, and lowered the window above it.

Life in a tin can on wheels, especially one parked in a campground with neighbors a few yards away on either side, lacked privacy. With the camper as closed to the world as possible, Emma cradled her phone and pulled up the missed call from her sister. But before she tapped the green button, a new question froze her.

Why was the body in the warehouse wearing Nell's clothes? Carrying her ID?

What had Nell done?

Dreading the answer but needing to hear it, Emma placed the call.

The ring-back tones played over and over in her ear. In her head, she prepared a voice message to leave at the tone. A simple "Call me" should suffice.

But the click on the end of the line signaled someone was answering. "Emma?"

She had known and loved that voice as long as she could remember. "Nell." While Emma had a voice message in mind, she wasn't prepared for this moment. "Is that really you?"

At another time in their lives, Nell would've laughed at the stupid question, but there was no humor in her tone today. "Yes." She choked a sob. "It's so good to hear your voice."

"Where are you? Are you still in Erie?"

"Yeah."

"Where?"

"I can't tell you right now."

Not this game again. "What the hell is going on with that dead body in the warehouse?"

A breathy sigh. "I figured it would've been found by now. Good."

"Good? Nell, she was wearing your dress, carrying your purse. Your identification."

"I know."

She *knew*?

"Listen, I can't go into it right now." Her tone sounded urgent, whispered, as if someone had come into the room. "I just wanted you to know I'm alive. But you can't let anyone else know, okay? And I do mean *anyone*," she enunciated each syllable. "Everyone has to believe I'm dead. I mean it, Em. It's a matter of life and death. Mine."

"What the hell are you talking about? This isn't something you can keep secret. The coroner will find out the minute he looks at your dental records."

"I know they'll find out eventually." Nell's voice dropped even lower. "But I need some time before that happens. I have to go. I'll call again soon. I promise. We'll get together, and I'll tell you everything. Love you. Bye."

Emma listened to dead air for several long seconds, a hundred questions racing through her mind, before setting the phone on the table. Nell was alive. But that was all Emma knew about this mess. A matter of life and death, Nell had said. "What the hell have you gotten yourself into?" Emma said out loud. She should be overjoyed that her sister was alive. Instead, all she felt was dread.

The phone rang, and she flinched. Nell again? No. It was Eric's name and face lighting the screen.

"I'm done with work," he announced when she answered. "Come pick me up, and I'll take you out to lunch. My treat."

"Okay. Be there in ten minutes." It should only take five, max.

"You all right? You sound odd."

Hell, no, she wasn't all right. "I'll tell you about it when I see you." Except after she ended the call, she realized she couldn't tell him. Nell had been emphatic on that point. Although she couldn't have known Eric was in town. He was a big brother to her. She might not have included him in her blanket *anyone* order.

No. Emma couldn't share Nell's secret. Not even with Eric.

Chapter Nineteen

"We got the dental records for Nell Anderson this morning. They don't match our victim. Not even close."

Matthias listened to the coroner's words and fought to make sense of the news. "The body from the warehouse isn't Nell?"

"Correct."

"If the victim isn't Nell, who is she?"

"At this point, Jane Doe."

Matthias's racing mind settled like a flock of birds coming to roost.

Gillian Watson.

The woman he'd expected to find when he first got the call. Still missing. Had to be her. She had no fingerprints in the system, either. Dammit. He needed to reach out to the mother and sister for another set of dental records. But one big question remained.

Why was she wearing Nell's dress and carrying Nell's wallet?

"Honeywell?" Hamilton's voice jarred him from his thoughts. "You still there?"

"Yeah. Thanks. I'll get back to you."

He ended the call, immediately pulled up Emma's number,

and hit send. Her voicemail greeted him. "This is Matthias. I need to talk to you. Call me back as soon as you receive this.

As he hung up, he realized Cassie stood next to him. "What's going on?" she asked. "You look...odd."

"Thanks," he grumbled. He told her about his conversation with Felix Hamilton.

"Huh," she said when he finished. "I wonder how your cute photographer friend is going to handle the news."

"I tried calling her. No answer."

He didn't look up at Cassie but felt her hovering, studying him. "Would you rather I talked to her?" she asked.

"No." Even he was surprised at the quickness of his response. "I also need to talk to the Watson family."

"Correction. *We* need to talk to them." Cassie looked at her watch. "I did reach Russ Carlisle. He agreed to meet us at the restaurant at two. We've got plenty of time before then. I'll call Mrs. Watson and find out if her other daughter can be there when we talk."

He was relieved Cassie had said she would make the call. "She's going to know what this is about."

Cassie rolled her eyes. "Of course she is. As sad as it sounds, she's been expecting this phone call for over a week."

Gillian's mother informed Cassie that she and her daughter, Stephanie, were at her house. "Poor woman sounded devastated," Cassie told Matthias as he descended the dark staircase to the lower-level parking garage and their assigned sedan.

Matthias surrendered the driving duties to his partner. During the ten-minute trip to the western suburbs, he tried Emma's number again with the same result and left a second message. For the remainder of the trip, he stared out the side window, imagining how Emma would react to their news. Would she be overjoyed? Obviously. But the continuation of her years of not knowing would likely dampen the relief. The real difficulty would come from the list of hard questions he had for her.

Mrs. Watson opened her door to them, appearing even more stooped than she had at their last meeting. The daughter stood behind her, a stoic statue. Once inside and seated around a vintage dining-room table, Cassie took the lead.

"A body has been found in one of the warehouses on Sixteenth," she said.

"Gillian?" the mother asked, her voice like jagged glass.

"Unfortunately, we can't say for sure."

Matthias noted the brunette sister's eye twitch. "Do you need one of us to come down to the morgue?" she asked, her tone begging Cassie to say no.

"I'm afraid we'll need dental records to get a positive ID."

Stephanie didn't speak, but her expression relaxed.

"Do you happen to know who Gillian's dentist was?" Cassie asked.

The mother shook her head, a slow back and forth.

"I do," Stephanie said. She glanced at her mother. "She and I use Dr. Hines. I know because Gillian hates going, so we try to schedule our appointments at the same time." The young woman's stolid mask dissolved. "I guess I'll have to get used to going alone."

Mrs. Watson patted her arm. "Maybe this isn't her. Maybe it's some other young woman."

The sister looked at Matthias. "Did you talk to Didi?"

"I did." He hated what he had to say next. "She's away on vacation but said Gillian wasn't with her, and she didn't know of any plans Gillian had for a getaway of her own."

"Oh." The sister exhaled and deflated like a balloon, her shoulders nearly matching her mother's.

"But it still might not be her. We don't know for sure yet. She might be…" Mrs. Watson's voice trailed off, and Matthias knew she was searching for an excuse, a reason her daughter would vanish without leaving word, without telling her mother, sister, or best friend where she'd gone.

He wished he could offer a glimmer of hope for her to hang onto. But his gut knew he'd been right the first time.

A third call to Emma resulted in yet another voicemail recording. Impatient, he left a shorter, brusquer message.

Cassie eyed him from behind the wheel.

"She's not picking up," he told her.

"Shall we swing by the campground?"

He pictured Emma and that Mr. Superhero friend of hers from back home, holed up inside the cramped trailer. Hell, they probably thought it was cozy. Cassie would have a field day, finding out Emma was involved with someone. "No."

"Why not? This is news better given in person than over the phone."

He didn't have a suitable reply.

Cassie exhaled loudly. "We're going to the campground."

If Matthias argued, she'd demand an explanation he couldn't give. He had no right to be jealous. He and Emma weren't a couple. He was a cop. He'd learned long ago that law enforcement and serious romance didn't mix. If it had, he and Melissa would've been married twenty years ago. Instead, she was happily wed to a lawyer.

A *lawyer*, of all things.

Cassie slowed to a stop at the red light on Peninsula Drive. He felt her gaze burning into the side of his face. "Care to talk about it?"

"About what?"

"About why you don't want to talk to Emma in person. Did something happen while I was off?"

"No." Not exactly a lie. He'd met Mr. Superhero yesterday, after Cassie was back on the job.

"Why don't I believe you?"

The light turned green, saving him from her undivided attention.

Even as they cruised through Sara's Campground, Cassie remained silent. When they made the turn onto Emma's road, he noted the empty spot where she usually parked and exhaled in relief.

They pulled into the vacant space, exited the vehicle, and knocked on Emma's locked door. No response, no movement from inside.

"Try calling her again," Cassie said once they were back in the car.

"I've left three messages for her. She'll call me when she gets around to it."

Cassie studied him. "Gets *around* to it?"

"You know what I mean." He looked at the clock on the dashboard. Half past noon. "It's still too soon to meet with Carlisle. Let's go down to Sixteenth Street and see if any of the homeless community is around."

"If they'll talk to us."

"One way to find out."

She shrugged. "The encampment's only a block from the restaurant. Might as well kill some time being shunned by the local vagrants."

───────

Nothing had changed at the crime scene except the yellow police tape was gone.

He and Cassie stood at the entrance to the alleyway and surveyed their surroundings. They had no reason to approach the pipe railing and what he knew were stairs to the subterranean level where the body had been found.

Regardless of whether she was Nell, Gillian, or some other Jane Doe, someone had moved her inside. Why?

Cassie elbowed him and gestured down the street to the east. "Let's go."

"Hello?" he called out as they approached the makeshift tent, trying to modulate his tone somewhere between authoritative and amicable. "Anyone home?"

No response. The fabric didn't so much as flutter.

On closer inspection, it wasn't one tent, but a cluster of three battered dome tents, like many campers used out in the wilderness, with a pair of large silver waterproof tarps covering the group, secured from the wind with stray bricks and blocks and assorted other heavy pieces of junk.

"Hello?" Cassie called out. Still no reaction from inside. She picked up a piece of tubing that looked like part of a broken bicycle and used it to lift a portion of the tarp. Bending, she peered in and wrinkled her nose. "Whoever lives here is not a good housekeeper."

"Well, they have no electricity or running water, so..."

"They also aren't home." She dropped the tubing. It hit the pavement with a clank.

Matthias gazed farther down the street to the east. A block away, the vacant warehouses were being reclaimed, reutilized, and repurposed. A few trendy shops had apartments upstairs, similar to his own place in the heart of downtown. And, around the corner, the Blue Pike Restaurant where Gillian Watson had worked.

Where Russ Carlisle worked.

Matthias started down the street toward the restaurant.

"Carlisle isn't going to be there yet," Cassie called.

"I'm hungry," Matthias called back. Which was true, but he also wanted to arrive ahead of Carlisle. Check the place out.

Maybe chat up some of the other co-workers. He'd already interviewed those who'd worked the night Gillian disappeared, but they might have remembered something since then. And they or one of the other employees might shed some light on Carlisle's relationship with the missing woman.

"I'm not leaving the car here," Cassie shouted after him. "I'll meet you there."

She had a point. In this neighborhood, they might return to find the sedan on blocks, missing vital parts.

Chapter Twenty

In Matthias's one-block walk, the world transformed from dystopian to elite. One warehouse hadn't been touched, while the next one's brick had been sandblasted. Doors and windows, which had never been there in the building's previous incarnations, opened to a clothing boutique, a metaphysical gift shop offering candles and crystals, and a store selling locally made chocolate and ice cream.

He rounded the corner at the end of the block to stand at the entrance of the Blue Pike. Massive windows, framed in black steel, occupied much of the restaurant's façade, but opaque blinds blocked the view. Matthias assumed management didn't feel the Blue Pike's patrons wanted to stare at the parking lot or still-untouched cinderblock building across the street. The bricks above the double door had been painted with a large blue image of a northern pike, a much sought-after catch of many Lake Erie fishermen.

He'd only been there a minute before Cassie wheeled around the corner in their sedan, and into the lot. He waited for her to join him before pushing through the door.

Inside, the brick and industrial décor, much like that of his own apartment, continued with exposed HVAC ducts overhead. A distressed wood counter greeted them along with a podium bearing a Wait to be Seated sign. Matthias ambled beyond the entry to assess the customers. A fraction of the tables were occupied. From what he could see, he didn't recognize any of the faces. No one he'd encountered in his law-enforcement capacity. He wished he could see into the kitchen to make sure he hadn't arrested any of the food preparers at some point. Revenge was a dish he did not want served to him, cold or hot.

A young woman in black slacks and a white blouse bustled past him with a scowl, apparently unhappy that he'd wandered beyond the *wait* sign. "Do you have reservations?" she asked.

"No, ma'am," he replied with an intentionally overdone grin and a healthy dose of the Oklahoman accent he only summoned when it served him.

She didn't appear fazed. "How many?"

"Two."

She studied an open appointment book on the podium. "There will be a twenty-minute wait."

He let the grin drop. "You have plenty of available tables."

Her unhappy scowl didn't waver. "They're all reserved."

He wasn't buying it.

Cassie stepped to his side, fists planted on her hips, which she angled to aim her badge at the hostess. "I'm Detective Sergeant Cassie Malone, Erie City Police. This is my partner, Detective Matthias Honeywell."

The hostess turned her displeasure in Cassie's direction. "How nice for you. There's still a twenty-minute wait."

Matthias wondered if Gillian had been this congenial.

Cassie raised her voice into crowd-control mode. "We're investigating the disappearance of your co-worker, Gillian Watson." If those in the rear of the dining room couldn't hear her, those closest to the front surely could. "Is Russ Carlisle here?"

The hostess's cheeks flushed. "He's off today. Come back tomorrow."

"No. He's supposed to meet us here. Today." Cassie continued to gain volume. "We've discovered a dead body on the next block. Our missing-person's case may have become a homicide investigation. Can we ask you a few questions? Miss…?" Cassie made a point of looking at the young woman's nametag. "Tiffany?"

Heads turned their way.

Tiffany shuffled papers on the podium and snatched a pair of menus from a bin on the side. "I can seat you in the back room until Russ gets here. Please follow me." She scurried away.

Matthias caught the amused smile on Cassie's face and bowed his head. "After you."

The room the hostess directed them to was enclosed by smoked-glass walls. Several small tables had been pushed together to create one long one. The hostess deposited the menus on one corner and pivoted to leave.

"Excuse me a minute," Matthias said, bringing her to a stop. She faced him, still looking annoyed. "Do you know Gillian Watson?" he asked.

"As you know, she works here. Or used to."

"Used to?"

Tiffany swept an arm in Cassie's direction. "She just said you found a body and it might be Gillian's. But even if it's not…even if Gillian shows up again, she's out of a job. You can't disappear and leave your fellow workers in the lurch, picking up the slack for over two weeks and still expect to keep your position."

"I gather you and she weren't friends."

"You gather correctly." Tiffany crossed her arms. "Gillian is… was…a bitch. All sweetness and smiles to the men, but to us women? She acted like she was better than us."

Considering Tiffany's unsweet behavior toward him and

Cassie, Matthias wondered if Gillian was indeed worse. Or if Tiffany saw her own attitude reflected back by Gillian.

Either way, Matthias was already concerned about who worked in the kitchen and what might happen to his food between there and the table. Now Tiffany was pissed at them too. He picked up the menus and handed them back to her. "Thanks, but we've lost our appetites. We'll just wait here for Mr. Carlisle."

She snatched them from his hand and stomped toward the door.

A thought flickered across Matthias's brain. "Hold up a minute," he called to the hostess.

Tiffany swung around and glared at him, her eyes and posture saying, "*Now what do you want?*"

He thumbed through the images on his phone and enlarged the picture of Nell. The one Emma had given him last month. Angling the screen toward the hostess, he asked, "You don't happen to recognize this woman, do you?"

"That's Nell Anderson. She used to work here as a bartender."

Matthias resisted looking at his partner. "When was that?"

Tiffany shrugged. "She quit three weeks ago."

"After working here how long?"

"I don't know. Five or six months, I think. Ask Russ. He'll know." Without giving Matthias a chance to ask anything more, she whisked out the door, leaving it open.

Cassie closed it, which blocked the dining-room chatter. They might be in a fishbowl, but at least their conversation would be private.

"Interesting," she said. "Nell had to know Gillian."

He agreed about Nell's employment at the Blue Pike being of interest but for so many more reasons than the link between the two cases. She'd been here the whole time Emma had been in Erie, searching for her.

"By the way." Cassie crossed her arms. "Nice of you to speak for me about my appetite."

"You don't want to eat here."

"Afraid someone will spit in your food?"

"Or worse."

Cassie chuckled. "Did you get a look at that menu? One entrée would blow my meal budget for the whole week."

"We'll pick up something when we're done here. My treat."

"Deal."

Matthias looked at his phone. No missed calls or messages from Emma. Frustrated, he keyed in her number again, aware that Cassie was watching. Same as the previous attempts, the call went to voicemail. He hit the red button before the beep and swore.

"It's odd," Cassie said, "that your photographer friend is avoiding your calls."

He kept his thoughts to himself.

Cassie tensed. "We have company."

A well-dressed man whose stride indicated a sense of purpose crossed the restaurant's dining room, headed straight for the smoked-glass private room. Matthias and Cassie had spoken with Russ Carlisle shortly after Gillian's family had reported her missing. At the time, they'd only known him as her manager here at the Blue Pike. He'd given them information regarding her schedule and when she'd left that Friday night. There had been no mention of a romantic relationship.

Matthias sized Carlisle up as he approached. Besides the dark suit and red tie, he wore a full, neatly trimmed beard. His dark hair was cropped close around the sides, longer and slicked back on top. Matthias calculated this guy spent more at the salon in one week than Matthias did in a whole year.

Carlisle pushed through the door into the private room. "I understand you've been trying to reach me." He didn't smile, didn't offer a hand to shake.

"Thanks for agreeing to take the time," Cassie said, giving him the smile he lacked. "I'm Detective Sergeant Malone. This is

Detective Honeywell. We spoke with you shortly after Gillian Watson went missing."

"I remember."

Carlisle turned his fierce glare on Matthias, who met it with the one he'd mastered long ago. No twenty-something with a trendy haircut could outlast Matthias where intimidating looks were concerned.

Although focused on Carlisle, Matthias picked up on Cassie's amusement in his peripheral vision.

Carlisle blinked, losing the stare-down, and shifted his gaze to Cassie. "How can I help you, detectives? I believe I told you all I know when we spoke the first time."

"I'm afraid that's not quite true." Cassie maintained her smile. "We've learned you were romantically involved with Ms. Watson."

His stony veneer momentarily showed signs of cracking, but he recovered with a shrug. "We may have gone out for drinks once or twice."

Cassie arched an eyebrow. "Oh, I believe it was a bit more than that. As I understand it, you two were involved for more like six months."

A muscle in his jaw twitched. "That's a lie. Who told you that?"

"Someone we consider a reliable witness."

Matthias could tell this guy wasn't accustomed to having his statements questioned. When confronted, he sucked at lying.

Carlisle fingered the collar of his charcoal shirt. "I don't see how my personal life has anything to do with it."

"Really?" Cassie said, exaggerating her disappointment. "Your girlfriend of nearly half a year vanishes without a trace, you don't even acknowledge the relationship until we call you on it, and now you can't see why we might question you about the personal nature of your involvement?"

Carlisle's powerful tough-guy veneer completely shattered.

"All right, yes. Gillian and I dated. But I honestly have no idea where she is. She's a free spirit. It's part of what I like about her. She's probably taken off with one of those girlfriends of hers. I expect her to walk back through those doors any moment now."

"According to Tiffany, you fired her."

He dismissed the statement with a wave of his hand. "That was all for corporate headquarters' benefit and so the staff wouldn't get ideas of their own. I'll rehire her the minute she comes back."

"When was the last time you saw her?" Matthias asked.

"Like I told you before. When she and I closed up that Friday night."

"She didn't tell you about these plans you claim she and her girlfriends had?"

"I didn't say she had plans. I said she's a free spirit. If one of those girls called, she'd be off in a heartbeat."

"One of those girls," Cassie echoed. "Such as Didi Reed?"

Carlisle snapped his fingers. "Exactly. You should check with her."

"We did," Matthias said. "She has no idea where Gillian is. In fact, she's the one who told us about your relationship."

Carlisle appeared perplexed. "I'm surprised. Not that she blabbed about our relationship, but that she doesn't know where Gillian is. Those two are usually all up in each other's business." He met Matthias's gaze and brightened. "I know. Check with the girls who were at the wedding."

"What wedding?" Cassie asked.

"Gillian and I went to a wedding the Saturday before she ran off. I can't remember the bride's name. She was one of Gillian's friends. But the reception was held at the Royal Palace Conference Center. Ask them. They could give you the bride's name. She was hanging out with a bunch of her high-school friends. If Gillian made plans to take off, I bet it was with one of them."

Cassie continued to ask questions, but Matthias's mind raced off on a different track. A wedding at the Royal Palace. On Saturday two weeks ago. The same day Nell had been spotted in the hallway.

He forced his jaw to unclench and his awareness back to the present. Cassie was asking for names of the women at the wedding, and Carlisle was claiming he didn't know.

Matthias interrupted. "Nell Anderson."

Carlisle shot a stunned look at Matthias. "Who?"

"You're not going to claim you don't know her, are you?" he said. "She worked here as a bartender."

"Oh. Yes. She did. She left a few weeks ago." Carlisle was beginning to act twitchy. Either he'd had too much coffee, or he was on the verge of coming unglued.

"Why?"

"I don't know. She just quit."

"Do you have an address for her?"

"No."

"Don't you need one?" Cassie asked. She'd picked up on Matthias's train of questioning. "For tax purposes."

"Oh, her employment records were all in order. You can check," he babbled. "I make sure all the proper deductions are taken. The government gets their portion." He seemed more upset about possibly being accused of tax fraud than of his relationships —personal or professional—with two missing women. One of whom was likely lying in the morgue at this very moment.

"Her address," Matthias said, reeling him back in. "You had to have one."

"Yes. I did. But it was one of those mailbox places." He looked from Matthias to Cassie and back. "Nell's homeless."

"You hired her anyway?" Cassie asked.

Carlisle shrugged. "I was trying to give her a hand *up* instead of a hand*out*. She always had clean uniforms. Sometimes she'd wash up in the bathrooms here before the rest of the staff came in, or after closing. She was always punctual. Polite. No complaining.

The customers loved her. I wish I had a dozen more employees like her."

His words were all perfect, but Matthias sensed Carlisle had prepared this speech and rehearsed it more than once.

"If you don't need me for anything else," Carlisle said, checking his expensive-looking wristwatch, "I have an appointment I need to get to."

Matthias stepped closer to him and held out his business card. "If you hear from either Gillian or Nell, call me." He fixed Carlisle with the same intense glare as earlier. Except Matthias's was still intact. Carlisle's? Not so much.

"I will." He slipped the card into one of his pockets, strode out of the fishbowl room, and, without speaking to any of his employees, out of the restaurant.

"Wow," Cassie said. "He's a piece of work. Caved like a house of cards in a breeze."

Matthias stared after the departed manager. "I'm not so sure."

"What do you mean? You saw him."

"He caved on the stuff he knew we'd already uncovered. I have a feeling there's still a lot he's not saying."

Cassie considered Matthias's words then shook her head. "Let's go get lunch. I'm starved. By then Emma might be home."

They left the private room and were headed for the exit when Matthias noticed Tiffany bustling toward them. He doubted she was going to insist they stay for a meal.

"Excuse me," she called, bringing them to a stop. As they faced her, she glanced toward the front door. Making sure Carlisle was truly gone? Edging close to them, Tiffany lowered her voice to a conspiratorial level. "What did he tell you about Nell Anderson?"

Matthias exchanged a glance with Cassie. "He confirmed what you told us, and he said she was homeless."

The slant of Tiffany's mouth told Matthias there was more. "Figures," she said. "He's such an asshole."

Matthias braced his hands on his hips. "Why don't you tell us what he left out."

She looked around at the customers seated nearby before meeting Matthias's gaze. "Come with me."

They followed her back the way they'd come, into the fishbowl. This time, she closed the door.

Facing them, Tiffany asked, "How did Russ react when you told him about Gillian's body?"

"We didn't," Matthias replied. "He claims she's off with some girlfriends. Until we get a positive ID on the victim, we'll let him stick with his story."

Tiffany scowled. "But you told me."

"We had to get your attention," Cassie said. "It worked, didn't it?"

"I guess. So you really don't know for sure that Gillian's dead?"

"Not until the coroner confirms it," Cassie said. "Or until she shows up alive and well-rested from her vacation."

Matthias brought them back on topic. Or at least the topic he wanted to address. "What about Nell?"

Tiffany appeared to weigh how much to reveal. She sighed. "I gather you know Russ and Gillian are involved. Sexually, I mean."

"We've heard as much."

"Do you know he was sleeping with Nell too?"

Matthias had been right. Carlisle's story about Emma's sister was a practiced pile of shit. But this wasn't what Matthias had expected to learn he was hiding. "No, we did not."

Tiffany didn't appear surprised. "I didn't think he'd tell you that part. Poor Nell. She told him no. More than once. I never really spoke with her much. I had a feeling she just wanted to keep her job and stay out of trouble. But Russ took her rejection as a challenge and cranked up the pressure."

Cassie folded her arms. "Sexual harassment."

Tiffany nodded. "Right in front of Gillian, too."

"Gillian must not have been too happy about it," Cassie said.

"I don't know. I suspect Gillian had her share of side action if you know what I mean."

Free spirit, Carlisle had said.

"What happened next?" Matthias asked.

"Nell gave in. It was a matter of sleep with the boss or be out on the street. And we all knew she was already out on the street." Tiffany made air quotes around the homeless reference.

"How long did this go on?" Cassie asked.

Tiffany shrugged. "Two or three months. Then she quit. It was the only way she could get rid of him." She looked toward the restaurant's front door. "And I'm not sure quitting was enough."

Matthias didn't like the uneasy expression on her face. "What do you mean?"

She brought her gaze back to his. "Russ isn't used to losing. He considered Nell to be one of his possessions. I truly believe he'd stop at nothing to track her down."

Tiffany's words and the image they stirred chilled Matthias. He knew they'd chill Emma as well. "Do you have any idea where Nell might be now?" he asked.

Tiffany shook her head vigorously. "No, and I don't want to know. If Russ caught wind I was keeping something like that from him…" She let the suggestion fade, but Matthias read terror in her eyes.

"Do you know any of Nell's friends? People she might confide in?"

Tiffany continued to shake her head. "Except for when Russ was putting her up, she lived on the streets. The people she was friends with wouldn't fit in around here." She gestured at the well-heeled patrons beyond the smoked-glass walls.

"Wait," Cassie said, cocking her head to one side. "Russ put her up? At his place?"

"No, but I heard rumors he was renting an apartment for her."

Tiffany gave a short laugh. "I bet having a nice place to stay was more of an attraction for Nell than the man himself."

Matthias pictured Emma's kid sister living in one of those tents a short walk from here and had to agree with Tiffany. Yet, Nell had given it up and taken off. Good for her.

Tiffany took another glance across the dining room. "I've told you all I know. Now I really need to get back to work."

They thanked the young hostess and watched her hurry out of the fishbowl and toward her post at the front door.

Matthias pondered the conversation they'd just had. "We need to find that apartment."

"I wonder if Nell Anderson might still be there," Cassie said.

"According to Tiffany, Nell quit to get free of the guy. Why would she continue to stay at his apartment?"

Cassie looked like she'd smelled something rotten. "Tiffany said it herself. She doesn't know a lot of things and doesn't want to. Everything she told us was supposition and rumor."

As much as he hated to admit it, Cassie was right.

"It makes perfect sense for Nell to quit. She's being taken care of, given a nice home. Why bother working? Especially if the jackass boyfriend's other babe is harassing her."

This wasn't the Nell Matthias had pictured, but he realized that unsullied image had been fed to him by Emma.

Cassie must've read his thoughts. "I think it's time we pay your cute photographer chick a visit." She reached over and wrapped her fingers around his forearm. "I also think she doesn't need to know about the jackass boyfriend just yet."

Puzzled, Matthias studied his partner's face. "Why not?"

"Think about it. Nell Anderson and Gillian Watson were both involved with the same man. Judging by the place he calls home, that suit he was wearing, and the Rolex on his wrist, Russ Carlisle might be a jackass, but he's a rich jackass. He was keeping formerly homeless Nell in a nice apartment. He was also sleeping with Gillian. Now one of those two women is dead. Maybe Nell got tired of sharing her sugar daddy."

"You heard Tiffany. Nell was scared of him."

"According to Tiffany," Cassie said with a hefty note of skepticism, "who admits she wants nothing to do with any of it."

"Are you suggesting that Nell offed her competition?"

Cassie shrugged. "Stranger things have happened. Love and money are strong motives for murder. And the love *of* money is even stronger."

Matthias thought about it and tried to argue against Cassie's scenario but ended up stuttering and falling silent.

"Look. I understand keeping things from Emma has never been one of your strong suits—"

He again opened his mouth to argue.

Cassie flashed a palm, stopping him. "Don't even try to deny it. You know damn well it's the truth. Just humor me. Okay? I want to see how Emma reacts to the news her sister's still alive."

He picked up on her insinuation. "You think Emma already knows?"

Without responding, Cassie headed once more across the dining area. Matthias remained in the fishbowl, his mind spiraling. He understood the look his partner had given him. Not only did she believe Emma already knew about Nell being alive, she thought Emma might be involved in Nell's mess.

No. He wasn't buying it. None of it. And if Emma knew anything, she would tell him.

Or would she? Was he once again placing trust where it didn't belong?

Chapter Twenty-One

E ric stood at the Forester's passenger door, looking across the roof at Emma. "What's going on? You didn't say two words over lunch. And you hardly ate anything either."

She avoided eye contact and climbed behind the wheel. "I'm grieving the death of my sister," she lied. She couldn't tell him the truth. Hiding behind bereavement seemed like a logical cover.

He climbed in beside her. "You've been grieving for three days."

"What? I'm only allowed two?"

Eric groaned. "No, of course not. But I never realized stony silence was one of the stages of grief. You talked to me the entire drive up here yesterday. Now you're shutting me out. What gives?"

"Nothing." She turned the key, shifted into reverse, and backed out of the parking space at the chain restaurant where they'd had lunch. "You said it. I talked all day yesterday. I'm talked out."

Emma refused to look at him but felt his dubious gaze.

"Something's happened," Eric said. "What is it?"

"Nothing's happened." She hated lying to her best friend in the whole world but had no other option. Not until she had a chance to talk to her sister. "I guess it's just starting to hit me. Nell's really gone. After all this time, not knowing where she was but at least hoping she was safe, now I know she's not coming back." Emma kept her head straight, shifting her eyes for a quick glance at Eric.

He nodded. "I understand."

She relaxed and turned onto Peninsula Drive.

"I've never had to go through what you have," he said. "Losing your parents. Your only sibling becoming an addict. Disappearing for years. I can't imagine what it's been like."

From her hip pocket, her phone vibrated. She shifted to the other hip, reached back, and dug the phone out.

Eric reached out to her. "Here, let me take it."

"No, thanks. I've got it." She angled the screen away from her passenger, hoping to see the number Nell had used. Instead, the incoming caller was Matthias. As she'd done with his previous calls that morning, she thumbed the red icon, sending the call to voicemail before re-pocketing the device. In doing so, she caught a glimpse of Eric's frown. At least he didn't continue asking questions.

As they made their way down the hill and under the roller coaster track of Waldameer Amusement Park, Eric's face was turned away from her. He was angry. She'd shut him out, something he wasn't used to.

Emma owed him a mega-sized apology.

"Any idea how long it'll be before the coroner releases Nell's body?" Eric asked.

"Nope."

He grunted. "I don't think you'll be able to find any peace so long as she's in the morgue. I know you hate funerals, but they do provide a sense of closure."

Emma kept silent. She made the right turn into the parking lot and through the gate of Sara's Campground. The aroma of wood smoke and grilling meat wafted from several sites. Fellow campers waved as she passed. She returned the gesture. As she approached the hill to her trailer, a new thought almost paralyzed her. All those ignored calls from Matthias. What if he was waiting for her return? He must have news about the case. She would have to pretend it was still Nell's case. Eric might buy her lies—barely—but she'd witnessed Matthias's ability to discern deception from fact. Would she be able to convince the detective that her edginess was a result of coming to grips with Nell's death?

She had no choice. She had to.

When her camp came into view and the parking spot in front of it was empty, she exhaled a relieved breath.

"Oh, there's something else I meant to tell you," Eric said as she parked. "During my virtual work meetings this morning, I told my team I'm taking the rest of the week off so I can be here for you."

Emma turned off the engine and struggled to pretend she was happy about the news when in fact, she now had to figure out how to get away without him once Nell called. "That's sweet, but it really isn't necessary. I'm not that fragile."

"I know you aren't. But you don't have any friends up here."

"There's Kira."

"Whom you've known exactly five minutes. Don't you dare tell me you don't need me. I'll be heartbroken."

Eric's exaggerated pout made Emma laugh. "You're right. I'm glad you're sticking around."

They climbed out of the Forester and onto her deck. The rumble of an approaching vehicle reached her but didn't garner her attention until Eric didn't follow her inside. Instead, he squinted toward the road.

"Your cop is here," he said.

"What?" She spun back toward the door, nudging Eric aside for a better view of the black Impala. Matthias must've grown impatient. Crap. Why hadn't she returned his calls? She should've known avoidance would result in him coming to look for her. Now she had to lie to Eric *and* Matthias at the same time. Then she noticed two cops in the car. Make that Eric, Matthias, and Detective Malone. How the hell could she pull this off?

As the Impala came to a stop next to the Subaru, Eric closed his hand around hers and drew her onto the deck. She jerked away. "Stop clowning around."

He eyed her and whispered, "Making him a little jealous can only help."

She considered choking her old friend, but right now she had two cops as witnesses.

Matthias led the way to Emma's deck. "You didn't return my phone calls." His stony expression and level voice gave nothing away.

"We just got back," she said, cringing at how chirpy she sounded. No way was she going to pull this off.

Matthias's gaze drifted to Eric but came back to Emma. He tipped his head toward his partner. "You remember Detective Sergeant Malone."

"Yes, of course." Emma attempted to smile and knew she failed.

Detective Malone maintained the same stoic expression as Matthias.

"We need to talk to you," he said. Looking directly at Eric, he added, "Alone."

Eric draped an arm around Emma's shoulders. "I'm not going anywhere."

She considered slugging him. Maybe later.

Matthias met her gaze. "I'd really rather this be a private conversation."

Private. Except he had Detective Malone with him. Leaning on Eric might not be a bad idea. "It's okay. Anything you have to say to me, can be said in front of him. He's known Nell almost all her life."

Matthias exchanged a look with his partner. "All right," he said to Emma. "Perhaps you'd better have a seat."

Knees already weak, she complied. Eric once again stood behind her, hands on her shoulders.

Unlike last time, Matthias didn't claim the second chair, choosing to stand instead. "The coroner called me this morning."

Emma tensed, realizing they knew. She'd been a fool to believe it would take longer.

"Your sister's dental records don't match with the victim in the warehouse."

She gripped the armrests, struggling to keep her face still. Nell said she needed to stay dead. She needed time. Her life depended on it. And now her time had run out much sooner than she'd hoped.

Emma wasn't a good enough actress for this kind of role.

Eric's grip on her shoulders tightened. He leaned over, speaking softly into her ear. "Hey, this is good news, right? Nell's alive."

Emma managed to squeak out, "Yes."

"I realize this is a shock," Matthias said, "but we have to ask you some questions."

She looked up at him, searching his face for some hint of the compassion he'd shown her in the past. Except his expression remained carved in stone. She'd seen this side of him before as well. When they'd first met.

"Do you have any explanation for why the victim was found wearing your sister's clothing? Or why she had your sister's purse and identification on her?"

Emma couldn't have formed words with her mouth as dry as

silica gel even if she'd had a reasonable answer. She shook her head.

"Have you spoken with her recently?"

Emma hesitated and immediately realized her mistake. He would take that hesitation for what it really was. An indication that she had to think before fabricating an answer. "No," she said, her voice still little more than a chirp.

If Matthias caught the lie, he didn't let on. "When was the last time you heard from her?"

Emma thought beyond the deception. "Last month. That message she left me."

"The one where she told you not to try to find her."

She nodded. Prior to this morning, that had been the last time she'd heard from Nell.

"Do you know who the victim really is?" Eric asked.

"We're waiting for a positive ID," Matthias told him. He brought his focus back to Emma. "You don't have any idea how we can reach your sister?"

"None."

Detective Malone edged forward. "It's vital that we speak with her."

Emma looked at Matthias's partner, whose face was even less readable than his.

"If you hear from her, tell her to call us. You have Detective Honeywell's number."

"I do. I will." But Emma didn't believe for one minute that Nell would make the call.

"If you hear from her," Detective Malone repeated with added emphasis, "*you* call us."

Emma gave another nod. Inside her head, she heard the litany of charges which were bound to be leveled at her. Impeding an investigation. Making a false statement. Lying to the police. Were any of those actual arrestable crimes? Did she need an attorney?

Detective Malone's phone pinged with a notification. She

thumbed the screen, read, then nudged Matthias. "Let's go," she said as she stepped off the deck.

But he didn't follow. He stepped closer to Emma and extended a hand. Thinking he was offering a supportive gesture, she took it. Except he closed his fingers around hers and hoisted her to her feet. Not roughly, but firmly. In the moment when Eric's grasp on her shoulders released, Matthias drew her close until his face was little more than an inch from hers.

The stoic mask cracked as he held her gaze in an even firmer grip than he held her hand, silently communicating something more intense. Fury? Disappointment?

She was only sure of one thing. Matthias knew she was lying.

But he was letting her get away with it. For now.

Once the Impala had disappeared at the bottom of the hill, Eric faced Emma and huffed. "That man is a brute. I'm glad you're not involved with him."

"He's not a brute." The words slipped from her lips before she had a chance to stop them.

Eric stood taller, scowling down at her. "You really do like him."

This time, she kept her mouth shut.

"Oh, my God. You *knew*."

"What?" Her voice was back to being a squeak.

"About Nell. You knew. You lied to the cops." A cloud of deep hurt passed over his face. "You lied to *me*."

Emma staggered over to her deck chair and collapsed into it. Denial was useless at this point. "I did. I'm sorry."

Eric's lips trembled like a child about to burst into tears. "You're not forgiven. You lied to me," he repeated, sharper this time. "About Nell. *Our* Nell. You let me go on believing she was dead. Why?" He crossed his arms. "How long have you known?"

"Not long." Emma told him about the phone calls. The one Nell had made to her and the one she had returned. "She was emphatic that no one could know."

Eric listened, still glowering. "No one doesn't include me," he said stiffly.

"I didn't get a chance to ask." When he didn't relinquish his angry stance, Emma went on. "She's my sister. She's in trouble. She asked me...no...*pleaded* with me to keep her secret. If you confided in me about something horrible and asked me to tell no one, you know damned well I wouldn't make exceptions."

Eric's mouth bunched to one side of his face.

She knew she'd reached him and needed to drive her point home. "How good are you at poker?"

"You know I suck."

"Exactly. If I had told you about Nell, and those detectives showed up asking questions, do you honestly think you could've faked your way through it?"

Eric gave her the side eye. "Probably better than you did. You didn't fake anything. You all but screamed *liar liar pants on fire.*"

"They bought it," Emma insisted. Didn't they?

"I highly doubt that."

"Okay, so I was a wreck, but they had to know I'd be in shock considering the news they were breaking to me."

"Emma, if they had been telling you Nell was dead, you could've gotten away with collapsing into a fugue state. They were giving you good news. She's alive. If you wanted to convince them this was the first you'd heard of it, you'd have jumped for joy."

She pondered Eric's words. As much as she hated to admit it, he was right.

Emma dug out her phone.

"You calling the brute?" Eric asked.

"No. I'm calling Nell." Emma pulled up the number she'd used earlier and hit the green icon. After several cycles of ring-back tones, an automated voice informed her the party she was trying to reach was currently unavailable. At the beep, she left her message. "It's me. Call me ASAP. It's important." She ended the call and closed her eyes. Important. Nell had told her keeping her secret was a matter of life and death. And now that the police knew, it was only a matter of time before whomever Nell was hiding from knew as well.

Chapter Twenty-Two

Matthias fumed in silence as he drove south along Peninsula Drive. Cassie was on the phone with Frazier, who'd sent the text reporting that one of Thomas Jenkins's credit cards had been used to make a purchase at an auto-parts store down on West 26th.

She ended the call. "Frazier will meet us there. He talked to the manager, who says they have security cameras near the cash register and is willing to let us view the footage."

Matthias grunted a response. He felt her gaze burning into the side of his face. "What?" he snapped.

"Emma is lying," Cassie said.

"I know."

"What do you think? Is she covering for the sister?"

He hadn't gotten that far in his ruminations yet. He was still hung up on why she lied to him. He'd believed they were beyond that, which, he realized, was stupid. He and Emma were barely friends. She'd known him a whole month, and part of that time, she'd been a person of interest in a homicide he was working. But much had happened since then.

Or had it?

Yes, he'd had a small role in saving her life. Yes, he'd helped get her a job. On the other hand, he'd dated a woman Emma considered a friend. Partly because Kira was hot. Mostly because he knew Kira had no interest in anything more than a sexual relationship. And maybe because he knew it would drive a wedge between him and Emma.

He had feelings for Emma. The kind that would ultimately break his heart. And hers.

Cassie jabbed his arm. "Hey."

He flinched. "What?"

"Do you think Emma is covering for her sister?"

He pulled his heart out of the equation and forced his brain back into cop mode. "Yeah. I do."

"Do you believe she knew the body wasn't her sister's all along?"

Matthias pondered the question, recalling the look in Emma's eyes when he'd broken the news. "No. She believed Nell was dead."

In his peripheral vision, he saw Cassie nodding. "Nell contacted her," Cassie said.

"Probably."

"Have they been in touch with each other before this?"

"No." He reconsidered his answer. "Maybe. Hell, I don't know." He braked as they approached the light on Peninsula and West 26th.

"I think Nell had something to do with the woman's death," Cassie said. "First, there's the romantic triangle. Add to that the fact Nell is a known drug addict. And addicts would do just about anything for their next score or for money for their next score. Maybe Russ hasn't merely been providing a nice apartment for her. Maybe he's her dealer."

Matthias hated every word Cassie was saying. Hated that it made entirely too much sense.

The light turned green.

"Therefore," Cassie continued to extrapolate, "since Emma knows Nell's alive, it's likely she knows what really happened."

Matthias wasn't ready to make that final jump in logic. He needed to get Emma alone. No Cassie.

And no Mr. Superhero.

Matthias eased into the Lake Erie Auto Supplies lot and parked next to Frazier's car.

They found him at the rear of the showroom, leaning on the counter and chatting with the beefy bald man behind it. Frazier straightened when he spotted them. "Detectives Malone and Honeywell, this is John Ingram, the store manager. Go ahead and tell them what you told me."

Ingram folded his arms across his expansive belly. "Fellow comes in around lunchtime to buy an alternator and core. I ring it up, and he hands me a credit card." He uncrossed his arms and leaned one elbow on the counter. "Did you know when a card is stolen and used before it's reported, the cardholder gets their money back? Meanwhile, we retailers have to eat it."

"I did not know that," Matthias said, hoping he'd get on with it.

"We've been burned on that little detail a couple of times. One man took us for several-hundred dollars a few months ago. Hey, we're a small business. We can't afford those kinds of losses, so now I require ID on credit card sales when I don't know the customer."

"And that's what you did?" Mathias asked.

"You bet. He started patting his pockets and said he must've left his wallet in his car. He supposedly went out to get it, but he never came back." Ingram picked up a credit card that had been sitting on the cash register. "That's when I really looked at the thing and saw the name on it. Thomas Jenkins. I remember seeing the news story about him getting killed last weekend."

Matthias pulled on a pair of Nitrile gloves and reached for the card. "May I?"

"Sure thing." Ingram shoved the piece of plastic at him as if it was scorching his fingers.

Matthias held the card so Cassie and Frazier could see it before sliding it into an evidence bag.

Frazier inclined his head toward a doorway behind Ingram. "You said you keep your video surveillance recordings back there?"

"Yep." Ingram waved to them. "Come on into my office. Pisses me off, people trying to rip off small businesses. I kinda miss the days when I helped my old man, and almost all transactions were in cash."

Matthias, Cassie, and Frazier passed between the counters and followed Ingram through the doorway, past rows of shelves holding boxes of all sizes. At the rear of the storage area, Ingram entered a surprisingly neat and clean office space. One wall was filled with more shelves. These held a digital recorder and a monitor showing four images. The first was aimed at the sidewalk by the front doors. Another captured images of anyone entering from inside the store. Two others were aimed at the area where they'd stood moments earlier, one camera high behind the counter, the other facing it.

Ingram rounded his desk where his computer sat. "Give me a second." He flopped into the chair and started pecking on the keyboard. "Here." He turned the screen so the three detectives could see it.

As they watched, Ingram played the video from the camera behind the cash register. A man approached the counter with his head lowered, a baseball cap's brim concealing his face. Ingram entered the frame, the camera capturing the back of his head. The silent movie continued, Matthias maintaining focus on the customer, willing him to lift his face. Instead, the transaction went on as Ingram had described. He retreated into the storage room. The customer looked left and right, but not up. Ingram soon returned with a box holding the requested part. The customer handed over the card. Ingram held it and spoke to the customer, who patted his shirt and pants pockets. He gestured toward the door, turned, and hurried out.

Without ever showing his face.

"Dammit," Matthias muttered.

"Can you show us another view?" Cassie asked.

"No problem." Ingram tapped the keyboard a few times and the angle reversed, now showing the view from the showroom toward the register.

The same sequence of events played. This time, they could clearly see Ingram's face and the back of the customer's head. Matthias thought about asking the manager to fast forward through the recording but feared he'd miss something. He waited and watched. Ingram brought the box out and set it on the counter. The customer searched for his wallet. From this angle Matthias noted rectangular-shaped bulges in both of the guy's hip pockets. Phone. And wallet. Then the customer pivoted to leave.

"Freeze it," Matthias and Cassie said simultaneously.

Ingram hit a key and the image stopped with the man's gaze lifted enough for them to recognize him.

"Sebastian Wilcox," Frazier said.

Matthias blew out a growling breath. "So much for Jenkins's wallet being empty when he found it."

Once they were outside, Matthias, Cassie, and Frazier gathered between their cars.

Frazier held the evidence bags containing a flash drive onto which Ingram had copied the security footage of Wilcox and the credit card. "He told us he was on his way to an interview at Lake View Real Estate when he found the wallet," Frazier said. "We haven't confirmed it with them yet though. Do you want me to head over there?"

Cassie tapped her notebook against her chin and gazed into the distance. "Yeah," she said after several moments. "You do that but drop off our evidence at the station first." She shifted her focus to Matthias. "Wilcox works at Erie Sand and Gravel, right? Let's you and me go over there and have a talk with him."

Fifteen minutes later, Cassie slowed at the entrance to the sand and gravel company. Matthias thought back to the last time they'd been here a month ago. They'd been searching for a missing victim of a home invasion whose abandoned car was found on these grounds. Unlike that evening, this time the massive cranes and earth movers rumbled and moved about the place, loading equally massive dump trucks.

Matthias led the way to a construction trailer near the entrance. Inside, a man and a woman occupied two desks and looked up. The man rose and circled to them. "How can I help you?"

Matthias made the introductions. "We're looking for a Sebastian Wilcox. I understand he works here."

"Yeah, Wilcox is here. You need to talk to him?"

"We do."

The man shot a glance at the woman, who kept her head down and was reaching for the phone. "Get Wilcox in here," he said.

"Already on it."

Five minutes later, Matthias and Cassie stood outside the trailer and watched Wilcox ambling toward them with a long easy gait. Then he must've recognized them. He stopped. Looked around as if searching for an escape route.

"Do not make me chase you," Matthias grumbled under his breath, knowing Wilcox couldn't hear him.

But Cassie could. She snickered. "You could use the exercise."

Apparently, Sebastian Wilcox decided against an attempted getaway. With slumped shoulders, he trudged toward them. By the time he closed the distance, his spine was again straight.

Matthias could well imagine the internal debate going on inside the guy's head.

"Detective Honeywell, isn't it?" Wilcox extended a hand, which Matthias grasped.

"Good memory." Matthias gestured to Cassie. "This is Detective Sergeant Malone."

Wilcox offered a pleasant nod, but Matthias sensed the ruby flush to his cheeks was not from working in the sun.

"We have a few questions for you," Cassie said without mirroring the forced geniality.

Wilcox crossed his arms. "Okay."

Cassie tipped her head toward the construction trailer. And Wilcox's boss. "How about we step inside."

He shot a wide-eyed look at the office. "I'm good right here."

"I'm not." Cassie wasn't using her mother hen persona today. "Tell you what, Mr. Wilcox. I'll give you a choice. We sit down and chat inside." She again indicated the trailer. "Or we can sit down and chat at the station."

Wilcox's lips tightened into a thin, pained line. No one ever wanted to "chat at the station," but his other option was airing dirty laundry in the presence of his boss. He didn't know—because Cassie hadn't told him—they would've asked the foreman and the secretary to step out while they had the room.

"I can't leave the site," Wilcox said uneasily. "I'll get fired."

Matthias plastered his best sympathetic expression on his face. "I guess the job interview didn't go so well?"

"It went okay. I just haven't heard anything yet. Seriously, I don't need trouble."

Well, dude, you've got it, Matthias thought.

"Can't we talk right here?" Wilcox pointed at his feet. "Or in your car?"

Cassie eyed Matthias, acting as if she'd never thought of that. "Okay," she told Wilcox. "The car it is. But we'll have to pat you down first." At his shocked expression, she added, "No one gets in my car without me checking for weapons."

Despite the nearby workers who stopped what they were doing to watch, Wilcox complied.

With the air conditioner running and Wilcox squirming in the back seat, Matthias and Cassie sat in the front, backs to the doors so they could keep an eye on him.

"Tell us about the wallet you found," she said from her position behind the wheel.

"I already told him and the other guy." Wilcox peered at Matthias as if he might save him from the pissed off Black woman. "Detective Frazier, right?"

Either Wilcox had a superior memory for names, or his time spent with Matthias and Frazier had been indelibly etched in his mind.

Cassie gave him a predatory grin. "Help me get up to speed."

Wilcox swallowed. "I was on my way to a job interview when I tossed an empty coffee cup in the trash. And my car keys along with it. While I was digging for them, I found a wallet." He shot a quick help-me look at Matthias. "I turned it in. Ask him."

Matthias was kind of enjoying playing good cop to Cassie's bad. It happened so rarely. "He did."

"What was in the wallet?" she asked.

"Thomas Jenkins's driver's license."

"Anything else?"

"I don't know. I didn't look."

"But you didn't notice any cash or credit cards?"

He shook his head emphatically. Too emphatically. "No."

Matthias's phone pinged with a notification. A text from Frazier.

Lake View Real Estate confirms interview date and time with Sebastian Wilcox.

He read the rest of the message and responded with a thumbs-up emoji. Instead of putting his phone away, he pulled up a still from the video John Ingram had provided. Matthias shifted in his seat and angled the screen so Wilcox could see the image from inside Lake Erie Auto Supplies. And his face caught on camera.

He leaned back in the seat, his expression melting into resignation.

"You know," Matthias said, still faking empathy, "this doesn't look good for you, buddy."

Wilcox lowered his face and nodded. When he looked up again, he appeared on the verge of tears. "It's been a rough year, okay? My junker of a car keeps breaking down. The old furnace went out in my house last January. You know how winters are in Erie. Buying a new furnace wasn't something I could put off. Then I had a plumbing leak in my upstairs bathroom. Hell, I can't get one bill paid off before another comes up. When I found that wallet with those credit cards in it, I figured I'd just use one. And only this one time. Then I'd shred all of them. I really needed that alternator." His chin dropped to his chest.

Matthias pocketed his phone. "You took the credit cards."

"Yes."

"What about the cash?"

Wilcox's head came up again. "There wasn't any cash in the wallet. I swear to God."

Matthias believed him.

Cassie apparently did not. "You've lied to the police at every turn. Why should we buy one word coming out of your mouth?"

"I admit I took those cards. But I'm not lying to you. I only tried using one card, one time. And there was no cash. None. Whoever killed that guy and took the wallet in the first place must've taken the money."

"Which brings me to my next question." Cassie glared at him. "Why should we believe the person who killed Thomas Jenkins isn't you?"

"What? No." Wilcox sputtered. "I would never...I could never kill anyone. I swear to God I didn't do that."

"You already swore to God. Not sure I wanna be in the same car with you when the Big Guy strikes you down with a lightning bolt."

Matthias battled down a snort of laughter. Cassie was in rare form today.

"I swear on my mother's grave. I swear on my kids' lives." Wilcox's voice rose in pitch with each sentence, finally reaching a crescendo with "I didn't kill anyone."

"Well, buddy, we do you know you committed credit-card fraud," Matthias said. He climbed out of the passenger seat and opened the back door.

"You're letting me go?"

He withdrew his handcuffs and gestured for Wilcox to stand up. "Afraid not. But you're under arrest and probably shouldn't say anything else until you get an attorney."

A crowd of workers, including the foreman and secretary, had gathered to watch as Matthias drew a passive Sebastian Wilcox's hands behind his back and clicked the cuffs on his wrists. Matthias felt sincerely bad for the guy.

As Matthias assisted him into the car again, Wilcox exhaled a sigh. "Not only is my job here toast, the real-estate place probably won't want to hire me now either."

Matthias thought of the rest of Frazier's text. "For what it's worth, Detective Frazier did some checking. He confirmed you had an interview at Lake Erie Real Estate. He also learned they hired someone else for the job."

Chapter Twenty-Three

E mma stayed in her camper all afternoon, her phone within easy reach. Eric tried to talk her into a walk around Presque Isle, but she'd already missed one call from Nell because of the poor cell service. She finally convinced him to take her bike, adjust the seat height for his long legs, and go without her, claiming she had photo editing to do. Her excuse wasn't yet another lie. She did, in fact, have almost a hundred images to sort through for an impending deadline. Whether she'd be able to focus on work, even with Eric gone, was up for debate.

She made the effort and managed to get through about a quarter of the photos before her phone rang. She snatched it, expecting to see Nell's number. Instead, the incoming call was from Matthias. Emma contemplated sending it to voice mail, but that maneuver hadn't worked earlier in the day.

"Hello." She made no attempt to cover her lack of enthusiasm.

"I need to talk to you." He was still using that low, gravelly tone.

"You've got me."

"I mean in person."

"We did that earlier."

His exhale sounded exasperated. "Just you and me. Without Cassie and your boyfriend."

Boyfriend? *Eric*? Emma almost laughed.

"Can you get away from him for a while?"

She looked at the clock above her table. Four-thirty. If Eric made the entire fourteen-mile loop as he'd planned, he'd be gone for another couple of hours. "I don't expect Eric back until after six."

"I'll be there in fifteen minutes."

Emma was sitting on her deck when Matthias's red Jeep crawled up the hill toward her camp. His personal vehicle, not one of the department's sedans. He parked next to her Forester and climbed out. Instead of his departmental polo shirt and trousers, he wore a blue T-shirt and jeans, both slightly on the tight side, revealing his well-toned gym-rat physique. Damn. Kira was right. He was hot.

He headed toward her. "Thanks for agreeing to see me," he said as he lowered into the other chair.

She replied with a nod.

They sat in silence for well over a minute, Emma tense, waiting for whatever was coming next. Matthias at least appeared relaxed, leaning back in his chair, studying his hands. Then, he lifted his gaze, his piercing blue eyes burning into hers, and in a low, almost whispered voice, he said, "You lied to me."

She opened her mouth, but words wouldn't come. If she denied the accusation, she was compounding the list of offenses she'd committed. And he knew, so why even try? She lowered her head and exhaled. "I did."

"How long have you known the body wasn't Nell's?"

This question was harder. But covering for her sister meant more lies, and Matthias would see through them. "Since this morning."

He waited, watching her.

"Aw, hell." Emma sighed and poured out the events of the

morning from the bike ride and the voicemail to returning the call and speaking with Nell. "She begged me to keep it quiet. Her being alive. She said she needed some time. That it was a matter of life and death. Hers. She's scared. I had to keep her secret."

Matthias's eyes shifted away from hers. "Did you keep it secret from your boyfriend too?"

Emma studied Matthias, who refused to meet her gaze. Was she imagining it, or did he sound more like a jealous suitor than an interrogating cop? She hated that she wished it was the case. Her first instinct was to quash the whole boyfriend thing. But maybe having Eric in play might keep whatever was developing between her and Matthias strictly professional. "Yes, I kept Nell's secret from Eric."

If Matthias's expression was any indication, her answer clearly surprised him.

"And he was pissed at me about it too." Emma attempted an apologetic grin.

"Do you know where Nell is?"

She let the grin fade. "No."

He looked skeptical. "Really?"

Emma huffed in annoyance. "Really."

"Did she mention how her clothing and ID ended up on a dead woman's body?"

"No."

"Did she mention the dead woman at all?"

"She told me she figured the body would've been found by now and that she knew her stuff was on it. But nothing more." Matthias's expression was growing more ominous by the minute. "What are you thinking?"

Instead of answering, he asked, "She didn't mention who the woman was?"

"No. Have you IDed her yet?" He seemed to weigh how much to tell her, which told her enough. "You have."

"Do you know where Nell's been working lately?"

"You know I don't. Why?"

Once more, he appeared to want to say something but decided against it.

As seconds ticked away in silence, Emma replayed the questions he'd asked and the answers he hadn't given. A realization hit her harder than if he'd thrown a punch. "You think Nell had something to do with that woman's death."

He kept his gaze on Emma, and she tried to read his face. No longer accusatory. No longer jealous. He looked...sad. Regretful.

"Well?" she prodded.

His eyes shifted, breaking contact. "We have to look into the possibility."

Emma leaned forward in her chair, wanting to shake answers from him. "Why would she kill a woman and swap clothes with her?"

He came forward, too, once more meeting her gaze. Once more accusatory. "As for the clothes swap, you said it yourself. She's trying to fake her own death. As for why she'd kill a woman? Greed. Jealousy. Age-old motives for murder."

Emma could tell he realized he'd said too much, but he didn't back down. Or back away. He stared at her, his face less than a foot from hers. She didn't back away either. "Who's the victim? You clearly believe Nell knew her."

Instead of sitting back, he let his chin drop toward his chest and rested his elbows on his thighs. When he lifted his face, he looked around as if searching for eavesdroppers. His eyes came back to Emma's. "Until recently, Nell was working as a bartender at the Blue Pike. We believe the victim in the warehouse is a woman who's been missing for over a week and who also worked there."

Emma had read about the missing woman. ErieLIVE had posted stories about her. "Gillian Watson?"

Matthias nodded. "Both Gillian and Nell were sexually involved with the restaurant manager, a man by the name of Russ

Carlisle. Carlisle let Nell stay in an apartment he paid for. Prior to that, she'd been living on the streets. I'm willing to bet Gillian wasn't too happy with the situation. Three weeks ago, Nell quit. It's possible, likely, that Gillian pressured her into it. Roughly two weeks after that, Gillian disappeared on her way home from work. I know you don't want to believe your sister is capable of murder...I wouldn't either...but if Carlisle was supplying her with drugs in addition to putting a rather comfortable roof over her head..." Matthias didn't finish the sentence but raised an eyebrow at Emma, silently telling her to do the math.

She'd been building up steam, building up an argument against everything Matthias was saying, until he mentioned drugs. Nell would never kill someone. But Emma knew how drugs took over an addict's mind. Nell under the influence might be capable of things a sober Nell would never consider. Unspeakable things.

Like murder?

Emma hated that she was even entertaining the idea. As she absorbed and processed Matthias's words, her phone broke out in the rock tune she used as a ringtone. She resisted the urge to react, presuming the call was from her sister. Matthias, the master at detecting lies, was mere inches from her, studying her. She made a conscious effort to keep her breathing slow, steady, recalling Kira's directions in yoga class. The same instructions Nell had given a lifetime ago when she too taught yoga and meditation.

Keeping her face neutral, Emma reached back, withdrew the phone, and, keeping the device angled away from Matthias, touched the screen to silence it and send the call to voicemail. She'd seen the number—the one Nell had been calling from—but didn't react.

At least, she hoped she hadn't.

She returned the phone to her pocket.

"Who was that?" Matthias asked.

At this point, what was one more lie? "Eric."

"I thought he was bike riding in the park."

"He is."

"You should've taken the call. He might have a flat."

She could tell from his tone that Matthias suspected she was lying again. But he couldn't know. Not unless she confirmed it for him. "He might. But he can wait."

Matthias didn't blink.

Neither did she. "You were saying Nell quit her job three weeks ago. Did you go to the apartment where she'd been staying?"

"We're still trying to get an address on it."

"Then she might still be there." Emma made no effort to hide her eagerness. She much preferred to think of Nell as a kept woman in nice, safe surroundings as opposed to living in one of those tents near where the body had been found.

"She might."

Another thought came to Emma's mind. "Have you talked to any of the homeless people camped on Sixteenth Street?"

"We've tried. They tend to vanish when law enforcement shows up."

She didn't doubt it. "Eric and I went to the warehouse before —" She ran a tongue over her lips. "When I still believed the body you'd found was Nell."

"I told you—"

She waved a hand between them to silence his warning about the wisdom, or lack of it, in venturing into that neighborhood. "I know what you told me. Listen. When we were standing back by the steps where she—Gillian—died, a homeless man appeared at the end of the sidewalk, out by the street. He yelled at us. At Eric. He said, 'Leave her alone,' or something like that."

"You shouldn't have—"

"I know that. What if that homeless man saw what happened to Gillian?" The moment Emma said it, she realized *what if that homeless man saw Nell kill Gillian?*

Matthias pulled out his notebook and pen. "Can you give me a description?"

A lead weight in the pit of her stomach, Emma shook her head. "He had a beard and was wearing a camo ball cap. I think he was tall, but he was too far away to really judge."

Matthias nodded as he scribbled on the pad. He closed it and put the pad and the pen away. Then he reached over and took her hand, same as he had earlier that day. But this time, he simply held it rather than hauling her to her feet. The strength yet gentleness of his grasp stirred a beehive of emotions. A rush of tears rose to the surface, startling her. She slid her hand free and scrambled to her feet, stumbling to put space between them.

He rose as well, but slower. "Listen to me." His tone was softer, less gruff. "When you talk to your sister, find out where she is and call me."

Emma blinked away the heat building behind her eyes. Call Matthias, she thought, and turn Nell in to the cops. Not very damned likely.

He closed the distance she'd created between them but didn't move to touch her. He held her merely with the intensity of his gaze. "Call me," he repeated. "Not Cassie. *Me.* You may not believe it, but I'm worried about your sister, too. Whether she's on the streets or with this Carlisle dude, she's not safe." He raised an eyebrow—the one just below the scar he'd gained last month trying to help her—and waited for her response.

"I will. I promise."

He stayed there, studying her, reading her as if her every thought was an open book, before stepping around her and striding off the deck.

Once she was sure he was gone, Emma frantically dug her phone from her pocket. Nell hadn't left a message but had texted,

Meet me @ the base of Bicentennial Tower @ 6am.

"I'm never leaving you alone again." Eric slumped in one of Emma's porch chairs and glared at her. "I can't believe that brute had the nerve to come back here and to suggest our Nell had anything to do with that woman's death."

Emma pressed her fingers into the space between her eyebrows to stave off a headache. She shouldn't have said anything to Eric. Lying to him infuriated him. Telling him the truth rankled him just as much.

"At least Nell texted you. When we see her tomorrow morning, we'll find out what really happened."

Emma lowered her hand. "Not we. I. When *I* see her tomorrow."

"I'm going with you."

"No, you're not."

"Nell is like my sister, too," Eric said, his voice growing louder.

Emma shushed him. She didn't want anyone else in the campground hearing her business. Hers and Nell's. "She doesn't know you're here," Emma said sotto voce. "If she sees anyone with me, she's likely to disappear without waiting around to find out who it is."

"I can wait in the car while you go to the tower."

"No. I can't take the risk of spooking her." The simple truth was, Emma wanted time alone with her sister. Eric might be the closest thing either of them had to a brother, but right now, close wasn't close enough. "I'll meet her. Hear what she has to say, and then I'll let her know you're in town. If she's okay with seeing you, I'll call."

"I don't like you going down there alone."

"It's the Bicentennial Tower. Not the abandoned warehouse district. I think I'll be safe."

Not that it mattered. She'd have walked into Hell's fury if it meant getting her hands on Nell.

Chapter Twenty-Four

Emma had promised to contact him if she heard from her sister, but Matthias knew the call she'd ignored was Nell. So much for their friendship and trust.

He knew there wasn't anything else he could do to convince her. Not right now. Instead, he drove downtown, parked on South Park Row, and entered the police department. Upstairs, the detectives' floor was quiet after hours. He wished he'd stopped for coffee but settled for starting a new batch in the break room's industrial-sized urn. While it brewed, he stepped through the doorway into Major Crimes, lowered into his desk chair, and fired up his computer.

He had two homicides on his plate, with no real progress on either. In fact, he didn't have a confirmed ID on the woman in the warehouse. The one wearing Nell Anderson's clothes and carrying her driver's license.

He picked up his phone and punched in Felix Hamilton's number. The coroner sounded exhausted when he answered. "Hey, Ham. It's Matthias Honeywell. Did you ever get a positive ID on the Jane Doe from the warehouse on Sixteenth?"

"Not yet." There was a shuffle and scrape on the other end of the call. "Aren't you off the clock? Don't you ever go home?"

"Do you?"

"Point taken. As for your Jane Doe, Gillian Watson's dental office promised I'd have the records on my desk first thing in the morning. I'll be in touch as soon as I know one way or the other."

Matthias thanked him and ended the call. For now, he was operating under the assumption Jane Doe was Gillian Watson, which meant following up on Russ Carlisle. And Nell.

But looking at his notes, Matthias realized there was someone else he could follow up with, possibly even tonight.

E.A. Dyson. When Matthias talked to him last night, he'd told Zeke that Nell was dead. He'd reacted strongly to the news. Matthias wondered if he knew the body wasn't really Nell and decided, no, his shock was genuine. Matthias traced the stubble on his upper lip. How would Zeke react to hearing Nell was, in fact, alive?

Matthias flipped back through his notes and stopped. Another lead he'd neglected to see all the way through was the housekeeper at the Royal Palace. Katie, last name unknown. Since he'd been there on Saturday, two of the three Katies had called as requested. Neither of them was the one who'd talked to Emma. He should go back to the hotel and try again. Not that he expected to learn anything new, but the housekeeper had provided Emma with the flash drive. He couldn't rule out the possibility that she knew more, and he wanted to talk to her source for the security footage.

Matthias made a note to visit Katie, last name unknown, tomorrow.

He moved on to the other homicide, Thomas Jenkins, and considered his persons-of-interest list.

Sebastian Wilcox claimed he'd found Jenkins's wallet in a trash can. He had a good story about why he'd been digging around in the garbage, and his reason for being in the area had been corroborated. But he'd lied about the credit cards. He'd probably lied about the cash as well. Why would anyone other than the shooter take Jenkins's wallet from the body and deposit it in the trash without first removing the victim's money and plastic?

Then there was the ex-wife and her new boyfriend, Pauly Nuccetelli, who also happened to be one of the last people to see Jenkins alive. Pauly had also lied. He had to know Jenkins used to be married to the woman he was dating.

Unless Olivia Petrovich didn't tell him. Which didn't look good for her.

Matthias tapped his notebook. They had yet to locate the woman who'd left the bar with Jenkins. She hadn't responded to the pleas they'd put out to the media. Nor had anyone else called with a plausible identification for her.

He mused over Frazier's theory regarding the ex-wife donning a wig. While Matthias had dismissed it, the idea of Jenkins and Petrovich playing some weird, kinky game with each other may not be so unimaginable after all.

Except that Pauly was there that night, which made that game even more kinky.

Matthias picked up a burger at a drive-through and ate it on his way to Pauly's Polynesian Pub. Eight pickups and a lone SUV occupied the lot. It was still early for the bar crowd, and it was a Tuesday night. Matthias parked and strode down the sidewalk to the entrance. As he reached the door, he caught a glimpse of a man shuffling down the next street away from him. From the back, he couldn't tell for sure, but the tall, thin figure reminded him of the scrawny guy he'd seen twice before in the neighborhood.

Inside, five men sat at the unattended bar, watching a Pittsburgh Pirates game on the TV. Two couples and another man claimed a trio of tables. Matthias approached the bar, watching the door behind it for some signs of Pauly or the bouncer or even a waitress. Without sitting, Matthias leaned an elbow on the dull, dark wood. He quickly pulled back when he realized his leather jacket was sticking to the surface.

A waitress, not the same one as he'd seen before, came through the door carrying two bowls of pretzels on a tray. She shot an expressionless glance at Matthias without saying a word. A few seconds later, the bouncer ambled out behind her. He spotted Matthias and pulled up short.

"Your boss around?"

The bouncer sniffed. "Hell, no. But he did call this morning."

"Did he say when he's coming back?"

"Tomorrow. Goddamn good thing too." The bouncer held his thumb and index finger a quarter inch apart. "I'm this close to walking out."

Matthias chuckled. "I'm kinda surprised to see you here at all. Yesterday, you said you were quitting if he wasn't back today."

"I told him that too." The bouncer shrugged. "He promised me a raise if I tended bar one more night. But this is it."

Matthias started to place his elbow on the bar again to strike a relaxed pose but remembered the tacky surface. "Don't suppose you've seen the blonde Tom Jenkins was with the last time you saw him, have you?"

"Nah. And I'd remember her, too." He blew a low, appreciative whistle.

"You said Pauly's out of town with his girlfriend?"

"Yep."

"And you said you've never seen this girlfriend."

"That's right. She don't come in here." He scowled. "Were you serious about her being Tom Jenkins's ex?"

"Yeah." Matthias gave the bouncer-turned-bartender a nod and walked out. He needed to get a photo of Olivia Petrovich. Maybe the disgruntled bouncer could settle the question of whether or not Tom Jenkins, his ex, and Pauly Nuccetelli were involved in some weird shit.

Matthias's next stop was the Mercury Tavern and Grill, which was doing better business than Pauly's, at least in the dining room. When he stepped into the dim bar, he surveyed the clientele and decided the Mercury only had one more drinking patron than the other place.

Behind the bar, Zeke Dyson had his back toward the door, chatting with a muscled guy. Matthias instantly identified the customer as a man he'd arrested twice for aggravated assault. As if sensing a cop's presence, the customer looked up and recognized Matthias, too. His lip curled and he pushed back. Matthias feared he might want a confrontation, but apparently, he wasn't that drunk. He slapped a twenty on the bar and headed toward Matthias and the door, muttering something as he brushed past.

Zeke's gaze followed the departure and settled on Matthias, who moved toward him.

"I got nothing to say to you," Zeke said, collecting the cash.

"Okay. But I have some news for you."

He didn't reply, instead focusing on ringing up his sale on the register.

"Nell Anderson is alive."

Zeke froze, his hand hovering over the cash drawer. As Matthias watched, the hand began to tremble. Zeke's eyes filled. He swallowed, stuffed the bill in the drawer, and swiped his face. "You shittin' me?"

"Nope. Dental records didn't match."

He lowered his face but not before Matthias saw him blow out a breath.

He was certain of one thing. Zeke Dyson wasn't faking his relief. "How do you know Nell Anderson?" Matthias asked.

Zeke didn't lift his head and his voice was strained as he replied, "Never said I did."

"We have her on video coming out of your hotel room. I don't believe your sudden bout of nausea had nothing to do with me threatening to show you a photo of a decomposing corpse. You definitely know her."

Zeke's face came up, his eyes looking everywhere but at Matthias. "I can't talk to you now. I'm working."

Matthias made a point of surveying the room. None of the handful of customers appeared to be waiting for service.

Zeke obviously understood what Matthias was thinking. "You're a cop. It doesn't look good, me standing here talking to you when I should be pouring drinks."

Matthias claimed one of the stools and leaned on the bar, which wasn't sticky like the one at Pauly's. "The only patron who recognized me as a cop just left." He indicated his attire. "I'm not in uniform. Hell, technically, I'm not even on duty. Pour me a draft."

Zeke gave him a side-eyed glare but did as requested.

With a foamy glass in front of him, Matthias shot him an exaggerated grin. "I'm a customer. You're a bartender. Let's talk. That's part of your job, right?"

"I got nothing to say to you."

"You don't wanna talk about Nell and the shared hotel room. Okay. Let's talk about what happened later." Matthias took a sip. "You called Emma Anderson. Told her you thought you'd seen her sister."

Zeke stiffened. Apparently, he hadn't realized Matthias knew about that conversation. "Yeah. I did."

"You knew who Nell was but didn't let on."

He squirmed but didn't speak.

"Why?" Matthias asked. "Why not simply tell Emma you knew Nell?"

Zeke met Matthias's gaze head-on for the first time. "Because I couldn't." He clamped his lips shut and looked away. "I can't. Look, I said it before. You wanna arrest me? Fine. But I'm not saying any more. I've already said too much." He pointed at the glass in front of Matthias. "That one's on the house. Drink up and get out."

Chapter Twenty-Five

The rising sun filtered through breaks in the clouds and shone through the Subaru's passenger windows as Emma coasted along the pier leading to the almost two-hundred-foot-tall observation tower at the edge of Presque Isle Bay.

Meet me @ the base of Bicentennial Tower @ 6am

Nell's text had read.

She knew better than to ask Emma to meet her on the observation deck at the top. As children, Nell loved racing up the exterior spiral staircase to stand at the rail and take in the breathtaking view while teasing Emma about her fear of heights. Besides, the landmark didn't officially open until ten. The clock on Emma's dash indicated it was currently 5:54.

State Street ended at Dobbins Landing, a one-way stretch of road, split by empty parking spaces. She kept right, driving slowly, past the docked paddleboat, toward the tower while keeping an eye out for Nell.

At the end of the road and the entrance to the exhibit, Emma swung the car to the left, under the elevated walkway and pulled into the first parking space. She shut off the engine and sat, terrified. Terrified that Nell wouldn't show up. Terrified she would. Terrified of what condition she'd be in.

It was more than two years since Emma had seen her sister. On that day, Nell was drunk, pale, and unsteady, her dark blonde hair drawn into a messy ponytail. She may have been high as well but wouldn't admit to it. Then again, she denied being drunk despite the pungent odor of alcohol seeping from her pores.

What about today?

Emma drew a breath, shook off the paralysis, and climbed from her car. A stiff breeze blew in from the bay as she stepped onto the sidewalk leading to the tower. The only sound was the waves lapping against the pier and her own footsteps.

The closer she came to the tower, the more she was convinced Nell wasn't going to show. Emma looked back in case she'd arrived too early, and Nell might be behind her. But the area was vacant, her Forester the lone vehicle in the lot. No pedestrians out for a stroll.

"Emma?"

The soft voice startled her. She spun back toward the tower.

Nell stood there, almost fifteen feet away, her hair loose and tossed in the breeze. She huddled in an oversized hoodie with her hands stuffed in the front pockets.

Emma closed the distance between them with long strides but stopped short. Nell didn't open her arms. Emma searched her face. Nell's eyes were wide—scared, Emma thought—but clear, as was her complexion. She didn't look drunk or high.

Nell appeared to be studying Emma as well, looking for... what? Judgment? Disappointment? Then she removed her hands from her pockets, took the final two steps between them, and flung herself into Emma's arms with a soft whimper.

Emma held her tight and buried her face into Nell's hair. She needed a shampoo but didn't smell of booze. She smelled like... Nell. Emma choked on a sob. "Thank God you're okay."

Nell shuddered and stepped back, not completely free of Emma's touch but out of her embrace. "Get me outta here," Nell said, her voice raspy and pleading.

"Where?" Emma asked.

Nell shook her head vehemently. "Anywhere but here." She swallowed. "The beach. Take me to Presque Isle."

"Okay." Emma slung an arm around Nell's shoulders. Together, they headed to the parking lot and the Subaru. Nell once again stuffed her hands in her hoodie's pockets and slouched as if trying to shrink. Or disappear. She kept step with Emma, leaning into her while sneaking glances left and right the whole time.

When they reached the car, Emma pressed the key fob, unlocking the doors with a series of chirps. Nell broke free and hurried to the passenger side.

"Drive," she whispered once Emma climbed behind the wheel. "And don't stop."

Emma did as Nell asked. Her sister's tangible fear seeped into Emma's skin, and she, too, started glancing around, looking for monsters. "Are you okay?"

Nell shook her head. "We'll talk at the park."

Emma drove in silence onto the Bayfront Parkway. A little over ten minutes later, she passed the entrance to Sara's Campground and entered the park. "Where to?"

Nell didn't speak but flapped one hand. Keep going. A few minutes later as they approached one of the bayside parking lots, she said, "Here."

Emma knew immediately where Nell wanted to go. The Feather. She pulled in. Unlike the Bicentennial Tower, Presque Isle was buzzing with activity. Early-morning walkers, bikers, and rollerbladers crowded the paved trail. Emma thought Nell might protest the abundance of people. Instead, she visibly relaxed.

Safety in numbers, Emma thought.

Once parked, they both stepped out. Nell moved to the trail

and stood, gazing out at the choppy bay, oblivious to the people sweeping around her.

Terrified in the solitude at the tower. Serene in the midst of exercise-seekers. She faced Emma and tipped her head in the direction of the Feather. Together, they ambled along the pavement.

When they'd been kids, they'd loved the rustic wooden observation deck with its primitive images of wildlife carved into the structure, an homage to the Native American people. Nell would slip away and come here in the early-morning hours, much like today, and practice yoga on the raised circular platform as she watched the sun rise over the bay. Emma wasn't surprised this would be the spot her sister wanted to visit now.

Except Nell veered off the trail just before the ramp leading to the deck. Emma followed her down a marshy path, usually used by fishermen, to the water's edge. Surrounded by trees and lush undergrowth, they were alone, shielded from the public. The path ended at a small patch of sandy beach. Nell again stood in silence, staring across the bay toward the marina. And the tower from which they'd just come.

Emma waited, never taking her eyes from her sister's back.

Nell turned to Emma, her face streaked with tears. "I'm in so much trouble."

Emma moved to a downed tree and sat, gesturing for Nell to do the same. When she did, Emma said, "Talk to me."

Nell blew out a breath and raised her gaze to the sky above. "I'm pregnant."

The words hung between them for a while. Emma tried to process the statement. Tried to weigh how she felt. Elation? But she saw no sign in Nell that joy was an appropriate reaction. Emma's gaze slid from Nell's face to her belly.

Nell looked down, too, and unzipped the hoodie. Beneath it, she wore a loose-fitting blouse that had seen better days. The bump was barely visible, barely there. But with Nell's slender frame, it could never be mistaken for anything else.

Their eyes met.

"This is good, isn't it?" Emma asked, unable to completely contain a silly grin.

For the first time in years, she saw her sister smile. A nervous one, but a smile nonetheless. "Yeah. I guess it is."

Questions tumbled through Emma's mind. Are you sober? Are you using? Who's the father? What are your plans? She debated which were vital and which might send Nell back into hiding.

Nell always could read her mind. "I haven't had a drink or used since the moment I found out." She shook her head. "I know. I should've quit even before then. But I wasn't planning on this." She tenderly caressed her belly.

"Okay," Emma said, and waited.

Fear danced across Nell's face. The same look from back at the tower. "The baby's father...terrifies me. He can't find out."

"Who is he?"

Nell shook her head. "I can't tell you."

Emma leaned forward, reached out, and took Nell's hands. "The body in the warehouse."

All traces of the smile vanished. Nell drew a tear-laden breath. "I know it was wrong. But she and I were the same size. Same build...well, she wasn't pregnant. I don't think. And she and I had the same color hair."

As Nell spoke, a chill crept up Emma's spine. "Don't tell me you killed that woman."

Nell choked. "God, no. What the hell? How could you think that?"

Emma immediately regretted the suggestion. But she had reason. "Not you. Not sober and straight. But..." She shrugged.

Nell studied her, visibly thinking about it. Finally, she looked down. "You're right." Her gaze came back to Emma's. "But I didn't. I swear."

Emma believed her.

"She was already dead. A friend of mine told me he'd seen a woman—" Nell looked away. "He told me he'd seen a dead woman at the bottom of those stairs. He knew I was in trouble and was hiding. We came up with the idea together. Drag her inside. Dress her in my clothes. Leave my driver's license on her. And hope she'd be unrecognizable before anyone found the body."

Emma tried to picture it. Her baby sister tampering with a corpse. The image, the thought of it, made her feel ill.

Nell again read her mind or saw the look on her face. "It was horrible. But I had to do it. I had to fake my death. I needed the baby's father to stop looking for me."

Emma took a deep breath of the slightly fishy smelling bay air to calm her stomach. "The cops know it wasn't you."

Tears gathered in Nell's eyes. "Are you sure?"

"Positive. And worse. They think you *did* kill her."

"What? Why?"

"You know who the woman was."

Nell leaned back, slipping her hands from Emma's. "Yes."

"Gillian Watson."

It took a few long seconds, but Nell nodded.

The moment Emma said the name, the rest of what Matthias had told her crashed into her consciousness. Gillian and Nell were both involved with their boss at the restaurant. "Oh, my God," Emma said under her breath. "Russ Carlisle is your baby's father."

Nell's eyes widened. She stumbled to her feet and staggered backwards, as if the mention of him would conjure the devil. "How—" she stuttered. "How did you find out?"

Emma debated revealing her source, but quickly realized she had to tell Nell all of it. "I have a friend who's the police detective working the case. He told me the body wasn't yours. I'd already heard from you, so I knew. He told me where you'd been working and about yours and Gillian's relationships with the restaurant manager."

Nell pressed trembling fingers to her lips. "The police know."

"Yes."

She looked around frantically. "Did you tell them you were meeting me?"

"No. I denied hearing from you at all." Emma didn't mention her doubts about whether or not Matthias believed her.

Nell grew still. Not quite relaxed, but not on the verge of bolting either.

"We need to call Matthias and talk to him."

"Who?"

"Detective Honeywell. The cop I mentioned."

Nell shook her head. "No. I can't."

"We need to clear you. Matthias is a good guy. He'll help."

"No." Her tone left no room to argue. "Listen to me. If the police know I'm alive, it means Russ does, too. Em, he beat me. And Gillian. I meant it when I said keeping my secret was a matter of life and death. He'll kill me." Nell fixed Emma with a hard stare. "And my baby."

Emma wanted to tell her sister she was exaggerating but couldn't. Not with her own past.

Once more, Nell knew Emma's thoughts. "He's like Clay."

The name sent ice down Emma's spine.

"You're hiding from Clay. Now I need to hide from Russ."

Emma blinked. Nell didn't know. "Clay's dead."

Nell inhaled sharply. "What? How?"

Emma closed her eyes, trying to shut out the memories. "I can't talk about it."

"I understand. But *you* have to understand how I feel."

"I do."

Nell's eyes brightened. "If Clay's gone, we can go home." Before Emma could grasp what Nell was saying, she continued, sounding almost buoyant. "That's it. You and me. We'll go home. We can move back into Grandma and Grandpap's old farmhouse. You can help me raise my baby. I know Eric would help, too."

Emma cut her off with a wave of her hand. "We can't. I'm sorry, sis. The farmhouse burned down."

"What?" Nell squeaked, tears reforming.

"There's nothing to go home to. Land, yes, but no place to stay."

Nell stumbled back to the fallen tree and collapsed onto it.

Emma followed, taking a seat next to her. "But Eric will definitely help. He's here, you know."

"Here?" Nell's gaze darted around again.

"Not *here* here." Emma made a loop with one finger, indicating the park around them. "In Erie. He wanted to come with me to meet you, but I made him stay at his hotel."

"He knows I'm alive?"

"Not at first, but he figured it out. He's worried to death about you." Emma watched as Nell thought about all she'd said. "I really think we need to talk to the police. Matthias. He'll help keep you safe from Russ."

"No police." Nell looked at her. "I didn't kill Gillian—"

Emma started to protest, but Nell stopped her with a raised hand.

"I didn't kill Gillian, but I'm not innocent. I helped move a body. I faked my own death by planting evidence. I'm no lawyer, but that's illegal."

"Not as bad as murder."

Nell shook her head slowly, insistently. "I don't want to bring my baby into the world in jail. Not to mention, they'll take him away from me. Put him in foster care."

"That's not gonna happen."

"I can't take the chance. This Matthias guy might be your friend, but he's a cop. He's not going to look the other way."

She was right. Emma leaned forward, bracing her elbows on her knees to keep from face-planting into the dirt and grass at her feet. Softly, she asked, "Where are you living?"

Nell scoffed. "Living? If you can call it that. The friend who helped me move Gillian? He's letting me stay in his tent."

Emma thought about the homeless community by the warehouse. The man who'd yelled at her and Eric. "On Sixteenth?"

"Yeah. But I can't go back there."

"It's too close to the Blue Pike Restaurant."

"Exactly. Russ could happen by at any moment. Although it's not likely." Nell's expression soured. "He wouldn't risk getting his shoes dirty."

Emma continued mulling over her sister's situation. "That's why you had me meet you at the tower."

"I don't have a car. I could walk there, but it was a risk. I could've been seen." Nell squirmed. "Please, Em. Can I stay with you?"

Emma wanted to laugh except there was nothing funny about the situation. "I live in a seventeen-foot camper at Sara's. You probably had more room in your friend's tent."

"I don't care. I'll sleep on the floor."

"That's not the real problem. You don't want to talk to the police. Matthias tends to just drop by unannounced." Nell gave her a look, and Emma realized how it sounded. "When he's working a case that might somehow involve me."

"Oh. No, I can't stay there then."

"How about Eric? He's staying at a hotel not far from here. Would you be okay if we asked him for help?"

Nell's face relaxed into a smile. "I don't trust your cop friend, but I do trust Eric."

Chapter Twenty-Six

M atthias found Cassie at her desk after trudging up the stairs to Major Crimes, a cup of organic coffee in hand. She looked up as he entered and sneered wordlessly at his beverage. She'd repeatedly made derogatory remarks about his choice of expensive coffee when a full pot in the break room was available.

"You're late," she said.

"Yes, I am." He claimed his desk chair and placed the recyclable cardboard cup next to his computer. "I was out last night, paying visits to Pauly's Polynesian Pub and the Mercury."

"Oh?" She rolled her chair to where she could see him. "Learn anything?"

"Pauly and the ex-Mrs. Tom Jenkins are still out of town. But they're expected back today."

"Add them to our to-do list. What about E.A. Dyson?"

Matthias told her about Zeke's response to learning Nell was alive. "He's not a good enough actor to fake that kind of reaction. He was shocked to learn she was dead. Equally shocked to learn she's not."

"Did he explain the room at the Royal Palace?"

"Nope. He may not know about Nell's life-and-death status, but he knows a whole helluva lot and is not willing to talk about it."

Cassie grunted. "To you. Maybe I should have a chat with him."

"Good luck with that." Matthias leaned over to look at the neighboring cubbies. "Where's Frazier?"

"Working a robbery case with Roth." She waved Matthias toward her. "Come take a look at what I dug up while you were out bar-hopping last night."

While Cassie wheeled back to her desk, he rose and moved to her side.

"Russell Carlisle is one rich son of a bitch." She indicated her computer monitor where financial spreadsheets filled the screen. "And he didn't come by his wealth by working hard. His daddy and granddaddy amassed the family fortune."

"What about the Blue Pike? Do they own it?"

"A reasonable question, all things considered, but no." Cassie's eyes held a mischievous sparkle, suggesting there was more.

Since she didn't volunteer, Matthias decided to play her game. "Who *does* own it?"

"I'm so glad you asked." She tapped the keyboard, bringing up another screen, this one a conglomerate website. "Erie Huron and Ontario Holdings owns dozens of businesses in northern Pennsylvania, eastern New York, northern Ohio, and all over Michigan. Those businesses include eleven restaurants in those same areas."

"Of which the Blue Pike is one."

"Ding-ding-ding. Give the man a prize. The biggest shareholder in Erie Huron and Ontario Holdings is a man named Elias Nelson."

Matthias searched his memory, but the name didn't sound even vaguely familiar.

"Elias Nelson had a daughter, who was also a major shareholder."

Matthias continued to wait. Cassie was having fun torturing him, and he wasn't willing to let his impatience show.

"The daughter's name was Havana Carlisle."

A chill settled over Matthias's brain. "Was. Carlisle. As in Russ."

"His late wife."

The chill worked its way down Matthias's spine. "How did she die?"

"A skiing accident out in Colorado."

"Was Russ with her at the time?"

"He was. They were alone on the slopes. Claims he saw the whole thing. Interestingly, no one else did."

"Was there an inquiry into the accident?"

"Oh, yes. I contacted the investigating agency and the detective in charge. He stated there was no evidence of foul play, although when I pressed, he admitted the husband's grief did not strike him as genuine. But the coroner ruled Havana's injuries were consistent with skiing into a tree. The death was ruled accidental. With no evidence to the contrary, no charges were filed."

"Let me guess. Russ Carlisle inherited his wife's shares in the company."

"You nailed it again."

Matthias stared at the monitor as Cassie clicked to another page on the Erie Huron and Ontario Holdings' website. A long list of the businesses under the conglomerate's umbrella filled the screen. The Blue Pike was there.

As was the Royal Palace Resort and Conference Center.

But that wasn't the listing Cassie pointed to. She placed a fingertip on another Erie business. Bay Front Place, the luxury apartment complex where they'd gone looking for Russ two days ago.

Cassie's eyes still twinkled as she looked up at him. "Guess where Russ Carlisle keeps several apartments reserved in addition to his own."

Matthias swore under his breath. "Nell Anderson."

Cassie leaned back in her chair. "Her name's not on any rental agreement I can find, but I'd bet a year's salary that's where she was staying. Maybe still is." Her phone rang, and she rocked forward to pick it up. "It's Ham," she said before answering the call.

While she chatted with the coroner, Matthias pondered the information she'd uncovered. Russ Carlisle had money to burn. Wealth from his family. Inherited wealth from the questionable death of his wife. Luxury apartments—plural—for his various love nests.

Cassie uttered an occasional "Uh-huh" into her phone. Matthias couldn't make out Ham's muffled, incomprehensible side of the conversation. Cassie tapped her pen on her desk. "Great. Thanks, Ham. Appreciate it." She hung up and faced Matthias. "Dental records matched. Jane Doe from the warehouse is Gillian Watson."

No surprise.

Matthias took two strides to his cubicle but didn't enter. He turned and took two strides back. "A dead wife. A dead girlfriend…"

"Coincidence?" Cassie raised a sarcastic eyebrow.

He grunted a reply.

"How does Nell Anderson play into this?" Cassie asked.

"If she plays into it at all."

Cassie made a sour face. "You're only saying that because of her sister."

Maybe. Not that he'd admit it to his partner.

"Nell is definitely involved. Her clothes and driver's license didn't just happen to find their way onto the body. She wanted to conceal the victim's identity. Why? To keep the heat off her lover,

Russ Carlisle? And in the process, make everyone...us...believe Nell was the one who's dead."

Matthias hated to admit Cassie's theory made sense. "Except she had to know we'd eventually find out."

"Nell's an addict. Her brain is addled. She probably didn't think that far ahead. Or she was just buying time. If she isn't still holed up in Carlisle's apartment, who knows where she is. Hell, he could've shipped her off to Cancun with plans to meet up with her later."

Which also made sense.

And he was one-hundred percent sure that Emma knew, if not all of it, part of it.

Matthias and Cassie had a long list of stops to make today. His preference was to start with a visit to Sara's Campground but knew the Watson family came first.

Stephanie, the sister, answered the door this time. She wore no makeup, and her face was void of any color except for bruise-like circles under her eyes. "Please come in." Her voice sounded like she'd swallowed ground glass.

She ushered them to the same vintage dining room table as yesterday. Gillian's mother sat there, clutching a tissue. A second young woman was seated to her left. Matthias had seen her photograph several times over the last week.

Didi Reed's tan stood out in stark contrast to the pallor of the Watson women. She looked from Cassie to Matthias, her expression dark. Angry. Or perhaps it was a cover, hiding her grief.

Stephanie made the introductions none of them needed.

"I thought you wouldn't be back until tomorrow," Cassie said.

"That was the original plan." Didi tucked a strand of dark hair behind her ear. "But once I learned Gillian was missing, I caught an earlier flight. Got in last night and came straight here."

Stephanie lowered into the chair on her mother's right. "I insisted Didi stay with us."

Mrs. Watson extended a hand toward the opposite side of the table. "Please, detectives, have a seat." As they complied, she said, "It's her, isn't it?" No indication of hope tinged her tired voice.

"Yes, ma'am, it is," Matthias said.

Mrs. Watson nodded. "I knew. After you were here yesterday, I knew. My Gillian would never have intentionally left us hanging like this."

Cassie interlaced her fingers and rested her hands on the table. "Are you up to answering a few questions? I know it's a bad time, but—"

"Please," Mrs. Watson said. "Anything to find out who did this to my girl."

Matthias dug out his notebook, but Cassie took the lead. "Can you tell us about Russ Carlisle?"

"Piece of shit," Didi muttered. Her eyes widened as if she hadn't intended to say it out loud. She glanced at Mrs. Watson. "Sorry."

"Don't apologize," Stephanie told her. "You're the one who should answer this question." To Matthias and Cassie, she said, "Gillian never said much to Mom and me about him."

Mrs. Watson worried her tissue. "She never said *anything* about him to me. She kept her romantic life to herself."

Didi sniffed. "I'm not sure I'd call Gillian's relationship with Russ romantic."

"What would you call it?" Cassie asked.

Didi gave the question some thought before responding. "Mutually beneficial."

"How so?"

"Gillian was drop dead gorgeous." Didi realized her poor word choice when Mrs. Watson cringed. "I'm so sorry."

Gillian's mother shook her head. "No, you're right. She was."

Didi brought her gaze back to Cassie. "Russ enjoyed having a beautiful woman on his arm. And in his bed, I'm sure." She shot another apologetic glance at Mrs. Watson. "For Gillian's part, she enjoyed nice things. Expensive trinkets. Russ had money and had no problem spending it to make her happy."

Matthias thought of the luxury-apartment complex. "And yet Gillian paid for her own apartment downtown."

"And walked to and from work," Cassie added, without mentioning the abandoned warehouses she passed along the way.

"Living arrangements were where she drew the line," Didi said. "He offered her a place over by the bay—"

"Bay Front Place?" Cassie asked.

Didi nodded. "That's it. But Gillian never held any illusions that Russ was 'the one.' She knew the relationship was temporary and said it would be too messy if she had those kind of ties to break. Jewelry, she could take with her. An apartment?" Didi shook her head. "Besides, she loved where she lived."

"Why did she walk to work?" Matthias asked. It was a question that had bugged him all along. "It wasn't a good neighborhood to be in, especially late at night."

"I know. I told her that all the time, but she wasn't concerned. Said she didn't see the sense in moving her car when it was only a few blocks. She loved to walk." A hint of a smile crossed Didi's face. "She said she was perfectly safe walking that route. She always took leftovers from the restaurant and gave them to the homeless who lived on the street. Said they loved her for it and would never hurt her."

But someone had. Matthias knew better than to mention that fact.

Cassie seemed to be considering her next question. She glanced at him, an odd look in her eyes. Then she brought her gaze back to the three women across the table. "Did Gillian ever mention someone by the name of Nell Anderson?"

Matthias looked at his partner. He shouldn't be surprised she'd bring up Emma's sister. It was a reasonable question that needed to be asked.

Gillian's mother, sister, and best friend exchanged looks. All shook their heads.

Didi spoke for the others. "No. Who is she?"

"She worked with Gillian," Cassie replied.

Mrs. Watson released Stephanie's hand to bring her tissue to her nose. "Gillian never talked about her co-workers."

Cassie acknowledged her with a nod and fixed her gaze back on Didi. "Did Gillian ever mention Russ seeing other women?"

Didi's jaw clenched. "Like I said, he's a piece of shit. Gillian mentioned how he loved beautiful women. All of them. He would openly flirt even when she was right there."

"*Just* flirt?"

Didi shrugged. "She didn't say. I think Russ likes the thrill of the game. Even better if there's a risk of getting caught."

Matthias exchanged a look with Cassie. He knew she was thinking the same thing. Bedding two women who worked at his restaurant at the same time definitely qualified as risky.

"Was Gillian jealous?"

Didi snorted. "Not at all. I told you. There wasn't anything romantic about the relationship. She knew Russ would cut her free sooner or later."

"Mutually beneficial," Matthias quoted what Didi had said earlier.

"Exactly."

"How about Russ?" Matthias asked. "Was he the jealous type?"

The question appeared to startle Didi. "I don't think so. Why would he be jealous? He could have any woman he wanted. Besides, Gillian was content to stick around and collect the bling he bought for her."

"Were you aware that Russ Carlisle had been married before?" Cassie asked.

This question startled Didi even more. "No."

"Did Russ ever get physical with Gillian?"

This question did not startle her. "She would never say, but I had a feeling he may have pushed her around on occasion."

Cassie echoed the words back at her. "Pushed her around?"

"Gillian could give as good as she got. She'd earned a blackbelt when she was a kid."

Mrs. Watson and Stephanie nodded their confirmation. "Although," the mother said, "she didn't keep up with it."

"True," Didi said. "Still, I got the impression Russ liked the rough stuff. Some guys get off on it, you know?"

The idea raised Matthias's ire. He'd like to show Russ Carlisle some rough stuff.

"Excuse me, detective." Mrs. Watson raised a hand like a kid in school.

Matthias and Cassie looked at her.

"Are you suggesting...do you think...suspect...Gillian's boyfriend might have..." The mother's tears filled in the rest of her question.

"We're looking at all possibilities," Cassie said softly. To Didi, she asked, "When was the last time you saw Gillian?"

The best friend's expression darkened. "She was with Russ. We were all at a wedding at the Royal Palace."

Chapter Twenty-Seven

On the way to Eric's hotel, Emma hit a fast-food restaurant's drive-through window and asked Nell what she wanted. Wide-eyed and salivating, she requested one of everything. Emma laughed and ordered enough food for five people. When she started to pull into a parking space, Nell made a looping motion with one finger. "Keep driving."

Emma recognized the fear in her sister's voice and eyes. With a nod, she headed for the exit. She drove around blocks, through parking lots, always moving except when a red light brought them to a halt. All the while, Nell devoured scrambled eggs, hash browns, oatmeal, and fruit. She left the coffee for Emma but drank two large orange juices. Sated, she tossed the trash into the rear seat, leaned back, and closed her eyes.

"You ready?" Emma asked.

"I guess."

Emma pulled into the parking lot of Eric's hotel and had no problem finding a space. She shifted into park, shut off the ignition, and turned to Nell. "Let's go in."

She squirmed and ran a hand over her hoodie. "I can't."

Emma suspected Nell wasn't as concerned about her tiny

225

bump as she was about her dirty and threadbare attire. "I'll call Eric and tell him to come to us."

Nell nodded. "That's better."

Eric picked up immediately. "Is she…"

"We're out in front in my car. Can you come down?"

"On my way." The call ended.

Emma smiled. Eric was as eager to see Nell as Emma had been.

Less than five minutes later, the passenger door flung open, and Eric almost dove in on top of Nell, throwing his arms around her. Emma smiled as her baby sister and best friend blubbered all over each other.

"We need to go," Nell finally said.

Eric pulled back, his eyes wide and questioning. "Where?"

"Anywhere."

Emma caught his gaze. "She's uneasy sitting still. Get in."

He appeared confused but didn't ask. Instead, he stepped back, shut Nell's door, and climbed in behind her. "Good heavens. A fast-food chain exploded inside your car."

Emma almost said Nell was eating for two but didn't. It wasn't Emma's news to share.

"Sorry," Nell said. "I haven't eaten in a while."

Eric looked at Emma, his eyes sad, glistening. He blinked the tears away. "Don't worry, baby girl." He gathered the trash. "I'll dump this and be right back."

While he strode across the lot to the garbage can, Nell gave Emma a weak smile. "Thanks, Em. For everything."

Emma blew a raspberry. "Where do you want to go next?"

Nell faced forward, the smile gone. "Anywhere but downtown."

They headed back to Presque Isle. Eric chattered the entire time, but Nell's responses were monosyllabic and noninformative. Emma drove until they found a beach without a lifeguard or a crowd. They settled on a picnic table with the nearest human soul barely visible, and sat in silence. The three of them perched on the table, their feet on the bench. Nell gazed across the lake toward Canada, well beyond the horizon. Eric's eyes never left her, but he'd clearly figured out she wasn't ready for his onslaught of questions.

Emma sat next to her sister, shoulders touching, content with the company. She closed her eyes, breathed in the damp air, allowed the breeze to toss her hair, and listened to the squawk of the sweeping seagulls. Blocking out the questions surrounding Nell, Emma felt at peace for the first time in ages.

"You've cut your hair."

Emma opened her eyes to find Nell looking at her.

"And it's not red anymore."

Eric shook a finger at Emma. "You know, I noticed that, too, but was afraid to ask."

She didn't want to talk about the measures she'd taken to fly under Clay's radar. "I needed a change."

Nell shook her head. "I love you, but I don't like it."

Emma snickered. "I plan to let it grow out."

"Good."

Eric's eyes shifted between them before settling on Nell. "Can I ask questions now?"

Nell smiled, looking as at peace as Emma. "I guess. But let me tell you something first."

Emma watched Eric's face when Nell told him her big news. He was rarely speechless but came darned close. He sputtered and choked before clamping his gaping mouth shut. Happy tears filled his eyes. He stood, stepped in front of Nell, and pulled her into his arms. "I'm so happy for you, baby girl."

Emma realized she'd been so engrossed in Nell's fear that she hadn't congratulated her sister. She reached over and rubbed Nell's back. "Me, too, sis."

A sob bubbled up from Nell's throat along with a barely audible "Thank you."

Another realization struck Emma. "I'm going to be an aunt."

Nell hiccupped a laugh. "Yeah, you are. And I'm going to be a mom."

Eric held her for several long minutes, as if afraid she'd disappear if he let go.

Emma knew the feeling.

When he released her, he reclaimed his perch on the picnic bench while still holding onto her hand. "Tell me everything," he said.

Emma listened as Nell shared what she'd already told Emma. Or at least part of it. She was clean and sober. And homeless. She didn't want the father to know about the baby.

"Zeke?" Eric asked.

Nell tensed. "Zeke? No." She glanced at Emma then returned her gaze to Eric. "What do you know about him?"

Eric scowled. "He's your boyfriend, right?"

"Why would you think that?"

He tipped his head toward Emma. "Her friend Kira talked to Rafael at the Mercury who said you were Zeke's girlfriend. And you two were having problems."

"Who's Kira?" Nell asked Emma.

"My yoga instructor. She didn't want me going to the Mercury by myself."

"Good for her. It's a dive."

Emma battled a laugh. This from a young woman who lived in a tent on a city street.

"Zeke," Nell said, "is a friend. Not a boyfriend. Just a friend. A very good friend."

"But you were having problems?" Eric asked.

"No." Nell shook her head. "He might have said that to keep people from asking too many questions."

Eric glared at her. "Like the questions I have?"

"Probably." Nell sighed. "When I found out I was pregnant, Zeke was the only person I could trust."

Emma battled to contain her ripping heart. Nell had known

Emma was in Erie, yet this Zeke Dyson was the one she trusted with her secrets.

"He hid me at his place. Helped me kick the drugs."

"You were using when you got pregnant?" Eric asked.

The same question Emma wanted to ask.

Nell lowered her head. "I'd been clean. Until…" She sneaked a glance at Emma. "Russ got me using again."

"Russ?" Eric asked, venom in his voice.

The same venom Emma felt. "The baby's father," she said, saving Nell from having to say it.

Eric's face darkened. "That son of a bitch."

Nell snorted a humorless laugh. "You don't know the half of it."

He shifted sideways on the table, facing her. "Tell me."

She didn't meet his eyes. Or Emma's. Instead, she studied the distant horizon. After several long moments of silence, Nell repeated the horrors she'd already shared with Emma. The abuse. The plot she and her homeless friend had devised to fake her death. All to keep Russ Carlisle from coming after her.

Emma's thoughts drifted to her own nightmare with Clay. He'd been abusive, controlling, threatening, but he hadn't gotten her pregnant. Nor had he supplied her with drugs. But he had come after her.

The parallel brought another possibility to the surface of Emma's mind. One she'd been too focused on her sister's situation to consider before.

When Nell finished her tale and fell silent, Emma faced her and asked. "You said Russ beat you and Gillian."

Nell lowered her gaze and nodded.

"Do you think Russ is the one who killed her?"

Nell's eyes came up, and Emma could tell she was thinking about—and not liking—the scenario. "I don't know. Maybe."

Emma could also tell there was something Nell wasn't saying.

She lifted her chin and looked from Emma to Eric and back. "Get me outta here. Take me home."

"To Sixteenth Street?" Emma asked, stunned.

"No." Nell sounded like she had when they were kids and Emma came up with what Nell felt was the stupidest plan ever. "*Home*. To the farm. I know you said the house was gone, but we can rebuild. Or we can get a mobile home." She snapped her fingers. "I know. You said you're living in a camper. We can move it down there. I don't need much space."

Eric nudged Nell. "That's not a bad idea. Although I've seen her camper. I doubt it's road worthy."

"Hey," Emma protested. "Don't go badmouthing my little home on wheels." She didn't mention he was probably right.

"Seriously, though," he went on. "Em, you got the insurance payout for the house. You can afford to rebuild. Nothing as big as what you lost, but it would be grand compared to how you've both been living."

Nell nodded enthusiastically. "And Russ would never find me there."

Emma didn't want to voice her doubts. "Running isn't an answer."

Nell clutched Emma's arm and shook it. "Running's the *only* answer."

Eric's expression suggested he was playing out the scenario in his mind and not liking where it was leading. "Nellie, honey, what happens when he finds out you're carrying his child? You don't think he'll be able to figure out where you went and will track you down?"

Tears glistened on Nell's dark lashes. "Okay. So let's go somewhere else. Anywhere else. Someplace we've never been before. Where he won't be able to find me."

Emma took Nell's trembling hand in both of hers. "There's only one way through this, and it's not running away. I tried that."

"Then what?" Nell's voice had risen to a frantic pitch.

"Matthias," Emma said.

Nell jerked her hand free. "The cop?"

"The brute?" Eric scowled.

"He's not a brute." Although Emma understood why Eric thought of Matthias that way. She would never forget the anger in those blue eyes the first time she'd encountered him. "He's working Gillian's homicide case. We tell him what you know. He'll arrest Russ for murder, and he'll never be able to hurt you or your baby again."

"No." Nell shook her head. "The one person he'll arrest is me. Russ will come after me. If not himself, he'll send someone to get me. Russ Carlisle has more money than God, for crying out loud. He'll make sure I get convicted of Gillian's death and then take my baby." Her voice shattered into a sob. She doubled over, burying her face in her hands.

Eric pulled her into his arms. "We won't let that happen."

But she jerked free, jumped from her seat on the picnic table, and spun to face them. "You won't have any say in it. You don't get it. Russ is evil."

Eric stepped down from the picnic table and moved toward Nell, but she backed away. He raised both hands. "Let's come to some kind of agreement for right now." He pointed at Emma. "You aren't going to the police." Then he faced Nell. "And you aren't disappearing. What you are doing is moving into my hotel room with me. I have two queen-size beds. You're welcome to one of them. We'll keep you safe and make sure you're fed. You are eating for two, you know."

"Have you seen a doctor?" Emma asked.

Still frantic but ratcheting down the panic in her voice, Nell replied, "Hell, no."

"Then we need to make sure you do that." When Nell appeared ready to argue, Emma added, "For the sake of the baby."

Nell stood immobile, thinking. She finally nodded. "You're right."

She didn't resist when Eric closed the distance between them and draped an arm around her. "Okay, then. Let's you and I get settled back at the hotel, while Em gets on the phone and finds you an obstetrician."

Emma forced a smile. "And I'm going shopping to get you some clothes," she told her sister.

That brought a grin. "I could just borrow some of yours."

At one time, they'd frequently traded outfits, but now Nell's shoulders and arms appeared bonier while her chest was definitely filling out. Then there was the bump, tiny though it was. Emma feared any joke she made about Nell's size might not go over well. "You could, but I don't have much of a wardrobe right now, either. I need to go to the store anyway. I'll pick up a few things for you."

Nell's sheepish smile led Emma to wonder if she'd had the same thoughts about her current shape. "Well, if you insist."

"I do."

"Good. That's decided," Eric said. "Let's go get you settled at the hotel."

Nell agreed.

As Emma led the way back to her car, she replayed the discussion they'd just had. She was relieved about her sister staying with Eric. She'd be safe with him. For now.

But Russ Carlisle would be looking for her the moment he learned she was alive. For all his good intentions, Eric wouldn't be able to protect her from a man like that.

Their only chance was Matthias.

Chapter Twenty-Eight

"Nell Anderson is involved up to her eyeballs," Cassie said once they were back in the car. "I'll bet you a month's worth of that high-priced organic coffee you're so fond of."

Matthias couldn't argue. Gillian Watson being found wearing Nell's dress and with her ID on the body was a start, and now they knew Nell and Zeke were at the Royal Palace at the same time as Gillian and Russ. For the same wedding? Matthias intended to find out. The Royal Palace had soared to the top of the priority list.

He pulled their Impala in front of the lobby door and turned off the ignition. If anyone complained about him blocking the spot reserved for guests unloading luggage, too damn bad.

The same skinny guy who'd been there Saturday was behind the reception desk. Matthias headed his way, but Cassie elbowed her way in front and reached the counter first. She showed her badge and introduced them. "We need to speak to whomever is in charge of events."

The skinny guy glanced at Matthias, who caught a flicker of recognition in his eyes, but he quickly returned his focus to Cassie.

"That would be Penelope Ortega. I'll call her and have her come out to meet you."

"Perfect."

Skinny Guy picked up the phone. A moment later, he told Cassie, "Ms. Ortega will be right out."

Cassie thanked him and started toward one of the groupings of couches and plush chairs.

Before Matthias could follow her, Skinny Guy leaned forward. "Excuse me, detective. You were asking about employees named Katie. Sandy-brown hair."

"I was."

"All three of them are working right now. That rarely happens, so if you're still interested..."

"I am. I already spoke with two of them." Matthias thumbed through his notebook and found the page. "I'm just missing Katie Tucker."

Skinny Guy nodded. "Do you want me to call her to the lobby?"

Matthias glanced at Cassie, who was watching him. "One interview at a time," he told the receptionist. "Unless she's going to be off duty within the next fifteen minutes."

"Nope. She's on until four this afternoon."

A dark-haired woman in a navy skirt and jacket strode across the lobby, her heels clicking on the wood flooring. The brass name badge labeled her as hotel management well before she was close enough for him to read a name. Penelope Ortega, he presumed.

Matthias smiled at Skinny Guy. "I'll be back after we talk with Ms. Ortega."

"Gotcha."

The navy-suited woman headed for Matthias, hand outstretched, and introduced herself. Cassie joined them. "Ms. Ortega, I'm Detective Sergeant Malone. This is Detective Honeywell. We're investigating a homicide—"

Ortega gasped. "We've had no deaths here at the hotel."

"No, but the victim and several persons of interest attended a wedding here less than a week prior to the homicide. We're hoping you can identify the bride and groom."

Ortega's eyes narrowed in an uncomfortable scowl. "Let's go to my office, if you don't mind."

Matthias and Cassie followed her down a hallway off the lobby to the first door on the right, which bore a plaque reading Head of Catering and Events. The office itself was small, crammed with shelves holding large binders. Ortega slipped behind a desk piled with papers surrounding a computer monitor and keyboard. "Please have a seat." She gestured to a pair of battered looking but functional chairs.

Cassie gave her the date of the wedding. Ortega fingered the keyboard, paused, and studied the screen. "We hosted one wedding reception that night. Bryce and Sterling Graham. Mrs. Graham's maiden name is Vincent." Ortega turned the monitor toward them. "Ordinarily, we don't give out guest information, but it was in the society section of the news, so it's not like you couldn't locate it elsewhere." She smiled tightly. "Of course, if you want a list of attendees, I can't help you."

"That's what we intend to ask Mr. and Mrs. Graham," Cassie said.

Matthias leaned forward. "Could you look up what room one of the guests, a Ms. Gillian Watson, may have stayed in? She may have been with a man by the name of Russ Carlisle." He spelled it out.

Ortega hesitated.

"If you want a warrant," Cassie said, "we can get one, no problem. But if we have to come back to execute it, we'll be forced to bring several marked police cars." Not really true but Ortega didn't know that.

She reached for her keyboard. "No need. We always cooperate with law enforcement, especially under such serious circumstances." She entered the information and squinted at the monitor. "No registration that night under Watson." She continued typing. With a shake of her head she added, "Nothing under Carlisle either. I'm sorry."

Matthias wasn't surprised. He was certain the guest rooms here were nice, but not as nice as Carlisle's apartment at Bay Front Place.

"No problem," Cassie told Ortega. "Would you be able to get us access to the security footage of the areas around the wedding reception?"

Ortega dropped her hands to her lap. "I'm afraid I have to draw the line there. We had too many guests present. I'm not comfortable violating the privacy of innocent parties on the slim chance of catching a glimpse of your persons of interest."

Cassie sighed audibly. "I guess we'll have to get that warrant after all."

"I guess you will."

With addresses and phone numbers for the bride and groom secured, Cassie and Matthias thanked Ortega and headed back to the lobby. "I hate to admit it," Cassie muttered, "but I'm afraid the judge will agree with Ortega. We don't have enough for a warrant. Yet."

Matthias grunted. He was thinking the same thing."

Cassie stopped and faced him. "What were you talking to the receptionist about?"

"Beige Katie," he said.

"Who?"

"The woman in Housekeeping who gave us the security footage showing Nell Anderson and E.A. Dyson's room number."

"You mean the woman who gave *Emma* the footage."

Matthias exhaled a growl. "Whatever. I've wanted to speak to her and find out what else she might know, and lucky for us, she's working today."

"Maybe we won't need that warrant, after all."

A young couple stood at the desk as Matthias approached.

Skinny Guy looked up. Matthias expected him to signal for him to wait, but instead, he pointed toward the alcove next to registration, which housed shelves of snacks and small packages of essentials that guests might have forgotten to pack. A woman in a beige uniform that matched her sandy hair stood at the coffee maker, her back to Matthias.

Beige Katie.

He shot a look at the skinny receptionist who nodded and gave him a thumbs up.

Matthias caught Cassie's arm, tipped his head at the housekeeper, and moved toward her.

"Excuse me," he said. "Katie Tucker?"

She wheeled to face them, her startled eyes widening as she took in their polo shirts with the police department badge embroidered on them. Her gaze darted to their sidearms on their hips before coming back up. "Yes?"

Matthias made the introductions and offered her a smile he hoped would put her at ease. "I believe you know a friend of mine. Emma Anderson." The smile combined with Emma's name should've put her at ease. It didn't.

"Yes?" she said again, looking like she was about to flee.

Cassie nudged him hard with an elbow. "Stop scaring the poor woman." She gave Katie a smile of her own. "I'm so sorry. He really isn't as mean as he looks. We wanted to thank you for helping Ms. Anderson track down her sister."

Cassie's mother hen act usually worked. But not this time. Katie's fingers trembled as she tucked an errant strand of hair behind one ear. "She wasn't supposed to tell anyone what I'd done."

Matthias offered an apologetic grin. "Don't blame her. I didn't give her an option. We are investigating a murder."

Katie glanced around before coming back to Cassie. "It's just, if my boss finds out what I did...giving her that information...I'd be fired."

"We're not going to tell anyone." Cassie winked.

"Besides, it was too late. By the time I found out anything useful, her sister was dead."

Cassie ran a hand over her short white hair. "Actually, she's not."

Katie's eyes widened again. "What?"

"It was a case of mistaken identity," Matthias said. "The body wasn't Nell Anderson's."

Katie made several failed attempts to speak before finally getting words past her lips. "Emma must be ecstatic."

"I guess that means you haven't seen Nell around here recently," Cassie said.

"No. But, I mean, I didn't see her the first time, either."

Cassie maintained her kindly mother façade. "Who did?"

"I'd rather not say. I don't wanna get anyone into trouble."

"We don't want to get anyone into trouble either, but we need to find her."

Katie scowled. "Why don't you ask Emma?"

"We have," Matthias said. "She says she doesn't know where her sister is."

"Oh." Katie dragged the word out. Her scowl deepened. "If the body you found wasn't Nell, who was it?"

"Another woman who was at the reception the same night Nell was spotted coming out of that room," Cassie said. "Gillian Watson."

Katie covered her mouth and cheeks with both hands. "How awful."

Matthias scrolled to a photo Gillian's mother had given him and held his phone toward the young housekeeper. "Do you know her?"

Katie took a quick glimpse before averting her eyes. "No. But the thought of someone who was a guest turning up dead? It's horrible."

"Emma told me how helpful you'd been when she was

searching for her sister," Matthias said, keeping his tone as gentle as Cassie's. Or as close as he could muster. "We need some help trying to retrace Ms. Watson's time here."

"I don't know what I can do. I was working the guest rooms that evening, not the banquet facilities."

"You gave Emma a flash drive of security footage. Maybe you could get us access to the footage from the wedding reception?"

Katie's face turned stony. "I can't."

"Why not?" Cassie asked with a voice like honey.

"I called in a favor to get that flash drive. I risked my friend's job, not to mention my own."

Cassie tipped her head and gave Katie a secretive grin. "Couldn't you ask your friend? The worst that could happen is he says no."

Katie shook her head. "The worst that could happen is we both get fired. I shouldn't have done what I did the first time. But I felt so bad for Emma. I'm sorry." She looked around nervously. "I have to get back to work." She sidestepped away from Cassie and scooted away.

"I'd really like to know who this friend is who she's protecting," Cassie said as Beige Katie disappeared around a corner.

"Unless she's protecting herself," Matthias mused. "I had the distinct feeling she knew more about Russ and Gillian than she was letting on."

"Funny. I had that same feeling."

"Either way, there's no chance she's going to help us."

Cassie started toward the hotel's front door. "Looks like we need to get a warrant after all."

Matthias followed, still looking in the direction Katie had vanished. She hadn't been willing to help the police, but she had been willing to do a favor for Emma once. Maybe she'd do so again.

"While I'm filling out the affidavit, you drive," Cassie said. "Let's pay a visit to Tom Jenkins's grieving widow."

Being away on vacation with her lover did nothing to improve Olivia Petrovich's attitude. She wore the same surly expression when she opened the door to Matthias and Cassie as she had when he and Frazier were there four days ago.

Matthias reminded her of who he was and introduced Cassie.

Olivia wrinkled her nose. "What happened to the other guy?"

"He's on another case," Cassie replied. "May we come in?"

Olivia responded by leaning a shoulder against the door jamb and reaching across to brace a hand on the opposite side, blocking their entry. Looking at Matthias, she asked, "Why? We've already spoken. You told me Tom's dead. I told you I haven't seen him in years. Nothing's changed."

Cassie turned to give Matthias a go-ahead nod. Sometimes looking scary worked in his favor.

"You failed to mention you're well acquainted with Pauly Nuccetelli, who was one of the last people to see your ex-husband alive," Matthias said. "We can discuss it here where all your neighbors can watch and listen. Or we can discuss it inside."

The glare she gave him made him glad Cassie was there for backup. Olivia lowered her arm, turned her back on them, and stalked into the house.

The already crowded living room's furniture had been joined by a pair of suitcases still boasting tags from the airlines. Olivia flopped into the same recliner as last time and folded her arms. Cassie took a seat on the oversized sectional, but Matthias chose to remain standing.

"Is Mr. Nuccetelli here?" Cassie asked.

"No."

"But you were away on vacation with him."

"Yes."

This was going to be fun. "Why didn't you mention your relationship with him when I was here previously?" Matthias asked.

"Because it was none of your business."

"Your ex-husband frequented the joint your current boyfriend owns, and you can't see how it might be something the police should know?"

"No. Neither of us had anything to do with Tom's murder."

Cassie came forward in her seat. "That's up to us to determine. What we need from you is everything you can tell us to help clear you and Mr. Nuccetelli *and* help determine who might've killed your ex."

Olivia's eye twitched. "Frankly, I don't care who killed him."

"Well, you see, that's a problem," Matthias said. "Because it makes you sound like you're happy he's dead. And that makes you sound guilty."

She breathed a growling sigh. "What you don't understand, detective, is that I sincerely mean I don't care. I feel nothing about Tom. I don't hate him. I don't wish him harm. I definitely don't love or even like him. I'm totally indifferent. That doesn't make me a good candidate for suspect of the year, now does it?"

She had a point.

"So it's only the police you hate?" Cassie asked.

"I hate having my time wasted."

"Great." Cassie sat back again. "Then answer our questions so we can get the hell out of here."

For the first time, Olivia appeared less hostile. "Fine. Ask."

Cassie took the lead. "Does Mr. Nuccetelli know you were married to Tom Jenkins?" she asked.

"I have no idea." When Matthias gave her his darkest scowl, she added, "Seriously. We don't talk about our past relationships. Ever."

"Have you ever been to his bar?"

"A few times."

Matthias wondered what she considered to be *a few*. "Have you ever run into your ex-husband there?"

"Never." She looked at Matthias. "I didn't know he was a regular at Pauly's place until you told me."

Her responses sounded reasonable. Still, Matthias couldn't shake the theory Frazier had planted in his brain. "I have one more question for you."

She kept her gaze on him.

"Do you own a blonde wig?"

"A what?" She barked a laugh. "Why on earth would you want to know that?"

He held her gaze and waited.

"No, I don't own a wig, blonde or otherwise." The reason for his question must've struck home. "Wait. You said Tom was seen leaving the bar with a blonde." Olivia choked. "You think it was me?" She laughed. When she determined Matthias was serious, the laugh grew raucous, and she doubled over.

Matthias looked at Cassie, who shrugged.

A good minute or so passed before Olivia sat upright, still snickering while wiping tears from her eyes. "I'm sorry. I haven't heard anything that funny in ages. No, I don't have a wig. No, I wasn't at the bar when Tom was there. And good God, no, I didn't dress up like a blonde and pick him up that night. Or any night."

Matthias's phone vibrated. He slipped it from his pocket with the intention of sending the call to voicemail. But Emma's name lit the screen. "Excuse me. I need to take this."

Olivia climbed to her feet. "We're done here. If you need to ask me anything else, let me know so I can hire an attorney."

He left Cassie to wrap up the visit, maneuvered around the furniture, and stepped outside. "Emma? Are you okay?"

"I need to talk to you."

"I'm here."

"No. In person. Alone."

He glanced over his shoulder at the door. He lowered his voice. "When?"

"Now?"

"Okay." Shaking Cassie would be tricky, but he'd manage. "Where?"

"My place."

"I'll be there in a half hour."

"You'll be where in a half hour?" Cassie asked from behind him.

He swiped the red button, ending the call, before spinning to face her. He debated what to tell her and decided she'd sniff out any lie he made up. "Emma's agreed to talk."

"Great. Let's go."

He reached out, stopping her. "To me. Not us."

Cassie opened her mouth to object, but he fixed her with a look. Not his scary one. One he hoped said *trust me*. She studied him. And nodded. "Fine. Drop me off at the office on your way." Then she jabbed a finger at him. "But use your head. You know better than to get emotionally involved with a person of interest."

He almost argued. Almost. "Yeah, I do."

Chapter Twenty-Nine

Emma paced the four strides from her camper's futon to the bathroom door and back again. Nell was safe with Eric at the hotel. Emma knew Nell would consider speaking with Matthias as a betrayal, and she couldn't really disagree. She'd promised to keep her sister's secrets. And yet, calling Matthias, asking him to come to her camper, broke that promise in a big way. If Nell never spoke to her again, she'd have only herself to blame.

But if Nell was alive, at least Emma had a chance at making amends. If Russ Carlisle killed Nell and their child, Emma would never forgive herself.

The decision hadn't been that hard.

Twenty-five minutes after she'd placed the call, the black Impala crawled up the hill and eased in next to her Subaru.

She went to the door and watched as Matthias climbed out, strode to her deck, and stepped onto it. She opened the screen. He entered without a word.

Once he was inside, she unhooked the bungee and pulled the exterior door closed. She'd already shut all the windows, creating as much privacy as possible.

He took a seat on one end of the futon, she on the other. She turned sideways, drawing both knees in, conscious of the barricade they created.

Matthias's granite expression was neither angry nor comforting. He kept his gaze on her, not saying a word.

Emma took a breath. This was even harder than she'd thought. "I've seen Nell." She watched for a reaction. There was none. "She made me promise not to talk to you. Or anyone."

"Even your boyfriend from back home?"

Not the question she expected. Under different circumstances, she'd have laughed. "Eric and Nell have a brother-sister relationship. She trusts him."

"That means you have told him."

"She agreed to it. And he can keep her safe."

Matthias's jaw tightened and his eyes shifted. He seemed to inspect every inch of the small camper, each window, before coming back to her, his face again still.

When he said nothing more, Emma dove in. "First, she didn't kill Gillian Watson. She tried to switch identities after one of the homeless guys told her about the body. She wanted everyone to believe she was dead. And by everyone, I mean Russ Carlisle."

The name stirred a reaction. One eyebrow raised in obvious interest.

"Nell's pregnant. Russ is the father. She's terrified he'll find out and kill her...and the baby."

The granite crumbled. Matthias's eyes softened.

Emma poured out the rest. Russ keeping Nell hooked on drugs, beating her. Her running away with Zeke's help. Staying with the homeless friend. Everything except Eric and Nell's current location.

As Emma told the story, she watched Matthias's expression morph from dark and dangerous when she spoke of Russ to curious when she mentioned Nell's escape.

"How is Zeke Dyson tied to all this?" Matthias asked.

"He's a friend who's been helping her. That's all she's told me."

Matthias turned sideways, mirroring her position, but with only one foot tucked under. "I've talked to Dyson a couple of times. I think he tossed his cookies when I told him Nell was dead. And he was floored when I went back and told him she was alive. But he refused to answer any questions."

Emma thought about it. "It's odd. He's the one who called me and said he'd seen her at the hotel."

"Without mentioning she was sharing a room with him."

"Right." Emma needed to question Nell about that.

"Can you do me a favor?"

"What kind of favor?"

Matthias took a moment to reply. "I can't believe I'm asking you this. Could you go to the Mercury and talk to Zeke? He may give you answers since you're Nell's sister and not a cop." Quickly, he added, "I'll take you there and wait at the door in case there's trouble."

"Okay."

He appeared surprised she agreed so easily.

Another of Nell's mysteries came to Emma's mind. "There's something else."

"What's that?"

"The homeless guy."

Matthias's chin came up. "The one you and—" He stuttered, his cheeks flushing. "You and your friend saw at the crime scene? Or the one Nell's staying with?"

Emma wondered what he'd been about to say when he changed his mind. He was probably catching himself from calling Eric her boyfriend again. She didn't ask. Instead, she considered his question. "I don't know. Do you think they might be the same person?"

"There is more than one vagrant on Sixteenth Street. Why don't you ask your sister?"

247

"Because she doesn't know who I saw either. But the one I'm interested in is the one who yelled at me and Eric." She pictured the figure, little more than a silhouette at the end of the sidewalk. "He shouted, 'Leave her alone.' I keep wondering if he meant Gillian Watson. Maybe he saw someone throw her down the steps."

Matthias's face grew stony again, but Emma knew his anger was directed at a killer, not at her.

She aimed a finger at Matthias. "I'm sure he won't talk to the cops either." Then she touched her breastbone. "But maybe he'll talk to me."

Matthias scrutinized her, and she wondered what he was thinking. He nodded as if coming to a decision. "All right." He flinched almost imperceptibly, slipped his phone from his pocket, and scowled at whatever was on the screen. He brought his gaze back to her. "While I'm using you as an informant, I have one more request."

She waited.

"Call your friend, Katie."

"Beige Katie?"

"That's the one."

"Why?"

He told her about his earlier visit to the Royal Palace. About asking for Katie's help in accessing security footage from the wedding reception in the hopes of tracing Gillian's time there. "Everything keeps coming back to that night at the hotel." He held up his phone. "That was a text from Cassie. Judge Wilks turned down our request for a warrant. We need that video to see if something happened between Gillian and Russ."

"You believe Russ killed her?"

"Let's keep him tagged as a person of interest. You say Nell's scared of him. Maybe she has good reason." Matthias's mouth slanted into a crooked smile. "Beyond him being an asshole."

Emma would've called him something worse than that. "Katie

has told me how much trouble she'd get into if she got caught sneaking the hotel's security footage to me. If she wouldn't do it for the police, I doubt she'd do it for me."

He shrugged. "She did it once. She likes you."

Emma sighed. "She won't like me if I get her fired."

He leaned toward her, his eyes intense. "There's another reason I'm asking for your help with this."

"Oh?"

"If the video shows what I expect...an altercation between him and Gillian or some other incident...it could help clear Nell."

The implication, shocked Emma. "You still think my sister may have killed her? Even after what I told you?"

Matthias shook his head. "It doesn't matter what I think. Right now, the evidence is stacked against her. The father of her child was sleeping around with the victim. She admits to being in the vicinity of the body." Emma opened her mouth to protest, but he raised a palm to silence her. "Her clothing and ID were found on the body, and she admits to putting it there. You can see how it would look if presented to the district attorney. Or a jury."

Emma leaned back, glaring at him. Right then, she didn't like him very much.

He reached out, placing a hand on her knee. "Listen to me. I don't believe Nell killed Gillian Watson. That's why I want to see the security footage from the night of the wedding. To *clear* her."

Emma studied him, wishing she could read his mind. Wishing her resolve wasn't melting from the touch of his hand and the blue of his eyes. She looked away. "Fine." Unfurling her legs, she rose and picked up her phone from the kitchen counter.

She scrolled back through her recent calls to locate Katie's number and tapped the green icon.

She answered immediately. "Emma?"

"Hi, Katie."

"I heard your sister's alive. That's great news."

"Yeah, it is. And I want to thank you for getting that video to me showing her at the hotel."

"I was happy I could help."

Emma glanced at Matthias, who watched without a word. "But now I have a big problem."

"What's that?"

"The police think Nell killed that woman. Gillian Watson."

Katie didn't respond for a moment. "That's awful."

"She didn't do it."

"I'm sure she didn't."

Something about Katie's tone struck Emma as odd. Maybe she *did* think Nell killed Gillian. And if Beige Katie suspected her sister was capable of murder, what chance did Nell have with the police? "I need to prove she's innocent."

"I don't know what I could do to help."

"I hate to ask, but is there any way your friend who supplied the video footage could look for film of Gillian that night?"

Emma's question was met with a silence so long she feared the call had dropped.

"Katie? You there?"

"Yes," she said, her tone chilly.

Emma's mind raced for some tidbit that might sway the young woman. "Nell's pregnant."

"Oh." Katie sounded surprised but Emma couldn't tell much more from one syllable.

"The baby's father was abusive, and she's terrified he'll find her and kill her."

"That's terrible, but I don't see what it has to do with Gillian."

"Gillian was at the wedding with him. I think he cheated on both of them. If he beat up my sister so badly that she fears for her life, he's probably done the same to Gillian. And maybe…" Emma let the insinuation hang, hoping Katie would put the pieces together on her own.

She fell silent yet again. This time Emma waited.

When Katie finally spoke, her voice was almost a whisper. "You believe this guy is the murderer."

"Yes. And if we could find something on video showing him getting angry or physical with her, it might go a long way to taking suspicion off my sister." Emma heard the pleading in her own voice and realized that while this phone call started as a favor to Matthias, it was now a genuine appeal for help.

"I told you before, if anyone found out, I would get fired. So would my friend."

"I know. I really appreciate you putting your job on the line for me. For Nell. But I don't know where else to turn."

The silence was shorter this time. "I'll see what I can do. No promises, though."

"Understood. Thank you."

The call ended, and Emma exhaled. She looked at Matthias. The expression on his face, a hint of a smile, made her reconsider her decision to avoid feelings for this man.

"She agreed?" he asked.

"She said she'd try but made no promises."

He gave one nod. "It'll have to do for now."

"What's next?"

"You up for talking to Zeke?"

Emma climbed out of Matthias's Impala across the street from the Mercury. He stepped out from behind the wheel and met her gaze across the roof. "You ready?" he asked.

"I thought you were waiting out here."

"No way. I'll stay in the atrium, right outside the bar, but I'm not letting you go in there alone."

Emma felt she'd be fine, that he was being overprotective, but she also realized she liked having him nearby.

They crossed the street and entered. Matthias found a spot

next to the bar's entrance and leaned back against the wall, his arms crossed, his expression stern. Emma couldn't help but think he'd scare away any potential patrons who wandered in.

"What's so funny?" he asked.

She hadn't realized she was grinning. Clamping her lips shut, she ducked her head. "Nothing. Back in a bit."

The interior of the Mercury was as she remembered it from last Friday. The guy Kira had flirted with was nowhere to be seen, but Zeke stood behind the bar, talking to a customer. He looked her way as she approached and excused himself.

He pointed at her. "Emma, right?"

His feigned effort to recall her name would've been totally believable if she didn't know it was an act. "That's right. Good memory." She could put on an act of her own.

He grinned. "Job requirement. You ever find your sister?"

She stood between two stools, braced a foot on the kick rail, and rested her elbows on the bar. "I did."

"Good."

"Why didn't you tell me you two were friends?"

The grin disappeared. "She told you about me."

"Why the act? Why not just call me and say what you knew?"

Zeke glanced around the room and tipped his head toward the end of the bar, farther from the other customers.

But closer to the door where Matthias waited.

She moved with Zeke and took a seat. "Well?"

He leaned toward her, keeping his voice low. "I didn't come out and tell you because I knew Nell didn't want you to know where she was. But I was worried about her." He paused to take another look around the room. "She and I have been friends a while. We worked together at another bar. I helped her get clean and sober. We both ended up moving on but stayed in touch. Then about a month or so ago, she showed up here, scared out of her wits." He closed his mouth and eyed Emma.

She had a feeling he was about to change his mind about

talking. "Because she was pregnant and the baby's father's abusive."

Zeke relaxed. "So you know about that."

"Yep. And I know you helped her get clean. Again."

He nodded and looked down at the bar. "It was harder this time. Maybe because she was already dealing with morning sickness. I don't know. But she fought through it. She was determined she didn't want the baby to be born addicted." He lifted his gaze to meet Emma's. "And she wants this baby like she's never wanted anything. In spite of who the father is."

The light in Zeke's eyes struck Emma. "You're in love with Nell."

He turned his head away as if terrified by what Emma saw.

She decided to let it drop but planned to question Nell about her feelings for this guy. "Why did you two end up at the Royal Palace?"

He sniffed and brought his gaze back to the bar. "She'd been cooped up in my apartment for so long, I could tell she was getting stir crazy. I'd been invited to a wedding. An old friend from high school. So I asked if she wanted to go with me. We made a pact. No booze. No drugs. Just a nice evening out. I don't have a car, so I sprung for an Uber. My buddy got us a deal on one of their swanky hotel rooms. And it was nice. Until we ran into *them*."

"Russ and Gillian?"

"Yeah." Zeke ran the back of his hand over his mouth. "I was pretty sure they hadn't seen Nell, but she freaked out. I gave her the key to the room and sent her back there while I snooped around to find out if she'd been seen."

"Had she?"

"Not as far as I could tell. I went to check on her, but she was gone. So was her overnight bag."

Emma spotted a glimmer at the corner of Zeke's eyes.

"She wasn't at the apartment. I waited for her to show up, but she never did. I knew you'd left that photo with your number on it here." He tapped the bar. "Nell, she talked about you a lot. How close you'd always been. How she felt she'd let you down so bad she couldn't stand to face you."

Emma struggled to keep from choking up.

"I knew if I gave you the tip about the hotel, you'd be able to learn more than I could. I knew you'd find her."

"You should've just told me all of it," Emma said, battling to force the words through a throat strangled with tears and regret. Nell thought she couldn't face her. Did she truly believe Emma would judge her? Think less of her because of her battle with addiction?

"In hindsight, maybe." Zeke leaned forward on the bar, his face inches from Emma's. "I needed you to find her and make sure she's safe. But I didn't want her to ever hate me for betraying her trust."

Which was precisely what Emma had done.

Chapter Thirty

Emma staggered from the bar into the atrium. Matthias pushed away from the wall, took one look at her and demanded, "What did he say to you?"

She could well imagine what she looked like. She knew how she felt. She'd let her sister down over and over again. To the point where Nell trusted a bartender with her secrets, but not Emma.

She shook her head at Matthias, pushed through the doors into the blazing sunshine, and tripped off the curb, wanting nothing more than to get into the car and go back to her camper.

Strong hands—Matthias's—grabbed her from behind and yanked her back as a delivery truck rumbled past, blaring its horn.

Emma gasped as he held onto her, and the breeze kicked up by the truck tossed her hair across her face.

She needed to get a grip. She may have betrayed her sister by calling Matthias, but getting flattened wouldn't help anyone.

Once they were safely settled in the car, Matthias started the engine and cranked the AC on high before facing her. "What did he say?"

She dug through her purse and came up with a tissue, which she pressed to her nose. "Nothing."

"Dammit," Matthias muttered. "He said *something*."

She sniffled and lowered her hands, still clutching the tissue, to her lap. After taking a few slow breaths—the kind Kira taught in yoga class—she offered him the abbreviated version of the conversation. She told him about Zeke helping Nell kick her addiction. About taking her to the wedding reception at the Royal Palace and encountering Russ and Gillian. She told him how Zeke had sent Nell back to the room and how that was the last he'd seen her.

"Why didn't he just tell you that instead of acting like he didn't know her?"

That part, Emma couldn't bring herself to admit. "He didn't say," she mumbled and knew Matthias didn't buy it. But he didn't press.

He faced forward, and they sat without speaking. She kept waiting for him to demand more details. Especially the big one. Nothing Zeke had said cleared Nell of murder.

Matthias finally broke the silence. "Do you still want to check out the homeless guy?"

She did. But did she want Matthias with her? What if they learned—

No. Emma couldn't allow herself to even consider that Nell had killed Gillian. Nell was the victim.

If she had killed anyone, it would've been Russ.

"Hello?"

Emma looked at Matthias who appeared more worried than angry or annoyed.

"The homeless guy. Do you still want to try to find him, or have you had enough for one day?"

"No. I mean yes." She shook her head to clear the jumble of conflicting thoughts and emotions roiling around in there. "Yes, I still wanna talk to the homeless guy." When Matthias looked doubtful, she added, "I'm okay."

He shifted the car into drive. "I need to make a stop first."

"Okay."

"I don't want you wandering around that homeless encampment by yourself, even if I'm nearby. I want to stop at my place and change into civvies. They might be less likely to take off or hide if I don't look like a cop."

Matthias parallel parked in front of an Irish pub on State Street, a couple of blocks north of the police station. Not far from Kira's yoga studio, Emma thought. Convenient.

He started to get out, but when she didn't move, he looked at her and pointed to the apartment windows above the bar. "You can come up if you want."

Her cheeks blazed as she imagined being alone with Matthias Honeywell...while he changed clothes.

Get a grip, she thought and climbed out.

He let them in through a street-level door next to the bar's entrance and led the way up a narrow staircase, which opened into an industrial-style loft space. Emma took it all in. Brick walls, floor-to-ceiling black-metal-framed windows, ductwork overhead. A wide-open living space with leather furniture and a huge TV. And the biggest kitchen she'd ever seen. Even bigger than Eric's.

Matthias must've seen her gawking. "I like to cook."

Not at all what she expected. "I like to eat." The words slipped out unedited, and she winced.

He shot a flirtatious grin at her. "I'll fix you dinner sometime," he said and strode toward a room at the rear of the space. "There's water and beer in the fridge. Help yourself."

Once he'd disappeared behind a closed door to what she assumed was his bedroom—a room she tried not to imagine—she wandered around the living space, taking in the décor. Comfortable. A touch of rustic. Definitely masculine.

She wandered over to a grouping of photos hanging on the brick wall. There were two of a much younger Matthias. In one, he wore a cowboy hat and sat astride a horse with an ease that suggested he'd been born to ride. In another, he and five others stood straight and stern in dress police uniforms.

Emma moved on to a time-faded shot of a woman on a horse, rounding a barrel, the horse digging in, leaning. The woman focused, stretching as if she could carry her mount through the cloverleaf pattern. Emma had tried barrel racing once, coming away with bruised shins from cutting too close. This woman in the photo looked like a pro.

"That's my mother."

Emma spun. Matthias stood in the bedroom doorway, tugging a blue T-shirt down over a pair of well-worn jeans. And watching her.

"I didn't mean to be nosy."

His grin seemed sad. "I did invite you up, you know. I didn't expect you to stand in one spot with your eyes closed."

Emma felt her cheeks flush again. She returned her focus to the barrel racing photo. "She looks like quite the horsewoman."

"She was." Past tense. Before Emma had a chance to decide if condolences were in order, he added, "She died when I was a teenager."

"I'm sorry. What about your dad?"

Matthias's expression darkened with an anger more intense than she'd seen from him. And she'd seen him plenty angry. But he quickly recovered…without, however, answering her question. "I'm ready to go if you are."

The photos held her, especially the one of him on the horse. "I didn't know you rode."

"It's been a while."

She thought longingly of the last time she'd been in the saddle. "I miss having a horse."

"Me too."

Emma looked at him and found him wistfully studying the same old photo of a younger him. "Maybe we can go riding someday." She almost choked. Almost took the words back. But decided to leave them there, hanging between them.

He brought his gaze to hers, a stony wall concealing his feelings. "Your boyfriend might not like that."

It took a second before she realized he again meant Eric. This time, she laughed and decided to come clean. "Eric," she said, "would be more likely to want a relationship with you than with me."

The stony wall crumbled as Matthias's face metamorphosed through a sequence of emotions, from confused to comprehension to flustered, before settling on what she interpreted as relieved. "He's gay?"

"Oh, yeah." She folded her arms. "And he thinks you're a brute or he'd probably have hit on you already."

Matthias choked and lowered his head as if studying his boots. When his gaze came back up to hers, his expression was softer. Sexier. Remembering the feeling of being in his arms, it was all she could do to not move toward him.

"Do *you* think I'm a brute?" he asked.

She swallowed. "No."

"Good."

She thought for sure he was about to close the distance between them, pull her close, and kiss her. And she'd have let him. Instead, he appeared to reconsider whatever was in his mind and his face grew unreadable once more. "We'd better go."

Emma nodded, disappointed. But he was right. This... whatever *this* had almost been...shouldn't happen. Not now. Possibly not ever. But definitely not now.

They needed to clear Nell.

He turned from Emma and strode toward the door, snagging a black hoodie from a hook next to it. She spotted a bulge under his shirt at his waist and recognized it as a gun. Of course he'd be armed. He was a cop.

Emma trailed behind, thinking of her sister. Thinking of Kira in this same apartment.

Thinking she needed to get a handle on these feelings she was having for Matthias Honeywell.

Chapter Thirty-One

M atthias drove in silence, grateful that next to him, Emma wasn't talkative either.

He'd come so close—too close—to giving in to his feelings for her. Letting her into his apartment was a mistake.

Except he didn't regret it.

Emma and Mr. Superhero weren't lovers. They were friends. Only friends. Meaning he still had a chance.

But first, he needed to clear her sister of murder.

God, he hoped Nell wasn't guilty of killing Gillian Watson.

Stop it, he silently chastised himself. Focus. Not on his feelings for Emma. Not on wanting to prove her sister innocent. But on the facts. If Nell was guilty, he'd be forced to collect evidence against her. Emma would hate him. Forever.

So be it.

"This may not be easy," he said and, in his peripheral vision, saw Emma look at him. "These folks may not want to talk to us. They're used to being hassled. In their experience, people, especially cops, want to force them out."

"I'll tell them I'm Nell's sister. That should help."

"If they stick around long enough." What had Didi Reed told

him? "Gillian would take leftovers from the restaurant and give it to them. Her friend said they loved her for it. That's why she never felt in danger walking home along Sixteenth. We should do the same."

Emma didn't reply. Instead, she turned to look out her window.

Matthias cruised past the crime scene and the encampment along 16th. He didn't see anyone around the tents. This might be another waste of time. He pulled into the lot across from the Blue Pike and parked. Emma unbuckled her seatbelt, and he reached over, touching her arm. "You wait here."

She looked over at the restaurant, and he knew what she was thinking. Nell had worked in there. Russ Carlisle still worked there. Emma wanted to see who this guy was.

Which was exactly why Matthias had to insist she stay in the car. "I mean it. You need to stay here."

"But—"

He shook his head. "I'm stepping over the line as it is, involving you in this investigation. I'm not about to put you anywhere near a man who might be a killer."

She gave him a look.

Matthias guessed her thoughts. She'd already been near a killer and not that long ago. He wanted to point out she should've stayed out of that investigation too. Instead, he forced his jaw to relax. "Please. Do not get me fired. Stay in this car."

With a sigh, she nodded.

He stepped out and headed across the street.

The sign ordering him to wait to be seated once again greeted him, but the hostess station was empty. He stepped into the dining room and looked around. Too late for the lunch rush and too early for the dinner crowd, over half of the tables sat empty. At the far end of the room, he spotted Tiffany. And Russ. He appeared to be lecturing her, and she appeared to be struggling to remain professional. Although Matthias hadn't planned on another chat with either of them, he strode across the space, weaving around tables.

Russ spotted his approach first with Tiffany following her boss's gaze. Matthias wondered if Russ had learned his hostess had ratted him out. Or if he'd learned his former hostess/girlfriend was dead.

Matthias plastered a big grin on his face. "Hey, there," he said, intentionally loud enough to draw attention from the nearest diners. "I don't mean to bother you, but I wanted to place a takeout order and there wasn't anyone up front."

Russ's jaw clenched so hard, Matthias expected to hear teeth cracking. "Tiffany," Russ said at a much lower, less obtrusive volume, "take Detective Honeywell back to the entrance and handle his order."

Matthias turned his smile on the hostess. "You go ahead. I'll be with you in a minute." Turning his gaze, minus the smile, to Russ, he added, "I want to speak with your manager for a moment."

Tiffany mumbled something incomprehensible and scurried away.

Russ was attempting to out-scowl Matthias again. "I have nothing more to say to you."

"I suppose you've heard the news about Gillian."

"I have. Terrible thing. But as I just said—"

"I heard you." Matthias held his gaze. As long as Russ didn't request a lawyer, Matthias wasn't backing down. He glanced toward the smoked-glass fishbowl room, which was once again vacant. "Shall we take this somewhere private or would you rather I asked my questions right here?"

Russ shot a look at the nearest occupied table where a gray-haired couple were watching them as if they were the afternoon's entertainment. "Fine. But make this brief. I have work to do."

"So do I."

Russ led the way to the private room and stepped inside but didn't close the door. Folding his arms, he faced Matthias. "What part of 'I have nothing more to say to you' don't you understand?"

"The part that wants to know about Nell Anderson."

Russ's brow furrowed. "I thought you wanted to ask me about Gillian?"

"We'll get to her. But first, tell me about Nell."

"I already did. She was a good employee. Then she quit."

"A good employee whom you kept in an apartment at Bay Front Place."

Russ's eyes widened. "How did you—" He clamped his mouth shut.

"How did we find out? We've found out a lot. Like how you like to bully the women in your life. Do you get off slapping them around?" Matthias moved closer and lowered his voice to a threatening growl. "Does beating women make you feel tough? I know you beat Nell. I'd be willing to bet you beat Gillian, too."

Russ's cheeks flushed as he took a step back.

Matthias moved with him, staying in his face, betting he was too much of a coward to take a swing at a man. But if he did, Matthias could handle him. Not to mention arrest him for assaulting a police officer. "What did you do? Offer to walk her home that night? Maybe she pissed you off. Called you out for cheating on her with Nell."

"No."

"For something else then. I don't suppose it takes much to push your buttons. So you took her into that dark walkway between the warehouses. Started shoving her around. Did you intend to push her down those steps? Or did she stumble and fall?"

"No," Russ said louder. "It wasn't me. It was Nell. She was jealous. Possessive. She hated Gillian. Begged me to fire her. She wanted me all to herself."

"Liar!"

Matthias hadn't noticed Emma enter the restaurant. Hadn't

seen her cross the dining room. Hadn't heard her reach the door of the fishbowl. Until her strangled, outraged cry.

"*Liar*," she repeated, fists clenched and trembling with rage.

"Who the hell are you?" Russ demanded, his own fists clenched.

Matthias was right. Russ had made no move to threaten Matthias despite the pressure he'd put on him. But he sensed if Emma took one more step, Russ might take a swing.

He also sensed Emma was ready to throw a few punches of her own.

"Nell's my sister," she said, "and she wants nothing to do with you."

She started to advance, and Matthias stepped in front of her, blocking her with an arm. "I told you to stay in the car."

Her eyes never left Russ. "I had to see him for myself."

"You're Nell's sister?"

Matthias shot a look at him. The bastard was studying Emma and wearing an appreciative sneer.

"I've always wanted to do sisters."

Matthias came around, trying to swing, intending to bash the smug son of a bitch in the teeth, but Emma clung to his arm.

"Don't," she whispered. "He's baiting you. If you flatten him—while I'd love to see it—he'll file charges."

Breathing hard, Matthias looked into her eyes. As much as she appeared to want to rip Carlisle's head off, she also didn't want Matthias to pay the price.

"She's one smart cookie, this one," Carlisle said. "You'd better listen to her. You lay one hand on me, and I'll have you up on charges of police brutality."

Matthias battled to relax the muscles in his hands and his arms. Not because of Carlisle's threats, but because of Emma still clinging to him. He could feel the rage radiating from her, yet she maintained control of herself. He fixed her with a look, silently asking: *Are you sure?*

She gave a minute nod.

He inhaled. Exhaled. And lowered the arm. "Let's go," he told her.

She gave another nod.

Matthias started toward the open door.

Carlisle gave a low chuckle. "I meant what I said. You and your sister and me. I'll show you—"

Before Matthias could react, Emma took one long stride and struck out. The crack of her palm connecting with Carlisle's face echoed like a gunshot. He reeled away from her, clutching at his cheek.

Emma may have topped out at five foot five, at most, but she looked to loom over the six-foot Russ Carlisle. "You try to file charges against *me*," she said, "and I'll bring down an entire law firm on you, beginning with a litany of drug charges and ending with sexual harassment and the rape of my sister." She wheeled away and brushed past Matthias. "I'll be in the car."

Matthias watched her storm across the dining room. He wasn't alone. Restaurant patrons' heads turned to watch as well. He looked to Carlisle, who still cupped his cheek, eyes wide with shock and pain. Matthias smiled. "Looks like you met your match. I'll be in touch."

He turned and followed Emma.

Matthias had Tiffany put together a large takeout order. When he pulled out his wallet, she waved it away. "I saw what your friend did back there," the hostess said with an evil grin. "The two of you can have free meals for life as long as I'm around."

He thanked her and carried the two oversized bags to the car, where Emma sat in the passenger seat.

Where she should have waited all along. Still, the image of her slapping Russ Carlisle brought a smile.

He climbed in, setting the bags on the back seat. Emma looked miffed as she cradled her right hand.

"What?" he asked.

"That hurt," she grumbled.

He snorted a laugh which brought a dirty look aimed his way. "Sorry." He reached out to her. "Let me see."

With a huff, she opened her hand, which he took and examined. The skin of her palm was bright pink. He suspected Carlisle's cheek wore a similar shade.

"Wait here." Matthias popped the trunk, climbed out, and strode to the rear of the Impala. He found a chemical ice pack in the first-aid kit stored there and slammed the lid. As he returned to the driver's seat, he punched the bag to break the inner one and shook it to mix the chemicals. Inside the car, he handed it to Emma. "Hold this. It should take the sting away."

She did as told but kept her head down. "I'm sorry. I can't believe I did that."

"Are you kidding? I'm proud of you."

She met his gaze, surprised.

"And thank you for stopping me from doing worse to him. You're right. I'd have been on desk duty if I'd done what I wanted to."

She lowered her face again but not before he caught her embarrassed grin. "I'm already responsible for the scar above your eye and for almost getting you shot. I don't want to be blamed for you losing your job."

"None of it's your fault." Matthias had a feeling Emma's slap carried some pent-up hostility toward Clay Bauer, the man who was responsible for the scar—and for a lot more—but knew better than to bring up his name. "Are you ready to track down this homeless guy?"

She nodded. "Let's do it."

They left the car in the lot and rounded the corner to the crumbled sidewalk on 16th Street. No one appeared around the cluster of tents. Matthias handed both bags to Emma and gestured for her to keep going. "I'm gonna cross the street and lay back a little. We don't want to scare anyone away, but if the man in question is home, I'll be close enough to grab him." Matthias nudged her with his elbow. "Or you can just give him a right to the jaw." He feigned throwing a quick punch.

She made a face. "You're not funny." But the hint of a grin said she thought otherwise.

He left her walking toward the tents and jogged across 16th Street. Head down, hands stuffed in his pockets, he paralleled her, acting like he was watching his step on the uneven pavement when in truth, he was on high alert, watching her and the canvas-covered huddle. Emma played her part well, never glancing over at him, striding along as if she was familiar with this path.

When she drew close, she called out, light and friendly. "Hello? Is anyone home?" No one responded and she stopped next to the encampment. "Hello? I'm not here to cause trouble. I brought you something to eat." She shook the bags, the paper rustling.

To Matthias's surprise, the canvas cover moved. He stopped and brought his phone from his pocket, keeping his head lowered as if scanning the device.

A gap appeared and a man's head popped out. He looked around warily, glancing at Emma. But his gaze settled on Matthias. Even with his head down and from that distance, Matthias could tell the man was leery.

Emma held out the bags. "Here. I know you must be hungry. I wanted to help."

The aroma enticed the man to focus on her rather than Matthias. He stepped out of the tent, a tall, thin man. Something about him struck Matthias as familiar.

He cautiously accepted Emma's offering. She said something to him, too soft for Matthias to hear. The man backed away a step, still gripping the bags. Emma held her hands open, palms up, imploring. For a moment, Matthias thought he was going to relax and speak to her. But then he looked across the road, directly at Matthias.

He realized where he'd seen this man before. The scrawny guy he'd encountered near Pauly's Polynesian Pub.

The man recognized Matthias as well. He dropped the bags and bolted in the opposite direction from the Blue Pike. Matthias launched after him, pounding across the street, angling toward the guy, who was fast. Damned fast. He darted into the gap between the warehouses, toward the stairs where Gillian had died. Matthias charged in after him.

The man was clearly outdistancing Matthias, arms churning like an Olympian track star. Matthias watched him racing toward the daylight at the far end. Reaching it. Disappearing from view.

Matthias arrived at the end of the red brick passageway. A ten-foot-high chain-link fence edged the property, separating it—and him—from the railyard. Beyond, long lines of freight cars waited to transport goods along the Great Lakes shores. He looked left and right, seeing no evidence of the homeless guy.

He leaned against the brick wall, breathing hard after the pursuit. Dammit.

"Are you okay?" Emma shouted.

He looked back the way he'd come. She stood at the far end, the deadly stairwell midway between them. "Yeah," he called to her. He pushed away and started toward her but sensed something wasn't quite right. She looked like a kid who needed to use the bathroom, shifting from one foot to the other impatiently. "What's going on?" he asked when he drew closer.

She held her phone in a vice-like grip and appeared on the verge of tears. "I just got a phone call from Eric. There's something wrong with Nell. He called the ambulance and is taking her to the hospital."

Chapter Thirty-Two

Eric's words didn't echo in Emma's mind as much as the tone of them. He was frantic. Scared out of his wits. Cramping, he'd told her. Nell was cramping and in pain.

And there Emma was, miles away without her car.

Matthias hadn't hesitated. He hustled her back to the Blue Pike's parking lot—she'd left the two bags of takeout tucked inside the tent for whenever someone returned—and insisted on driving her to Hamot's emergency department. And then, instead of dropping her off as she'd asked, he parked in a restricted space, left some sort of placard on the dashboard indicating he was law enforcement, and escorted her inside.

They tracked down Eric in a waiting room, bent over, his head in his hands.

"Eric," she called to him.

His head came up and he popped to his feet, throwing his arms around her. "I'm so glad you got here," he said, his voice ragged. "Our poor Nellie. I didn't know what to do."

She held him for a minute, uncertain who was comforting whom, before she pulled free and held him at arm's length to study his tear-streaked face. "What happened?"

"I don't know. Nothing. I mean, she didn't fall or anything. She'd had a nice nap. I had a pizza delivered. She ate like…well, like she was eating for two. When she said she didn't feel well, I thought it was the pizza. I even teased her about eating too fast." He inhaled a sob. "Then she just doubled over and started crying in pain. She said she thought it was the baby. I called 911. I mean, I didn't have a car."

No, of course he didn't. Her Subaru was back at the campground.

"You did the right thing," she told him. "Has the doctor talked to you?"

"Not yet. They took her right back and said they'd be out to get me when they had her settled." A sheepish grin shone through his tears. "She told them I was the father. Otherwise they might not have let me in."

That sounded like Nell.

Emma noticed Eric's eyes shift, looking behind her, and he straightened. She followed his gaze to Matthias, who stood a few feet behind her. Under different circumstances, she'd have laughed. Eric, shattered as he was, was attempting to morph into his straight alter ego to keep "brutish" Matthias at bay.

She gave Eric a shake. "It's okay. He knows."

His questioning gaze met hers. "Knows what?"

"Who you are."

Trying—and failing—to appear threatening, Eric glared at Matthias. Emma again followed Eric's gaze. Matthias, to her relief, had dropped the scary cop, jealous "brute" act. Instead, his expression matched the softer, concerned side of him that she'd come to know after the chaos of last month.

She came back to Eric who was studying her with a healthy dose of skepticism.

A woman in a white lab coat breezed in through a door. "Nell Anderson's family?"

Eric and Emma wheeled toward her. "That's us," Emma said.

The woman approached and gestured to a round table in one corner. "Please. Sit," she said as she lowered into one of the chairs. Emma and Eric sunk into the chairs opposite her, while Matthias hung back.

"I'm Dr. Thornton," the woman said. "You are…?"

"Emma Anderson. Her sister." She pointed at Eric and went along with the story he and Nell had already concocted. "This is Eric Baker. The baby's father."

He flushed but shot a grateful smile at her.

The doctor folded her hands. "I'm afraid Nell's blood pressure is extremely high, which is affecting the fetus. She also informed us that she's an alcoholic and was not only intoxicated but was using narcotics early in this pregnancy."

"But she's clean and sober now," Eric said.

"Which is good." The doctor looked from him to Emma and back. "But damage may have already been done."

Emma's mind spun. "What does that mean? Is she going to be okay? Is the baby?"

The doctor shook her head. "I wish I could give you definite answers. We're treating her for pre-term labor as well as for the high blood pressure." Her gaze fixed on Emma. "Nell is also undernourished and underweight for as far into the pregnancy as she is. She admitted she hasn't sought medical help and isn't on any prenatal vitamins."

Emma suddenly saw the situation through the doctor's eyes. Or at least how she imagined the doctor saw it. Nell's addiction, her lack of nutrition and medical care…why hadn't the sister or baby's father done more?

Before Emma could speak, the doctor silenced her with a raised hand. "I'm not accusing you." She looked at Eric. "Either of you. Nell told me she lied about you being the father. The real father is no longer in the picture. Nell's been living on the street of her own accord. You're both trying to help. You got her here quickly. We're doing all we can. I'm just not sure it will be enough."

Emma tried to breathe around a knot in her throat. "You're saying you don't think you can save her baby."

"I'm saying no such thing. It's too soon to tell." The doctor rose. "One of you can go back to see her for a few minutes."

Eric placed a hand on top of Emma's. "That should be you."

She nodded and stood.

Before she could follow the doctor, Matthias stepped in, took her hand, and leaned close, whispering into her ear. "I know the timing sucks, but if you can get Nell to tell you who's been taking care of her on the street…"

Emma looked into his eyes. There was no sign of the tough cop, demanding information no matter what. He was genuinely concerned. But he was also trying to catch a killer. If the homeless guy witnessed Russ Carlisle push Gillian to her death as Emma suspected, Matthias would arrest the son of a bitch who got Nell back on drugs. Emma gave a quick nod.

He tipped his head toward her, his forehead lightly touching hers. The simple gesture brought a rush of tears. Choking, she leaned into him, burying her face against his neck, seeking solace. Seeking strength. Seeking…

When his arms started to envelop her, she drew back. As much as she'd been fighting it, she realized she was falling in love with this man.

And it couldn't happen at a worse time.

Nell looked tiny in the hospital bed, connected to oxygen and IV tubing. Wires led to a heart monitor perched next to her. Emma took note of the blood-pressure reading. One eighty-six over ninety-nine.

Nell must've seen her looking. "And that's lower than it was."

Emma moved to her side and closed her fingers around Nell's hand. "How are you feeling?"

"Better. Not great, but better. At least the cramps have stopped." Nell managed a weak grin. "And there wasn't any bleeding. That's good, right?"

Emma had no idea but agreed. "Very good. You just need to rest and get pumped full of vitamins for a while."

Her phone rang. She yanked it from her pocket, prepared to send the call to voicemail, but she recognized the number lighting the screen. She swiped the green icon. "Katie?"

"Emma, hi—"

"Can I call you back? My sister's in the hospital and—"

"Oh, no. Nothing serious, I hope."

Emma didn't want to simply brush her off after asking for her help. "Serious enough to put her in Hamot."

"Aw, I'm sorry. You don't need to bother calling me back. I just wanted to let you know my friend isn't willing to help with those videos."

Right now, the hotel security footage was way down on Emma's priority list. "No problem. I appreciate you trying."

"I hope your sister feels better soon. Bye."

Emma ended the call and brought her attention back to Nell.

Her gaze had shifted. "This is all my fault. I shouldn't have given in to Russ. I shouldn't have accepted those pills from him. I shouldn't have left Zeke. At least he was trying to help me."

"I spoke with Zeke."

Her gaze snapped to Emma. "When?"

"Today. He's worried about you."

Nell looked away. "He's a good friend."

"Why did you run away from him?"

"He told you about seeing Russ at the wedding reception?"

"He did."

Nell fingered her IV tube. "I freaked out, seeing Russ again. I was afraid. Not just for me and my baby but for Zeke, too. People

275

ANNETTE DASHOFY

who go up against Russ either end up in a hospital or disappear altogether."

Emma's nerves went on high alert. "What do you mean? Disappear?"

"Just that. He pays them to leave town. Or threatens them. Whatever. Zeke and I met in AA. He helped me get clean back then, too. I was afraid Russ would do something to get Zeke hooked again."

Emma wished she'd let Matthias slug the bastard.

Nell's words sunk in even deeper. Russ made people disappear. Like Gillian had disappeared?

"I need to ask you something," Emma said.

"Okay."

"Your homeless friend...the one you were staying with...the one who helped you move Gillian's body—"

Nell shushed her with a loud hiss.

"Sorry." Emma lowered her voice. "Did he see Gillian's murder?"

Nell averted her gaze. "I can't tell you."

Emma took the response as a yes. "I need to know his name."

She shook her head. "I can't."

Emma held her sister's hand and squeezed. "You have to, Nell. He has information that could help the police put Russ away."

Nell kept shaking her head like a pendulum. "I told you what happens to people who go up against him."

"Which is exactly why we need to stop him."

Nell hiccuped a laugh. "We need to stop him? We can't. He'll kill us."

"I don't mean we, you and me. I mean the police."

"You a cop now?"

"No, but I have a friend—"

"The cop? He'll never talk to a cop."

"You mean your friend in the tent?"

Nell nodded.

She was right about that much. The homeless guy had already proven he wasn't about to speak with Matthias. Voluntarily. "Give me his name. That's all."

"No."

"Nell, I'm your sister. You've not let me protect you since Mom and Dad died."

The bedside monitor started emitting an ear-piercing shriek.

Nell ignored it. Her face flushed in anger. "That's not true. I asked for your help. You turned me down."

Emma couldn't argue. Why had she ever listened to Clay? Damn him and his tough love. "Let me help you now. Russ is a snake. He's going to keep hurting women if we don't stop him. If your friend saw him kill Gillian, the police can put Russ where he won't hurt anyone ever again."

The door burst open and a woman in scrubs bustled in and crossed to the monitor. To Emma, she said, "You have to leave."

Emma looked up at the screen. 220 over 150. "Oh, God. I'm so sorry."

The woman jerked a thumb toward the door. "Out. *Now.*"

Emma scrambled to her feet, sputtering apologies to Nell and to the nurse. She scrambled backward, keeping her eyes on her sister. Then she turned away.

"Jacob," Nell called.

Emma spun to face her.

"I don't know his last name. Everyone just calls him Jacob."

Chapter Thirty-Three

"That must've been some talk." Cassie glared at Matthias from her desk when he strode through the doorway to Major Crimes. "Did Emma tell you her entire life history?"

He'd taken time to change back into his regulation polo shirt and trousers before returning to the office, knowing Cassie would've jumped to all the wrong conclusions had he shown up in street clothes. "Jacob," he said.

The name derailed Cassie's haranguing, which was what Matthias intended. "Who?" she asked.

"It's the name Emma's sister gave us of the homeless man who's been helping her out. I don't know if he's the same one who spoke with one of the uniforms early in the investigation. But he or one of his friends may have witnessed Gillian's murder."

Cassie perked up. "Do we have a last name?"

"Nell didn't know it."

"What else did you find out?"

He leaned against the wall across from Cassie's cubicle and started telling her about the last few hours. Nell's pregnancy. Her relationship with Russ Carlisle. Filling in a few gaps where Zeke Dyson was concerned. The conversation with Russ, although

Matthias left out the part about almost punching him in the face and Emma's slap.

As he talked, Frazier appeared from his cubby and listened, arms crossed.

When Matthias got to the part about the homeless man—possibly Jacob, possibly not—and his foot chase, he turned to Frazier. "Remember the scrawny guy we kept running into near Pauly's?"

"The one who was scared of you?"

"Or scared of the police in general. Yeah. Well, that's the guy I chased this afternoon."

"Really?" Frazier fingered his mustache. "Interesting. That's quite a hike from Pauly's over on Walnut all the way to Sixteenth Street."

Cassie rocked back in her chair. "What's even more interesting is that this guy can be placed near two crime scenes."

Matthias had been thinking the same thing.

"If Nell Anderson knows him by name, maybe she'd be willing to take us to him," Frazier suggested.

"She's in the hospital," Matthias said and told them how he'd left Emma there with her sister and their friend.

Cassie's eyes glazed with tears. "That's horrible. What are the doctors saying?"

"They're making no promises."

"Poor Nell. Poor Emma. They both have shitty taste in men."

Matthias eyed her, searching for any hint of sarcasm. Finding none, he looked at Frazier. "Don't you have a friend who works a soup kitchen downtown?"

"Yeah."

"We need to get an ID on this Jacob guy. Maybe your friend can help."

"I'll call him." Frazier ducked back into his cubby.

Cassie rose, her coffee mug in hand, and crooked a finger at Matthias. "A word, please."

He followed her to the break room, sensing she had more than one word for him.

She refilled her cup before facing him. "What the hell were you thinking, involving Emma in the investigation?"

"She's already involved."

Cassie shook her head. "You should have talked to her and nothing more. Letting her interview Dyson? That should never have happened."

"She didn't 'interview' him. He wouldn't talk to me. But he *would* talk to her. I just tagged along and stood outside the door in case there was trouble."

"And then you took her to see Russ Carlisle?"

"No. I told her to stay in the car while I picked up some food for those homeless people. I did not want her to confront Russ. She did that on her own."

Cassie set her mug down and crossed her arms. "Was there any blood drawn?"

Matthias stuttered. Paused. "Not by me."

She raised an eyebrow. "Is Emma okay?"

"I had to ice her hand."

Cassie fought a smile and didn't completely succeed. "How's Russ?"

"He had to find his own ice."

This time, a chuckle escaped Cassie's throat. "Good for her." She grew serious again. "Nevertheless, it was irresponsible of you to drag Emma down to Sixteenth Street."

"I was right there."

"And what if Jacob or whoever he is had pulled a gun? Or a knife? Bad things happen fast. You know that. You put Emma's life in danger. And your own as well. You may have been protecting her, but who was there to protect you? That is not a neighborhood to go into without backup."

"It was daylight."

"Even in the daylight."

He looked away. Dammit, she was right.

"And then there's her sister. I'm sorry to hear about Nell, I truly am, but being pregnant and hospitalized doesn't make her any less viable a suspect in Gillian's death."

"Russ Carlisle is the killer, and you know it."

"No, I do not."

Matthias met her gaze. "Cassie, come on…"

"Come on, yourself. You're fixated on this guy because he's an ass. But being an ass isn't enough for a jury or even the DA. We need evidence."

"I need to track down Jacob," he said, more to himself than to Cassie.

"That's one possibility." She tipped her head toward the office. "While you were gone today, dragging Emma all over the city, Frazier managed to get a warrant for the Royal Palace's security video for the night of the wedding."

Matthias brought his full attention back to his partner.

"Turns out Judge Hurley's his uncle. Anyhow, we've been going over the footage for the last hour."

"And?"

"It's a lot of ground to cover." She picked up her mug and headed back to her desk.

Matthias followed.

Frazier stepped away from his desk. "My contact didn't know anyone who goes by Jacob but is asking around and will get back to us. But I thought of something." He looked at Matthias. "We've seen him twice over by Pauly's. He knew Pauly's schedule. Maybe Pauly knows him too."

"That's a good point," Cassie said. "And we still need to talk to Pauly about his relationship with Olivia Petrovich." She checked her watch. "Why don't you two head over there now and see what you can find out. I'll stay here and keep going over the hotel's video. Then, when you get back, you—" She pointed at Matthias. "—can start doing a deep dive into Russ's financials. You're so convinced he's our man in the Gillian Watson case, find us the evidence to prove it."

By the time Matthias and Frazier stepped out of the car in Pauly's parking lot, dark clouds were rolling in from the north. The breeze carried the promise of rain. Matthias thought of those living in the tents on Sixteenth, trying to stay dry. Trying to keep their homes from blowing away in the storms. He thought of Nell. Emma's little sister had been one of them, struggling to survive. At least tonight she would have a warm bed and a roof overhead.

"Figures," Frazier said.

"What?"

Frazier extended his arms, gesturing all around. "It figures. Now that we want to run into that scrawny guy, he's nowhere to be seen."

Matthias hadn't expected to encounter him. It had only been a few short hours since Jacob—or whoever he was—had led Matthias on a foot chase. Then again, that was less than two miles away. Jacob was clearly accustomed to walking at least that far.

A quick look around confirmed Frazier's assessment. No Scrawny Guy AKA Jacob.

Inside Pauly's Polynesian Pub, a trio of men sat at one table, nursing beers. Two more perched at the bar. It clearly was five o'clock somewhere. The bouncer, who'd been tending bar, was absent today. Pauly was back. He spotted Matthias and Frazier and scowled. "I hear you've been hassling my girl."

"You've heard wrong," Matthias replied, keeping his tone light. "We just had a few questions for her. Now we have a few for you too."

He crossed his arms. "I'll save you the trouble. No, I didn't know Olivia used to be married to Tom. She goes by her maiden name. We agreed early on to not dig into each other's past. She ain't proud of hers, and I sure ain't proud of mine. No, they never crossed paths in here. And no, it wasn't her in a wig that night. I told you. I never saw that blonde before."

"I gather she told you about our visit this morning," Matthias said.

"You bet she did. And I don't appreciate you cops suggesting she's guilty of killing her ex. I can promise you she did not."

Matthias nodded. "Okay."

"I mean it. She had no reason to want him dead. She's over him. Her and me, we're happy together."

"Good for you," Frazier said and sounded sincere.

Matthias leaned his forearms on the bar, noticing it wasn't sticky today. "Tell us about Jacob."

The change in direction had its desired effect. Pauly appeared puzzled by the question. "Who?"

Frazier waved a hand toward the windows. "Homeless guy. Hangs out around here. Seems to know a lot about the hours you keep."

Pauly's eyes widened. "Oh. That Jacob."

"What do you know about him?"

Pauly scratched his head as if trying to scrape up his memories. "He used to live a couple blocks from here and was a regular. Then he fell on hard times. Lost his job. His car. His home." Pauly looked past them and nodded at a patron who'd raised a hand. He grabbed a glass and filled it from the tap. "Jacob's an all-right guy, but he's bipolar, you know? Has his good days and his bad. I don't know where he's staying now. A shelter maybe? I try to help him out when I can. I pay him to do odd jobs. Mop the floors. Take out the trash. That sort of thing. And I give him any extra food we have at the end of the night." Pauly excused himself and stepped from behind the bar to deliver the draft to his customer. When he returned, he grumbled about his waitress calling off, then glanced from Frazier to Matthias. "Why you asking about Jacob, anyway?"

Matthias shifted, keeping one elbow on the bar. "He ever mention seeing something bad?"

"Bad? Like how?"

"Like seeing a young woman get hurt?"

Pauly looked stunned. "No. Never." He wrinkled his nose. "But, you know, now that you mention it, he has been acting kinda squirrely recently."

"How recently?"

"I dunno. Couple weeks? Maybe a little longer."

Matthias looked at Frazier who gave a nod. About as long as Gillian had been dead. "Are you expecting he'll be in tonight?" Matthias asked.

"Hell, I don't know. He don't have a regular schedule. Maybe he will. Maybe he won't. I hope he does, to be honest. I'll pay him to wait tables."

Matthias reached into his pocket and came up with a business card, assuming Pauly had tossed the previous one. "If Jacob comes in tonight, tomorrow night, whenever, call me."

Pauly took the card, and Frazier reached out, clamping a hand on Pauly's arm. "And don't tell him, okay? He's scared of this guy." Frazier tipped his head at Matthias and grinned.

Pauly returned the grin. "Maybe I should call *you*."

Frazier handed him another card. "Either way. Jacob isn't in any trouble, but he might be able to help us lock up someone who's out there hurting young women."

Pauly stepped back and waved the two cards. "You'll hear from me as soon as I see him."

Back at the station, Frazier rejoined Cassie watching video of hotel guests coming and going along various hallways. Glad not to be wrangled into sharing the job, Matthias sat at his computer, running searches on Russ Carlisle. The DA had refused to subpoena Carlisle's financial records without more to go on. "More to go on" was exactly what he wanted to find.

As afternoon progressed into evening, Cassie left to spend time with her husband and granddaughter. Frazier, rubbing his eyes, headed out as well, mumbling something about getting a fresh start in the morning.

Matthias couldn't blame them. All he'd uncovered so far was a longer list of properties owned by Erie Huron and Ontario Holdings but none of them came up as crime-scene locations or being involved in criminal activities.

Which brought Matthias back to Russ's late wife, Havana Nelson Carlisle. She'd had an active social-media presence. Matthias had to scroll through hundreds of condolences and posts by friends sharing memories to arrive at Havana's last entries. There were lots of selfies of a bubbly Havana with girlfriends. A few with Russ, but they'd been posted by others who'd tagged her. The strain in her face was obvious in those, as if standing close to the man she'd married was an insufferable chore. Posed photos of the two, dressed for the nightlife, also revealed tense smiles rather than genuine ones. At least on Havana's part. Russ looked proud. *Look at me and the gorgeous woman on my arm.*

They were a handsome couple. Matthias could imagine them walking the red carpet at one of those Hollywood premieres. But only one of them was happy.

He scrolled back further and further into the past. At some point—about two years prior to Havana's death—she did look effervescent in Russ's arms. Young and in love. She clung to him, laughing. Joyful. Russ, however still looked more proud and smug than enamored of his bride.

What happened to change Havana? Had there been one humiliating incident? Or simply months of suffering? Matthias searched, but whatever it was, she hadn't made it public.

He made a list of Havana's social-media friends who appeared in photos with her, who lived in Erie, and those who were identified as family.

He switched to Russ's profile, scrolled back to that same period, and came to a realization. The only photos of Havana on Russ's page were those they'd both been tagged in. He shared no pictures of his wife. Most of Russ's photos were of real estate. Bay Front Place. Construction images labeled as the future site of the Royal Palace Resort and Conference Center. A few were of Russ with wealthy-looking businessmen and women. Russ wore the same smug and proud expression with his business associates as he did with his wife.

Had Havana been nothing more than another "holding" in his eyes?

Russ made no mention of his wife's death. Others had expressed their sympathy. He hadn't responded, commented, or even clicked "like" on those posts. But he became more active after Havana died. Assorted women on his arm, his smile still prideful and smug. Even in the last six months, he posted selfies with various gorgeous women, including but not limited to Gillian.

No photos of Nell, though. Had Russ considered her too special, preferring to keep their "relationship" private? Or had he not wanted the world to see him with a homeless druggie. Yeah, Matthias thought. That was more likely the case.

Matthias leaned back and scrubbed his face, his eyes burning from too much screen time. His observation about Nell sent his mind reeling to the hospital. And Emma.

He pulled out his phone.

If he felt exhausted, Emma sounded completely spent when she answered.

"How's your sister?" he asked.

"The same," she replied, her voice as soft as a sigh.

"How are *you*?"

Her breathy laugh almost tickled his ear. "Scared."

"Is Eric still with you?"

"Yeah. He's stranded too."

Matthias winced. "That's one reason I'm calling. I can pick you up and take you home whenever you're ready."

"Thanks, but we're going to stay here tonight. I'm hoping Nell and the baby will be in better shape by morning. We may hit you up for a ride then."

"You have my number."

"I do."

She sounded so beat, Matthias considered driving to the hospital and sitting with her, holding her so she could sleep. The thought of her in his arms, her head against his shoulder, her breath against his neck, stirred a tsunami of emotions he hadn't felt—hadn't allowed himself to feel—in almost twenty years. He closed his eyes. Reined in his heart. Steadied his voice. "If anything happens, call me."

"I will." There was a long breathy pause. "Goodnight, Matthias."

"Goodnight, Emma."

Chapter Thirty-Four

E mma tried to sleep.

She and Eric were alone in the obstetrics department, similar in layout to the emergency department waiting room but quieter and more comfortable. They each had a recliner. A nurse had given them access to a closet containing blankets and pillows.

Emma's request to sleep—or attempt to—in a chair in Nell's room was shot down. She needed her rest, the nurse said and promised to come get Emma should anything change.

The lights had been dimmed. Eric seemed to have no problem with slumber. Buried beneath the borrowed blankets, he snored softly from his recliner. Emma, however, couldn't get comfortable and gave up trying. She lay with her legs raised, stared at the acoustic-tile ceiling, and listened. The same nurse had closed the doors leading to the hallway, but sounds filtered through. Voices of passing staff. Distant beeping. The occasional squeal of an alarm. The first thirty or forty times, Emma had tensed. Was that coming from Nell's room? Was there a problem with the baby? But no one came for her, and she eventually acclimated to the sounds.

Instead, she replayed the phone call from Matthias. His tired but whiskey-smooth voice was balm to her anguished soul.

ANNETTE DASHOFY

He hadn't mentioned the investigation. Or Jacob. Had he learned any more about him? Emma hadn't thought of asking until after the call ended. She considered calling him back but decided it could wait.

Everything could wait until Nell and her baby were out of danger.

At some point, Emma must've fallen asleep because she became aware of being shaken awake. She jolted upright, blinking. Where was she? What was going on? Her fogged brain cleared when she saw Nell's doctor above her. From the look on the doctor's face, Emma knew it was bad.

"I'm so sorry," the doctor said in hushed tones. "Your sister suffered a miscarriage about an hour ago." She continued to speak, but Emma only registered fragments. "...Fetus not viable... Nothing anyone could've done... Shouldn't affect future pregnancies..."

None of it really mattered to Emma. "Can I see her?"

"Yes, of course." The doctor looked at Eric, still sleeping blissfully. "Do you want me to tell your friend?"

"Please." Emma climbed out of the recliner and charged out of the room.

She found Nell curled into a ball on her side, weeping. Emma moved to her, touching her arm, wanting to hold her. But Nell flinched at her touch and pulled the covers over her. "Go away. Leave me alone," she said, her voice muffled by the sheets.

A couple of minutes later, Eric joined them. "Oh, Nellie," he said, leaning over her, trying to wrap her in his arms.

She thrashed, shoving him away. "Leave me alone," she wailed.

Eric recoiled. He met Emma's gaze, tears gleaming. Nell wouldn't let them touch her, so they fell into each other's arms, watching the Nell-sized lump beneath the hospital blankets.

Emma's emotions bounced from numb to shock to anger and back, on a repeating loop of despair. She wanted to comfort Nell, but Nell was having none of it. At least when they'd lost their parents, they had clung to each other, mourning together. Recovering together had been more challenging.

Eric gave Emma's shoulders a squeeze. "Let's get some coffee. Give her some time."

Emma agreed, but feared time wasn't enough.

The morning light was filtering through the cafeteria's windows once they settled at a table. Eric had turned his concern to Emma, insisting they both needed nourishment. He left her sitting there while he browsed the breakfast offerings.

She placed her phone in front of her and stared at it, debating whether to call Matthias. She decided she couldn't talk to him. Not yet. She clicked on her text-message icon and stared at the blank message box. If she texted him, he would call her to offer sympathy, which again meant talking. She closed the app and turned the phone face down on the table.

Eric returned with a tray laden with plates of scrambled eggs, toast, English muffins, orange juice, and one with sausage links. Aware that Emma was a pescatarian, he placed the latter in front of himself before fluttering a hand at her. "Take what you want."

"I'm not hungry."

"Eat. We need our strength. Nell's going to be relying on us for a while. We can't fall apart when she needs us most."

Emma picked at the food. Eric let her eat in silence for once. She'd finished about half of her eggs when her phone rang. She picked it up and looked at the screen. As she expected, Matthias's name filled it. She silenced the call, sending it to voicemail.

"That was him, wasn't it?" Eric asked.

"The brute?" Emma tried to smile but couldn't. "Yeah."

Eric tipped his head. "Oh, he's not as brutish as I first thought. He seemed sincerely concerned for you and Nell last evening."

Emma didn't reply. She replaced the phone on the table.

"Why didn't you answer?"

She shook her head. "I just…can't. Not right now."

"I understand."

She was glad Eric did. She sure didn't. "This is all Russ Carlisle's fault, you know."

Eric met her gaze without speaking.

"I don't mean the pregnancy. Nell wanted the baby in spite of the father. But she'd been clean and sober. He robbed her of that. And the drugs and the alcohol are why she miscarried."

"I know that."

"She was afraid of him. Afraid he'd kill her and the baby. Well, he didn't kill *her*. But…"

Eric placed a hand on hers. "I don't know what, if anything, the police can do about it though."

"About the baby? Nothing." A rising surge of heat burned Emma's throat. "But we can see that he pays for killing Gillian Watson."

Cloud cover kept the heat down during their thirteen-block hike along State Street from the hospital to 16th Street. It was a couple more blocks to the encampment where Emma had seen Jacob—or the man she assumed was Jacob—yesterday. She'd expected more of an argument from Eric when she told him her intentions. Instead, he'd squared his shoulders and agreed to come with her.

As they turned onto16th, though, he seemed to reconsider. "I'm not so sure this is a good idea."

"It's early," she said. "The people who live in the tents should still be home." The word home made her wince.

"That's part of why it's not a good idea. We don't know how many of them there are. There're only two of us."

"We'll be fine."

They passed the walkway between the warehouses. The one with the stairs where Gillian had died. The one where Matthias had lost Jacob in their foot chase. Ahead, the fabric covering the tents fluttered. One piece lifted and a man's head appeared, looking their way. The same man she'd seen yesterday. He appeared to say something to an unseen person still inside their makeshift home before leaping out and sprinting away from them.

"Wait!" Emma ran after him, shouting, "I'm Nell's sister! She's in the hospital!"

He stopped and turned to face her but still looked like a coiled spring, ready to flee at a moment's notice.

She halted as well, waiting.

"You were here yesterday," the man called. "You were with the police."

Emma realized he was looking beyond her to Eric. "Yes, but this guy isn't a cop. He's a friend. Of mine and Nell's."

"What do you want with me?"

"Are you Jacob?"

Even from the distance, Emma could see him react. "How do you know my name?" he demanded.

"Nell told me. Please. We need your help."

Chapter Thirty-Five

Matthias managed a couple hours of sleep but spent most of the night lying awake, thinking of Russ Carlisle. Well before dawn, he tumbled out of bed, showered, dressed, and headed out. He picked up coffee at his favorite place along his walk to the station.

Major Crimes was vacant. He even beat Cassie to work. He settled at his desk and began searching for contact information on the list of Havana's friends and family he'd created yesterday.

Matthias was convinced Russ had killed his wife, just as he'd likely killed Gillian. But he needed a nugget of evidence. Something to share with the police in Colorado.

Something to take to the Erie County District Attorney.

Locating the phone number for Mr. and Mrs. Elias Nelson, Havana's parents, was easy. But it was a bit early if Matthias wanted their cooperation. By the time Cassie ambled in, he had almost a dozen numbers scrawled in his notes.

"Did you even go home last night?" she asked.

"Uh-huh," he grunted. "Couldn't sleep."

She flopped into her chair, tucked her purse in the bottom desk drawer, and slammed it. "I know the feeling."

He checked the time. Seven-thirty. Cassie was in early too. He took a break from his computer to call Emma, but it went to voice mail. He hoped she was getting some rest. For a moment, he considered calling the hospital to get an update on Nell, but would they even give out that kind of information to non-family members? He decided against it. Emma would call him back when she had a chance.

Was it still too early to call the Nelsons? Elias was a businessman. Surely he'd be up by now on a weekday. Matthias keyed in the number.

A woman answered, her voice soft and sleepy. "Hello?"

"Mrs. Nelson?"

"Yes. Who is this?"

"Detective Matthias Honeywell, Erie City Police," he said and added quickly, "There's no emergency. I didn't mean to alarm you."

The sleep cleared from her voice. "How can I help you, detective?"

"I'm investigating a case that may have ties to your daughter's death—"

She cut him off. "You mean that prick husband of hers has killed someone else?"

The words and the venom stunned Matthias into momentary silence. "You believe he's responsible for Havana's death?"

"You're damned right I do." Mrs. Nelson breathed a growling sigh into the phone. "Forgive my profanity. I've been so frustrated these last couple of years. I despised the man from the moment Havana first brought him home. But no one else could see in him what I did."

"Which was?"

"He's evil. Soulless. I saw it in his eyes. But my daughter was smitten. And my husband thought he was the second coming. I was just being foolish according to Elias. No man would ever be good enough for my girl. Isn't that usually what the father says?

But, oh no. Not my husband. All he saw was Russell's business savvy. He supported their marriage every step of the way."

"Disliking a man and believing him guilty of murder is still a big leap," Matthias said. "Is there something in particular that made you suspect Carlisle?"

"Lots of things. He never grieved for my daughter. He started dating within a month of her funeral. Then again, I'd put money on him having cheated on her from day one. That ski trip to Colorado? It was all his idea. Havana didn't want to go. She'd only skied a few times and wasn't good at it. He wouldn't take no for an answer."

"She wasn't a strong skier?"

"No. And do you know what slope they were on when she died? The most challenging one at the resort."

"Did you tell that to the Colorado investigators?"

"Of course I did. But a mother's intuition doesn't count for anything where the legal system is concerned. To be fair, the lead detective listened and really wanted to make a case against Russell. Unfortunately, he couldn't find any solid evidence. And once the coroner ruled it an accident, the case was considered closed. I wouldn't be one bit surprised if Russell made a substantial contribution to the coroner's retirement fund, if you know what I mean."

Matthias scrawled notes to look into Mrs. Nelson's accusations.

"You didn't answer my question. Has Russell killed another woman?"

"That's what I'm trying to determine."

"He has," she said firmly. "I knew it was only a matter of time. Please, detective, don't let him get away with it again."

Matthias knew better than make promises he couldn't keep. "I'm going to do my best, ma'am."

Once the call ended, he went over his notes, clarifying a few points where he'd been writing so fast he couldn't read his own scribbles. Before he could move on to the next person on his list, his phone rang. Emma's name filled the screen.

"Good morning," he answered. "How's Nell?"

"She miscarried this morning."

He closed his eyes. "Oh, God. I'm so sorry."

"That's not why I'm calling." She sounded out of breath. "I need you to come down to Sixteenth Street. The encampment."

His eyes flew open. "Are you okay?"

"I'm fine. I'm with Jacob. He's agreed to talk to you, and you need to hear what he has to say."

"I'll be right there."

"Matthias?"

"Yeah?"

"Bring coffee. Lots of it."

Matthias didn't tell Cassie where he was going. She asked, but all he said was he needed to follow up on something. She was so busy watching security footage, she didn't press the issue.

He made a stop at a nearby convenience store and bought eight large coffees. It took him two trips to get them all out to his car, but Emma had said "lots."

Matthias parked on the street across from the encampment. Emma, Eric, and the Scrawny Guy AKA Jacob stood on the sidewalk next to the tents. He could make out someone else sitting inside one of the shelters with the canvas drawn back. They all looked at him when he stepped out of the car with two of the coffees. "I could use a hand here," he called.

Emma and Eric broke away and jogged toward him. Matthias expected Jacob to take off in the opposite direction yet again, but he stayed where he was.

Matthias handed the two cups to Eric, who immediately returned to the tents. Matthias reached in for two more but held onto them when Emma held out her hands. He fixed her with a hard gaze. "Are you okay?"

A parade of emotions marched across her face before she replied. "No. But I'm not in any danger." She took the cups.

"How many of these do we need?"

"How many did you bring?"

"Eight."

She tipped her head toward the tents. "Bring 'em all. These folks aren't used to an abundance of anything."

Hugging the last four cups, he kicked the car door shut and crossed the street.

Jacob eyed Matthias with the same trepidation as he had over by Pauly's Polynesian Pub. Matthias needed to ask him about that too, but first things first.

A man and a woman appeared from within the makeshift shelter—the one who'd been sitting there when Matthias arrived and one other who was clearly the oldest of the trio. Emma introduced him as Pops and the woman as Blue.

She gestured to the three of them. "They've been looking after Nell since she ran away from Zeke."

Another question, Matthias needed to ask. Why had Nell left Zeke?

"When I told Jacob I was Nell's sister and what happened last night, he agreed to talk to me." She pointed to Matthias. "And to you." She gave him a look that was easily translated. *Don't scare him off.*

He nodded to the man. "Thanks. I appreciate that."

Emma looked at Jacob. "Tell him what you told me."

He lowered his head. "I adore Nell. We all do. She's a sweet kid who's had a rough time of it. Makes me sick to hear she lost the baby. In spite of the bastard who got her pregnant, she really wanted that child."

Emma put a hand on Jacob's sleeve. "Tell him about that night."

His face tensed at the memory. "That woman—Gillian—she came past here all the time. She worked at that fancy-ass restaurant up at the end of the street."

Matthias gave him a kind smile. "I understand she'd bring you leftover food at the end of her shift."

Jacob blew a disgusted breath. "If you could call it that. She'd dump a box of bread that was hard as a rock on the sidewalk." He indicated the pavement at his feet. "Or half-eaten meals that should've gone in the trash. Hell, I think some of it *was* trash. Not fit for a dog. Yet she thought she was doing us a big favor."

Matthias thought of his conversation with Didi Reed. *"She always took leftovers from the restaurant and gave them to the homeless who lived on the street. Said they loved her for it and would never hurt her."*

"I was told," he said, "that you all loved her for bringing food to you."

Jacob made that noise again. "We had no reason to love her. The woman was a bitch. But even a bitch doesn't deserve to die like that."

"You saw her get killed?"

"I did. She walked past here that night. Pulled open the tent flap and threw a couple of takeout boxes inside. Then she laughed."

"Sounded like a witch." Blue cackled while waving her fingers. "I'll get you, my pretty," she said in an exceptional impersonation of the character from the old Judy Garland movie.

Pops snickered.

Jacob narrowed his eyes. "That's enough. The woman is dead. Have some respect." He brought his gaze back to Matthias. "I watched her keep walking after that."

Matthias interrupted. "Was she with a man? Well dressed. Slicked-back hair?"

"Nope. She was alone. At least until she got up there." Jacob pointed toward the opening between the warehouses.

"Did she meet someone?"

"In a manner of speaking." Jacob paused to take a long sip of coffee and wipe his mouth with the back of his hand. "I'd seen this person hanging around for a couple of days. Seemed odd to me. She never bothered us, but I could swear she was following that Gillian woman."

"Wait." Matthias held up a hand. "*She* was following Gillian?"

"Yep."

"A woman?"

"Yep."

Matthias shot a glance at Emma, hating what he had to ask next. "Nell?"

"Oh, hell, no. Nell was inside with us, sick as a dog. Morning sickness doesn't happen only in the morning, you know."

He couldn't read Emma's expression. Not quite vindication for having her sister alibied. But if a woman killed Gillian Watson, that also cleared Russ Carlisle. Matthias brought his focus back to Jacob. "Tell me exactly what happened."

Jacob took another sip of coffee. "Like I said, I watched her— Gillian—walk toward downtown. But then this other woman stepped out of the canyon. That's what we call that walkway you chased me down yesterday."

Matthias winced.

"She startled Gillian, but Gillian didn't seem scared of her. I couldn't make out what was said but it sounded like Gillian was sassing her. The other woman sounded pissed. Really pissed. Gillian waved her arms and tried to keep going, but the other woman blocked her. Shoved her hard. Then they both started tussling. Pushing. Shoving. Pulling hair. You know. Cat fight. They disappeared into the canyon. I ran down there, thinking I'd better try to break it up before someone got hurt."

Matthias noticed Jacob's hand, the one holding the coffee, was trembling.

"By the time I got to the corner, they were by the steps. They were still yelling. All I could make out was the other woman saying something like 'you can't bully me anymore.' And then she pushed Gillian. Gillian tripped and fell down the steps. I heard her scream but then nothing. I ducked back before the other woman could see me, but I got a good look at her when she came back out."

"Did you recognize her?"

"Just from watching her follow Gillian those couple of days."

"Would you know her if you saw her again?"

Jacob nodded. "I did see her again."

"When? Where?"

"At Pauly's place. She was wearing a wig, but I know it was her. She was with that guy who got shot."

"I'll drive you back to Sara's so you'll have your car." Matthias buckled his seatbelt. Emma had already done the same from the passenger seat. Eric sat directly behind her.

"Just take us back to the hospital. I need to check in on Nell," Emma said.

Matthias stared straight ahead, toward the intersection at the Blue Pike. His mind raced through all he'd learned within the last thirty minutes and all he needed to learn. Still, he couldn't simply leave Emma without transportation. It was bad enough she'd walked all the way here through some sketchy parts of the city, but it was at least a five-mile hike from the hospital to the campground. "Fine. But we're making one stop along the way."

"That was nice of you, back there," Eric said once Matthias had turned the Impala around and headed to State Street. "Giving Jacob, Blue, and Pops money. Is it like in the TV shows? You carry a wad of cash designated to pay off informants?"

"Something like that." Matthias wasn't going to tell them he'd emptied his wallet of his own spending money so the people who'd taken care of Nell could have a few hot meals.

"I take it back," Eric said. "You aren't a brute after all."

Matthias choked. "Thanks. I think."

"I'm serious. I apologize for every bad thing I've said about you."

Emma shifted in her seat to look back at Eric. "If you're about to ask him out on a date, I'm pretty sure he's straight."

"It never hurts to ask," Eric said.

Emma laughed—a light, bubbly sound Matthias had only heard a couple of times.

"Sorry, dude. Emma's right."

"Darn." In the rearview, Matthias saw Eric feign an exaggerated huff as he crossed his arms. Then he met Matthias's gaze in the mirror, grinned, and gave a nod. Matthias didn't know him well but interpreted the expression as approval.

No one spoke during the drive north on State. They passed the police department, but instead of continuing through Perry Square Park toward the hospital, Matthias turned left onto South Park Row. He noticed Emma turn her head to look at him, but she didn't ask. And he didn't say anything until he eased up behind his red Jeep in one of the diagonal parking spaces. He shifted the Impala out of gear, tugged a key from his pocket, and held it out to her.

"What's this?" she asked.

"Take my Jeep."

"I can't."

"Yes, you can. I don't want to worry about you..." Matthias shot a glance at Eric. "Both of you...traipsing around the city on foot. This way, you can head straight to the hospital instead of me taking you all the way out to the campground and you driving all the way back here." He held her gaze and lowered his voice. "It'll give me an excuse to see you later."

Her cheeks flushed. "You don't need an excuse."

He wanted more than anything to lean over and kiss her, but he was aware of Eric watching from the rear seat.

Emma reached over and took the key, her fingers brushing his, lingering for just a moment. Then she turned away and stepped from the car along with Eric. She spun back and bent down before closing the door. "Thank you."

———

Matthias charged up the stairwell and through the break room to be greeted by an equally excited and agitated Cassie standing at her desk. "About time you got back. I found something interesting on the hotel's security footage."

"I learned something interesting too."

Frazier stepped from his cubicle while Cassie crossed her arms expectantly.

Matthias told them about Jacob's tale of seeing Gillian pushed down the steps to her death and about the killer *not* being Russ Carlisle.

Cassie's eyes grew brighter as Matthias spoke. "Did you get a description on the woman?"

"Not a good one. Jacob may be observant but he's not great on details. All he could say was she was average height, average build, brown hair. But I haven't told you the best part. Jacob swears he saw this same woman, in a blonde wig, leaving Pauly's Polynesian Pub with Tom Jenkins the night he was shot."

Frazier swore. "That matches the description we have."

"Yeah."

Cassie wore a Cheshire Cat smile and beckoned Matthias and Frazier with the wag of a finger. "Check this out." She returned to her chair and tapped her keyboard as they gathered behind her. She paused the video on an image of a housekeeping cart and three women standing in a hallway lined with guest rooms before zooming in.

Matthias leaned closer. Gillian Watson and Didi Reed were clearly identifiable. Both had hotel towels tucked under an arm. The third woman had her back to the camera but was obviously wearing a housekeeper's uniform.

Cassie tapped a key and the silent video played. The housekeeper wheeled away from the other two, her face now visible.

Katie. Emma's Beige Katie.

Gillian and Didi caught her by the arm, spun her around. While there was no sound and Matthias couldn't read lips, he could read expressions. These two were having a grand time taunting Katie, poking at her, gesturing at her attire, and laughing. Every time Katie tried to get away, they grabbed her and held her there, forcing her to be the source of their amusement.

Matthias watched, his anger growing. He thought of Didi telling him how the homeless loved Gillian and how Jacob had refuted the claim. Matthias recalled his conversation with Tiffany, the hostess at the Blue Pike. *"All sweetness and smiles to the men, but to us women? She acted like she was better than us."*

From what Matthias had learned from Jacob, Gillian was only sweet to *rich* men.

Cassie pointed to the computer monitor, which she'd again paused. "You recognize her, don't you?"

"Katie." Something else about the footage puzzled Matthias. "What's with the towels?"

"Watch this." Cassie reversed the footage and hit play. Gillian and Didi sashayed into the frame and stopped at the cart, where they began rummaging through it, helping themselves to several clean towels. Then Katie stepped from the guest room she'd been in and confronted the pair. "That's how it all started."

"We need to talk to her."

"I called over to the Royal Palace the minute I saw this. According to them, Katie left work early yesterday. In fact, she left right after we spoke to her."

"What about today?"

"She has today off."

Matthias looked at Frazier. "Didn't you say both Gillian Watson and Tom Jenkins went to Erie High School?"

Frazier's eyes widened and he backtracked to his desk. "What's Katie's last name?"

Matthias yanked out his notebook and skimmed to the page from yesterday, when he'd spoken with the hotel's skinny desk clerk. "Tucker."

While Frazier hunkered over his computer, Cassie gazed up at Matthias, her dark eyes gleaming. "I want to have another chat with Didi Reed."

Chapter Thirty-Six

When Emma and Eric returned to the hospital, Nell had been moved to another room. They tracked her down and found her sitting up in bed, a tray of untouched food in front of her. At least she wasn't curled into the fetal position any longer.

"Hi," Emma said softly as they approached. "You look better."

Nell didn't lift her gaze but simply held a spoon in a loose grip, moving mashed potatoes around on the plate.

Eric rounded to the opposite side of the bed from Emma. "Hey, Nellie. That looks truly disgusting."

Actually, Emma thought, it looked rather good for hospital food.

"I'll run out and smuggle something in for you," he said. "What do you feel like? Tacos? How about a big cheeseburger?"

"I'm not hungry."

He crossed his arms. "To be honest, I'm not surprised. You ate like a pig all day yesterday."

Nell looked at him, daggers in her eyes. "I was eating for two yesterday."

Eric reacted as if he'd been slugged. He took a step back and turned away, one hand going to his face.

Emma wanted to chide Nell. There was no reason to be cruel to Eric. Except Emma couldn't fathom the pain Nell was feeling. Emma crossed to Eric and placed a hand on his back. He glanced at her with tear-filled eyes but dismissed her concern with a quick wave. Nell's words may have stung, but he understood.

Emma gave him an encouraging smile before returning to her sister's side. "We're going to get through this. Together. Eric and I will be with you every step of the way. We're not going to let you handle this alone. We'll find a good therapist for you, if you want."

Nell laid the spoon down but kept her fingers resting on it. "I wanted this baby more than anything I've ever wanted in the world. After losing Mom and Dad and everything else that's gone to hell, my baby was the one bright spot of hope in my life."

Emma searched for words, but everything that came to mind sounded like a cheesy greeting card. "I'm so sorry."

Eric returned, his eyes clear. "I am, too. And yes, what Emma said. I'm right here. No matter what."

Nell stared at her plate. "Have they arrested Russ yet?"

Emma exchanged a worried glance with Eric. "No. Not yet." She couldn't tell her sister that there wouldn't be any charges against Russ. Not for Gillian's murder at least.

"I can't do this," Nell said, her voice a whimper. "Russ will kill me the minute he gets a chance." She lifted her head and met Emma's gaze for the first time since yesterday. "Unless...can we go home. Please? Back to the farm. I know the houses are gone, but hell, I've slept in a tent on concrete. I can sleep on the grass, no problem."

"Okay." Emma nodded, thinking. "We talked about this before. I'll buy a mobile home. Maybe a double-wide. We can put it near the farmhouse's foundation. The electric meter and well are right there. It'll do until we decide if we want to rebuild." She looked at Eric, surprised to see him frowning. Ignoring his scowl, she said,

"Eric will be there, too. We'll help you get through this. No matter what it takes."

Nell didn't smile, didn't appear excited or eager about Emma's proposal. But at least she didn't appear despondent.

Emma pointed at the tray. "First things first, though. You need to eat. Either that or, like Eric said, he can bring something in for you."

Nell shook her head and pushed the tray away. "I'm not hungry. What I need is sleep." She turned from them, pushed the button to lower the head of the bed, and curled up on her side.

"Okay. You get some rest." Emma looked at the pair of guest chairs placed on either side of the window. One for her, one for Eric

He took her by the wrist and tipped his head toward the door. "We'll be right back," he told Nell, who didn't respond.

In the hallway, he drew Emma well away from the door, away from Nell's ears.

"What are you doing?" Emma demanded.

"That's exactly what I want to ask you. You're going to move back home to take care of Nell?"

"Yes, of course."

He shook his head. "I agree home is where Nell needs to be. My place is huge. She can have my spare room. I'll make sure she gets counselling."

"I appreciate that, but she's my sister."

Eric's chin came up. "What about Matthias?"

The question, the mention of Matthias, brought a knot to Emma's throat. She'd been intentionally blocking him from her mind as she spelled out her plan to Nell. "What about him?"

"Look, Em, I know I was hard on you at first where he's concerned, but I was wrong. I think he could be really good for you. I'm not blind. I can see how much he cares about you. And I know you care about him too."

She lowered her gaze to her feet, unable to look into Eric's eyes. She thought of another pair of eyes. Those stunning blue ones. She thought of how Matthias looked at her less than an hour ago when he dropped them off, loaning her his Jeep. Only Eric's presence in the back seat had kept her from climbing over the Impala's center console and into Matthias's arms. "The timing's not right. I can't get into another relationship. Not now."

"Sometimes we don't get to pick the right time."

Emma steeled her nerves and lifted her gaze. "Nell needs me. I won't choose a man over my own sister ever again."

Eric opened his mouth to argue. Closed it. Opened it again. And gave up, pressing his lips into a thin line of surrender.

Emma took Eric's hands in hers. "Nell needs both of us. You and me. As soon as she's well enough, we'll take her home. No arguments. Okay?"

He clearly wanted to argue but couldn't. "Okay."

Chapter Thirty-Seven

"Bingo," Frazier called out from his cubby.

Matthias stepped from his. Cassie hung up her phone and joined him next to Frazier's desk. "What'd you find?" she asked.

"Kathryn Tucker, aka, Katie, graduated from Erie High School the same year as Gillian Watson and Didi Reed," Frazier said. "Thomas Jenkins and Olivia Petrovich were a year ahead of them."

"What about Ezekial Dyson?" Matthias dug out his notebook and thumbed back through the pages.

Frazier squinted at his monitor as he typed. "Nope."

Matthias found the page where he'd jotted names from the wedding. "Check for Bryce Graham." He spelled it out. "And Sterling Vincent."

Seconds rolled into minutes. *God, grant me patience,* Matthias thought. *And hurry.*

"Okay, Sterling Vincent was also in Gillian's graduating class." Frazier tapped a few more keys. "And I found Dyson. He and Bryce Graham were classmates at Iroquois High School."

That made sense.

"I found Katie's yearbook photo," Frazier said and pointed at his monitor.

Matthias and Cassie slipped in behind him, looking over his shoulder.

Kathryn Tucker's seventeen-year-old self was almost unrecognizable from the young woman Matthias had spoken to. While Katie was average, the kind of person who would disappear in a crowd, high-school Kathryn was the kind of girl who would've attracted all the wrong kind of attention. Her face was soft and very round with rolls down her neck. Her shoulders were also round. Even though the photo was a simple headshot, her obesity was evident.

Cassie pointed at the monitor. "Print that out. And find a current picture of her, either from her employment records at the Royal Palace or from the DMV. Print it, too."

Frazier's fingers flew over the keyboard. "On it."

Cassie faced Matthias who wondered what she was up to. "I just got off the phone with Didi Reed."

He feigned shock. "She answered?"

"Apparently, she only shuts off her phone when she's on vacation. I wish I could do the same. Anyway, she's agreed to meet with us."

"Where?"

"She suggested the Watsons' house, but I don't want Gillian's mother and sister to be in on this line of questioning." Cassie opened the bottom drawer of her desk and removed her purse. "It's a nice day out. I suggested we meet at Perry Park by the fountain. She said she's on her way."

Within a few minutes, Frazier had the photos printed out and handed them to Matthias. A few minutes more and Cassie and Matthias descended the stairs, stepped outside, and crossed the street to the park. Being a weekday morning and too early for alfresco diners, only a few tourists and pedestrians strolled the walkways, pausing to read the inscriptions on the monuments.

Matthias liked Cassie's decision to meet near the fountain. In addition to being easily located, the hiss of the spray kept words from carrying. Any conversation they had with Didi would be enveloped in a haven of privacy.

Cassie selected one of the black benches, while Matthias stood, keeping watch. About five minutes passed before he spotted Didi crossing the park. "Here she comes," he said.

She spotted him and picked up her pace. "Hello, detectives." She shook hands with both of them before taking a seat next to Cassie. "I assume you have news about the case."

"We've uncovered some information and hoped you could help us make sense of it," Cassie said with her easy smile.

Didi opened both palms. "Whatever I can do to help."

Cassie withdrew her notebook from her purse signaling that Matthias was to watch Didi's reactions. "When we spoke before, you mentioned the last time you saw Gillian was at a wedding reception at the Royal Palace."

"That's right. She was with that rat bastard Russ Carlisle. Have you found any evidence that he killed her?"

"We're still investigating. We've been going through CCTV footage from the hotel, trying to see if there was any kind of incident between Russ and Gillian that could've triggered aggression."

Didi nodded in approval.

"We came across another incident though and hoped you could explain it."

"Sure. If I can."

"There was a confrontation in one of the guest hallways involving you and Gillian and one of the housekeepers."

Matthias expected Didi to deny everything. Maybe even jump up and storm off.

Instead, she laughed and waved a dismissive hand. "Oh, that was just Plain Jane."

"Excuse me?" Matthias said, trying and failing to keep the growl from his voice.

"Well, that's what we called her in high school. Her real name is Katie...something. We hadn't seen her since graduation and were shocked. She lost like a whole person in weight."

"And you were congratulating her?" Cassie asked.

Matthias picked up on his partner's sarcasm, but Didi didn't. She laughed again. "Right," she said with her own palpable sarcasm. "Honestly, we didn't recognize her at first. Gillian and I needed clean towels and were taking some from a cart in the hallway when this maid came out and started yelling at us." Didi acted appalled. "Over towels for crying out loud. But then Gillian recognized her. Plain Jane, all grown up. And she really *made* something of herself. Get it? Maid?" Didi threw her head back, chuckling. When they didn't join in Didi's jocularity, she fell silent and appeared miffed, probably thinking they had no sense of humor.

"I gather you and Gillian found Katie to be amusing in high school, too."

Didi huffed. "She made it so easy. At least we only called her Plain Jane instead of Tubby like some of the other kids. She was the perfect target." Didi snickered. "I remember one of the big school dances our junior year. One of the seniors...the football team's quarterback...asked her to be his date. She thought he was serious. Can you imagine? So they show up at this dance, him all decked out in a suit and tie. Plain Jane all dolled up in some kind of red dress. I still don't know where she'd have bought it. The thing looked like a crimson tent. Everyone howled, it was so funny. Tommy and his football buddies got the biggest laugh out of it. I mean, she really thought he would want to be seen with her?" Didi shook her head. "Too funny."

"Tom Jenkins?" Matthias asked, making no effort to hide his contempt.

"Yeah." Didi froze, her mouth open. "Wait. Did I hear he died recently?"

Cassie's jaw was so tight, Matthias expected to hear her teeth crack when she replied. "Yes, he did. He was shot to death a week ago."

Didi shook her clueless head. "How tragic."

"I've heard of mean girls before, but that one beats all," Cassie said as she and Matthias climbed the stairs to the detective division.

He grunted. "Yeah. And Tom Jenkins makes me ashamed to have been a high-school quarterback."

Cassie stopped two steps from the top and turned to look at him. "I didn't know you were a high-school jock."

"It was a very long time ago." He gestured for her to keep going.

She did. "I'll bet you never humiliated some poor girl in front of the whole class."

"No. But teenage boys are notoriously stupid."

"Makes me dread the thought of Alissa growing up and having to deal with them," Cassie said, referring to her eight-year-old granddaughter.

"You and your daughter will make sure she can kick the ass of any teenage boy or mean girl who messes with her."

Frazier must've been listening for their return. He stood in the doorway between the break room and Major Crimes, looking as eager as a kid on Christmas morning. "What did you learn?"

Cassie caught him by the shoulders, turned him around, and marched him into the office. "Maybe we should ask what did *you* learn?"

"You first."

Matthias took a seat at his desk while Cassie told Frazier about their conversation with Didi and about her callous stories of Katie Tucker's tortured life as a teen. "At some point, she lost so much weight as to be unrecognizable to her tormentors."

Frazier listened intently, but still appeared ready to burst.

"Okay." Cassie extended an arm toward him. "Your turn."

He smiled and hurled himself into his desk chair, fingers on his keyboard. "After graduating high school, Kathryn Tucker went to Penn State where she studied..." Frazier lifted his gaze to glance from Cassie to Matthias and back. "Get this. Criminal justice." Continuing to read from his screen, Frazier said, "She earned her degree but wasn't an outstanding student. She then moved to Pittsburgh and attended their police academy but washed out. From what I've been able to tell so far, she lacked the ability to command and didn't do especially well at following orders, either. She did, however, have above-average scores on the shooting range. After she left the academy, there's a record of her purchasing a Ruger .357 and acquiring a carry permit. She's been a member of several gun clubs over the years."

Matthias looked at Cassie. "Three fifty-seven. Same as what killed Tom Jenkins."

She nodded and asked Frazier, "Do you know what brought her back to Erie?"

"I do. Her father passed away. Her mother never worked outside the home, so it appears Katie moved back in with Mom about the same time Katie took the job at the Royal Palace."

Cassie met Matthias's gaze. "What do you say we pay a visit to Katie Tucker?" he said.

"Yeah. And I think we take a search warrant for that Ruger with us."

Chapter Thirty-Eight

E mma sat in one of the visitors' chairs in Nell's room, attempting and failing to read the paperback she'd picked up in the gift shop. Nell was either asleep or pretending to be. Her lunch remained untouched on the tray.

Eric had a Zoom meeting for work. He'd claimed he didn't need to participate, but Emma could tell otherwise. She tried to persuade him to take the Jeep, but he refused. "I don't want to be responsible for something happening to your cop's car." He waved his phone. "I'll order an Uber." On his way out he added, "I'll bring my laptop back with me. That way I can work from here."

"You don't need to babysit us," Emma told him. "Stay at the hotel for a while. Take a nap."

He merely snorted a laugh and strode away.

"Bring back some Chinese takeout with you," she'd called after him. He'd waved in response.

After re-reading the same page for the fifth time without any of the words sinking in, Emma stretched out, leaned her head back against the wall, and closed her eyes, knowing she was too wired to sleep.

But soft footsteps in the room jarred her awake. Fuzzy-brained from the interrupted slumber, Emma sat up. The paperback slid from her lap to the floor with a soft thud.

Katie stood halfway between the door and the foot of Nell's bed and jumped at the sound. She spun toward Emma, her hand pressed to her chest. "I'm so sorry I woke you," she said, her voice little more than a whisper. After a glance at Nell's unmoving form beneath the white blankets, she added, "At least I don't seem to have disturbed her."

"Katie?" Emma rubbed her eyes. "What are you doing here?"

Katie stuffed her hands in the pockets of her khaki slacks and took two steps toward Emma. "You said your sister was in the hospital. I called to check on her, but they wouldn't tell me anything because I'm not family. I was downtown so I thought I'd stop by. How's she doing?"

Emma rose quietly, collected her phone from the chair's arm, and touched her finger to her lips. Nell needed her sleep. "Let's go out to the waiting room."

Katie nodded and followed, but Emma noticed she took a long look back at the bed before stepping into the hallway.

Two older adults and two small children had set up camp in one corner of the waiting room. Grandparents watching the grandkids, Emma thought and fleetingly wondered if the mom was visiting the dad or vice versa.

Katie slid into a chair well away from the other family. "How's your sister doing?" she asked again.

Emma took a seat kitty-corner to her. "Not well, I'm afraid. She lost the baby."

Katie's eyes widened in horror. "Oh, my God, how terrible. You've been through so much. So has she. And now this."

Emma looked down at the phone in her hands. "Yeah. She's having a hard time with it."

"You mentioned the baby's father was abusive?"

The mention of Russ stirred a flood of memories from last

night. She rubbed the hand she'd used to slap his smug face. "Yes."

"Do you still believe he's the man who killed that other woman?"

Emma almost told her no, that Jacob had identified a woman instead, but Matthias's voice whispered in her brain. It was an ongoing police investigation. She and Eric had been privy to information Matthias probably wouldn't want made public. At least, not by her. She lowered her eyes. "Yes. I do."

"Do the police still suspect Nell?"

"I don't know. I just hope they catch the real killer soon."

Katie sighed. "I wish I could help."

Emma shook her head. "You've done all you can. I appreciate that you put your job on the line for me and Nell."

When Katie grew quiet, Emma lifted her head to find Katie gazing out the windows, her expression pensive. "You know," Katie said, "you've been nicer to me than most of the people in my life."

The plaintive statement surprised Emma. She searched for a proper response. *I'm sorry* didn't seem to be it.

Katie's gaze shifted from the windows to Emma. "I mean it. I genuinely like you, Emma. And I appreciate how much you care for your sister. I wish I had a sister like you."

"Do you have any siblings?"

"No. It's just me and my mother. And the only reason she's ever cared about me is because of what I could do for her." A razor-sharp edge of bitterness crept into her voice.

This time, Emma did say, "I'm so sorry."

Katie blinked and smiled. "You're kind. Most people aren't." Before Emma could come up with a reply, Katie said, "Nell's boyfriend...the father of her baby...What all do you know about him?" The sudden shift in topic came with a definite shift in tone. Not melancholy, not bitter, but dark.

Very dark. Emma and Nell's mom used to tell them to trust

their intuition. To listen to the little voice in their heads warning of danger. The voice was whispering in the dark recesses of Emma's brain, but she couldn't make sense of it. "Not a lot really," she said. "Nell doesn't like to talk about him."

"But he bullied her, right?" That tone again. Low and…deadly.

Emma shifted uneasily, the whispers growing louder. She shook her head to clear it.

"He doesn't bully her?" Katie sounded shocked.

"No, he does. Did. But she's not with him anymore. I'm going to take care of her from now on."

"That's good." Katie's voice returned to normal. "That's why I like you, Emma. You care for your sister and want to protect her."

Emma relaxed, certain she was merely jumpy and imagining things.

Katie's gaze shifted toward the hallway and Nell's room. Her expression and her voice once more grew menacing. "Men like your sister's boyfriend eventually get what's coming to them."

Emma was definitely not imagining things. Jacob's words slammed into her. A woman pushing Gillian to her death after saying *"you can't bully me anymore."* Then he saw the same woman with another murder victim. Now, Katie was voicing concern about Nell being bullied.

The whispered words fell silent, replaced by an icy chill. Emma needed to get a message to Matthias.

She flinched, acting—she hoped—as if her phone had vibrated. She looked at the blank screen, carefully concealed from Katie. "Oh, that's my friend, Eric. I sent him for Chinese takeout, and he can't decide what to order for Nell."

Katie's dark expression brightened. "Chinese takeout sounds great."

Emma swallowed. "I can tell him to bring something for you, if you like."

"That's so sweet. But no thanks. I have dinner plans."

Relieved, Emma opened her contacts, selected Matthias's name, and tapped a message.

With Beige Katie at the hospital. Any chance she could be the woman Jacob saw?

Emma prayed he would text back telling her she was wrong. She really wanted to be wrong.

Katie gathered her purse. "I should be going. I just wanted to let you and Nell know that everything is going to work out. I have a strong feeling that man who hurt her won't be a problem much longer." She stood.

Emma came to her feet. She needed to keep Katie here long enough for Matthias to respond. "Stick around a while. I haven't had anyone to talk to about this. It's nice having someone to chat with."

Katie moved toward the door. "I wish I could, but I have some things to take care of." She gave Emma an odd, enigmatic smile. "I have a date."

"Oh." Emma winced at the surprise in her voice. "That's nice. Who's the lucky guy?"

But she realized she already knew.

Katie crossed to the elevators with Emma trailing. "I don't know about lucky," Katie said. "He's someone I met recently. Very handsome. Very rich."

Russ Carlisle.

The elevator dinged, signaling the car's arrival. In that same moment, Emma spotted Nell, wrapped in her hospital gown, round the corner, headed for the waiting room. Until she saw Emma and veered in her direction.

Katie looked toward her, smiling. "Here comes your sister."

Nell spotted Katie and hesitated. She looked puzzled. Pointing at Katie, she asked, "Where have I seen you before?"

The elevator doors opened.

"I remember now." Nell strode toward them. "You were hanging out down on Sixteenth Street." Realization dawned in her eyes. "You were following Gillian."

So much for Emma being wrong. Frantic, she stepped in front of her sister, arms extended to stop her.

Nell continued forward until Emma caught her by the shoulders. "Em, stop her. She might've seen Russ kill Gillian," Nell said.

Emma shushed her with a hiss. "She didn't see Russ kill Gillian. *She* killed Gillian," she whispered. But not softly enough.

Behind her, Emma heard a gasp. She wheeled to see a wild-eyed Katie inside the elevator car, clutching her purse as the doors whooshed shut.

Chapter Thirty-Nine

Matthias and Cassie arrived at the Tucker house accompanied by five, marked police units. Two more were in position on the next street should Katie make a run for it. Backed by enough firepower to take out a small militia, Cassie pounded on the front door. "Kathryn Tucker, this is the Erie Police. Come outside with your hands up."

His sidearm in hand, Matthias waited. They all waited. There was no sound from inside for several long moments before a frail voice called out, "Don't shoot!"

The mother, he thought, but no one let their guard down. The deadbolt turned with a *snick*. Another lock clunked, and the door creaked open. A stocky woman in a faded housedress stood there, clearly puzzled. Her pale eyes grew wide as she took in the police presence. "Good heavens, what's going on?"

"Step outside please," Cassie said and then asked, "Is your daughter home?"

The woman shuffled over the threshold. "No, my daughter isn't home. What's this about?"

Cassie unfolded the search warrant and handed it to Mrs. Tucker as Matthias holstered his weapon. He and several of the officers streamed into the house. He could hear his partner explaining the legal document to Katie's mother as he moved from the entryway to a room on the right. The living-room's carpet and furniture appeared as faded as the woman's house dress. A sofa and one matching upholstered chair faced a moderate-sized television. A pair of side tables were stacked with magazines. Matthias put on gloves and thumbed through those on the first table. He'd noticed the same titles on the racks at the grocery store check-out lines. He moved to the second table. The top few magazines were more of the same, but then he came to a half-dozen covers featuring firearms and ammo. The type put out by gun and paramilitary organizations.

"Holy crap," Cassie said from behind his shoulder. He turned to see her looking at the publications.

He handed an issue to her. "Katie kept up with her favorite subject from the academy."

"Her mother said she owns a handgun but doesn't know where she keeps it or what kind it is."

"Do you believe her?"

"The mom?" Cassie shot a glance at the open door where an officer was standing with Mrs. Tucker. "Yeah. I get the impression she doesn't know much about her daughter and doesn't want to know."

"Nice," he said with a healthy dose of sarcasm.

They made their way through the first floor, finding nothing unusual beyond the magazines. A two-piece powder room behind a closed door showed a layer of dust. Matthias judged the two women rarely hosted company who might use the guest bath.

From upstairs, an officer called down, "Detectives, you might want to see this."

Matthias led the way up the steps to a second story which held two bedrooms and a full bath. The uniformed officer stood inside the room on the left, holding an open box. The gun case was fitted with foam, cut to support a revolver, which was missing. A box of ammo was stuffed in a second cut-out. Matthias removed it and lifted the lid to find the box half empty. "Three fifty-seven," he said. Matthias replaced the box into the foam. "Bag it and tag it," he told the uniform.

Two officers were going through the dresser drawers and closet shelves in the second bedroom. Cassie stayed with the officer in the first one. Matthias moved to the bathroom at the end of the hallway.

With a green cast-iron tub and pink tile, it hadn't been updated in over fifty years, if he was any judge. But there was no soap scum, no water spots anywhere. Someone was a good housekeeper. The mom? More likely Katie, who cleaned for a living.

He reached up and opened the mirrored medicine cabinet door. The bottom two shelves contained toothbrushes and a tube of paste as well as a few over-the-counter products. The top shelf held an assortment of prescription bottles. One at a time, he took them down and studied the labels. All had been dispensed to Betsy Ann Tucker, Katie's mother. Matthias was no pharmacist but could tell they were mainly meds for high blood pressure and high cholesterol. One was for a drug he'd seen advertised on television for insomnia.

He started to put that bottle back, but something didn't quite feel right. Squinting at the small print, he realized the script for thirty tablets had been refilled two days ago. He uncapped the bottle, dumped the contents into his hand, and counted. Eight pills remained.

Matthias tromped down the stairs and out the front door to the porch where Mrs. Tucker had taken a seat on an ancient glider. A uniformed officer stood nearby.

Matthias approached Katie's mother and held up the prescription bottle. "Mrs. Tucker, are these yours?"

She dug a pair of readers from the pocket of her house dress, settled them on her nose, and reached for the bottle. Matthias didn't release it but held it closer so she could read the label. "Yep, those are my sleepy pills."

He was aware Cassie had joined them on the porch. "This says it was refilled on Tuesday," he said, pointing at the date.

"Okay." The woman looked at him over her glasses.

"Is that right?"

She made an uncertain face and shrugged. "I guess so. Katie takes care of my meds."

"How many have you taken?"

Mrs. Tucker frowned in thought. "Oh, I don't know. I took one last evening. Not sure about the night before."

"But you don't take any more than one a night?"

"Oh, no. My doctor told me. No more than one. And never with alcohol. Not that I'm a drinker. That was my late husband's bad habit. Not mine."

Cassie joined them on the porch, and Matthias angled the bottle toward her. He removed the lid to show her the contents. She shot a look at him before turning to Mrs. Tucker. "Do you have any idea when Katie will be home?"

"Nope." She made a sour face. "That girl. Used to be home every evening after work. I could count on her. Lately, she's been out 'til all hours. I wouldn't mind if she was with a nice gentleman, but I don't think that's the case."

"Why don't you think she's with a nice guy?" Cassie asked gently.

"What would she need that wig for if she was out with a gentleman? She thinks I don't know about it. Or that outfit she bought. The kind of thing a streetwalker would wear." Mrs. Tucker gave a disgusted sniff. "It's just not proper for a nice girl like my Katie."

Matthias thanked her for her time and drew Cassie back inside. "You helped search Katie's room, right?" he asked.

"I did."

"Did you find a blonde wig?"

"No, I did not." Cassie ran a hand over her short white hair. "And I went through her closet. Unless her mother thinks white blouses, khaki pants, and hotel housekeeping uniforms are the stuff hookers wear, Katie's 'new outfit' is missing as well."

Matthias rattled the prescription bottle. "Not to mention twenty or so sleeping pills." His phone vibrated in his pocket. Emma's name on the screen started an avalanche of questions and concerns. He opened her text.

With Beige Katie at the hospital. Any chance she could be the woman Jacob saw?

"Dammit." Matthias handed the prescription bottle to Cassie. "What's going on?"

"We have to get over to the hospital," he said as he typed out a reply.

I'm on my way.

Chapter Forty

Nell wrested free from Emma's grip. "She's getting away."

"No, she's not. I know who she is." Her phone pinged, and she read the text. "Matthias is on his way." But how long would it take him to get here? Emma needed to catch up to Katie. To stop or delay her. "Go back to your room and stay there."

Emma rushed to the buttons. Pressed the down one. It lit. But when she looked up at the floor indicator, none of the cars were close. None of them would arrive in time.

She looked around, desperate, and spotted the exit sign above a steel fire door. Jogging, she headed for it. Before punching through, she turned and pointed at Nell. "Go back to your room," she repeated. Then she pushed through the door and started down the steps. Clutching the railing, she hit the first landing, wheeled, and continued down. She stumbled. Caught herself. And kept going. Flight. Landing. Pivot. Flight. She noted each floor number she passed.

Gasping for air, she burst through the door to the main level. The lobby opened before her. Families, worried friends, all gathered at the elevator doors. Had Katie gotten here first? Emma looked around and didn't see her. But she did spot Eric striding toward the elevators, a pair of takeout bags in hand.

Emma maneuvered around the clusters of visitors and medical personnel and jogged toward Eric, whose face paled when he saw her.

"What's wrong? Oh, my God. Nell?"

"She's fine. Have you seen Katie down here?"

"Katie?" His gaze swept the lobby. "No, but I just got back. Why are you looking for Katie?"

"Because she's the one who killed Gillian Watson. And she was just upstairs to check on Nell."

"What?" Eric sputtered. "But—but—how? Why?"

Behind Emma the elevator dinged. She spun.

The elevator doors opened. Six, seven people stepped out.

The eighth occupant was Katie, her head down.

"There she is." Emma started in her direction.

Katie lifted her face, spotted Emma, and cut to the left, nearly knocking an older woman off her feet. Before Emma could react, Katie raced for the glass doors leading outside.

Emma shoved her phone at Eric. "Call Matthias," she shouted and bolted after Katie.

"Wait!" she heard Eric call out. "What should I tell him?"

Emma didn't answer. She slammed through the main entrance doors and was struck by a wall of heat and humidity. Ahead, Katie dashed past a puzzled-looking valet and sprinted along the front of the building toward the parking garage. Emma charged after her.

If Katie made it to her car, Emma wouldn't stand a chance of stopping her. But if Katie struggled with her keys, fumbled in any way, Emma was close enough, she might be able to grab her.

Instead, Katie cut left toward the emergency department entrance, weaving her way through parked ambulances. Emma kept her in sight but tried to take a more direct path. Her dad always used to tell her *the shortest route between two points was a straight line.* Was she gaining on Katie? Emma didn't think so. But at least she was keeping up.

At the end of the alley reserved for emergency vehicles, Katie darted straight across the street into a parking lot. Emma followed. The heat of the sun radiating off the pavement, combined with the oppressive humidity, began taking a toll. Emma struggled to pace herself without falling behind.

Katie dodged parked cars. Emma kept up with her but glanced off a parking meter. Ignoring the pain, she kept going. At the lot's 2nd Street entrance, she looked to the right. Katie remained well ahead of her, sprinting down the sidewalk like a track-and-field star.

Emma's lungs burned. Sweat stung her eyes. Her legs ached and grew weaker with each stride. Her morning walks and bike rides around the park had failed to provide her with the stamina for a full-out foot race. Especially on a sultry June afternoon.

Well in front, Katie veered into another one of the parking lots surrounding the various medical and professional buildings along 2nd Street. She cut the corner and raced across the intersection with Holland.

Emma knew she wasn't gaining ground but kept going, struggling to find a rhythm between her strides and her breath. She bore down on the intersection and hit a patch of grass sloped steeper than she realized. She nearly fell onto the sidewalk but recovered. The misstep was enough for Katie to pull away. She was already across the street and into yet another doctor's office parking lot.

Sheer determination drove Emma onward despite an inner voice begging her to stop. To catch her breath. If Katie was out to kill Russ Carlisle, why the hell was Emma trying to stop her?

She stumbled across the street, crossed the curb and sidewalk, expecting to see Katie well ahead of her. Instead, she saw no one. Emma wrapped an arm around a light post and leaned against it, sucking air into oxygen-starved lungs. The breeze coming off the bay a few blocks to the north felt delicious against her sweat-soaked shirt. She was tempted to collapse onto the curb at her feet.

She caught a flash of movement to her right. The impact felt like she'd been tackled by one of the Pittsburgh Steelers and sent her sprawling. Pain seared her knees and sliced into her palms as she slammed the pavement.

"I'm trying to save Nell from the man who bullied her."

Emma rolled to one side and gazed up at Katie, who was backing away.

"I don't want to have to hurt you, so stay there."

Before Emma could react, Katie pivoted and took off again.

Emma tried to push up and yelped. She looked at her hands, lacerated and bloodied. Where the hell had Katie come from to blindside her like that? She must've ducked down between parked cars. Battling through the pain, Emma made it to her feet in time to see Katie skimming down the sidewalk.

Ignoring the exhaustion and the slicing twinges in her knees, Emma loped after her, knowing Katie had too much of a head start, not to mention speed. Emma caught a glimpse of her as she skirted left at the next intersection. By the time Emma reached the corner and surveyed the residential street, Katie had vanished.

Chapter Forty-One

With Cassie driving, they were closing in on the hospital fast but were still about five minutes out when Matthias's phone rang, and Emma's number lit the screen. He skipped all pleasantries and answered, "We're almost there."

But it wasn't Emma's voice on the other end of the line. "Detective, this is Eric Baker—" His tone was panicked.

"What's going on?"

"Emma told me to call you. She's chasing Katie!" Eric sounded hysterical in Matthias's ear.

Matthias put his phone on speaker so Cassie could hear. "Where?"

"They just left the hospital." Eric was breathing hard, as if Emma wasn't the only one chasing the suspect.

"Is Katie in a car?"

"No. They're both on foot." The sounds of shouts and a car horn in the background confirmed Matthias's suspicion.

"Which direction are they headed?"

Eric swore. "I'm not from here. I don't know the street names or which way they run."

"Are they going toward the bay or away from it?"

"Um…" He was starting to huff, and Matthias imagined him trying to talk and run. "Away. Away from the bay. No. Parallel to it."

"You're following them?"

"Trying to. Damn those girls are fast."

Cassie took a turn, squealing tires. "Call out the landmarks you see," she shouted at the phone in Matthias's hand.

"Okay." Breath. Breath. "McGee Women's is on my left."

"He's on Second," Matthias said to Cassie.

A moment and more heavy breathing passed, then Eric cried out.

"What's going on?" Matthias demanded.

"Emma's down. Katie did something to her."

Icy fingers of fear-driven rage crept up Matthias's neck. If Katie harmed Emma…

"Katie's taking off." Breath. "Emma's up again. And moving." A moment later, Eric shouted, "Holland. They're on Holland Street. Going away from the bay."

"We're two streets over," Matthias said.

Eric mumbled something about a fancy church and seeing Emma ahead at the next corner.

"That's the Church of the Holy Trinity," Cassie said. "The corner he's talking about is Holland and Third."

She wheeled the Impala onto 3rd, a narrow one-way street. Matthias leaned toward the windshield, watching for Katie running down the sidewalk or lurking between houses. But there was no sign of her.

They found Emma sitting in the grass beneath one of the big shade trees edging a neighborhood park. Eric stood over her and waved to them. Matthias bailed out before Cassie brought the car to a complete stop. He dropped to his knees next to Emma. "Are you all right?"

She looked equal parts exhausted and pissed as she showed

him two scraped and bloody hands. "I'd be better if I'd caught up to the little bitch."

Eric placed a palm on her head. "Stop it. You're in better shape than Gillian Watson was after getting into it with her."

Emma wrinkled her nose. "Can't argue with that."

Matthias noticed the knees of Emma's blue jeans were as shredded as her hands. "Seriously, do you need me to call an ambulance?"

"For this?" Emma chirped a sarcastic laugh. "No. Some soap, water, and antibiotic cream and I'll be good as new."

Cassie came around the now parked Impala. "Did you see where Katie Tucker went?"

Emma glanced back toward the intersection. "The last I saw her, she turned the corner onto this street. By the time I got there, she'd vanished.

Matthias stood and surveyed the area. Houses with cars. The park they stood next to stretched across to Second. Katie could've cut through and doubled back or cut between houses over to Fourth.

She could be anywhere.

"She's going after Russ," Emma said, bringing Matthias's attention back to her.

"What did she say to make you think that?"

Emma closed her eyes. He could tell she was trying to remember. "She was fixated on Nell's boyfriend being abusive and asked a lot of questions about him. Including did the police still suspect him in Gillian's murder. Then she said something about having a date with a rich, good-looking guy. And she told me the man who hurt Nell won't be a problem much longer."

Matthias met Cassie's gaze and knew she was thinking the same thing as he was. Katie had been bullied and saw Nell as a victim of bullying too. Getting rid of Russ Carlisle would be payback for his bad deeds.

"Did you happen to see a gun?" Cassie asked Emma.

Her eyes widened. "No. But she was holding onto her purse for dear life the whole time. I did think she had something in there she didn't want to lose."

"The gun," Cassie said flatly.

"Good God," Eric whispered.

Emma's face paled, but she scowled up at her friend. "She didn't want to hurt me."

"You can't know that for sure," Eric said.

"More than once she told me she liked me. That I was kind, and not many people were. She appreciated my concern for my sister and wished she had a sister like me. I asked if she had any siblings, and she said it was just her and her mother. And her mother only cares because of what Katie can do for her."

Eric shook his head. "You sound like you feel sorry for her. I saw her flatten you back in that parking lot."

"And if she has a gun, she could've shot me there and then." Emma brought her gaze to Matthias. "She didn't."

"Thank God," Eric said.

Amen, Matthias thought. "Let's get you back to your sister so we can focus on tracking down Katie."

Eric nodded. "Good idea."

Both Eric and Matthias reached a hand down to Emma to help her up.

She looked from one to the other and gave them a weak grin before holding up both bloodied palms. "Thanks just the same." She shifted to one hip, curling one leg beneath her, and bringing the other foot to the ground in front.

Matthias contained a chuckle as she pressed up to stand. "Look, Ma, no hands," he said, catching her by one elbow to steady her when her knees seemed ready to dump her back to the grass.

Eric caught her other elbow. "We gotcha, Em. Me and your cop friend. We gotcha."

At the hospital's main entrance, Matthias helped Emma from the back seat. "Better get some ice on those knees," he whispered into her ear and was surprised and pleased when she touched the side of her face to his. The contact was fleeting, but enough to fan the embers within his chest.

She stepped away and met his gaze with a tired smile. Holding up her palms, she said, "These, too."

He wanted to take her home and minister to her injuries himself. But he had work to do, a case to close, before he could think of taking the next step with Emma.

He watched them disappear through the doors, Eric supporting her. At least Matthias wasn't dealing with jealousy anymore. What had Eric said?

"Me and your cop friend. We gotcha."

Matthias liked that. It meant they'd discussed him. And Eric, who'd known Emma forever, approved.

"Let's go," Cassie called from the driver's seat.

He slid in and slammed the door.

She waved her phone. "While you were getting cozy with the cute photographer, I called Frazier."

"And?"

"They didn't turn up anything else at the Tucker house. The gun and wig remain missing."

Matthias thought about it. "Let's head over to Pauly's Polynesian Pub. See if he can positively identify Katie as our mystery blonde."

"You have any doubt?"

"Not about that, no."

Cassie eased the Impala forward and pulled onto State Street. "Sounds like you do have doubts about something, though."

For the first time since the excitement with Emma and Katie, he had time to think. Something was bothering him, and it took a minute to realize what. "Emma's conversation with Katie."

Cassie glanced over at him before bringing her gaze back to the road. "You doubt Emma?"

"No. It's something she mentioned. Something Katie said to her. Katie asked if the police still suspected Russ of Gillian's murder."

"Yeah. So?"

"Yet we believe Katie's next target is Russ because of what he's done to Nell."

"Yeah," Cassie repeated, slower this time. "So?"

"If Katie is clueless about us suspecting her, wouldn't you think she'd want to throw blame his way? Make him look guilty so he takes the fall for Gillian's homicide?"

Cassie's eyes remained straight ahead, but Matthias could tell she was studying more than the downtown traffic. "Frame Russ for Katie's crime."

Matthias fell quiet, letting Cassie mull over the possibility.

"There are a few problems with that theory," she said.

"For instance?"

"Tom Jenkins."

"She's not aware we're interested in her for that one. Yet."

"Granted. But there's one other thing. She all but laid out her plan to Emma. And left Emma alive."

Definitely a problem. Matthias's jaw clenched. They'd just dropped Emma off at the hospital. Where Katie knew she'd be. Would Katie come back to correct her error? He pulled out his phone.

"Emma will be fine," Cassie said, as though she could read his mind. "Katie isn't stupid. Emma was right. If Katie wanted her dead, she would've shot her back there when she fell. Katie has to know enough time has passed for Emma to report everything that happened to the police."

Still uneasy, Matthias placed the call.

"What's wrong?" Emma answered her phone, sounding equal parts scared and exhausted.

"Probably nothing. But if you see or hear from Katie again, call me. Immediately. And don't leave the hospital with her."

Emma promised and threw in a vow to not chase her on foot either.

"You happy now?" Cassie asked with a grin when he ended the call.

"No." He watched the city buildings fall away to residential housing as Cassie drove. The question of what Katie had planned continued to replay in his mind.

Until he remembered something else.

"The missing sleeping pills."

Cassie scowled. "What about them?"

"Katie wants to frame Russ, kill him, and not become a suspect herself. She doesn't know we've searched her house."

"Right."

"She has a disguise and a bunch of sleeping pills."

Cassie braked at a stop sign and turned to look at him. A slow smile crossed her lips. "She wants to make it look like Russ Carlisle committed suicide."

Chapter Forty-Two

"What happened to our food?" Emma asked as she and Eric crossed the hospital lobby.

"Oh. I forgot about it." He made a sharp turn, taking her with him. "I basically threw the bags at a poor woman working in the gift shop and told her I'd be back."

The woman in question appeared puzzled but smiled as she retrieved the takeout bags from behind the counter.

Eric peered into them. "I'm afraid everything's going to be cold."

Emma inhaled the aroma of soy sauce and spice. "I don't care. I'm starved."

They made it up the elevator and stepped onto Nell's floor when Emma's phone rang. "It's Matthias. Now what?" She answered the call with a question. "What's wrong."

His obvious concern might have worried her if she wasn't so weak from racing a crazy woman for blocks. She assured him she wasn't going anywhere with anyone and would call if Katie showed up again.

"You two are so cute together," Eric said after she pocketed the phone, and they strolled down the hallway.

"I thought you said he was a brute."

"Yes, but he's *your* brute."

They passed the nurses' station on their way to Nell's room. No one looked up. "I wonder if they have a microwave we can use," Emma said.

"Should I ask?" Eric started toward the counter.

"Let's check on Nell first."

They passed two more rooms and made the turn into the third. The bed was empty, the sheets thrown back. Emma looked around. The patient restroom door was open. No Nell.

Emma fought down the rising panic. "Where'd she go?"

Eric set the bags on the rolling bedside tray. "They must've taken her down for tests. I'll go check. And I'll ask about the microwave while I'm at it."

Emma didn't stop him but looked around hoping her sister might materialize from thin air. Her gaze landed on her own purse, which she'd left hanging on the back of the chair when Katie had shown up. Now it was sitting on the chair's seat, unzipped and wide open.

Aching knees forgotten, Emma crossed the room, snatched her purse, and started digging through it. Her wallet was there. She unsnapped it and found it devoid of cash. There hadn't been a lot—a couple of twenties and some singles—but it was gone.

"Dammit, Nell." She tossed the purse back onto the chair and threw open the closet door. Nell's clothes—borrowed from Emma —that she'd worn when Eric brought her in yesterday, were also gone.

Eric charged back into the room on the heels of Nell's nurse. "She didn't have any tests scheduled." He sounded as frantic as Emma felt.

The nurse, whose name badge identified her as Heather, looked around the room, her gaze settling on Emma and the empty closet. "I'll contact security."

Emma jogged after her, Eric on her heels. "You can't mean to tell me she's gone," he said.

Heather ducked behind the counter, grabbed the phone, and punched in an extension. Other nurses and aides drifted over to her as word of an escapee reached them.

"Oh my gosh." One young nurse with wide brown eyes pressed her fingers to her lips. "I think I saw her. She was in street clothes and with a guy, so I thought they were visitors."

"A guy?" Emma felt a leaden weight crushing down on her. She looked at Eric. "Russ." Back to the nurse. "What did the guy look like?"

"Kinda scary. But not."

"What does that mean?"

"He was really muscled." She fingered her lip and chin. "He had a goatee. And lots of tattoos." She rubbed her arms. "Reminded me of a biker, but he had kind eyes."

The weight lifted. Slightly. "Not Russ," Emma said to Eric. "Zeke."

"The guy who helped her get clean?"

"Yeah." For that, she was grateful.

Heather hung up. "The hospital security cop at the front door remembers seeing them leave about ten minutes ago, but there didn't appear to be anything wrong. He thought they were visitors, same as I did."

Ten minutes. She'd just missed them.

"If it's any consolation, Nell was doing well. Physically. The doctor was planning to release her later this afternoon."

Emma thanked her and wandered back to the room.

Nell had been sleeping—or so Emma thought—when Katie arrived. Then Nell came looking for her and found her with Katie at the elevator. Emma told her Katie, not Russ, was the one who killed Gillian. Had she been so upset she'd called Zeke to come get her? Or had he conveniently shown up at the perfect time?

A memory from Emma's last conversation with Zeke rose to

the surface. He said they took an Uber to the wedding reception because he didn't have a car. "Oh, crap."

"What?" Eric demanded.

She grabbed her purse and dumped its contents on the bed, praying the keys to the Jeep were still there. Pushing aside the emptied wallet, she sifted through everything else. Tissues. Breath mints. A pen. Nail clippers. A canister of pepper spray that she'd forgotten she had. Loose change. Hand sanitizer. Crumpled receipts. A spare memory card for her Nikon.

No keys.

But a scrawl on one of the receipts caught her eye. She flattened the crinkled paper against the bed. The handwriting was undeniably Nell's.

I'm sorry. I need to deal with this loss in my own way.

"*What?*" Eric repeated louder, as if she hadn't heard the first time.

"She stole my money." Emma sighed and stuffed the note into her pocket. "And Matthias's Jeep."

Chapter Forty-Three

Matthias stood, arms crossed, in front of the Blue Pike, while Cassie explained the situation to a disdainful Russ Carlisle. He listened impatiently for a couple of minutes before flashing a palm at Cassie. "Let me get this straight, Officer—"

"Detective Sergeant," she corrected.

He smirked. "Whatever. You know who killed Gillian. Another woman. You don't know where she is, but you think she's coming after me next."

"In a nutshell," Cassie said.

"You admit I'm not guilty of anything, yet you want me to lock myself up at home rather than go about my business."

Not guilty of anything was a stretch, Matthias thought. From what he knew of Russ's past, the man was far from innocent.

"We're asking that you stay home tonight," Cassie told him for the second time. "We'll have officers watching your place, but we believe the suspect will show up here. Once we take her into custody, you're free to do whatever you want."

"You think I'm afraid of some little woman?"

"She's already killed twice," Matthias said. "Size doesn't matter when she's carrying sedatives and a gun."

Russ crossed his arms, mirroring Matthias's stance. "I'm not afraid of anyone, especially not some girl. Now if you'll excuse me, I have a meeting with local suppliers. Then I'll be back. I have a business to run." He pointed from Matthias to Cassie. "You two do your job and arrest this woman before I get back, because I'm damned sure not going to hide."

They watched him stride away to the parking lot.

"That," Cassie said, "is a waste, taking up air the rest of us could be breathing."

"Too bad you weren't here to see Emma slap him."

Cassie snickered. "Okay. On to plan B."

Tiffany was much more cooperative this time. Instead of sticking Matthias and Cassie in the fishbowl, she set them up at a table with a clear view of the Blue Pike's front door as well as the bar. She also fulfilled their request for concealment by having a pair of large, leafy, potted plants positioned in front of them. She even brought them several plates of food and a pitcher of iced tea.

"In case anyone spots you, you'll look like guests," the hostess told them. Her expression turned sour. "I know I shouldn't say this in front of cops, but I don't think any of our staff would be terribly disappointed if you don't catch this woman. Russ wouldn't exactly be missed around here." Tiffany pivoted and strutted away.

Cassie tilted her head to see through the greenery. "I'm beginning to think no jury would convict this woman."

"Gillian Watson's mother and sister might disagree."

Cassie considered his words and shrugged.

Unlike their first visit, Matthias was tempted by the food. But not the beverage. The last thing he needed during a stakeout was the urge to use the restroom.

A blonde in a short dress entered the front door, pausing to speak with Tiffany at the hostess station.

Cassie tipped her head toward them. "Is that Katie?"

Matthias studied the woman in question. From the distance, he couldn't see her face. "I'm not sure."

Tiffany stepped from behind the podium and let the blonde to a table already occupied by a man, who stood at their approach and bussed the new arrival on the cheek.

"Nope," Matthias said. "Not her."

In the next half hour, two more blondes entered the Blue Pike, drawing Matthias and Cassie's attention. In both cases, they determined the women weren't the one they were seeking.

Russ Carlisle swept into the restaurant and assessed the dining room like a king surveying his kingdom.

"There's our man," Cassie said.

"I see him."

Russ exchanged a few words with Tiffany. If her reaction was any indication, he hadn't cheered her with "good job." Her head turned as she watched him stride to the bar. She shot an obvious look in Matthias and Cassie's direction before greeting a group of new patrons.

Matthias picked up a fork and moved some shrimp around on his plate. "Now there's bait in the trap."

Earlier, they'd stopped at Pauly's place to show him a photo of Katie. At first glance, he claimed he'd never seen the woman before, but Cassie encouraged him to look closer.

He squinted at the image for several long moments before nodding. "Yeah. Yeah. That's her. That's the woman who Tom left with that night."

"You sure?" Matthias had asked.

"One hundred percent."

Minutes ticked into an hour. Then two. The food in front of them had grown cold and congealed while the ice in the tea pitcher melted. Matthias began to question whether Katie would really show up. She had to know Emma would've reported her to the police. They had uniforms watching her house in case she went home. The wise move would be to run. But where would she go? Other than her years at college, she'd lived her entire life in that house. Still, starting over—or attempting to—somewhere else would be the smart choice.

Matthias became conscious of Cassie watching him instead of the restaurant's door. "What?" he asked.

"What are you gonna do about your Jeep?"

Emma had called earlier to inform him of Nell disappearing yet again, this time in his car. "I put out a BOLO on it. It's only a matter of time before someone finds it. Maybe we'll find Nell and Zeke at the same time."

"You aren't upset at Emma?"

"Why would I be? None of it's her fault."

A sexy brunette sauntered into the now packed restaurant, drawing Matthias's attention.

Cassie followed his gaze. "Not a blonde but…"

Having seen Katie up close, he almost dismissed the woman. The new arrival would've been considered a bombshell by any of the heterosexual men he knew. Yet he looked beyond the long, sleek hair and perfect makeup, imagined her in a housekeeper's uniform instead of the lowcut, form-fitting top, short skirt, and high heels.

Beige Katie? Hardly.

"It's her," he said. "She must know we're on the lookout for a woman in a blonde wig, so she swapped it for a brunette one. But that's definitely her."

Cassie shifted for a better look through the leaves. "Damn." She dragged the word out to three syllables.

Matthias took in the packed restaurant and the line of patrons waiting for tables. If Katie had her gun on her, things could get ugly fast. "I don't want to take her down in here."

"Agreed. We wait until she—they—leave."

Matthias fired off a quick group text to Frazier, Roth, and the other officers waiting unseen on the streets around the Blue Pike.

She's here. Hold position.

Katie hesitated and looked around. Matthias held his breath. He knew they were well hidden but feared she'd spot them or grow suspicious about the large plant arrangement. She aimed her gaze their way for a moment too long. But her head turned. Her search continued until she spotted Russ standing at the bar, chatting with the female bartender. Nell's replacement.

Was he working on her as his next conquest as well?

Brunette Katie took one step in his direction before Tiffany, holding a menu, cut her off. Matthias remembered his first visit there, Tiffany asking if he had reservations. Did Katie? Had she planned for this?

Katie smiled and pointed at the bar. Matthias wasn't a lip reader but could tell what she was saying. "I just want to get a drink."

Tiffany swept the menu in that direction. He imagined her saying, "Go right ahead." Neither woman looked their way. Tiffany didn't suspect Katie. Katie didn't suspect two detectives were watching her every move.

The sexy brunette sashayed to the bar and chose a stool near Russ, leaving an empty one between them. She slithered onto the seat, hiking one hip, flashing a lot of thigh, crossing the other leg over. Flashing even more thigh.

Russ would've had to be dead not to notice. And Russ was not dead.

Yet.

He wasn't remotely subtle about eyeing the brunette's legs along with the rest of her anatomy. With a movie-star smile, he claimed the empty stool next to hers. She placed her small handbag on the bar top.

Was her Ruger inside? Matthias felt fairly certain she wouldn't pull it in here. As long as she was unaware of their presence, there was no need. She'd hooked Russ. Reeling him in would be easy.

He raised two fingers toward the bartender, ordering drinks.

She leaned toward him, leading with her chest. He reached over, touched her cheek, let his hand trail down her neck to her collarbone. Teasing, she shifted away and laughed.

"Damn, she's good," Cassie said.

Matthias was thinking the same thing. If the ice in the tea hadn't melted, he'd have taken a long slug of it.

The drinks arrived. The seduction dance went on. They chatted and flirted. Russ's hand eventually came to rest on Katie's thigh. She placed her hand on his and encouraged it higher.

Their glasses were almost empty when she tipped her head toward the door, then leaned toward him, whispering in his ear.

Matthias didn't know if she was suggesting her place, his place, or the back seat of a car. It didn't matter.

Russ stood and offered her a hand. She took it, stepped down from her stool, and wrapped both arms around one of his, clinging.

Matthias texted the rest of the team.

As the pair reached the doors, Matthias and Cassie rose and started around the plant barricade. He noticed Russ wobble. Katie bolstered him. Anyone else would've thought he'd had too much to drink.

Except Matthias knew about the missing sleeping pills. He'd watched Katie's every move. There had been a few instances when her body or Russ's blocked the view of her purse, but Matthias hadn't thought it was long enough for her to slip something into his drink.

He also knew it only took a second.

He looked over at the bar where Russ and Katie had sat and where the two not-quite empty drink glasses remained.

"Dammit." Matthias broke into a lope. "She's drugged him

already." Diners' heads turned as he charged past their tables. Behind him, Cassie's footsteps pounded. As he passed a shocked Tiffany, he waved a hand toward the bar. "Don't let anyone touch those glasses!"

He shouldered through the doors to see Russ and Katie in the middle of the road, headed for the parking lot, his arm around her shoulders, leaning heavily on her.

"Katie!" Matthias shouted.

She spun, nearly dumping Russ into the street. Her eyes widened in recognition, and Matthias saw rather than heard her say, "No."

Frazier and Roth exited their car in the lot, and Matthias was peripherally aware of other officers heading their way. Katie looked around frantically. He could see her considering her rapidly diminishing options before reacting.

She released Russ, kicked out of her heels, and sprinted toward 16th Street. Her intended victim did a slow pirouette, his knees buckling as he spun to the pavement. Something slipped from Katie's grasp, clinking onto the street.

"Call for medics!" Matthias shouted to the others as he launched after Katie. "Police! Stop!"

He didn't expect her to comply and wasn't disappointed. She raced ahead of him into the twilight shadows of the warehouses. No wonder Emma hadn't been able to catch her. Even barefoot, she was fast. But no way was he going to let her escape.

Two other officers, who'd been parked nearby as backup, joined the chase.

Katie flung one arm, sweeping the brunette wig from her head. Matthias charged past the thing lying in the street like roadkill. He was gaining. Not a lot, but definitely gaining. He hoped her race with Emma had drained her stamina.

As they neared the homeless encampment, she drifted toward the other side of 16th. Matthias swore. If Emma's failed chase earlier was any indication, Katie would veer into the nearby

351

residential area and vanish. He dug deep, calling up a little more speed.

She reached the first house well ahead of him.

But not ahead of the figure, who appeared from the tent. Jacob bolted across the street, tackled her, driving her down onto the sidewalk. She clung to her purse's strap, but its contents, including a revolver, spilled into the street. Shrieking and cursing, she struggled and broke free long enough to scoop up the firearm. Jacob grappled with her, dragging her back as Matthias closed the distance between them.

She extended the arm with the gun. Jacob tried to grab it. She flailed wildly away from him. The loud pop of gunfire echoed off the brick warehouse wall.

Matthias was three strides away when Katie's eyes—and the gun—swung toward him. He reacted. Too late. Another pop. The blaze of a muzzle flash. Intense heat seared his arm.

But adrenaline and momentum continued to carry him forward. He dove for the gun.

Jacob beat him to it. The scrawny guy who'd taken great lengths to avoid Matthias in the past, wrapped long fingers around Katie's wrist and slammed it to the ground. At the same moment, Matthias landed on top of them. The gun clinked on the pavement and skittered across the street.

Katie let out a wail as Matthias rolled off, coming to his knees. Four more officers jogged up to them, encircling the young woman, grabbing her wrists, taking the task of restraining her from Jacob. Someone radioed a request for additional EMS.

Matthias wasn't sure if the call for medical help was for him or for Katie, who was keening like a wounded bird.

"You okay, man?" Jacob asked as the other officers wrestled with a squirming Katie.

Matthias reached over and touched his burning left arm. The bullet had ripped his sportscoat just below his shoulder. His hand came away warm and sticky. But he successfully wiggled his left fingers.

Another scar.

"Yeah. Thanks to you." Matthias wiped the blood on his already ruined jacket, climbed to his feet, and offered a hand to Jacob.

He waved off the help, stood, and looked down at Katie. Shaking his head, Jacob said, "That Gillian woman was a bitch. But that don't mean she deserved to die."

A tearful, handcuffed, and Mirandized Katie Tucker sat in the back seat of one of the patrol cars. Paramedics had determined her injuries were superficial, especially compared to Matthias's. Except he refused their offer of a ride to the emergency department. He shrugged out of the unsalvageable sports jacket and allowed them to bandage his arm while promising to have his partner drive him there after their work at the crime scene was completed.

Cassie and Frazier walked down the middle of the blocked-off street to join him a few minutes later.

"How's Russ?" Matthias asked, not sure how much he cared about the answer.

"On his way to the hospital." Cassie eyed his bandaged arm. "Where it looks like you should be."

"I will. Later."

"Carlisle was pretty out of it," Frazier said. "Responsive to pain but unable to answer questions. The paramedics said his vitals weren't good at all."

Cassie wandered over to Katie's purse and its spilled contents. All except the gun.

Matthias gestured at the mess. "We already got photos."

Wiggling her fingers into a pair of nitrile gloves, Cassie

squatted for a closer look. He did likewise. From the agglomeration of the ordinary daily needs a woman carried in her handbag, Cassie retrieved a neatly folded sheet of paper. Matthias zeroed in on a small baggie containing pills matching those he'd discovered at the Tucker residence. He held the bag on one palm and smoothed it so he could count.

"Look at this." Cassie held the unfolded paper so he could see.

I'm so sorry for the harm I've done, the lives I've destroyed. I didn't intend to kill Gillian, but I lost control. I've done it before and know I'll do it again. I can't go on living like this. Please forgive me.

There was no signature, but the name Russ Carlisle was typed at the bottom.

"I was right." Cassie's solemn expression told Matthias she felt no desire to brag about it.

Matthias pinched a corner of the baggie and held it up. "The script at the Tucker house was for thirty pills. Her mother took one or two of them. There were still eight in the bottle. Katie has fourteen left here. I think we can assume Russ ingested at least five times the normal dosage."

"She probably intended to give him more if needed."

He gazed toward the patrol car holding their suspect. "Or Russ was supposed to shoot himself. All she needed was to have him knocked out enough to not protest."

Cassie handed the note to one of the officers. "Bag and tag that, will you?"

Matthias stood and offered her a hand. Unlike Jacob, she accepted. "Let's go have a chat with our meek housekeeper."

Katie was slouched in the back seat, her hands cuffed behind her, her face streaked with mascara-stained tears. No longer Beige Katie nor a bombshell, she looked more like a pitiful teenager who'd been busted for sneaking out of the house. She looked up, her gaze shifting from Cassie to Matthias. "Why are you doing this to me?" She sounded like a pitiful teenager, too.

"You honestly have no idea?" Cassie asked.

"None."

Matthias kept the anger from his voice when he said, "You shot me."

"I was defending myself. I didn't know you were a cop. I thought you were going to mug me. That other guy, too. I thought I was going to be raped."

Cassie hiked a thumb in the direction of the restaurant. "What about the guy you drugged?"

"I didn't drug anyone. He was drunk. I was helping him to his car."

"And you don't know who he is?" Matthias asked.

"No." Katie's voice was a squeak.

Matthias leaned down, bringing his face to her level and no longer blocking his anger. "Russ Carlisle. The man you told Emma was going to get what's coming to him. The one you said wasn't going to be a problem much longer." He held up the baggie and watched her eyes shift to it, darken, and come back to him. "Want to explain these?"

"Those aren't mine."

"You're right. They belong to your mother. The suicide note you wrote on Russ's behalf, though. That is yours."

Katie sank back into the seat, eyes gleaming with a fresh supply of tears. "Emma did this. She told you. I can't believe she betrayed me like that. I was just trying to help her and her sister. Russ was a hateful bully. He beat Nell. He beat Gillian, too."

"But he didn't kill Gillian. You did that."

"I did not. It was him. I just wanted to get him relaxed enough to admit it. I was trying to help Emma and Nell."

"For starters, Emma didn't have to tell us anything. We already knew. And we have a witness who saw you push Gillian down those steps."

Katie's eyes grew wide. She shot a look toward the spot where Jacob had tackled her. Matthias didn't confirm what he knew she was suspecting. Let her hear his testimony in a courtroom. "Care to tell us about Tom Jenkins?"

She inhaled sharply. Matthias judged that until now she didn't think they knew about her part in that case. "I don't know what you're talking about."

"We have a witness who identified you with him the night he died. And I'll bet two month's salary the bullets that killed Tom match the gun you shot me with."

From behind him, Cassie said, "No bet."

Anger and fear mingled in Katie's eyes. She choked out a defeated sob and lowered her face. In a voice so soft Matthias could barely hear it, she said one word. "Lawyer."

Chapter Forty-Four

Four days had passed since Nell had run away. Again.

The late afternoon sun cast long shadows as Emma sat alone on the deck of her camper, torn between grief and anger. Nell had been safe. Emma and Eric would've kept her that way. Would've helped her with whatever she needed. Instead, she'd vanished without giving them a chance.

A vintage purple VW Beetle rumbled up the hill. As Emma watched, it pulled into the spot usually occupied by her Subaru. Kira, dressed in jeans and a tank top that matched her car, climbed out and looked around. "So this is where you call home."

Emma extended both arms. "Camper, sweet camper." She lowered her hands to her lap. "What are you doing here?"

Kira joined her on the porch and took a seat in the spare chair. "You missed yoga class on Saturday. And this morning. I decided to come looking for you."

"Sorry. I haven't been in the mood."

"Which is exactly when you need yoga."

Emma tried to smile and failed. "Yes, ma'am."

Kira draped one arm languidly over the back of the chair. "Any word on Nell?"

"None. Eric and I checked at the homeless encampment, but Jacob hasn't seen her. He promised to contact me if he did. Then we went to the Mercury, looking for Zeke—"

"He quit," Kira interrupted.

"How'd you know?"

"I called Rafael."

Zeke's co-worker who'd become Kira's latest conquest.

"He told me Zeke took off without giving notice, other than telling Rafael he wouldn't be back."

Emma lifted her gaze to the deck roof. "I really do believe Zeke loves her. I should be glad to know Nell's with him rather than being alone."

"You don't sound glad."

Emma brought her eyes back to Kira. "Nell met him in rehab. I hope he can keep her clean, but I worry it'll go the other way, and she'll drag him down with her. I already know she doesn't handle grief well. Now she's lost her baby, too."

Kira studied Emma. "From what Rafael has told me, you're right. Zeke does love Nell. And I think he's strong enough for both of them. Nell needs time to heal. She'll come back to you when she's ready."

"I hope you're right." Emma looked away and wondered if this was how her relationship with her sister would always be. Nell running off only to reappear and then disappear again.

"How about you?" Kira asked. "How are you holding up?"

A sob bubbled up unexpectedly, choking her reply. "Not very well."

"Where's Eric?"

"He took my car to the hotel for a Zoom meeting."

"How long is he staying?"

"I'm driving him home tomorrow." Before Kira could ask the inevitable question—*Are you staying there or coming back?*—which Emma had no answer for, she decided to change the subject. "There's something I want to know."

"Which is?"

"You flirt with every good-looking guy you meet."

Kira grinned. "It's my hobby."

"But you never so much as batted an eyelash at Eric."

She shrugged. "He's gay. Why waste my energy?"

"How did you know? I mean, I've known since we were kids, but most people can't tell."

Kira grinned. "I have gaydar."

For the first time in what felt like a decade, Emma laughed. A full-throated, doubled-over, belly laugh.

Smiling, Kira turned toward the camp road. "Speak of the devil, here he comes now."

Emma brushed tears from her eyes and watched her Forester ease in next to the purple bug.

Eric stepped out and joined them on the deck, nodding to Kira. "Namaste, Madam Yoga Instructor."

She brightened. "Namaste. And why haven't you come to one of my classes while you've been in town?"

"My loss. Next time. I have to get back to work tomorrow."

"So I've heard." Kira eyed Emma but directed the question to him. "Are you going to keep her down there with you or are you sending her back to us?"

Emma avoided their eyes, wishing she could avoid answering.

"I'm not sure," Eric said. "I think it depends on you."

"Me?" Kira sounded stunned.

"Are you and Detective Honeywell still an item?"

Emma choked and shot an *I'll kill you* glare at her friend. *Former* friend.

"No, we are not." Kira glared at her. "And she knows that. Matthias Honeywell is besotted with her. I didn't stand a chance."

Emma sputtered, trying to come up with a retort, but caught a glimpse of yet another vehicle making its way up the hill. This time, it was a red Jeep. For a heartbeat, she thought it might be

Nell, but as it drew close, she could see Matthias behind the wheel.

Kira spotted the car too. "Damn." She looked at Eric. "I mentioned your name and you show up. Then we talk about Matthias, and *he* shows up." She looked toward the heavens and shouted, "George Clooney!"

"Hell, yes, girlfriend." Eric held up a palm, and they high-fived.

Emma covered her eyes. This was not happening. Matthias was not walking into the middle of this madness.

"Well, I should go." Kira rose and threw her arms around Eric. "Next time you're in town, make her bring you to my studio for a class."

"Will do."

Then she whispered something to him, which Emma couldn't hear. She stood as Kira released Eric and turned to her, arms open. "You come right back here after depositing him back in farm country." Kira held her in a tight embrace. "You hear?"

"I hear."

Emma watched as Kira strode toward her purple VW, her movements, as always, lithe as a panther. She paused, waiting as Matthias climbed out of his Jeep and moved to her. He gave her a quick, friends-only hug, and she whispered something to him too. He responded with a low chuckle.

Emma knew she'd never get him to divulge what Kira had said. But Eric might. Emma faced him. "What was with all that whispering?"

He raised both hands, palms toward her. "I don't know what you're talking about."

Kira's car door thunked shut, and she backed out, heading down the hill. Matthias watched her go, then approached the deck.

Damn, he looked good. Faded jeans. A red T-shirt snug enough to show off his powerful chest and arms. Including the arm

360

bearing a bandage. Emma had heard he'd been grazed by a bullet that night.

"You got your Jeep back," she said.

He glanced at it over his shoulder. "Yeah. It turned up in a parking lot near the airport. Keys in it. Not so much as a dent."

So Nell and Zeke had taken good care of their stolen property. But...

"The airport?" Emma repeated. They could've taken a flight to anywhere. If she hadn't been able to find her sister when she'd been in Erie, how was she supposed to track her down when she could be halfway around the globe?

Matthias seemed to read her mind. "We checked flight manifests. There's no evidence either of them boarded a plane. If you ask me, they wanted us to believe they had so we'd stop looking."

Eric nudged her. "Nell's still in Erie. You have to stay here. She knows how to find you as long as you're here."

"She has my phone number. She can find me anywhere."

He breathed an exasperated sigh and looked at Matthias. "Would you please convince her to stay?"

The look Matthias gave her turned her knees weak. She swallowed hard and focused on pouting at Eric. "You don't want me around anymore."

He leaned over, planted a kiss on top of her head, and said, "I want you to be happy." He moved toward the edge of the deck where Matthias stood. "I think I need to take a walk."

Matthias kept his gaze on her, still giving her the look that melted her resolve. "I was hoping to take you to meet a friend."

"Go," Eric said. "Don't mind me. I'll go hang out at Sara's Restaurant." Without looking back, he ambled away.

That left no one for Emma to look at—except Matthias. His eyes and hint of a smile were softer than she'd seen before, making her even more curious about whatever Kira had whispered to him. "What friend?"

361

"Come on." He tipped his head toward the Jeep. "You'll find out soon enough."

Matthias cast a glance at Emma beside him in the Jeep as they reached the top of the first traffic light on Peninsula Drive. She faced straight ahead, her nerves evident in the way she chewed her lip.

Hearing that she was strongly considering going home to Washington County and her family farm shouldn't have surprised him. What surprised him even more was his own reaction to it.

He didn't want her to go.

"Take care of her," Kira had whispered to him.

He wanted to. For the first time in many years, he wanted to take care of someone. Not for a night or a week. But for the foreseeable future. Or longer. The idea terrified him.

Losing Emma terrified him more.

She didn't say anything until he made the right turn on West Lake Road and put his turn signals on to make the left into Trinity Cemetery. Then she laughed softly and shifted to face him. "I think I've met this friend before."

"But you've never been properly introduced."

The cemetery road weaved and looped through trees and monuments. Matthias parked in his usual spot, shut off the engine, and stepped out. He reached into the back seat and grabbed three cans of beer. Emma had climbed down and stood at the front fender, watching him. He tipped his head. "Come on."

One relatively new grave lay in the middle of a grouping of older Tucci family plots. Matthias stood in a spot he was familiar with, in front of the glossy granite stone inset with a badge very much like the one he carried.

"Emma, meet Nick Tucci. My old partner."

At Matthias's shoulder, Emma nodded at the stone. "Hi."

He chuckled and gestured at the ground. "Have a seat."

Once they were both settled on the cool grass, he set one can in the middle of the red and white geraniums Nick's widow had planted. He popped the tops on the other two and handed one to Emma.

"This is where I first saw you," she said, her voice almost timid.

The meeting hadn't been friendly, although other than her apologizing for interrupting his ritual, no words had been exchanged. He'd thought she was taking photos of him. For what, he didn't know. He'd given her that look he knew sent terror into the souls of the bad guys he dealt with on a daily basis. It had done the same to her. He wasn't sure she'd recovered from it even now.

"You told me about him," she went on.

Nick had taken a shot that by all rights Matthias should've taken. An innocent man had caught that bullet and died. Nick, unable to handle the guilt, took his own life. "Nick and I used to go to a bar after a rough day. Now I come here."

Emma nodded. "I remember you saying that." She looked at him. "I gather today was a rough day. What happened?"

Matthias grinned and took a sip. "I learned a woman I care about might be leaving town." As soon as the words left his lips, he regretted them. Too much. Too soon. "But no. You're the one who's had a rough week. That's why I brought you here."

She looked at the can in her hands. "To have a beer with the guys."

This wasn't going right. He bent one knee and came forward, resting an elbow on it. "I hoped you'd feel...peace...here."

Emma continued to stare at the beer, then took a drink. She swallowed and licked her lips before speaking. "I do."

Matthias remained silent, wishing he could read her thoughts. Wishing he had the right words. Dammit. He was never at a loss for words with women. Other women.

Once he finished his beer, he crushed the can and set it next to the one in the flowers. Ordinarily, he would pick up the second one and drink it too. Instead, he looked at Emma. "Are you leaving Erie?"

He watched her eyes fill. She turned away and blinked before meeting his gaze. "I don't know. I've been thinking about it. Moving back home. That's where Nell wanted to go to keep her pregnancy a secret from Russ." Emma frowned. "How is he?"

"Still in the hospital. He'll live. For what it's worth, he got a good taste of what an overdose can do to you."

Emma's teal eyes turned stormy. "Would you think I'm a horrible person for believing he got off easy?"

"I thought that and worse while we were working the case."

"He may not have killed Gillian, but he's guilty of supplying my sister with drugs, not to mention beating her."

"He might be guilty of a lot more. His late wife died of a supposed skiing accident out in Colorado." Matthias thought of the visit he'd paid Russ in the hospital that morning. Alone. He'd made sure Russ knew Matthias would be keeping a close watch on him from now on.

"Supposed?"

"So far."

"You're still looking into it." She said it as a statement, not a question.

"Let's just say I'm not done with Russ Carlisle."

"Good." Emma nodded. "What about Katie?"

"She's been charged with two counts of homicide, one count of attempted homicide, and a few other odds and ends that will likely be dropped."

"I almost feel sorry for her." Emma's gaze drifted to his arm and the bandage still covering the stitches. She lifted a hand and touched his bicep for a brief second. "Almost."

He reached up and caught her hand, expecting her to pull it

away. She didn't. "Katie liked you. I think she wished she had what you had with Nell."

Emma's short laugh carried the threat of tears. "I wish I had what Katie *thought* I had with Nell."

"I'd like to tell you I'll get her back, but I seem to recall promising that before."

Emma shook her head. Her gaze settled on Nick's gravestone. "Does he ever give you any good advice? Because I could sure use some right now."

"He used to. These days he just listens. But sometimes that's enough."

Her gaze remained on the stone. Her hand remained in Matthias's. After what felt like hours, she looked at him, her expression agonized. "Tell me what I should do."

He leaned closer to her. "What do you want to do?"

She made two false starts, lips moving but closing again. On the third attempt, she whispered, "I want to stay."

Matthias made no effort to fight his smile. Or his relief. He leaned in even closer, until his forehead touched hers. "Good. Because I want you to stay too."

And he didn't think Nick minded being witness to their first kiss.

Author's Note

While I've set this story in a real city, Erie, Pennsylvania, not all of the locations are real. The warehouses, both abandoned and renovated along Sixteenth Street, are completely made up. The last time I drove around that area, the blocks involved in the story were nothing more than rubble. Therefore, The Blue Pike Restaurant is also completely fictional. I've also made up Pauly's Polynesian Pub and plopped it onto a street where it doesn't exist.

But many of the landmarks and features do exist. Sara's Campground is real, and I'm beyond grateful to the owners for allowing me to use it as a setting. However, the area where Emma's camper resides is a figment of my fertile imagination. Don't drive around the campground and try to find her campsite. It's not real.

Acknowledgments

As always, I have a whole team of support staff behind me as I write this book, and I owe them all a huge debt of gratitude.

Erie City Detective Sean Bogart has answered all my multitude of questions about his department, whether they're about procedure or what an interview room looks like. I couldn't bring Detective Matthias Honeywell to life without Detective Bogart. Also vital to my knowledge of police and investigation is Detective Adam Richardson, who heads up the Writer's Detective Bureau. If you write police characters, look him up on his website, his podcast, or his Facebook group.

Retired Coroner Chris Herndon is always my go-to expert on dead bodies. She's been helping me with all the gory details for years.

If you find mistakes in these areas, don't blame them. The errors are all mine.

Helping me hone my writing craft throughout the years and throughout this book are two fabulous organizations. Pennwriters and Sisters in Crime. I wouldn't be published without them. Special thanks to my fellow Pittsburgh Sisters in Crime retreaters who critiqued early pages and made them so much stronger: Carole Lynn Jones, Mary Sutton, Carol Silvis, and Jodene Weber (who hosts the true crime podcast, Caught in My Web—check it out!) And of course, my beloved critique buddies, Liz Milliron, Jeff Boarts, and Peter W.J. Hayes. They're incredible writers. Do yourself a favor and check out their books, too.

Sending my undying gratitude to my awesome agent, Dawn

Dowdle, my editor Jennie Rothwell, and the crew at One More Chapter. Thank you all for believing in me and helping to make my words shine.

To the owners of Sara's Campground and Sara's Restaurant, thank you for giving me your blessing to use your businesses in my series. If you're ever in Erie, you have to stop at Sara's Restaurant. It's iconic for a reason.

And to Ray, my husband and best friend, who makes it possible for me to spend my days holed up in my office, talking to my make-believe friends. Thank you, my love.

ONE MORE CHAPTER

The author and One More Chapter would like to thank everyone who contributed to the publication of this story...

Analytics
Emma Harvey
Maria Osa

Audio
Fionnuala Barrett
Ciara Briggs

Contracts
Georgina Hoffman
Florence Shepherd

Design
Lucy Bennett
Fiona Greenway
Holly Macdonald
Liane Payne
Dean Russell

Digital Sales
Laura Daley
Michael Davies
Georgina Ugen

Editorial
Arsalan Isa
Charlotte Ledger
Nicky Lovick
Jennie Rothwell
Emily Thomas
Kimberley Young

International Sales
Bethan Moore

Marketing & Publicity
Chloe Cummings
Emma Petfield

Operations
Melissa Okusanya
Hannah Stamp

Production
Emily Chan
Denis Manson
Francesca Tuzzeo

Rights
Lana Beckwith
Rachel McCarron
Agnes Rigou
Hany Sheikh
Mohamed
Zoe Shine
Aisling Smyth

The HarperCollins Distribution Team

The HarperCollins Finance & Royalties Team

The HarperCollins Legal Team

The HarperCollins Technology Team

Trade Marketing
Ben Hurd

UK Sales
Yazmeen Akhtar
Laura Carpenter
Isabel Coburn
Jay Cochrane
Alice Gomer
Gemma Rayner
Erin White
Harriet Williams
Leah Woods

And every other essential link in the chain from delivery drivers to booksellers to librarians and beyond!

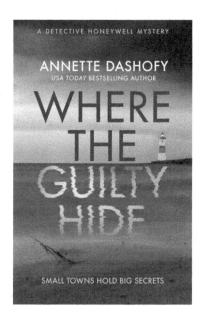

A DETECTIVE HONEYWELL MYSTERY

ANNETTE DASHOFY
USA TODAY BESTSELLING AUTHOR

WHERE THE GUILTY HIDE

SMALL TOWNS HOLD BIG SECRETS

On the shore of Lake Erie, Pennsylvania, a body lays half hidden, the waves slowly moving it with the rising tide...

In the early morning mist, freelance photographer Emma Anderson takes pictures of the rocky coastline. She moved to Erie to escape a past that haunts her but the last thing she expects to capture is a dead body.

Available in eBook and paperback now

ONE MORE CHAPTER

One More Chapter is an
award-winning global
division of HarperCollins.

Sign up to our newsletter to get our
latest eBook deals and stay up to date
with our weekly Book Club!
<u>Subscribe here.</u>

Meet the team at
<u>www.onemorechapter.com</u>

Follow us!
 @OneMoreChapter_
 @OneMoreChapter
 @onemorechapterhc

Do you write unputdownable fiction?
We love to hear from new voices.
Find out how to submit your novel at
<u>www.onemorechapter.com/submissions</u>